ENSHROUDED

JEFF TREDER

ENSHROUDED

TATE PUBLISHING
AND ENTERPRISES, LLC

Enshrouded

Published by Tate Publishing & Enterprises, LLC
127 E. Trade Center Terrace | Mustang, Oklahoma 73064 USA
1.888.361.9473 | www.tatepublishing.com

Tate Publishing is committed to excellence in the publishing industry. The company reflects the philosophy established by the founders, based on Psalm 68:11,
"The Lord gave the word and great was the company of those who published it."

Cover design by Blake Brasor
Interior design by Lucia Kroeger Renz

Published in the United States of America

ISBN: 978-1-62024-089-2
1. Fiction / Romance / Suspense
2. Fiction / Romance / Contemporary
12.06.11

DEDICATION

For Judy—

God's servant,
My wife,
Their mother and grandmother,
Our delight.

Soli gloria deo.

Early on Sunday morning, while it was still dark, Mary Magdalene came to the tomb and found that the stone had been rolled away from the entrance. She ran and found Simon Peter and the other disciple, the one whom Jesus loved. She said, "They have taken the Lord's body out of the tomb, and we don't know where they have put him!"

Peter and the other disciple started out for the tomb. They were both running, but the other disciple outran Peter and reached the tomb first. He stooped and looked in and saw the linen wrappings lying there, but he didn't go in. Then Simon Peter arrived and went inside. He also noticed the linen wrappings lying there, while the cloth that had covered Jesus' head was folded up and lying apart from the other wrappings. Then the disciple who had reached the tomb first also went in, and he saw and believed—for until then they still hadn't understood the Scriptures that said Jesus must rise from the dead.

John 20: 1-9, NLT

OPENING: QUEEN'S GAMBIT

PROLOGUE

Inside the cathedral it was cold. There was a cold, majestic beauty about the architecture and sculpture, and it was literally cold too. I was wearing a suit jacket but could have used an overcoat. The Cathedral of St. John the Baptist seemed larger on the inside than it looked from outside and was more impressive than attractive. That's probably how it was meant to be.

"This way, please," said Monsignor Damiani, the graying prelate who was our guide. He spoke English with an Italian accent—the accent because this was Italy, and the English, I suppose, because it was the main international language for the time being, and we were a mixed group. He led us down a colonnade to the right of the central nave toward the rear of the cathedral. There were eight of us, five men and three women, plus two hefty security guys wearing those rather baroque uniforms favored by Italians. I was here on account of being a scholar and more specifically on account of special arrangements having been made, strings having been pulled.

Our footsteps on the ancient marble floor clopped as if we were iron-shod. The prelate's assistant walked beside him, a severe-looking woman in a plain burgundy suit, carrying a clipboard. She looked back to make sure we were following. I thought she ought to trust the two guards for that.

Damiani led us behind the filigreed screen at the rear of the high altar and into the Chapel of the Holy Shroud. The Shroud of Turin—that's what we were here to see. It was shown to the public around once a decade, and private viewings weren't a lot more frequent. I assumed that my fellow viewers had also pulled strings, but we hadn't shared that kind of information during the brief time after we arrived and before the no-nonsense assistant greeted us.

I'm not much of an art appreciator, but even I could tell that the chapel was exquisite. It had been badly damaged in a 1997 fire, probably the work of an arsonist. The Shroud itself was rescued, just barely—at least the second time in its epic history that it was nearly incinerated. The chapel had since been restored and the Shroud returned to what might manage to be its final resting place.

It rested in a fifteen-foot-long, three-ton, air-conditioned conservation case. Normally it was kept horizontal, but it could be tipped toward the vertical for viewing, as it was now. Damiani arranged us behind a purple velvet rope about ten feet from the softly illuminated Shroud and said in mild tones, "Here is the Holy Shroud with which, we believe, our Savior Jesus Christ was covered during his three days in the tomb. In it you can see what you can see, with your natural eyes or with eyes of faith or with both. This viewing will last for fifteen minutes, after which I will answer any questions as best I may."

I had seen the famous photographs of the crucified man imprinted on the linen cloth, with that serene look about him, studious almost, undeniably mysterious. I had read a good deal about the Shroud and the controversies surrounding it. But none of that quite prepared me for the real thing. Except where a fire in 1532 had seared holes in it, the ivory-colored cloth looked to be of fine quality and in good condition, with a distinctive herringbone weave. The image itself, though, was strange. For one thing, it was both easy to discern and hard to see. It made you want to look at it askance to see if it would come into sharper focus. With that in mind, I moved around behind a couple of the other visitors to get a different angle, causing one of the guards to glare at me. But the image on the cloth remained elusive, half there, half not there.

All of the questions swirling around this remarkable object boiled down to a simple alternative. Either it really was what the true believers thought it was, the burial shroud of Jesus of Nazareth, or else it was an extremely cunning medieval forgery. I already knew enough about it to figure that out. Now if I could figure out just how the forger had pulled it off, I could climb out of this deep, dark excretory hole I'd dug for myself.

CHAPTER 1

How this came about. I teach history and philosophy—actually I'm a full professor—at Columbia University in the Big Apple. I teach a few courses and seminars, hold some tutorials, serve on too many committees and boards, and do a lot of research—one of those perpetual students. I've published four books and more articles than I can remember.

My office is comfortably large but, even so, overstuffed with books, journals, computer, printer, fax, files, a small conference table piled with stuff, two potted plants, some chairs, and a fair-sized but utilitarian desk. Two tall windows look out on a grassy quad that's green and pretty in the spring and summer, gorgeous in the fall, and frigid and desolate all winter.

On one of those desolate afternoons late in February, with spring waiting silently in the wings, a man stopped outside my open door and peered in. I looked up from whatever I was doing and said, "Can I help you?"

He stepped inside and scanned all around. No surprises, I would think. He was a large, stoop-shouldered guy with a bloodhound face and a trench coat over his gray suit, maybe around sixty. By now the adrenaline rush made it hard for me to breathe—he had to be one of *them*, coming to collect.

After taking in everything else, he looked my way and said, "Maybe so. Professor Hult, I presume."

"Like it says on the plaque," I said, motioning toward the doorway while fantasizing about a button on my desk releasing a trapdoor in the floor. Drawing breath as steadily as possible, I stood and held out my hand. He reached across the desk and shook it. "Tom Freebinder," he said. He had a smoker's voice and tanned teeth to match.

"What can I do for you, Mr. Freebinder?"

He sat down heavily without waiting to be asked. "I'm here on behalf of a third party, a lady by the name of Doris Ballaster." He let that hang between us. So much for small talk, but the adrenaline backed off a bit.

"All right ... "

"I know you don't know her, but do you know of her?"

The name Ballaster seemed vaguely familiar, but I couldn't place it. "Not that I can recall."

He leaned back in the chair, which groaned briefly. "Then let me fill in the blanks. Doris Ballaster is the widow of Curtis Ballaster, who passed away nearly ten years ago. He was a fund manager with Lehman Brothers. His demise, perhaps fortunately, preceded Lehman's demise, and he left a large estate, even by Wall Street standards. Mrs. Ballaster lives fairly frugally, but she doesn't have to."

"I remember the name now, but this is all news to me."

"Right. The thing is, Mrs. Ballaster thinks there may be something you can do for her. She would like to make you a proposition, which has both academic and business aspects."

I waited for him to explain that in more detail, and he waited for me to respond. We both waited. I blinked first. "What's the proposition?"

"Mrs. Ballaster would like to explain it to you herself, if you could pay her a visit at home, at a mutually convenient time. As soon as possible."

"I see," I said, though I didn't see much. "And what's your role in this, Mr. Freebinder? Are you her lawyer?" The question was almost sarcastic. He didn't give off lawyerly vibes; he gave off cop vibes.

"A friend of the family. Longtime friend. Now, would you be willing to hear Mrs. Ballaster out on this?"

"I don't know. This proposition, it wouldn't involve an offer I can't refuse, would it?"

He showed the first indication that he could be amused. "No, Mrs. Ballaster isn't in that kind of business. Or family."

I nodded as if reassured. What did I have to lose? (Don't look there.) "Okay, I'll come and see her. Where and when?"

"Would tomorrow evening suit you?"

That would be Thursday evening. I had a sort-of date with Lara, my current but probably expiring lady friend—a breakable date in a winding-down affair. "I could do that," I said. "At her home?"

"Yes. She lives at the Paterno, eighth floor."

That raised my eyebrows. "Right in my neighborhood. On the better side of the tracks."

"Small world, the Upper West Side. But that's by sheer coincidence. Mrs. Ballaster has considered candidates from all over the map."

Candidates? "And my number came up?"

"You could say that. I'll let her explain it to you. Tomorrow evening then. Would eight o'clock suit?"

We agreed on that, and he levered himself up, shook hands again without a wink or a nod, and left. I swiped at the sweat beading on my dome. It's not healthy, living on the edge. Coronary before forty?

I went back to whatever I had been doing, but it was hard to concentrate with the distraction of this proposition. With both academic and business aspects. From the rich widow of a Wall Street tycoon. Enough to distract Leonardo from the *Mona Lisa*. Pretty soon I gave up and decided to call it a day, work-wise. I got out my cell phone and speed-dialed Lara—Lara Martinez, ferocious ad exec in Lower Manhattan, smart, sarcastic, burning the emergency flare at both ends.

"Adam," she said, "what's going on?" She was at her office, where she worked long, irregular hours.

"Hi, baby. Look, something's come up for tomorrow night. Can we do this evening instead?"

"What's come up?" I could tell she was also carrying on a conversation with someone else, presumably someone she could see and touch.

"I'm not sure, but even though it couldn't be more important than us, it's not something I can pass up. So this evening? Maybe at Zib's?" Zib's was a favorite restaurant of Lara's, and I liked it too, which was fortunate since I didn't cook.

"That means changing my plans."

"So ..." I heard more muffled conversation, probably slandering my good name.

"Okay, plans changed. But not for a couple more hours. Say about eight."

"I'll see about a reservation," I said and switched off (you don't hang up any more). I called Zib's and was told they could squeeze us in at eight fifteen.

I stuffed some things into my briefcase, plucked my overcoat from the coat rack, shrugged into it, turned out the light, and left. Outside, the only light was manmade even though it was barely 5:00 p.m. The temperature was a little above freezing, with a light mist making things almost as wet as rain. Students and other collegiate types hurried to their destinations, chins tucked down unhappily. I joined them in the same spirit, but luckily I didn't have too far to go since I lived in an apartment building just across 116th Street from the university campus. It was quite a classy residence when it went up during those "last golden years" before the First World War, and all things considered, it had aged well. Suited me fine.

Thomaz, the doorman from one of the Central Asian stans, greeted me, as always, as "Doctor Prof." I took the antique elevator, which works about as well as it ever did, up to my floor, the fourth—*Half as high*, the thought niggled my brain, *as that Wall Street cookie who wants to proposition me.* Once in my apartment I turned on several lights, turned up the heat, hung up my coats, and put on a CD of Hoagy Carmichael singing his own songs. Then I took a shower, as hot as I could stand, and while I was still toweling off, my cell rang. Caller ID id'd Ari Halevi, my best of best friends since we grew up together in Brooklyn.

"Hey, Ari."

"Hey, man, what's bitin'?"

"Not much. Maybe an odd nibble. I'm home. Just finished showering."

"Play some chess tonight?" He always thinks he can beat me, and often does.

"Not tonight. I'm doing dinner with Lara and then, if Venus smiles, having a little dessert too."

"You old killer. What's the odd nibble?"

I considered what to say. Ari knew just about all my secrets, but I'd kept one of them to myself, or tried to.

"Funny thing. This guy comes into my office a couple of hours ago, a big older guy in a trench coat, with eyes like surveillance cameras, definitely not from academia. Do you recall the name of Curtis Ballaster?"

"Yeah, but I think he's dead, and he wasn't all that big."

"Right, some high-flying fund manager for Lehman Brothers before the crash. Anyway, this guy who came to see me says he's representing Ballaster's widow. Says she has a proposition for me."

"She's probably too old for you. Besides, you're stuck with Lara."

"Money always talks loudest. Not that sort of proposition, though. Something combining academics and business, this guy says."

"Well, academics is fun, but business pays the rent. He say any more about this proposition?"

"Nope, closed as a clam. But I'm going to be entertained by the widow Ballaster tomorrow evening. Then we'll see what's what."

"Money's the root of all evil. Just keep reminding yourself."

As if I needed reminding. I splashed on some aftershave lotion without shaving and then dressed and put the Hoagy CD back to track one, popped a bottle of Bavarian Black Lager from Heartland Brewery, and sat back in my comfy recliner to think about things.

CHAPTER 2

Dinner with Lara at Zib's started out bad and didn't get much better. She turned up late and in a contrary mood. At least she looked good, as usual—sexy in a hard-edged way. She was about five seven, just a little shorter than me, with dark eyes and blonde hair that she was always having restyled. A Martinez with blonde hair? It could be natural, I guess—as with just about everything else about females, I could only guess.

Why would she be attracted to me? Not tall, not slim, not handsome. Balding, nearsighted, and not even especially nice. Okay, I had a solid job at a world-class university—reliable breadwinner (amazing breadloser). But she made plenty of bread herself, so what was left? Whatever, it seemed to be wearing off. This relationship, such as it was, might suggest why I never married. Always by choice, hers and mine. Perhaps more hers than mine.

We both ordered exotic seafood—Zib's only does exotic—with a bottle of white Bordeaux. Lara complained about her boss, who she called "that crab" and I regarded as a good businesswoman, more experienced than Lara and certainly no crabbier. After a while, she switched gears and turned sensual and suggestive, which I took as a good sign but not one I could bank on. She made a reference to how we got together in the first place. If either of us was at all romantic, tonight might be thought of as our first anniversary, since it was just about a year ago that we met at a cocktail party, a fundraiser for Democratic politicians. Did we flirt, either of us? Did we make eyes? No, we argued politics—not candidates or people but issues, things like financial regulation and carbon taxes. Neither of us could definitively out-argue the other. In the process, though, we got drunk together and wound up in her bed, where we hit it off splendidly. Our relationship had been pretty much like that ever since.

After dinner at Zib's, we finished up in the same place, and the sex was as lively as ever, but a romantic affair probably needs at least a bit of romance to keep it from losing its tread. I left for home around 1:00 a.m. without any future promises on either side.

In the morning, fortified with plenty of French Roast, I taught a class on the early Roman Republic and a seminar on the philosophical roots of the French Revolution, then did a couple of graduate tutorials. I had lunch with several students at a local sandwich place, trying to loosen them up and get them to say what they really thought instead of what they thought might impress Doctor Prof.

That afternoon I read half a dozen student papers and talked with about that many drop-in students. Later I spent a few hours at Butler Library, doing some research on the last years of the Mogul Empire. Coming up for breath at one point, I noticed it was going on seven o'clock. Panic! I had almost forgotten all about my date with Doris Ballaster. I exited the library with all deliberate haste, snagged some takeout Chinese at one of the university cafeterias, and made it to my apartment by seven-twenty, at which point I realized there was time enough to eat my noodles and chicken and veggies sitting down. I did so at the breakfast nook in the kitchen, washing it down with a Sunset Red Ale from the Chelsea Brewing Company.

The Paterno, which Mrs. Ballaster called home, was a genuine Manhattan landmark, combining elegance and luxury and architectural pizzazz. It was seated, monarchically, on the corner of 116th Street and Riverside Drive, with an outward-curving facade that leaned toward the similarly curving facade of the building's regal twin across the street, the Colosseum. Less obsequious locals have likened them to two pregnant women comparing notes. But as I'd realized when Tom Freebinder dropped the name, the Paterno really was within walking distance of my place, just a few blocks down the street.

Walking distance, though, was easy or not, depending on the weather. This evening it was raining, with a cold, gusty wind blowing up from the river. I thought about taking a cab but rejected that as too wimpy. Overcoatted once more, I unfurled my umbrella and headed out into the elements. By leaning into the gusts, the umbrella a shield before me, I was able to keep up a brisk pace, though it was tricky avoiding collisions with other, similarly militant pedestrians.

Before too long, the imposing porte-cochere of the Paterno hove into view, and after shaking most of the water off my umbrella, I gave my name to the doorman—several cuts above Thomaz, with an accent from close by Buckingham Palace. Evidently Doris had apprised him of my coming, since he pointed me toward the elevators. I followed his direction through the stained-glass vestibule and across the magnificent marble lobby.

At her apartment door, I rang the bell. I couldn't hear anything—good soundproofing—but immediately it was opened by a dark, handsome man in an immaculate white achkan. "Good evening, sir," he purred in lilting Indian English, his palms pressed together in the polite *namaste* greeting. "It is Professor Adam Hult, is it not?"

I confirmed this, and he took my umbrella and overcoat and led me through a broad entryway into something that the word *apartment* doesn't bring to mind. *Townhouse* would be too casual. *Luxury suite* sounded uncomfortably ostentatious; this place was luxurious without ostentation. It was the cat's silkiest meow.

If this lady lived frugally, as Tom Freebinder had claimed, it didn't show.

There was a large living room with a picture window that would have looked out over Riverside Park on nice days; now it was covered with drapes in muted shades of red. The furnishings were mostly in shades of ivory and pale peach. There were paintings—modern impressionist?—that were undoubtedly originals. Freebinder was planted on a chair in a far corner, wearing a different suit but the same well-broken-in trench coat and the same shuttered look. He didn't rise to greet me.

Neither did Doris Ballaster, but that could be explained by the wheelchair she sat in, as the polite valet moved solicitously to stand at her side. She was probably in her seventies, with a round face, pale blue eyes, and well-coiffed white hair. A blanket covered her lap, above which she wore a green blouse that might have cost more than all I was wearing. My first impression was of physical frailty but mental toughness, though that remained to be seen. A lot remained to be seen.

"Good evening, Dr. Hult," she said, holding out her hand. "It's so kind of you to come on such short notice. I am Doris Ballaster, and, of course, you've already met Tom."

I came across the thick Oriental rug and took her hand, deciding at the last moment that a gentle squeeze was probably more appropriate than a cavalier kiss.

"Please, have a seat," she went on, motioning toward a sofa that looked too good for me. "Would you care for something to drink? Some whiskey perhaps, or perhaps something lighter—some wine or coffee or tea?"

"Coffee would be good," I said after sinking into the sofa's embrace. Her coffee would doubtless be better than good.

She nodded to the valet, and he glided from the room. Then, adjusting her wheelchair to face slightly more toward me, she said, "I know that Tom has told you that I've invited you here in order to offer a proposition to you. I will get to that in due time, but it might be good if I set forth the reasons why I am offering it to you and not someone else."

She tilted her head interrogatively, and I said, "Sure."

"Very well, then. I shall take the liberty of reviewing some facts about you—all in the public record, of course." She said that with a prim smile, but I didn't believe her. I got the uncomfortable impression that she knew facts about me that weren't open to the public, the kind of facts that old family friend Tom Freebinder might have access to.

"You're thirty-six years old. To begin near the beginning, you were quite a child prodigy. Humble beginnings, in the good American way, but you graduated from high school and were accepted at Princeton by age twelve. There you took a double major in both mathematics and philosophy. Not a usual combination, is it?"

"I suppose not," I replied, and when she seemed to expect something more, I added, "I started out in math, which has always fascinated me—the arcane beauty of its unpredictable byways—but there came a point at which it seemed to me that where mathematics stretches our understanding to the limit, as it does at every point of the compass, those are regions where philosophy might begin. Gödel's incompleteness theorems are one such region. But it is philosophy of a certain kind. It's hard to explain."

"Impossible to explain to me, but not necessary either," she said graciously. "Ah, Gopal, please serve us now."

The valet brought out coffee and accoutrements on a cart made, I would guess, of mahogany inlaid with ivory. He asked how I took it, and I said, "The better the bean, the blacker I like it," which drew a smile, though he would also have smiled if I said I preferred instant. The coffee, served in china cups with real handles on them, tasted every bit as good as brewing coffee smells.

"And then," she continued when Gopal had withdrawn, "having graduated *summa cum laude* at age sixteen, you went on to doctoral studies in history at Harvard, receiving your PhD at twenty. Not quite a record, but close. Instead of pursuing mathematics or philosophy, however, you switched to history. Just out of curiosity, why the change?"

"Good question. Math and philosophy have never stopped fascinating me, but they only comprise a small segment of the whole pie—I mean, that is, the whole of human experience. I wanted to broaden, and history seemed the best way to go."

"I see," she said, "and it makes sense to me. Continuing with your curriculum vitae, then, you were an associate professor at Amherst for five years before you moved on to your current post at Columbia. All of this is excellent—you are certifiably smart—but it isn't the main reason you are here this evening."

I sipped the heavenly coffee and raised my eyebrows, hoping to be ready for anything.

"There are other things that are even more interesting to me. You compose large crossword puzzles with few black spaces in them. You are a master-strength chess player. In other words, you are a problem poser and a problem solver. And more to the point, there is the matter of your published books. Four of them."

"And lots of articles."

"Yes, but the articles are purely academic for the most part. The books, I believe, are addressed to a wider audience."

"I'd agree with that. I think wider is better."

"As do I. Now, four titles—*Dreaming Scientists*, *Not Bacon or the Earl*, *Old As It Looks, A Christian Nation?* Catchy titles."

"Editors help with that."

"No doubt. But the books themselves ... Is even one of them on a subject in your field of expertise?"

"Not exactly. I'm something of a generalist."

"To say the least. *Dreaming Scientists* is a lively investigation into certain medieval alchemists—"

"Excuse me," I interrupted, "but have you read it? One of the main points is that alchemy came to full fruition in the Renaissance, not the Middle Ages. The alchemists and the new scientists were born as twins. Both were seeking ways for humans to exert control over nature. Same ambition, different techniques. One technique worked; the other didn't. But the ambition tells us more than the techniques."

If this rebuke fazed her, she didn't show it. Smiling, she said, "I stand corrected. But I have read it. I don't always express myself as accurately as I should. Perhaps I can do better with *Not Bacon or the Earl*—the book that may put to its final rest the hard-to-kill idea that someone else wrote Shakespeare's plays."

"No, you can never kill it. I put a big stake through its heart, but Hollywood is still wringing cash out of the popular old fantasy."

"The public prefers fantasy and pays for it, one way and another. And then, next there is *Old As It Looks*, your comprehensive refutation of the belief that the earth was created less than ten thousand years ago. Another formidable argument in terms that the average reader can comprehend. Not all readers will agree, of course, but to disagree, they have to ignore all manner of evidence."

"Readers, and people in general, are accustomed to that," I said, in tune with her cynicism.

"Indeed. Finally we have *A Christian Nation?* This, if I may say so, is my personal favorite, where you refute the idea that America is or ever was a 'Christian nation.'"

"The phrase really is a sort of oxymoron," I said. "The irony is that I had to read the Bible to become sure of that. In the Bible, the 'nations' are the various ethnic groups all across the world, much the same as we use the term today. And the 'kingdom of God,' especially as preached by Jesus, is a spiritual kingdom or authority which intends to supersede all national or other political authorities."

"Exactly," she said acidly. "Take over the world for Jesus."

"But not, if I understand it rightly, by military or even political means. I think the idea is a voluntary shifting of allegiance—upward, I suppose you'd say."

"No, I wouldn't say. And in *A Christian Nation?* you apply this idea to our nation's history."

"Yes. The seventeenth-century Puritan colonists mostly had their fill of an official state religion in England and just wanted a place where they could farm the land and practice their faith freely. Some among them, however, certainly had the dream of founding a 'Christian nation' in the wilderness. As I've suggested, though, insofar as their ambition was to unite the kingdom of God with an earthly political authority, they misunderstood their founder's blueprint. They would have been repeating the same error they had escaped from. And, of course, their dream has never come to pass."

"Thank God," she sniffed sarcastically.

"Well, whatever, by the time they got around to having a revolution and founding a government, the leaders were only conventionally religious or, like Franklin and Jefferson, non-religious freethinkers. Their novel brainwave, ironically anticipated in a way by Jesus, was to separate the political and religious authorities for the good of both. And the country's subsequent history has mostly borne that out. Christianity has flourished under that policy and become the dominant religion, and yet many outspoken Christians keep complaining how non-Christian the rest of their supposedly 'Christian nation' is. They're like cats complaining that dogs aren't cats. That's *A Christian Nation?* in a nutshell."

"A pistachio. Now, along with your books, Dr. Hult, we have the variety of courses you have taught as a full professor at Columbia. It's the same pattern as with your books, all over the ballpark. How, if I may ask, do you manage that?"

I finished the cup of coffee, and before I could set it down, Gopal appeared at my side and refilled it. I wondered if he moonlighted as a stage magician.

"How do I manage it? I'm a generalist, as I said. I have broad interests."

"As do many of us, but they don't turn us loose teaching upper-level courses at Columbia University on everything from Alexander to Zorro. My point is—and I have no interest in flattering you—you are a phenomenon, Dr. Hult. You get away with it because you're just so good at it. All right, so much for that. I have one more observation about your professional life to date. What one word best characterizes your books, particularly the last three?"

I thought about that. "Truth telling? Exposure?"

"Yes, but the word I have in mind is *debunking*. You are drawn to debunking, Dr. Hult, and you are very good at it."

I bowed as best I could from deep in the sofa. "I appreciate your good opinion."

"Let me repeat, this is not flattery. I am, I think, every bit as interested in truth telling as you are. One truth is that I believe you may be capable—more capable, perhaps, than anyone else—of meeting a certain challenge I have for you. Which brings me," she said with a real smile, "at long last to my proposition."

CHAPTER 3

Doris leaned forward as if to concentrate my attention. "Tell me, Dr. Hult, what do you know about the Shroud of Turin?"

Not a question I was expecting. Collecting my thoughts, I answered, "Not a whole lot. It's one of those sacred relics, purported to be the burial shroud of Jesus Christ, with his image somehow imprinted on it. Haven't scientists dated it to the Middle Ages?"

"Yes, but that finding is hotly disputed. Disputed, of course, mainly on religious grounds. Even so, though, the Shroud is more than just one more sacred relic. A fragment of the true cross may be just a hunk of old wood, probably is, and who can prove otherwise? A finger bone of St. Stephen may be any old finger bone—again, the whole burden of proof rests on the believers, while the skeptics rest their case without a qualm. But there is an image on that length of cloth in Turin, and no one denies that it's an image of a naked, bearded, crucified man. So, quite understandably, the believers point to that image and challenge skeptics to explain how it got there. The burden of proof shifts somewhat."

I shrugged. "Painted on or stained or otherwise put on there by some clever graphic artist hoping to score some francs or piasters. It looks like he succeeded."

"Beyond his dreams. Thus far, however, modern attempts to explain or demonstrate how the forger did it have fallen short of the mark. At least, let me put it this way: more and more people, some of them rather important people, have come forward recently, expressing skepticism about the skeptics. There is a very real danger of belief in the Shroud's authenticity spreading from the religious fringe to a much broader range of people—ordinary religious people, people open to any new spiritual twist, people fascinated by the paranormal. Before long, it could be spreading to just plain, ordinary curious people."

She paused to let that sink in. It didn't sink in very far. I said, "So what? If it's a forgery, eventually we'll figure out the how."

"Of course it's a forgery, and of course *eventually* we'll figure it out. In the meantime, though, as I trust you've noticed, the human race is stampeding toward self-destruction. Failing states, revolutions, terrorism, famine, flooding, drought, disease, nuclear proliferation, drug trafficking, slavery, child prostitution, global warming—need I go on? Our global civilization is in desperate straits, and our main responses, increasingly, are denial and religious consolations. Religious 'solutions'—salvation crusades, pilgrimages to Mecca or the Ganges, advice from the Dalai Lama. Perpetual prayer, mass meditation, fanatical fundamentalism. All of this, however ignorantly well meant, drains energy from genuine efforts toward improvement, even toward actual solutions. Rational solutions, scientifically valid and effective solutions."

Again she paused, aware, I think, that she might be sounding rather fanatical herself. Then she went on in a quieter tone. "You see that this matters to me, Dr. Hult. I'm an idealist without apology. I wish more people were. I thought you might be, but it doesn't much matter whether you are or not so long as you are an extremely capable debunker. And not only capable but successful, even renowned. What you have, and I need, is world-class intellectual clout. If you can expose the Shroud as a fraud, there may be some hope of turning the tide.

"So here's my challenge, Dr. Hult. If you will take on this assignment, I will give you a fifty thousand-dollar retainer. In regard to this, please forgive me for bringing up one more personal matter. Your financial portfolio is a house of cards, a house of illusions. You have a problem with the IRS, quite a sizable problem. How that came about is interesting in itself but doesn't concern me now. The fifty thousand could help you there, but not enough. If you succeed in this challenge, however—if you successfully persuade both the general public and the intelligentsia that the Shroud is a fake, a distraction from our terrible problems rather than a solution to them—I will make your problem with the T-men vanish like a summer mist. Or, more practically speaking, our mutual friend Tom Freebinder will."

I was flushing, as both of them surely noticed, with a potent brew of embarrassment, anger, and either greed or hope. Temporizing, I asked breathily, "How would he do that?"

She turned to him. "Tom?"

He stood up, went over to the window, and moved the drape aside, as if checking for a peeping namesake (eight stories up). Apparently satisfied, he turned to me and said, "I'm retired from the FBI. Thirty-five years of snooping into secrets and making a lot of enemies and a few friends and, most relevant to you, some uncollected IOUs. There are skeletons that have skeletons. You don't want to know."

That seemed condescending. "I don't need Mr. Fix-It," I retorted. "I need a big bill paid, a financial settlement. I don't need an arm-twister."

"Yes, you do. Once their fangs are in you this deep, they keep on sucking. They don't care how smart you are. To them, you look pretty dumb. Hell, to me you look pretty dumb. But you've got a lawyer working on this. What's he got to say?"

I almost pleaded confidentiality but realized the absurdity of it. "He's working on that financial settlement."

"Working with *his* retainer, *your* money, where *his* whole financial incentive is to string out the negotiation, and on top of that he's overmatched against those hardheads. Oh, he'll present you with a 'final best deal' one of these days. Only it won't be final. Won't ever be, unless some strings are pulled, real tight."

I stared at him then back at Doris Ballaster. "We aren't talking—"

"No, no," she assured me, "Tom enjoys colorful metaphors. There are ways of applying pressure apart from thumbs on throats. But now, Dr. Hult, with most of our cards on the table, what do you say? Fifty thousand up front, all your investigative expenses paid, and then, if I am satisfied with your results, your tango with the government no longer even a bad dream. All in a good cause—and, I should think, for a professional debunker, a worthy challenge. What say you?"

What could I say? "I suppose, Mrs. Ballaster, you could start calling me Adam."

▪ ▪ ▪ ▪ ▪ ▪

I walked back home with my umbrella furled in my fist, letting the cold rain be a cleansing stream. I had that feeling that my life had just turned a corner, and I had evidence to back up the feeling. I was walking away with a great big promise—contingent on my "satisfying" the rich widow and her spooky friend—and I had her check for fifty large in my wallet. Who could blame me, though, for feeling manipulated as well as x-rayed?

A bar called Silvio's approached on my left. I'd been in there before, though I didn't frequent bars much. Tonight I felt like frequenting. Inside it was dim and smelled alcoholic. Quite a few patrons either kept to themselves or murmured among themselves or blathered without inhibition. I took a stool at the bar and, when the bar chick came over, ordered a double Jack Daniels on the rocks. When it came, I took a gulp and relished its burning course down into my gut and, immediately, up into my brain.

What rankled most was that big thick cop agreeing with the feds that I was dumb. What rankled, I mean, was that he was right. All my life I'd been a genius about almost everything but money. Money I sort of took for granted. Probably with some soul searching I would discover I'd always felt intellectually superior to money. I was supposed to be, as Doris said, this ultra-rational phenom, but my attitude toward money wasn't rational; it was loony, counterproductive, self-defeating, the road to ruin. Did I need snooty Doris and tough Tom to tell me this? Hell no, I'd known it for years. I could see it like I could see my glasses were greasy. But knowing and doing could be worlds apart. The wisdom of Solomon. But he had it all together, didn't he? Why not me?

I rapped my empty glass on the counter and ordered a refill. A new customer came and sat on the stool next to me, an older gent with a white goatee who started trying to engage me in conversation. I ignored him and took my first sip of the renewed Jack Daniels.

When I thought about it, I knew I had no good reason for money problems. Plenty of reasons, just not good ones. I'd never learned to cook or cared to learn, so I ate out all the time. I attracted women with rigorous analytical arguments combined with lavish spending on dining, beach hotels, shows, cruises, jewelry and such, and I was smart enough to know which ploy worked best. I traveled a lot to faraway places, both for scholarly reasons and often just for fun. Travel may enrich the mind but not the bank account. All in all, during my wild twenties, I shredded lots of lettuce. And well into my thirties. What they call a cash-flow problem.

To do myself credit, I had spent money in some meritorious ways as well. My parents, for one thing, Gus and Bernadine Hult—the proverbial deserving poor. My pop was sprung from that last generation of men who felt a moral imperative to be the single provider. He drove trucks for various companies in the New York and Jersey area, and in the early seventies he poured his savings into the down payment on a smaller, older house in a decent Brooklyn neighborhood east of the Washington Cemetery. That was his gift to his new bride, my mom, who was an orphaned survivor of a hopeless upstate hippy commune. They were rough but dogged people who lived by fifties American values in the seventies American economy. I came along with the bicentennial in '76, and my brother, Sam, came three years later. Pop, a heavy smoker, had health problems that laid him up from time to time, a body blow to the family income. We ate a lot of hot dogs and hamburger-potato fry-ups. Even so, when I started reading and spouting arithmetic around age three, they arranged for some private tutoring. I don't know how or even whether they paid for it. Then I zoomed through high school and Princeton and Harvard and became a college prof at a starting salary larger than Pop brought home in his best years, which were long behind him by then, though the Marlboros still hadn't killed him yet, amazingly. I wanted to move them into better digs—the old homestead was wearing out—even though I couldn't really afford it. But they were firmly entrenched and honestly didn't want to move, so I compromised and took out a bank loan to pay for an Extreme Makeover, Small Box Edition. (Sam, by the way, took off for Florida before his senior year of high school to be a surfer and beach bum. Booze and babes. It hasn't turned out well.) Mom and Pop kept soldiering on. He was mostly housebound by then with a respirator, but they didn't have much savings to speak of or retirement income, and neither of them was quite old enough to get Social Security. So I helped to support them—see halo.

So much for expenses; what about income? Substantial and increasing salary from Amherst and then Columbia. Some stock market investments (smart guys know how to pick 'em). Royalties from the sale of those four books that Doris enthused about. Which reminds me of that nasty matter of taxes. Smart guys also know how to master all those syntactical obfuscations and legal conundrums that the IRS tries to snow you with. We know how to finesse their unreasonable and extravagant claims on our legitimate earnings. We are so good at this that they, those hardheads that Tom mentioned, might not even notice it for some time. They might not ever notice it.

Or else, at some point, they might. Then they might salivate over things like interest and penalties. Serious money. Meanwhile, sometime around the great crash of 2008, most of those Wall Street picks might have fallen off the table. Coincidentally, all those credit cards might have maxed out and started bumping up the compound interest. I *understand* all this perfectly.

I finished off the second whiskey and looked at my watch, but due to the dim light and my greasy glasses and addled brain, I couldn't make out what it said. How late could it be? Not all that late. This train of thought had me gazing lustfully toward the bar chick, when somehow my better angel took over and I dug out a twenty, flipped it onto the bar like Jack Nicholson would, and sauntered like the Duke out through the door. I didn't even forget my umbrella.

CHAPTER 4

I caught myself looking at Benny's eyes, trying to decide if they were owl eyes or vulture eyes. He was sitting across the table from me, looking over my shoulder at infinity. Benny Halevi was Ari's father, a medium-size guy in his early seventies with rawhide for skin, who still played soccer with middle-school kids. He didn't talk any more than he had to.

Everyone else did, though, except maybe for Shelley, Ari's thirteen-year-old niece, who chattered among her own set but tended to be more subdued around adults, like most barely teen-agers. We were finishing up, in a leisurely way, a Saturday morn-ing brunch at Ari's century-old brick rowhouse in the Windsor Terrace section of Brooklyn: boiled eggs, kosher sausages, fresh strawberries from someplace sunnier and warmer, and Hannah's cinnamon rolls that could corrupt Francis of Assisi.

Hannah was Ari's older sister, a plump, gregarious woman with a natural-born orange mop like Orphan Annie. When we were kids, they teased her by calling her Hannie, but she frus-trated them by accepting it good-naturedly. Now she was rins-ing off dishes in the kitchen sink, just inside from the sun porch where the rest of us were lounging around the messed-up table, enjoying coffee and fourth-quarter nibbles and the blessed sun-shine that had broken through at last.

"*Pulp Fiction*," said Ari. We had gotten on to favorites—res-taurants, songs, and now movies.

"*Pulp Fiction*! You can't be *see*-rious! It smells, Ari. Flush it down the toilet! Only a man could love it." This was from Lara in a good mood—yes, that Lara. Soon after she started seeing me, she naturally met Ari and his family, and she and Hannah struck up an improbable friendship. They each seemed to admire what the other had. Lara had style, chutzpah, looks, and sharp edges, while Hannah had a dependable husband, a lively daughter, and niceness.

"Sorry," Ari said. "Change that vote to *The Sound of Music*."

"Ha!" Lara snorted.

"Over to you, Adam," said Ari. "Whatcha got?"

I was working on one more cinnamon roll. "I guess I'll go for *Duck Soup*, the Marx Brothers. Can't get much better than that. What about you, Benny—and don't claim you never see any movies, with a TV and satellite dish."

Benny tapped his spoon gently on the tablecloth, as though gathering his thoughts. My impression was that his thoughts were always pre-gathered. "Okay," he rumbled in his carefully articulated, faintly Hebrew-accented bass, "what about *Life Is Beautiful*, with that great Italian comic. Deal with the worst kind of evil by making fun of it."

"Good choice," said Lara, while fixing Ari with a teasing smile. "Great film."

"What do they know from great films," Hannah pronounced, stepping back onto the sun porch and wiping her hands with a dishtowel. "My Shelley sees more movies every week than the rest of you see in a year. Tell us what's the best, baby."

Shelley flashed her self-conscious, metal-studded grin. At this point she was all nose and ears and elbows, with dark-red hair cut short and spiky and with one of those stiff, velcro-fastened casts on her broken left wrist. In five years she would be a looker, and in ten she would be strawberry ice cream. She blurted out, half-laughing, "*Kick-Ass*!"

"*Kick-Ass*!" Ari trumpeted, slapping a high five with Shelley and then with Lara. "How come the kids get all the good flicks?" *Kick-Ass* was a popular teen-screen a few years back.

"More coffee, anybody?" said Hannah, scooping up the coffee pot and offering it around the table.

"Speaking of Saudi Arabia, what happens if the Saudis can't hold it together?" Ari asked.

"Who's talking about that?"

"You know, kick-ass. Kick-ass all over the whole Arabian universe, finally coming to a theater near you if you live in a palace in Riyadh. What if they can't hold it together and oil starts costing real money, and everything else with it?"

"We'll hold it together," I said. "We'll have to—no other choice, really."

"We? Who's we?" Lara posed.

"I mean the US. I'm not being patriotic, just trying to be realistic."

"Up till now, recently at least, we've been siding with the rebels, the underdogs, the little guys," she went on. "With encouraging words, if not with guns and bombs. Democratic values and such. But this time, with the huddled masses clamoring and dying in the streets, we prop up the regime because we need their oil?"

"Probably won't matter in the end what we do," Ari said. "Haven't Iraq and Afghanistan taught us there are places we can't control no matter how many guns and bombs we have?"

Hannah heaved a theatrical sigh. "Oh, this is no fun. Men are no fun. Come on, girls. Let's go do it."

She meant go shopping and maybe take in a movie or something else that turned up. That was the plan for the day. The three of them got up and bustled around the house, perfecting costumes and makeup. Shelley bustled right behind Lara , whom she idolized. Pretty soon the front door closed behind them and the vocal trio dwindled into quietness. Benny went out through the sliding glass door to the patio to smoke one of his unfiltered Camels.

He lived with Hannah and her husband, Chuck, an insurance agent, in the same Midwood neighborhood where Hannah and Ari and I had grown up, a few blocks away, but he spent quite a bit of time here with Ari. His wife, Abby, died of a brain tumor four years ago. She was a second mother to me, and I missed her like crazy. So did Ari, of course, and now, with just the two of us there at the table, the house seemed too empty. His mother gone, his wife gone—through divorce a couple of years ago. They'd had two children, but their son, Amos, died of childhood leukemia just before his fifth birthday. Their daughter, Lucy, now nine years old, lived with her mother but stayed with Ari most weekends, though today she was at a roller-skating birthday party.

All in all, too much death, too much separation. Probably par for the human course, however.

Ari drank from his coffee cup and made a face. "Lukewarm, yuck. Okay, bro, tell me about the mysterious proposition from the rich elderly widow. And don't tell me there's nothing to it. I can tell."

"Nothing to it, really. Well, maybe a little something. She made me a challenge, gave me a sort of assignment."

He made a circular hand gesture. Give more …

"She, this Doris Ballaster, she's a woman of, I guess you'd say, passionate convictions. She thinks people depend so much on religious faith to solve the world's problems that it detracts—drains energy, as she put it—from real, more practical solutions."

"So? Sounds about right to me." His warm brown eyes twinkled. He was a bit taller than me, and he kept himself in shape, running and pushing weights.

"She has a particular thing about the Shroud of Turin. You know about that?"

"Catholic relic. Highly venerated. It's turned Turin into a major pilgrimage site, even though the Shroud is seldom shown to the public."

"But there is the occasional private viewing for the privileged few with serious pull at the Vatican. For instance, *moi*."

"The Ballaster heiress has arranged that? Why?"

"Ah, now we get down to it. She thinks the Shroud is a special case, a relic whose phoniness is harder to establish than most such things. Harder because of the nature of the image on it and, for just that reason, more necessary to debunk. She's afraid it may become a sort of talisman around which energy-draining religious devotion will grow."

"So naturally she turns to the great debunker. She must have tempted you with more than just an intellectual challenge."

Benny came back inside and poured himself another cup of coffee from the insulated holder before sitting back at the table. I used the interlude to calibrate my response.

"Fifty thousand dollars up front, plus expenses. Then another fifty if I satisfy her expectations."

Benny stared at me. Personal probing wasn't his bent, but I had his attention.

Ari was frowning. "Only another fifty if you expose the most famous Catholic relic of the last five hundred years? You didn't hold out for more?"

"She says the fame itself will bring fortune, and undoubtedly it would, were I to succeed." I despised myself for fudging the truth with my best friends, but when it came to this money problem, I was like an alcoholic in denial.

But Ari let it pass, saying, "When are you supposed to start? You've already got a job."

"Well, right away I'll start with the basic research, getting oriented. Other current research projects get shelved. Of course, I'll finish all my stuff with spring term at the U, but after that I'm full time on the Shroud. And if that takes me into the fall, Doris tells me a sabbatical will be arranged. Maybe she's such a platinum-level underwriter that she could actually make that happen."

"So you'll be digging into the Shroud of Turin?" Benny asked quietly.

"That's the new plum."

"Interesting," he said.

Ari suggested that we should finish doing up the dishes and then maybe he and I could go play some handball. Besides chess, handball is our other mano a mano, more literally. We usually play on a court over at the high school in his neighborhood. We're fairly evenly matched—I'm a bit better at chess, and he usually wins at handball. We've been honing each other at both since we were in fifth or sixth grade, around the same time we also got into martial arts. That was really Benny's doing, or rather, the two of us dragged it out of him. Benny was, I think, an officer or operative in the Mossad, the elite Israeli intelligence outfit. He never confirmed that—Benny and the Mossad are equally secretive—but we naturally devoted all our intelligence to ferreting out his father's secrets, and eventually we pegged it (as I still believe) with close to 90 percent certainty. Among our discoveries was his expertise in Israeli unarmed combat techniques, and we bugged him to teach us until finally he did. Like in *The Karate Kid*, though, he made us understand the heart of the matter. Not fun and games but responsibility.

Benny and Abby had moved from Israel to Brooklyn in 1978, when Ari was three. After that, Benny was "away" quite a bit, which was one of the clues Ari and I pursued in trying to figure out how he put food on their table. He retired, as far as we could tell, seven or eight years ago, but with Benny, you never knew. As for Ari, he was many-sided. He did gigs as a clarinetist, jazz and classical, and also earned money as an ad-hoc, top of the line bodyguard. His main income source, though, was as a computer consultant, which involved ordinary fixes and also sophisticated tweaking and hacking.

So anyway, after the three of us cleaned thing up, Benny said he would do some gardening, and Ari and I headed over to the handball court.

CHAPTER 5

The next three months—the rest of spring semester—kept me hopping. I'm conscientious enough about my teaching responsibilities, I think (still employed), and as I've indicated, I have an appetite for research. I wasn't far into my new, potentially make-or-break project when I realized it was going to be far from simple—as Doris had implied.

I started by checking out online Shroud sites—mostly produced by believers, naturally—and following out their links. I checked Google, Wikipedia, and Amazon for leads and references. They led me to numerous books and articles. Morningside Heights, where Columbia is located, was crammed with good bookstores, and I quickly tracked down and bought three books that seemed to offer a good introduction to the subject. Two of the authors concluded that the Shroud might well be the real thing, while the other book, an in-depth history of the Catholic Church in the late Middle Ages, included a chapter investigating the Shroud's provenance.

One of the first things I looked into was Jewish burial customs around the time of Christ. I had always assumed he must have been wrapped like a mummy, rather than having the cloth draped over him lengthwise. But, I found, my assumption was wrong; lengthwise was in accord with their tradition. Another relevant piece of lore I turned up was an ordinance in their law that if a corpse was contaminated with blood, it must be interred without washing. The forger I was tracking must, somehow, have known these things also.

Otherwise, my research confirmed most of what I thought I already knew. Of the many questions surrounding the artifact, the primary one—the one it made sense to look into first—seemed to be the question of carbon 14 dating. A 1988 testing of small swatches cut from the Shroud determined that the fabric itself dated from no earlier than the thirteenth century. If that result was held up under further scrutiny, then the image on the Shroud could only be a very clever counterfeit, and the problem would resolve itself into figuring out how it was done.

I wasn't a physicist and had only the average child prodigy's understanding of radiocarbon dating, but I knew at least one physicist, Chou Li-Cheng. Chou was a fellow Columbian, a fifty-something nuclear physicist from Taiwan. He and I had served time together on a faculty committee and hit it off pretty well, so in the last week of March I gave him a call and arranged for a lunch meeting a few days later. Meanwhile, so as not to appear too unlearned, I read some layman's explanations of the technique and boned up on the particular controversy regarding the 1988 testing of the Shroud.

Chou was already there when I showed up, on time, at Panicci, a high-toned, pretentious pizza joint on Claremont Avenue, a block from the campus. He rose to greet me, beaming a smile. One thing I liked about him was that I towered over him, as he was only an inch or so over five feet and weighed around a hundred pounds.

"Adam, what pleasant thing to hear from you other day! How you keeping yourself?" He spoke fairly fluent English but spoke it fast with a thick accent and fractured grammar, so I had to listen hard.

"Couldn't be better even if I didn't try. You ordered yet?"

"No, man, waiting for you."

"Well, I appreciate it." We sat down, and I waved a waiter over. Table service was one of Panicci's high-toned amenities, along with the prices. After we ordered—Greek salad for him and lobster and artichoke pizza for me—I asked, "How's the family, Li-Cheng?"

"Wife is okay, but she got stomach problems. Can't eat hardly nothing. Thinks guy like me that knows about quarks and pi-mesons oughta know better than medical guys." He shook his head, laughing. "Son is working tail off in first year grad school at Berkeley, studying economics—crazy stuff. They try making science out of it. They make it sound like science, but not really science. All about human behavior, you know? Totally unpredictable, you ask me. But Wang, he don't ask me. He sweating bullets thinking he not gonna make it, and then he always come out top of class. Got his mother's worry gene."

I laughed along with him. He was the kind of person that just made you feel good—seemed to be free of that worry gene.

After our food came, I told him I was looking into a historical matter, an ancient but well-preserved piece of cloth that involved carbon 14 dating. He nodded vigorously and went into an explanation of the three isotopes of carbon—12, 13, and 14. Carbon 12, he said, makes up almost 99 percent of naturally occurring carbon, including the carbon in living things like cotton and linen. Living things also have minute amounts of the unstable isotope carbon 14. The ratio between these isotopes remains constant as long as the organism is alive, but when it dies—when cotton or linen is made into cloth, for instance—the carbon 14 isotope begins to decay, to disappear, at a constant rate. It has a half-life of about 5,730 years, meaning that if the cloth was made that long ago, only half of its original carbon 14 would remain. This constant rate of decay provides a reliable way to measure the age of dead organic things, like wood or bones or cloth. Only a small bit of the object is tested, since the testing process destroys the bit.

This is a simplified version of what he told me, and what he told me, he said, was a simplified version of the truth. I couldn't handle the truth.

Okay, but was it simplified so much as to be falsified or misleading?

No, he said, this version was accepted in court all the time. It was true enough.

I took a swallow of my Sam Adams Boston Lager. "All right. But now, this ancient piece of cloth I'm concerned with, there are allegations that the radiocarbon testing on it might be wildly off base. How likely is that?"

Chou made a face like something tasted bad, not his salad. "Two things," he said after a moment. "One, what they call chain of evidence. Maybe, if people not watching real close, or better, if camera not watching, somebody slip some foreign source of carbon into sample, either by accident or on purpose—to screw things up for some reason. Not often, but could happen. Two, contamination of this cloth itself, not just sample. Whole thing contaminated by foreign carbon that have got into cloth sometime after it first made."

"Foreign carbon?"

"Sure. Carbon from some, any other source. Your old piece of cloth, maybe it lay on ground some time, or maybe under water, for some few weeks, maybe four hunnerd years ago. Microorganisms, millions of them, make home in there, eat each other in there, poop in there. Could have happened. Lots of things like that."

"And that could throw off the dating?"

"Oh yeah, little bit or way off, no way to tell. That why when testing done, small sample goes through special cleaning, for clean out foreign carbon, make cloth as close to new as can be."

Now I thought we were getting down to it. "So, this special cleaning, how reliable is that? I mean, how sure can they be that they're getting out all the foreign carbon? Or else, maybe going too far and restoring the cloth to newer than new, different from what it originally was?"

He pondered this, chewing the last bits of his salad. "Okay, this what I think. This dating technique about sixty, seventy years old now. Like with other things, scientists learning as they go, getting technique better, making it work better. Better controls, better ways to determine how reliable results are. In 1960, who knows? Today, pretty darn reliable."

▪ ▪ ▪ ▪ ▪ ▪

"Fishy, Adam. Your deal with this babe gives off a certain odor."

That was Lara's assessment, or rather her first impression. She was wrapped in a green and purple quilt (and nothing else), lounging on the couch in my living room, holding a glass of Oregon Pinot Gris elegantly with her long fingers. I was working on a bottle of Guinness on the same couch, my mediocre physique covered with a fleecy bathrobe. The lamps were low. It was after midnight, just beginning the second day after I lunched with Chou, and I was in that post-coital lassitude where thinking comes slowly. I had been vaguely wondering if maybe the affair still might have some life in it.

"Think so?"

"You think? A hundred grand may be pocket change for her, but she knows it's going to light you up. And for doing what? Quite a few religious addicts may think that shroud's the real thing, but they're still religious addicts. Proving it's a fake should be easy pickings for someone like you. It doesn't quite compute, Adam."

Untypically, I didn't feel like arguing, but I said, "According to la Ballaster, any number of efforts to prove it's a fake have already fallen short. Maybe it won't be all that easy."

"Swamp gas! You say that, and you'd like it to be true because you want everything to work out according to the script. You succeed where all have failed, you cut the mystical knot, and your grateful patron forks over the full amount while cameras flash, fade to close with strings. Swamp gas!"

I took a long pull on the bitter brew. "I don't see the problem, Lara. So maybe I'll be able to prove it without too much difficulty. Lady B. won't care how easy or hard it is. She just wants it done. As you say, it's pocket change to her."

She shook her head, annoyed. "You don't get it. There's a script here, some kind of fiction. That whole scene you described in her fairy queen palace, that's the opening scene. Breathtaking scenery, some pageantry, a little sleight of hand, and plenty of intrigue. These strangers who know you better than you know yourself. And then there's her Rasputin, this shadowy counselor, what's his name?"

"Freebinder."

"Freebinder—who's got a name like that? Okay, maybe it's real, maybe not, but who is he? He claims to be ex-fibbie, but for all you know, he's with the mob or the KGB. You don't know much at all here, Adam. And all the scripting sounds like a setup."

I was at a disadvantage in this chat, since I'd given her the same version I gave Ari. Nothing about the real terms of the deal or their apocalyptic diagnosis of my personal finances or, for that matter, the fact that they were right. There was way more to the script than Lara knew about or than I wanted her to know about. But her speculations suggested that I might have let slip more than I wanted. So I had to tiptoe.

"I don't know, sugar. What kind of fall would they be setting me up for? Why? Sounds more likely to me that Doris wants what she says she wants, basically for the reasons she gave. You're imagining conspiracies here."

"I could Google your friend Freebinder, just like he probed you. Or better yet, Ari could, and Freebie wouldn't have a postage stamp to hide behind. Let's do it, Adam."

"Hey, girl, we just finished doing it."

Through her empty wine glass, she gave me an evil leer.

CHAPTER 6

I descended the cathedral steps slowly, in somewhat of a daze. It was a cool, sunny April day with swirling breezes and a sprinkling of cotton clouds, a pleasant day, and I felt inclined to walk and think. It had been two months since Doris propositioned me and two weeks since she handed me the plane ticket for Turin, via Paris. I didn't know how she wangled the viewing—don't ask, don't tell. Possibly she had pull in the New York archdiocese. It didn't matter how; now that I'd seen the Shroud, I had much to ponder.

This was the second day in a whirlwind weekend squeezed in between university duties. I hopped the pond yesterday, Friday, checking in late at the Grand Hotel Sitea, a plush accommodation only about a mile from the cathedral. Tomorrow I had an appointment with a medieval historian in Milan, but for the rest of today I was fancy free.

But not really. Walking, I drifted south, in the direction of my hotel. Turin is a beautiful old city—beautiful, at least, in its older parts—but I was too distracted to appreciate it properly. I wandered past a large ornate Renaissance palace, the Palazzo Madama, and then past the equally sumptuous Egyptian Museum. I came to my hotel but kept going down toward the Po River.

You have to understand, the image on that cloth has a haunting quality, no matter what you believe about it. A naked, apparently crucified man, covered with what looks like gashes all over his body, and bloodstains on the cloth. If this was the work of some sort of artist, he was an imaginative cousin of Hieronymus Bosch. Beyond that, my investigation was jumping off into more directions and complications than I expected. If the Shroud was a forgery, just exactly how was it done? Even with Dr. Chou's elucidation, there were still questions about the radiocarbon dating. The date of the dating, for instance. If such tests were iffy in 1960 but had evolved since then into greater reliability, what about a test done in 1988?

Then there was the historically known provenance of the artifact. It first appears with any certainty in the historical record during the mid-fourteenth century in the possession of a minor French nobleman, Geoffroi de Charny. Prior to that there are tantalizing hints that it might have been held and venerated by the secretive order of the Knights Templar. And back before that, there is a theory that it might be one and the same as a mysterious "Image of Edessa," one of the most deeply venerated relics during the long centuries of the Byzantine Empire.

I came to an extensive, lush municipal park extending down to the banks of the Po, the Parco del Valentino. There were ancient stoneworks and fountains, trees and shrubbery, lawns and ponds and flowers of every variety, only a few of which I could name. Strolling here seemed to "still my beating mind," in Prospero's phrase—odd bits of Shakespeare clung to me ever since I did that book on him.

A memory came to me from my childhood, when I was six or seven and our school class went on an outing to the Statue of Liberty. It was a cold, foggy day, and we took an excursion boat from Brooklyn across the bay. The other kids were all a couple of years older and looked on me as a freaky little runt, so naturally I had socialization problems. Anyway, I'm sure I was more focused on the goal of our journey than they were. I was peering into the mist when the Big Lady suddenly emerged, ghostly at first but then clearer in her form and her majestic stance and her sheer towering size. I shivered, not from being cold. Seeing the Shroud this morning must have been what sparked that reminiscence.

Standing by a pond, I noticed a young woman inspecting some roses around a bend of the pond. Not especially beautiful or eye-catching, she drew my attention nevertheless. I looked away, at other things—there were a number of people walking by, small children playing, older children flying kites on a green hill—but my eyes kept wanting to return to her. She moved in a slow, desultory way in my direction. She wore what looked to my unskilled eye to be a fine-quality brown wool skirt, a pale yellow blouse, and a tan jacket, perhaps of calf's leather. A small beret was perched atop jet-black curls that brushed her shoulders. Now she was walking toward me, and our eyes met. She didn't lower hers, and by now mine were ... what? Not exactly captivated but certainly interested. She came in hesitant steps up to me, the hint of a smile on her otherwise serious oval face. I noticed that she was more petite than I had first thought, not much over five feet.

She stopped and said in a small, quiet voice, "Dr. Adam Hult, is it not?"

I hope my jaw didn't drop. Here I was in a random part of a North Italian city, half a world away from home. I had to say something, so I said guardedly, "Yes?"

"Please don't be alarmed. I know who you are, Dr. Hult, because ... well, because you are a known figure among historians internationally, as well as among other people who have read your books, and because ... let's just say, for other reasons. I am Sareen."

She held out her small, ungloved hand, and I took it briefly. Her fingers were cold. Her fluent English was accented, but from somewhere other than Italy that I couldn't place just then. Her explanation left a lot unexplained. Did she just happen to recognize me here at the park? Had she been following me?

"Sareen. Is there something I can do for you?"

"Perhaps if we could talk?" Now she sounded diffident, timid, as if her self-confidence had been worked up and was deflating.

I looked around and saw an unoccupied bench not far away. I motioned toward it, and she nodded. We went over and sat down, neither of us at ease. She had lovely eyes, dark Mediterranean eyes. How old was she? Twenty-five? Thirty-five? Was it only down to my male obtuseness that I couldn't tell?

"Would you consider me a mind reader," she began, "if I told you what you are thinking about?"

"I suppose I would if you got it right."

"You are wondering about, and troubled by, the Shroud of Turin."

Okay... mind reader? No, there would be some more mundane explanation. But not necessarily a more pleasant one. Obviously she knew where I had been that morning.

"And what gives you that idea?"

She ignored that question. "You are wondering, I think, as do many people, what to make of it. A despicable fraud? An astounding work of art? A piece of inexplicable mystery? The actual burial cloth of Jesus of Nazareth? But you, Dr. Hult, weigh these questions quite differently from most people. Very much more systematically."

She paused, crossing her hands in her lap. A few birds took noisy flight from a tree branch overhead. An elderly couple walked past us, murmuring a greeting. Children's shouts and laughter came from different directions. I decided, for now, not to pursue how she knew all this about me or why, even though I was plenty curious. She didn't seem threatening, unlike certain others. There would be time enough for further revelations. At least (flutter of intrigue) there might be.

"If I can call you Sareen, you can call me Adam."

"Madam, I'm Adam?" she intoned, the small smile appearing again at the simple palindrome.

"But not Eve?"

The smile disappeared. "No, not Eve. But tell me, please, whether I am not correct about what is upon your mind."

"All right. Quite amazingly correct. But what's your interest in all this?"

"That I can tell you. I love the man in the Shroud." She said this with simplicity, without intensity.

"I see. So you believe ... that it's really him?"

"Oh yes, really him. Of course, it's only an image of him, but it's ... a real image. Truly him. It's hard to explain, even to myself."

"And so you believe that the Shroud, that length of cloth, is two thousand years old, and actually ..."

"Yes, Adam, actually."

All this while I was looking at her the way you might look at a portrait by Raphael. She was hard for me to define. Exotic but plain, plain but attractive, attractive but unusual. What Audrey Hepburn might have been if she were Egyptian or Moroccan or Persian. I had a strong inclination to uncover her secrets, but direct inquiry seemed at this moment like a violation.

"Okay, lots of other people believe that too, millions of them probably. But why me? Why are you talking to me about it?"

She shook her head as if that puzzled her. "As I said, you are a widely known historian, a popular writer on such subjects. You are influential. I thought you should know—"

"That the Shroud is the real thing?"

She negated that more emphatically. "No, not that. You must decide that for yourself. But you should be aware that there is more to this ... more to this than you know. Than any of us knows."

I waited a few moments, and when she didn't continue, I said, "That's pretty enigmatic. Can you elaborate?"

"As I said, more than any of us knows. More than I know. But I do know the power of the man in the Shroud. Power like that is ... is not safe."

Again I waited and then told her, "I don't understand that. I don't know what you mean."

She gave a little laugh. "You? *I* don't even understand. I only know what I have to do. Or, to tell the truth, what I *think* I have to do. I apologize if I don't make myself clear. How could I?"

She stood up suddenly, seeming flustered. "I must go now. I'm sorry—I'm sorry, Adam. Thank you." And she hurried off along the path, not looking back.

▮ ▮ ▮ ▮ ▮ ▮

I remained seated on the bench. *Process, process!* I told my mind. But the more I worked at processing, the less clear things became. I found myself half-wondering whether I'd just imagined that brief encounter. No, of course not. This whole Shroud business was starting to play with my imagination—"that way madness lies"—but it was annoyingly difficult to assess who this Sareen was and what her game might be. Was she just what she seemed, a simple, innocent, mystically inclined young woman who, just by chance, recognized me here in the park? Was she a sinister Mata Hari whose veil of innocence cloaked some ulterior agenda? What agenda would that be? Was she trying to nudge me toward belief in the Shroud or, with the obscure warning, away from belief in it? Either possibility, or some third or fourth possibility I couldn't yet grasp, seemed about equally likely.

Would I ever see her again? No doubt about it, I wouldn't mind seeing her again. But that prospect was up to her—she apparently knew how to find me—and I had no idea whether she would want to see me again.

My stomach was reminding me that it was well past my usual lunchtime. Near the park entrance I had passed a busy trattoria with sidewalk tables. I found my way back there, obscurely troubled in mind. The place was still bustling, but a few tables were open. I took an outside one under the green and yellow awning, and a waiter placed a menu before me. My Italian was limited but good enough when it came to food. When the waiter came back,

I ordered some agnolotti, a pasta stuffed with beef and vegetables, with some chewy Italian bread, washed down with a velvety Barolo.

I wondered what the odds were that Sareen wasn't acting alone. If the chance meeting wasn't really by chance, she was almost certainly not acting alone. That would mean some group or organization was tracking me for one reason or another. The reason had to be connected with my inquiry into the Shroud. This brought to mind her disjointed references to something going on that none of us really understood. I suspected that she understood a good bit more than I did at this point.

I got out my iPhone and called Ari. After a short while, his voice came through with only a little static.

"CIA hotline. State your business."

"Delighted to hear from you too. What time is it there?"

"A little after nine. That would be a.m."

"And you're up already?"

"We never sleep. How's life over on the Riviera?"

"Embarrassing as hell. They go naked on the beaches here, especially the females."

"I should have warned you. Keeping yourself covered?"

"No, I've succumbed to peer pressure. What a life—almost wish you were here."

"Yeah, sure. What's up, bro?"

"I'm not really sure. Some funny business related to the not-so-funny business I'm here about. I saw the Shroud this morning, right on schedule."

"Tell me about that."

"Impressive. Unforgettable, actually. Strange. Mesmerizing, I suppose, if you're susceptible to that sort of thing."

"But you're not."

"I wouldn't have thought so … Check that, absolutely not."

"That's comforting. Now, about that funny business …"

"Right. Okay, I took a walk after the viewing, down to this big park by the river. While I was there, minding my own business, this woman comes up to me and tells me she knows who I am and what I'm doing here. Even tells me what's on my mind."

"Let me guess. She was right on all counts."

"Creepy, huh?"

"So this woman, maybe along with some others, had been following you. You asked her about that?"

"Naturally. She claimed just to have recognized me. So, coincidence? Accident?"

"Close to zero chance of that. What sort of woman is this? Old or young? Rich or poor? Seductive?"

"Fairly young, well dressed. Middle Eastern or something, hard to tell exactly. Speaks good English with some accent. Seductive? Not overtly, but hardly repulsive. She claims to believe the Shroud is authentic."

"And wants to persuade you to agree."

"Not quite. At least, again, not overtly. She said I need to make up my own mind on that score. But she seemed to want to warn me about something. At that point, though, she got rather mystical and incoherent. Then she took off, leaving me in the dark."

"Figuratively speaking. Did she seem afraid toward the end there?"

"No, I don't think so. Upset about something, but not afraid."

"And you're puzzling over who she is and what she's up to."

"Ah, but I can turn to the answer man."

"Sorry, dude, way too little information. She's playing with your mind—or they are. But you've already figured that out. You'd better be prepared for Act One, Scene Two. Keep your powder dry."

"Watch my back?"

"Trust no one. But seriously, the threat, if any, would seem to be psychological. They know something, if not everything, about your little mission over there. Possibly about who put you up to it and why. But I wouldn't expect bullets to be flying."

"Good, I'm slow at ducking. She did tell me her name—first name anyway. Sareen."

"Not helpful, especially since it's probably an alias. Anything else, bro?"

"Any movement on Agent Freebinder?"

"It's coming. The Bureau keeps its cards to its chest, but your humble inquisitor has learned a few things. He was indeed a career man, like he said. His last stint before retirement was in antiterrorism. Since retiring four years ago, he's been a sort of consultant or PI for a few very rich clients, such as your patroness. Quiet stuff, under the radar, but effective. If I played poker with him, I wouldn't figure him for a bluffer."

"That warms my heart."

"We aim to please. Keep me posted, okay?"

"As ever."

I switched off, took the last swallow of wine, paid my bill, and tried to forget about the whole thing, at least for the time being.

CHAPTER 7

Shortly after ten the following morning, my train, *Torino a Milano*, pulled into Milan's Central Railway Station. On weekdays, the train would have been packed with commuters, but on this Sunday morning it was only half full. Milan Central was a large, impressive structure, not unlike New York's Grand Central. From the platform, I made my way out to the street, where I waited my turn for a taxi. The sun was out, but a chilly wind was blowing down off the Alps.

My destination was the University of Milan, a couple of miles across the city center. I had an eleven o'clock appointment with Agnella Lozio, a prominent historian specializing in the transition from the European Middle Ages to the Renaissance. I had met her a couple of times, once at a professional conference and the other when she was a guest lecturer at the City University of New York. Normally she wouldn't be keeping office hours on a Sunday, but she graciously agreed to a meeting, accommodating my tight schedule. I had suggested a coffee house or something like that, but she stipulated her office. Keeping it professional, I guess.

What could I learn from her that I couldn't learn from straight research—books, articles, and websites? Maybe a little something, maybe next to nothing, but I've found that you can often learn things from talking to people, especially highly informed people, beyond what you can find in print. Angles, attitudes, nuances, vectors. Doing research is like fishing; wild fish are harder to catch than fish planted in a pond, but they taste better.

My taxi driver seemed to be glad I didn't speak much Italian, as it gave him an opportunity to practice his English, which, on balance, was the closest we had to a common language. We sped aggressively past the Public Gardens and then the spectacular Gothic spires of the Duomo, the great cathedral of Milan. Dr. Lozio had given me good directions to the right building within the university complex, and my driver dropped me off as close as he could get to that. I was a few minutes early, so I took a stroll around before zeroing in.

Her office was on the second floor—what Europeans call the first floor. The door was open, and I knocked on the jamb to announce myself. Dr. Lozio rose from her desk and came over to greet me. She was in her fifties probably, tall and buxom, with dark-brown hair pulled back into a bun, wearing a brown damask suit with a black shawl over it.

"Dr. Hult, it's good to see you again," she said in her Italian-flavored contralto.

"Thank you so much for making time for me, Dr. Lozio."

"*Dio!*" she laughed, drawing me by the forearm to a well-upholstered chair. "Let's not 'doctor' each other. I'm Agnella, you're Adam. I have no coffee to offer you. Is it too early for some amontillado?"

"Sounds good to me, Agnella."

She went over to a credenza to pour the wine into small crystal glasses. Her office was about the same size as mine, but there the similarities ceased. Hers was neat, elegant, and classy. No doubt these differences bespoke essential differences between us, but I didn't want to dwell on that. Handing me the wineglass, she sat down not at her desk but in the chair next to mine.

"Now, Adam, your e-mail mentioned an interest in the known provenance of the Shroud of Turin. Since you're looking into it, I expect you've already done some reading on the subject."

She ended on an interrogative note, and I replied, "Yes, I have, but different sources say different things. It's hard to tell where knowledge ends and speculation begins."

She sat back, swirling the pale-golden sherry in its sparkling crystal vessel. "As it so often is in historical matters. But speculation is valuable, even necessary. It's like pointing a torch deeper into the darkness—you don't know just where to point, so you have to try various directions. You know about Geoffroi de Charny and his widow, Jeanne de Vergy?"

"The first definitely known owners and exhibitors of the Shroud."

"Exactly, and as we peer back in time, that's just the point at which knowledge veers off into speculation. Geoffroi was born around 1300 and was killed at the Battle of Poitiers in 1356. He was, by all accounts, the very embodiment of Chaucer's 'verray parfit gentil knight,' a man sincerely devoted to putting the ideals of chivalry into practice, in war as in peace. He wrote a treatise on chivalry which became the standard guide in his day. But he had the bad fortune of living during the Hundred Years' War—or, one might say, of living in the real world. In any event, it was an anarchic and cynical time."

"The Black Death had a lot to do with that," I said.

She grimaced. "Yes. The plague. It arrived from somewhere in Asia in 1347 and devastated Europe for the next several years. According to most modern estimates, it killed around a third of the population, much more than that in some places, and always in the most gruesome and terrifying way. They had no idea what was actually causing it; mostly they saw it as God's judgment on all their sins."

"And in the ensuing decade the Shroud makes its first appearance."

"That we know of, at least."

I thought this over and said, "With all that religious terror in the air, the time would have been ripe for the offer of salvation through relics."

"Absolutely, although the physical conditions were so chaotic and ravaged that it's hard to imagine how an artifact as sophisticated as the Shroud could have been produced under such circumstances. However that may be, there is documentary evidence that Geoffroi exhibited it at least once at the church in the village of Lirey, on his estate southeast of Paris, a year or so before he died, which places these showings around 1355. There is confirmatory evidence, in the form of a pilgrim medallion, that the showings attracted visitors from all over France and even beyond. The several strands of evidence put it beyond doubt that the item exhibited was the same Shroud now residing in Turin. But, of course, Geoffroi was killed in battle shortly thereafter—he had the singular but highly dangerous honor of carrying the Oriflamme, the royal battle standard, which made him an obvious, standout target for the enemy.

"His death left his widow, Jeanne, in very difficult circumstances. She had a young son, also named Geoffroi." Agnella shook her head in amusement and then explained, "There are no less than three Geoffroi de Charny's in this story. The knight we have just discussed is usually referred to as Geoffroi I, and his son as Geoffroi II."

"And his grandson as Geoffroi III?"

"No, the third Geoffroi was the first in sequence. I'll get to him in a moment. Are you well enough confused by now?"

"I'm on my way, but please go on. This is the stuff I want."

"Very well. So then, Jeanne and her young son are in trouble. Her husband is dead—he was buried near the battlefield at Poitiers—and marauding bands of English soldiers, no better than brigands, are roaming the countryside. On top of that, the ownership of the Shroud is now up for grabs, and several powerful churchmen are reaching out for it. Jeanne seems to have shared her husband's valor, however, for she packed up her son, the Shroud, and other essential belongings and made a tactical retreat. We don't know just where she went at that point, but we do know that within a few years she was remarried to a wealthy nobleman in the region of Savoy, which was relatively secure from the ongoing turbulence. There the Shroud apparently remained until this second husband died in 1388. In the very next year, 1389, however, it was once again being exhibited back at the church in Lirey, this time under the auspices of Geoffroi II, who by then was securely in his father's footsteps as a soldier and official of the crown."

"Back to Lirey and farther from Turin," I put in.

"Yes. As you suggest, Savoy was nearby the Shroud's final home in Turin. Therein lies the tale I will now recapitulate for you. Making a long, eventful story reasonably short, this second round of Shroud displays in Lirey provoked even more political controversy than the first one a generation earlier. There was controversy over who held the authority over showing the Shroud and whether it should be presented as the genuine burial shroud of Christ or a replica of it."

"Ah, as far back as that."

"Yes, but the point in dispute wasn't quite the same as today. They weren't so much arguing over whether the Shroud was genuine as whether, even if genuine, it would be sacrilegious to present it as such. Many church officials were concerned that such relics—which of course were a dime a dozen then—would attract and foster idolatrous worship. I think they were aware that the Shroud, as a relic, was in a class by itself."

I finished my sherry and declined her offer of a refill.

"In a class by itself," I said, "it looks like they were right about that. But now, this Geoffroi, the son—or his father, for that matter—do you think they knew how that image got put onto the Shroud?"

That question animated her. "Oh, but how I wish I knew! I mean, I wish I knew the origin of the image, of course, but just as much, I wish I knew how much they knew about it. So far, however, we have yet to discover in the written records any indication of that—nothing to indicate whether they knew it was a forgery. It's frustrating, but we just don't know what they knew."

"I see. And no one knows how Geoffroi I came into possession of it?"

"Well, that's another deep subject. I'll get to it in a moment. Let me first finish summarizing what happened after the second round of showings in 1389. In a curious way, the son's history repeated his father's. He too was a distinguished knight-at-arms, he too held possession of the Shroud and exhibited it at the Lirey church, and he too met an untimely death, probably as a result of wounds or infection suffered in battle in 1398. Once again too, it was his child who took legal possession of the Shroud—this time a daughter, Margaret. She grew up to be a pious, strong-willed woman, and all the evidence indicates that she took her responsibility as guardian of the relic very seriously. Over the next half century, amid turbulent political broils, she outlived two aristocratic husbands and was often on the move, just ahead of trouble. Through all this peril, she kept the Shroud secure and exhibited it publicly several times. She was childless, though, and on that account she became increasingly concerned for its safekeeping after her death. Her quest for a new guardian forms another intricate and fascinating tale, but she ended up deeding it to one of the few men she trusted, Louis, Duke of Savoy."

"So back again to Savoy."

"Back again, and back to stay, for the next five hundred years and more. Within the territories of the dukedom, it continued moving around until, in 1578, it finally found harbor in the Turin Cathedral, where, as you have seen, it remains to this day."

"Yes, I *have* seen. Have you seen it?"

"During the public showing in 2010. I would certainly not have missed that opportunity."

"No, of course not. What did you think? It's too vague a question, I know..."

She smiled, or maybe winced. "I think, as many people do, that it is beautiful, enigmatic, perplexing, disturbing. One of a kind."

"Otherworldly?"

That brought a short laugh. "That *is* the question, isn't it? Of course, I don't know. I'm not especially religious, but... In this research you're doing now, isn't that what you're trying to answer?"

"Basically, yes." I hung back from saying I'd actually been hired to prove something rather than to find something out. Agnella Lozio would understand the difference and would think the less of me.

"I'll be interested to learn of anything new you may discover and what conclusion you reach. A central part of the mystery is the question you raised previously. Our earliest definite knowledge of the Shroud is its showing by Geoffroi I around 1355. But how did he come to possess it? Through inheritance, in the same way he passed it on to his son? From the artist or forger who created it? If the latter, was Geoffroi in collaboration with the forger?"

"Well? I'm all ears."

"Ha! Must be an Americanism. In your researches thus far, have you come across a document known as the D'Arcis Memorandum?"

"I've read about it in books and online. Different sources, different assessments, though."

"That document is the prime—virtually the only—direct source of information about a complicated and fascinating episode. Pierre d'Arcis was Bishop of Troyes—the nearest city to Lirey—at the time when Geoffroi II, the son, was having his priests display the Shroud publicly at the church in Lirey. That was in 1389, as we know from the memorandum that d'Arcis wrote to Clement VII, the current Avignon pope."

"And d'Arcis was not pleased."

"He was furiously indignant. He leveled two distinct charges against Geoffroi. First, he, Bishop d'Arcis, had not approved the exhibition. Second, a previous showing of the same object had occurred at Lirey 'about thirty-four years ago,' as he put it, and the then Bishop of Troyes, Henri of Poitiers, had investigated the incident and discovered that the Shroud was a fake."

"So I've read, but what was his evidence?"

"That's the problem. The evidence is hearsay upon hearsay, so much that we may never get to the bottom of it. Unless, of course, you, Adam ..."

"No effort will be spared. So this hearsay, it's information that d'Arcis allegedly got from Bishop Henri ..."

"For which we only have his testimony in the memorandum. And Henri allegedly had got a confession from an unnamed 'artist' who allegedly admitted to making the forgery. As to how Henri elicited the confession, we don't know. We don't know what, if anything, this supposed artist said about his technique, or whether Henri just invented him out of spite. You could write a book about all the things we don't know—although that project, I suppose, wouldn't interest you."

"It certainly wouldn't interest my publisher. But now, you mentioned a third Geoffroi, the one who came first?"

"Ah yes, the first Geoffroi de Charny, at least the first that we know of. According to the conventional notation, we might refer to him as Geoffroi Zero—though no one does. There is some evidence, though no proof, that he was an uncle or great-uncle of Geoffroi I. He was one of four French masters in the military-slash-religious order of Knights Templar formed during the Crusades to protect crusaders. When, in a major power play, King Philip cracked down on the Templars and effectively destroyed the order, Geoffroi was taken into custody, and in 1314, alongside the grand master, Jacques de Molay, he was burned at the stake."

"But there's no evidence that Zero ever had the Shroud." This much I had gathered from my own research.

"No evidence, but plenty of theories. Templar lore, as you know, is a thriving cottage industry."

"So, bottom line, two possibilities are most likely. Geoffroi I either inherited the Shroud, possibly from this Templar knight of the same name, or he got it from some forger, as d'Arcis claimed. But there's no solid evidence either way."

"Not as yet, at any rate. A person's answer to that prize question tends to follow from his or her religious views."

"Unsatisfying."

She sat back. "Unsatisfying," she agreed.

CHAPTER 8

On the previous afternoon, following my encounter with the cryptic Sareen and my long-distance confab with Ari, I had taken a taxi and returned to the cathedral. When I was there that morning, I noticed a souvenir shop outside, but I hadn't thought I would be interested in any of their offerings. Afterward, though, one thing occurred to me that might be worth a look. They might have—probably would have—prints of photographs taken of the Shroud.

The photographic history of the Shroud is a story in itself. For some time after photography came along in the second half of the nineteenth century, the Vatican was averse to exposing the Shroud to the new technology. But then in 1898, an accomplished amateur photographer, Secondo Pia, was given permission to photograph it. Owing to some primitive wiring, he had difficulties with his lighting, but he managed to get some good exposures. When he developed them, he got the *aha!* moment of a lifetime. The photonegative looked like a photopositive. The man who, in the image on the Shroud, looked vague and indistinct now looked much more clear and well defined, like an actual man who had been brutalized but now, dead, was "resting in peace." The significance of this was immediately plain to Pia: the Shroud image was in fact a photographic negative. But how could that be? Could a medieval artist have produced such an effect? How? And still more, why? Or did some medieval genius invent a proto-photographic process five hundred years ahead of time? How did this genius come up with a scourged and crucified corpse to take a picture of? Well, the times, they were violent and grisly.

As for Secondo Pia himself, he was a pious man and took this remarkable discovery as a clear sign that he was looking at the very face of the Savior.

Not surprisingly, the souvenir shop had a variety of photographic images. I chose a 16-x-30-inch poster reproduction of the classic 1931 black-and-white shot taken by Guiseppe Enrie, a professional photographer. My poster included only the front view. The Shroud itself, I should point out, has both a front and back view of the man, and these lie head to head on the fourteen-foot-long cloth. The idea is that he was laid supine with his feet near one end, and then the rest of the cloth was draped over his head and back down over his feet. Somehow, somewhere, and somewhen—those are the questions—the whole front and back figure was painted or daguerreotyped or transferred or whatever onto the cloth.

For the second time that day I legged it back to my hotel—if nothing else, I might get into better shape—and this time I went up to my room. I tossed my suit jacket over a chair, took off my tie, and then unrolled the poster on the elegant bedspread. The room was opulently furnished—the sort of place I imagine Doris Ballaster would choose for herself—and I used two books from an antique bookcase to hold down the ends of the poster, two volumes from a French edition of Flaubert's novels.

I took some time studying the photo. I couldn't help being impressed by the uncanny skill with which the Shroud image had been done, however it was done. Even in death, it was eerily lifelike. Having seen the original only five or six hours ago, I was struck by much the same things that must have struck Pia and Enrie and countless others ever since. What I was looking at now was really a negative, but since it was a negative of a negative, it came out positive, like squaring a negative number. All sorts of details that were mistily indecipherable in the Shroud itself were distinct here—the face puffy with bruises, the nose swollen and slightly bent, the full mustache and forked beard, the puncture wounds and blood spatters on the forehead, the numerous wounds that either were scourge marks or were made to resemble scourge marks, and the wound in the left wrist (the right wrist is covered by his left hand). Oddly, the most easily noticeable marks on the Shroud, the burn marks from the 1532 fire, seemed to recede into the background when you inspected the man himself.

How was it done? In my reading, I had come across a theorist who speculated that it really was a photographic image and that the genius who pulled it off was none other than Leonardo da Vinci. The trouble with that idea was that Leonardo was born in 1452, almost a full century after the first well-documented public showing of the Shroud. If it was proto-photography, the genius was earlier and rather less celebrated. But from the research I had already done, I knew how long the odds were against that possibility, given the chemicals and glassware (for a lens) available in Europe around 1350. Getting a bearded corpse and mutilating it to mimic a scourged, thorn-crowned, crucified man would be the easy part. Figuring out the theory and practice of primitive photography and doing the deed on just this one occasion in pursuit of a chancy hoax instead of pursuing fame and riches as the inventor of a miraculous new technology—all of this added up to an extremely long shot. Exposure time, for one thing—the corpse would have to have been strung up vertically for several days' worth of bright sunlight. And no notice was taken of this, no official inquiry? That *might* have happened, but almost certainly it didn't.

But negative . . . a negative image. That bothered me.

▪ ▪ ▪ ▪ ▪ ▪

My homeward flight landed at JFK before ten o'clock on Sunday evening, and I caught a cab. The subway would be about as fast and almost as safe, but long ago I got into the N'Yawk taxi habit. By the time I got to my apartment, I was a little blurry from travel and time zones and mental puzzles, so I just stripped down to my Hanes, turned off the lights, and flopped into bed. If I dreamed, I didn't remember it.

On Monday morning, I taught two classes. If you ask about when I prepped for these, that's a good question. The answer is that I have nearly total recall of preparation I did months ago. Does relying on that ability amount to cutting corners? Well, don't we all cut all the corners we can? Am I too cynical? You are what you are.

Also that morning, I called my parents and arranged to go over there for lunch. I'd been neglecting them lately, for the usual reason. I loved them, or so I assured myself, but they were depressingly consistent, living this stifled, monotonous existence and never complaining or considering dullness as anything other than the natural norm. What's to complain about? Maybe their impervious stoicism ought to be admired, but it gave me claustrophobia.

I took a cab over to Midwood in Brooklyn, and after paying the driver, I paused a moment on the crumbly old sidewalk and contemplated the house I grew up in, a small, square house built with Depression-era economy in the 1930s. Before I got to the porch, my mother opened the door and said excitedly, with a hand to her cheek, "Oh, Adam!"

I had no idea how to read her greeting. It's so wonderful to see you? What became of your hair? Why didn't you come sooner? Her pinched expression suggested the last option. She was sixty but looked older. Chubby in her prime, she had lost weight and now sagged all over. Her long hair was gray, unkempt, unhealthy.

I gave her an awkward hug and went inside into the main room of the house, which at one time really was a living room but not so much any more. The makeover I had funded didn't include most of the furniture, since they were so attached to the dowdy stuff I grew up with. My father was sitting in his favorite easy chair—originally burnt orange and fuzzy, now brown and threadbare. Seeing him, I thought I understood my mom's greeting. He was a bit taller than me and burly as a tree stump, or anyway he used to be. Now he looked scrawny, wasted, clinging to life by his fingernails. I had gotten used to the respirator tubes curling around his face, but today they seemed more conspicuous. Was it lung cancer? Emphysema? I didn't really know and was reluctant to ask. That's the kind of relationship we had.

"Hey, kid," he wheezed, raising one hand but not the forearm.

"Hey, Pop." I went over and laid a hand on his bony shoulder.

"Ain't … all here any more. But don't … pay me no mind. Bernadine … tells me you been … over in Europe again."

"Yeah, I just got back yesterday. Short trip. The usual research stuff."

"Lunch is all fixed," my mom said. "I'll just set it out." With what might have been a meaningful glance at me, she went into the kitchen. I pulled a chair over to sit close to my pop.

"World traveler," he commented.

"It gets old after a while, like everything else." I regretted these words as soon as they tumbled out, but he didn't seem to notice anything.

"Last night," he said, "they lost again. Three in a row. Two games under … five hundred."

That was the Yankees. He was a fervent fan. He started out life with the beloved bums, the Brooklyn Dodgers, but in 1958 they broke a million hearts by moving out west to LA. It took him a while to get over that, but when he did, he underwent a radical conversion to the Yanks.

"Still early in the season," I pointed out.

"Nah ... they all got old ... Jeter, A-Rod, the others ... Hall-of-Famers but too old ... heh, ask me about that." He did seem to be picking up the *old* theme. It was probably never far from his mind.

"They've got good, young players—Teixeira, Cano, Granderson ... "

"Yeah, but ... not enough. Half the teams ... got more."

"What the league wants, probably. Competitiveness."

"Screw that. Ain't been the same since ... the old guy died ... What's his name?"

"Steinbrenner?"

"Yeah. George. The old guy, not the kid."

I looked around the room. Totally familiar, but it seemed to be getting gradually smaller. It smelled musty and medicinal. There were some family photos on a sideboard, none of them less than twenty years old.

"You been to ... any of the games ... this year?" he asked.

"No, not yet."

My mom brought a couple of metal TV trays—again, same ones I grew up with—and put them in front of Pop and me. Then she brought sandwiches on plates, tuna sandwiches with chopped celery mixed in, with pickle wedges on the side, and some iced tea. She had her own sandwich on a plate, without the tray. There was little or no conversation while we ate. Pop ate the pickles and nibbled at the sandwich. Back when, he would devour three of them.

"Adam," Mom said, "have you heard anything lately from Sam?"

My derelict brother, last known whereabouts somewhere on the Florida coast. Asking about him must have cost my mother, since it implied she hadn't heard from him. The last I heard, he had a job as a bail bondsman in Fort Lauderdale. But that was two years ago, and I had only his word for it, which was worth about as much as one of my credit cards.

"No, not lately."

"Oh. I just wondered."

My cell phone vibrated, and I took it out. Dina Pallas, my book editor. I got up, nearly bumping over the TV tray, and excused myself and went to the kitchen to take the call.

"Adam," she said, "my favorite hunk in all the world, but why don't you keep in touch with your friends?"

"Keep in touch? Didn't we talk, what was it, just last week?"

"Three weeks and five days, Adam; call it one whole month. I love you like a rib-eye steak, but you're making me nervous."

Me making *her* nervous? Dina was a great editor, a lanky energizer bunny somewhere in her forties who wore bold colors with baubles, bangles, and beads. Along with her two nerdy young female assistants, she had virtually coauthored my last three books. But she was one of those people who increased my apprehension about the other sex.

"What's on your mind, Dina?"

"The wave, my pet, remember?"

"Oh yeah, the wave."

"Let it pass you by, and what?"

"It passes you by." I remembered my catechism.

"That it does. But I can't give you ideas, sweetheart. I'm not the creative one; you are. You're one of the most creatively beautiful people on the planet. Like the Good Book says, though, time and tide wait for no man."

"That's not in the Bible."

"Don't be evasive, please, angel eyes. Now, the last time we schmoozed, a whole month ago, you were holding out on me. Playing coy—don't deny it. Something's up with you. The hairs on my neck are twitching. You can't fool Mother Nature, sugar. Out with it."

I lacked the strength to resist this perfumed tsunami. "There might be something," I allowed.

"That's my boy. Okay, come across, the full monty."

"The Shroud of Turin. I've started looking into it—"

"Gotcha, Adam, with you all the way. Famous Catholic relic, like the Weeping Madonna. An ATM for the Vatican. Is there an exposé here?"

"I'm looking into it."

"And? Come on, toots, what got you going with this?"

My mom brought the lunch dishes to the kitchen sink, tossing me a quizzical or maybe a wounded look.

"Sorry, Dina. I'll have to get back to you about it."

"You're not stiffing me, are you?"

"No, but I can't—you know."

"Oh, that. Is she hot, Adam? An animal?"

"No, not that. Bye for now."

"The Shroud—go after it, baby."

And I switched her off, the only way.

I didn't stay long after that. I couldn't take much more of it. I'm not the prodigal son—Sam has monopolized that—but I'm not really the good son either. I don't think I'll ever develop into a hand-holder. Out on the front porch, though, my mom said, "What can I do, Adam? He's going ... he's going ... "

I couldn't think of anything to say except to finish the thought with "gone," so I clenched my teeth and gave her another awkward hug and buggered off. I was hot under the collar with emotions I didn't understand—frustration, guilt, anger, and who knows what all. Who was I angry with? Not poor old Mom and Pop, for sure. Myself? In a way, but probably it was more about what than who. I was steamed about the whole pathetic situation. I would have been mad at God if I thought he had anything to do with it.

In this frame of mind, I kept walking hard, halfway back to Manhattan, trying to get whatever it was out of my system. After a few miles, though, my legs were tired and my feet were sore, and I finally flagged down a cab somewhere out on Washington Ave.

CHAPTER 9

Life goes on. For people in my trade, university life goes on, which includes a depressing amount of politics—administrative politics, faculty politics, student politics, and departmental politics. If only we didn't have people, I sometimes muse, we wouldn't have to mess with politics.

On the following afternoon, Tuesday, we had our regularly scheduled history department meeting. It included all the usual rigmarole, most of it necessary but tedious. At one point, though, a question was raised about my weekend fling in Europe. It was a nuisance question, really, brought up by a colleague who should have retired in the last millennium. Was I engaged in genuine academic research, or was I running off again during the academic term in pursuit of yet another popular potboiler? Was I, that is, continuing my moonlight career as an academic prostitute? Assenting murmurs drifted around the table—an enormous table that could seat around thirty. I wasn't just imagining this whisper of righteous disapproval and stifled envy. Celebrity has its trials, particularly in the ivory tower.

As straight-faced as I could manage, I mentioned that during this academic year I had published three papers in academic journals. (How many, I didn't ask, had he?) Were there any pertinent complaints from my students? No, there didn't seem to be. At that point, the issue petered out, and we slogged on to something else.

In relating such things, I'm sure, I sound like a spoiled twit. Maybe I am; from time to time I worry about it—but not much, not for long, not very often. Guilty as charged. Of course, nobody at that department meeting asked if I'd been hired (or bribed or blackmailed) to do off-the-books research by a rich old lady with an ax to grind. Nobody asked because nobody knew or even imagined, and I didn't bring it up.

Then that evening, around nine, buoyed by my most recent tryst with Lara, I gave her a call. I didn't know where she would be, but I figured if my timing was inconvenient, we could cut it short.

Inconvenient?

"Adam!" Everyone has caller ID now.

"Hey, babe, is this a good time?"

"For what?"

"Well, I mean, for starters anyway, to talk."

"You mean sex talk."

"Yeah, that maybe, but almost any kind will do. Good time?"

"I don't know. It depends."

"On what?"

"On you."

Ah, woman, the mysterious gender.

"So, what about me?"

"You tell me, Adam."

"Okay, let's see. I resemble what Henry Kissinger might have looked like at my age if he'd lost most of his hair. I'm almost as clever as Henry but nowhere near as worldly-wise. I can recite the Pledge of Allegiance backward. I'm still searching for the perfect microbrew. Second to you, Shirley Jones is the most beautiful woman I've ever seen, and that was only in the movies."

"That's supposed to be funny? Who the hell is Shirley Jones?"

"Never mind. Hey, I'm trying at least."

"Did you enjoy France and Italy?"

"Enjoy? I saw the Shroud of Turin. You don't do that for fun."

"What *do* you do for fun, Adam?"

Land mine territory. I tried, "Jump between the sheets with you?"

"Is that a question?"

"No! More like a proposition."

"More like a subpoena. I'm sorry, Adam. There's an attitude here I don't want to deal with right now."

Click. (It doesn't click any more, but the lights and sound went out.)

▮ ▮ ▮ ▮ ▮ ▮

"But ... I didn't do *anything*. I hardly even *said* anything."

Ari had been playing, perhaps improvising, a soft, plaintive Hebrew melody on his clarinet. Now he paused and said, "That may be the problem. Passivity can be perceived as indifference. It may in fact *be* indifference, a waning of interest. Consult your heart, if you have one, not your loins."

I groaned. He was probably right. My problem was that loins speak louder and clearer than hearts do. I wasn't even sure I had a heart in the romantic sense that Ari seemed to mean. I cared about certain people—my parents, Ari, Benny. I cared about them enough to qualify as a human being, if only just barely. For better or worse, though (okay, worse), what I cared about most was ideas. Like the so-called "aliens from the fourth dimension," which are not grotesque science fiction life forms but a purely mathematical, but weird, branch of Yang-Mills theory, one of those mathematical regions that veer off into philosophy. Or the meaning of randomness. Or the meaning of "history." Or the meaning of meaning. It wasn't Lara's fault that she had never been galvanized by the meaning of meaning.

It was late in the evening, the next day, and Ari and I were unwinding at his place. I was setting up the pieces for a game of chess. We were both working on bottles of Pennant Ale from the Brooklyn Brewery and munching on cashews. He cleaned off his clarinet and set it in its case and then tuned in an FM station where what sounded to me like a Miles Davis combo was doing it right.

I said, "I don't think what Lara and I have had between us is the kind of thing that lasts. Or really ought to last."

"Okay. Doesn't matter what she thinks then."

"Oh, come on. It takes two to tango, especially if the dance goes on more or less forever. You know what I mean. We would both have to be all in."

Ari sat down on one of the straight-backed chairs at the dining table, where the chessboard was set up, and straightened his pieces precisely, the white ones.

"So," he said, "you're going to break the good news to her pretty soon?"

"I don't know. Call me indecisive." I took a deep swallow of the ale.

"Indecisive. On the other hand, too much decisiveness can lead to trouble too."

"Voice of experience?"

He nodded. Playing the black pieces, I countered his king's pawn opening with a Sicilian Dragon, an aggressive defense, not for the faint of heart. See? I've got plenty of heart when it comes to things like chess.

"Doing anything this weekend?" I asked.

"Probably doing something." He moved his rook pawn to h4, an attacking move against the Dragon fianchetto. Undoubtedly planning to castle long. I would have to accelerate my queen-side counterattack.

"What I mean, of course, is anything out of the ordinary."

"Ah, but as you know better than most, one person's ordinary is another's extra."

"All right, all right, out of the ordinary for *you*."

"No, not unusual for me."

This rather mindless conversation was interspersed between bouts of intense, silent calculation. The position on the chessboard was getting complex, knife-edged.

"So what is it?" I asked.

"The weekend? I'll be babysitting a Russian businessman on his first visit to New York."

"Businessman?"

"Oligarch, then. With Gazprom, their natural gas monopoly."

"Why you? Don't guys like that have their own private KGB?"

"They don't know the territory like I do."

"Fair enough. But how did he know about you?"

He clipped my knight on h5 with his rook, an exchange sacrifice meant to expose my king to nasty pressure.

"The world of custom personal security is a small community with a high degree of insider knowledge. Like, perhaps, the world of top pole vaulters or *origami* masters. We're more secretive, but at the same time, we're intelligence mavens, so it evens out. Word gets around."

How did Ari get to be an elite bodyguard? Back when I was getting my academic career under way at Amherst up in Massachusetts, he spent two years over in Israel getting training from their intelligence services or special forces, maybe both. In most areas, he and I share secrets like teenage girls, but he's always been guarded about that part of his life, as I'm sure he's supposed to be. Benny's connection with the Mossad was certainly Ari's way in. My impression is that Benny would have preferred not to have his son follow his footsteps so closely, but Ari was very determined, and Benny acquiesced. The result was a young man highly skilled in unarmed combat, small arms, surveillance, counter-surveillance, and professional driving, including extreme driving—I've seen some of this. He was also schooled in the psychology of power and violence, an Israeli specialty that they share sparingly with foreigners, even Americans. As for Benny, it was never clear if he was more Israeli-American or American-Israeli, and it's much the same with Ari. But he's a private contractor rather than an agent of any government. I think.

"So what danger would there be for this Russian tycoon in the city?" I asked.

"Other Russians mainly. It's important to know all the neighborhoods, down to the last nightclub and shuttered door."

"A lot to know."

Studying the position on the board, he didn't respond to that, or to my suggestion of another bottle of the excellent ale. I went and got one for myself. Then he moved his queen, slammed it actually, onto a square in the center of the board, a powerful spot but one in danger of attack from my pieces. I hadn't expected this, so it forced some furious recalculation.

"Any more sign of this mystery woman who calls herself Sareen?" he asked, obviously intending to distract me.

"No."

"There will be if you keep going with this."

"Okay by me." I decided my best defense at this point, chesswise, was to intensify my queenside attack and do it fast. Burn my bridges. On an adrenaline high, I sacrificed a knight on c3.

"Think it through. Think it through," he said. I wasn't sure if he was referring to the game or my Shroud investigation. Maybe both. With a delicate touch, unlike his last move, he moved his king out of check, to the corner square—declining my sacrifice.

"I always think things through."

"Yes, I think you do. That's why I wonder about this current venture. It's a worthy goal, exposing hoaxes and defusing superstition, but isn't there a danger in being paid up front to do it? Being paid, I mean, not to find out the truth but to prove what is assumed in advance to be the truth?"

"What, you think the Shroud might be genuine?"

"I think the odds are mightily against it, as they always are with things like this. But that's not the point. Prejudice, prejudgment, that's the point."

"But I'm not prejudging. I'm a historian, a philosopher; open-mindedness is my reason for being. I really am coming at this with an open mind."

"With an open mind and an enlarged bank account and the promise of even bigger bucks if you prove what you're supposed to prove. Much bigger bucks, I suspect."

I made a noise, a growl or a groan. I saw it now. My attack on his king was stymied for the moment, and my moments had run out. On his next move, he was going to rip open my king's defenses with a sacrifice of his own, and no matter what I did, I was going to be prodded off the plank in five or six more moves. I was manly enough not to sweep all the pieces off the board; I just toppled over my king.

"Think about it," he said. "Selling off your academic integrity to the high bidder. Can she pay you enough?"

I hoped so. I hadn't yet told him the full terms of the deal. He was suspicious, obviously, and maybe he didn't need to be told.

CHAPTER 10

By the beginning of May, a stormy spring with lots of rain interspersed with a few sunny and windy days was giving way to summer. The trees were fully in leaf and flowers bloomed all around, and for their part, Columbia students got a week to cram for final exams.

For months now, the online Shroud sites had been promoting a conference to be held in Antwerp, Belgium, from May eleventh through the thirteenth. Attending that conference would be the best way for me to get a feel for who was who and what was what in this affair, to penetrate beneath surface impressions to whatever truth was underneath. Despite Ari's qualms about my being bought, I really did intend to discover the truth and let the chips fall either way, into my lap or out of my pocket. At least that's how I thought of myself. But then, who understands the bottom line of his own motives? "Know thyself," Socrates taught, but he knew it's the hardest thing of all.

The conference dates overlapped the study week dates, and although I was supposed to hang around and make myself available to students the whole week, I knew I could disappear for two days and not be seriously missed. So, a few days in advance, I phoned Doris and ran the plan by her—not to get her blessing but to get a first-class plane ticket and hotel room paid for. She was entirely agreeable, but the last thing she said was, "Tom will want to see you."

Oh, joyous day. Sure enough, the day before I flew off to Belgium, Tom phoned and told me (not asked me) that he would see me in my office at four that afternoon. I would have thought about fending him off, except that he was delivering my plane ticket.

As it turned out, when he showed up at the stroke of four, there was a drop-in student in my office, a girl with bulgy eyes and a mane of frizzy hair who talked in one unending sentence without ever breathing in. When Tom Freebinder stopped in the doorway and looked at her with a look that, for him, was not unkind but could nevertheless peel off makeup, the girl, Brandon (first name), gasped and stuffed her notebook in her backpack and, apologizing pointlessly, made an athletic move around him and out the door.

"Am I interrupting?" he said, deadpan. It might have been his form of humor; he certainly didn't care about interrupting.

"Not at all. She just remembered an urgent appointment with her dentist."

He sat down on the same unfortunate chair he'd sat on the last time and said, "How is it progressing?"

"It's progressing. These things take time."

"I understand that. Take your time. Do the job right. Dot the i's and cross the t's. Make sure your exposé doesn't rebound on you."

I nodded slowly. "Sound advice."

He scowled a little more. "Be cute all you want, Professor, but keep in mind the difference between this good life you like living and debtors' prison."

"We don't have—"

"Yeah we do. You get dropped from this cushy perch and go to the back of the employment line. Long lines these days, especially for blackballed mandarins. The revenue boys seize all your remaining assets. You can't afford an apartment with a doorman anymore. In this town, you pretty much can't afford anything.

That crowd out on the street is a rough crowd. Hobbesian. Smart fellow like you knows what that means."

This guy certainly knew how to get under my skin. I breathed deep and said, "When I need motivation, I'll ask for it. What I need now is that ticket."

Probably because it was a mild May day outside, he wasn't wearing the trench coat over his dust-gray suit. From the inside jacket pocket, he drew out the ticket and dropped it on my desk.

"Hotel information is in there too. Have a nice trip. And try to remember, Mrs. Ballaster isn't your enemy; she's your friend. Could turn out to be a very good friend for you. But she's getting old, and while she still has all her marbles, she doesn't deal too well with disappointment."

I didn't say anything. He levered himself up, and with a wink and sort of a smile, he turned and left. I had a plane ticket for a European holiday, where I could pursue the kind of question I was born to pursue. I had a promise, however conditional, of financial freedom. Why wasn't I having fun?

. . . . . .

The morning sun was dazzling, beating down on the busy plaza outside Antwerp's International Airport. It would have been less dazzling if I had spent a longer and different night. After my flight for London took off around 6:00 p.m., I got out an old Agatha Christie mystery to pass the time as painlessly as possible. Airlines barely feed you anymore, so I had already eaten, but this was the first-class compartment, and the comely hostess offered me a mini steak filet and my choice of cabernet or champagne. French champagne? No, Napa Valley, but top of the line, Schramsberg Reserve. I gave in easily to this temptation and had my little strip of medium-rare tenderloin washed down with that chilled sparkly stuff that goes down so smoothly, so pleasantly. I was feeling considerably better by then and had sorted out the suspects in the poisoning death of the wealthy old miser, and when the hostess kept offering refills, I kept on accepting. It was a nighttime flight, and I intended to sleep through most of it; what better way to get sleepy than with a few more slugs of that soothing nectar? At some point I lost the thread of Dame Agatha's plot and went off into dreamland. The hostess, I presume, switched off my reading light and covered me with a blanket, because when I woke up—from the plane bouncing on British tarmac—it was dark and I was cozy warm.

When you travel eastward through the time zones, time goes by faster. I had only slept for a couple of hours when I had to change planes at Heathrow. It was nearly 4:00 a.m. local time. Groggy and still half-plastered, I lurched around in the airport and managed to find my connecting flight for Antwerp. Thanks to the goddess Ballaster, this one was first class too, and even at that ungodly hour they offered free (or prepaid) booze. Not knowing any better, I had some more champagne, French *ordinaire* this time. This leg of the journey was only an hour or so, and I didn't figure on getting any more sleep. The truth is, I wasn't figuring anything very clearly.

The morning sun in Antwerp, as I said, was dazzling, but I was already pretty dazzled. I flagged down a taxi, which sped me to my hotel, the Dortmunder, not far from the airport. I checked in, and when they told me I'd have to pay for an extra day because it wasn't yet noon, I nodded gratefully, ordered a pot of room-service coffee, and took a long hot shower. After a vigorous rubdown with the hotel's giant towel and two cups of coffee, I felt, if not chipper, at least up to four on a scale of ten.

The conference was in another hotel near the old city center, a sleek twentieth-century high-rise surrounded by architecture out of a painting by Vermeer. Another taxi dropped me off there around nine thirty, and along with quite a few other people, doubtless mostly Shroud junkies, I headed into the main lobby. The various conference activities didn't start until ten, so I grabbed a brochure and went into the hotel coffee shop. I wasn't hungry, but a double-shot cappuccino couldn't hurt.

The plenary opening session was held in an ornate auditorium seating close to a thousand, and it was filling up when I took a seat near the rear. There were about as many women as men, and the crowd seemed to have the usual distribution of types—Sneezy, Sleepy, Dopey, Doc, Bashful, Happy, Grumpy. Clerical collars and nuns' habits were plentiful. I was making small talk with a woman seated next to me who might have been a nun in mufti when the emcee, a man with snowy hair and a booming voice, welcomed us and gave us a rundown of what the conference would include—just what the brochure said. He introduced several people whose efforts or money had made the conference possible, and then introduced the featured speaker for this plenary session, a Dr. Toomey. Toomey was professorial looking (much more than me), tall and a little stooped, with wispy gray hair and a long nose supporting reading glasses over which he peered at us pedantically.

He spoke better than he looked, however—with energy and enthusiasm for his subject. He was a botanist who had been part of the team of experts who were permitted to give the Shroud its first, and thus far only, thorough scientific examination over several days back in the 1970s. They called themselves the Shroud of Turin Research Project, acronym STURP. Toomey had studied microscopic pollen samples lifted from the Shroud with a special adhesive tape. Pollen grains, he said, are virtually indestructible and can remain intact for many millennia. The individual characteristics of each species show up under the microscope, and from the Shroud samples, he had identified several species not found in France or Italy but native to Palestine, the Jerusalem area in particular, and others native to what is now eastern Turkey. These he showed on the big screen, magnified so that they resembled cacti the size of cantaloupes. It was an interesting presentation. If what he said was true, the Shroud would seem to have spent some of its life over in Palestine and areas north of there. Unless maybe there was beaucoup funny business going on here.

Besides the plenary sessions at the beginning and the end, there were lecture/study sessions in various hotel meeting rooms and also the main event, held in a huge multipurpose room. This was where the whole gamut of interest groups had their booths, displays, and sideshows, like a state fair that was all about the Shroud. From my review of the brochure, I had decided there was only one study session I wanted to attend, the one discussing various theories about how the image might have gotten onto the linen cloth. That was at three this afternoon. Mostly I wanted to explore the booths and displays and interact with the people there. The best clues to this kind of mystery are found in or reflected through people—Hercule Poirot was right about that. Especially if there is funny business afoot, like a six-hundred-year-old hoax.

So I went strolling with all the fans and critics and tourists, all of us that P.T. Barnum would have called suckers. I saw at once that at least a third of the displays were explicitly religious, either with a Roman Catholic flavor or a Pentecostal flavor or other flavors I wasn't so sure of. Others had a more scientific slant, or sometimes pseudo-scientific, like the effect of gamma rays on dead bodies. Several booths presented the Shroud's putative connection with the Templar Knights, a trendy focus for medieval mystery enthusiasts. And quite a few of them offered their ideas on my main interest: how the crafty medieval craftsman might have done it.

The first display that grabbed my attention was a different one, though. Its subject was the analysis and conclusions of several forensic pathologists who had studied photographs of the Shroud image. Apparently the image was clear and detailed enough that they could examine it just as they would an actual corpse. The first thing I noticed here was a Roman *flagrum*, probably a modern copy of one, spread out on a table. The *flagrum* was the whip they used to punish serious offenders. It had several leather thongs attached to a handle. Fastened to the tip of each thong was a lead pellet about two centimeters long, shaped like a dumbbell. When the malefactor (or victim) was flogged, these pellets embedded themselves and then tore out bits of flesh. The relevance of this gory information was that the pellets could be precisely aligned with the approximately one hundred scourge marks visible on the man in the Shroud image. One pathologist was quoted as saying he could tell from which direction, the right or the left, many of the blows were delivered.

Then there were the puncture wounds all over the scalp, many of them trickling blood (the bloodstains on the Shroud are not just images, like the man himself, but actual human blood, type AB). These wounds, the pathologists agreed, were fully consistent with wounds that would have been made by the crown of thorns said to have been jammed onto Jesus's head by the sportive soldiers.

The crucified man also has a wound in his right side, such as a spear thrust would make, which caused a large flow of blood and watery fluid. Such a flow, according to the pathologists, would occur from a spear thrust up into the heart of a man who had died within the last hour. The exhibit quoted a few verses from the Gospel of John describing a soldier spearing Jesus to make sure he was dead.

One point emphasized in the pathology reports was that the crucified man had been nailed through his wrists, not his palms. That was the Roman method, because only thus could the nailing be sure to bear the man's weight without tearing loose. Christian artists depicting Christ's crucifixion many centuries later, when crucifixion had been supplanted by other ingenious tortures, always show him nailed through the palms.

How had the Shroud forger known better than all his contemporaries? How did he manage to get everything just right? I wanted to ask some questions about this, but there was only one person manning, or rather womanning, the booth, and a clutch of inquirers had her cornered, so I ambled on.

There were, of course, food and drink stands at an event like this. When I came to one offering sausage sandwiches and Belgian beer, I suddenly realized how hungry I was. And thirsty. You would think that after my binge last night… but no, the body needs food, and Belgian beer is among the world's best. So I took a time-out with a brat in a bun and a frothy cup of Flemish Red, then continued my quest in a better frame of mind.

They were piping in music over the sound system, what sounded like a monastery choir singing Gregorian chants. Not my kind of music usually, but it seemed fitting here.

"I don't say you know nothing about it, mate, but if you haven't actually *done* it, well then, what?"

I heard that spoken in a penetrating male voice, and looking back over my shoulder, I saw that it came from a slender black man whose kinky hair was arranged in geometric patterns around his skull. He was gesturing eloquently to press his argument with a short, fat, fair, freckled, sweating man who shook his head and punctuated each negation by slapping his straw boater against his leg. This fellow had his back to me, so I couldn't hear his rejoinders. I stopped and moved closer to them and heard the black man saying, "… couldn't tell a pigment from a pigsty. Yunesky and his crowd, they're just as feeble. Trial and error, trial and error—none of them have the patience or persistence to stick it out. One trial, one error, and they hold it up and say, 'Look! This is it! I've got it!' What have they got? Piss on a bedsheet."

His accent would have fascinated Henry Higgins; to me it sounded like cockney spiced with some variety of African. At this point, his antagonist gave up in disgust and trudged off, clapping the boater back on his head. The black man, I now noticed, was minding a booth, which also featured a display of photos or other prints in both color and black and white. These resembled the Shroud image to some extent.

He saw me looking and waved me over and said confidingly, "Some cheeky blighters always turn up at an event like this. But you, guv, have the appearance of a more discriminatin' class of trade." He offered his hand. "Boki Mubala, sir, at your service. Call me Bob—everybody does, north of the desert."

I shook his hand and introduced myself as Adam Hult, no title. People often recognize my name from my books, but Bob seemed blessedly untouched by my modest fame. I asked about his display, and he was eager to explain it.

"First off, I take it that a well-educated man such as yourself"—this was flattery, but more accurate than he could have known—"understands that what we are concerned with here is a monumental feat of flummery. Truly monumental, unparalleled. That it is not *actually* what it is *claimed* to be does not detract from its artistic pre-eminence. Its creator may have been a con man to his marrow—indeed, must have been—but he—probably not she; this was the middle ages, after all—he was a phenomenal artist. Phenomenal. Are you trackin' with me, sir?"

"Tracking with you so far."

"You aren't . . . you know, scrupulously religious?"

"Not scrupulously, no."

"And, if you don't mind my askin', are you familiar with what the scientists, or most of them, say about that image on the Shroud?"

I shrugged with semi-feigned modesty. "That there is no evidence of painting or staining? No residue?"

He clapped his hands like a gratified teacher. "Quite so, quite. And the depth of the image?"

"It is only on the very outermost fibrils of the linen. If you could scrape off the top millimeter, the image would be gone."

"Excellent! You are indeed well up to speed. So then, how did the wily artist do it?"

"There are some who would give a small or medium fortune to know."

At this hint of remuneration, however insubstantial, he perked up even more.

"Is that a fact? It's a puzzler, ain't it? But there is a way; there is a way. As the famous old British puzzle solver Sherlock Holmes put it, 'When you have eliminated the impossible, whatever remains, however improbable, must be the truth.' And here we have lorry loads of impossibility. Not a religious miracle. Not a photograph—if you're with me there, I won't trouble you with that. Not a painting using any pigment known in the fourteenth century or, for that matter, any time since. So we eliminate those. I ask you, sir, what is left?"

Without either turning or pointing, he nevertheless managed to draw my attention unmistakably to the array of photos all around him.

"All right," I said, "I'll bite. What's all this you've got here?"

"Ah! Since you ask, and since you seem an honest gentleman, I'll tip my hand. This"—and now he did wave his hand around like an impresario—"this is how our foxy forger made it happen. I'm not keeping secrets here; the world needs to know. Very clever indeed he was, our old master, inventive in the extreme. He invented the green vitriol powder rubbing method for impressin' an image on a piece of cloth, but so sly, so super subtle that it's barely on there at all, and it gives that shadowy, ghostly look and feeling to the viewer."

He paused to let this sink in and allow me to survey his display.

"Why just photos?" I asked. "Why not bring the thing itself?"

Now for the first time he got cagey. "Oh no, guv, that would not be prudent, not prudent at all. Not everyone in this crowd is as honest as yourself." His eyes flickered around the passersby as if to identify potential thieves or vandals, and I was, unexpectedly, reminded of Sareen's portentous remark about the Shroud's capacity for causing trouble.

"Green vitriol?" I queried.

"Old name for iron sulfate, what they called it back then—a sort of green rust. You heat this up, you see, and it turns to a reddish ash, which is easily ground to powder. In the process, the sulfate turns to iron oxide, traces of which have been found all over the Shroud, not just where the image is."

"Right. You've got a lab or studio where you work on this?"

"Lewisham. South London. Upstairs over the antique shop we keep, the wife and me."

All this time I was examining his work on a pseudo-Shroud. The photos included both positives, showing his artifact as it actually was, and negatives, intended to resemble the negative images of the Turin Shroud. All in all, it was impressive but not quite convincing. If the Shroud was the work of an old master, Bob's stuff was like the attempts of a talented apprentice. That, of course, might be the actual relationship.

"So, with this powder, how do you paint it onto the cloth without leaving any pigmentary traces?"

He beamed a toothy smile. "That's the secret, which, as you see, I'm disclosin' to the captains of science and art. For the 3D effect, you start with a sculpture. I've got a friend who's a bit of a sculptor and works with me on this. He did a sculpture—the head and face are the most important part. Then you dampen the linen and form it over the sculpture. After it dries, you daub the vitriol powder *very* gently over the raised portions, barely touching it, so that only the surface of the linen is affected. That's how it's done."

"And that's how it was done in the first place?"

"Must have been. I've never seen a better way."

"Okay. What I'm wondering about is the photonegative character of the image. I see that's how you made it."

"Too right."

"Because that's how the original was done."

He regarded me quizzically. "Well, natch."

"But why? I mean, why did the original artist, the forger, make a photonegative image? How would he, or anyone else in the fourteenth century, have any idea what a photonegative image was?"

He gave a palms-up shrug. "He was a genius?"

CHAPTER 11

A few displays along the way from Bob Mubala's I came to one with a large, red-lettered banner reading *"Angels Preserved It! The Pope Stole It!"* Three women sat on folding chairs behind the counter, looking eager for customers. The crowd, though, was milling on by, either oblivious of them or avoiding them. I could see why. What their booth mostly featured were floral arrangements, Bible verses, and religious paintings of angels and people wearing robes. The largest such painting was of winged angels carrying the full-length Shroud. The total effect was so fulsomely sentimental that it grabbed my attention just long enough for one of the women to make eye contact and bounce up to greet me. She was chubby, and her dress, with round pink polka dots of various sizes, made her chubbier. Her expression, shining through foundation and plenty of powder, exuded ingenuous friendliness.

"Good morning, sir, or is it good afternoon already? I have no idea," she gushed in Deep South American. "Welcome to our little corner of this mighty great event. Oh my, here I am rushing on and I don't even—do you speak English?"

"Most of the time," I said. I should have just shaken my head apologetically.

"Oh, wonderful. One never knows, you know, over here and all. I'm Henrietta Harvey, *Mrs.* Henrietta Harvey." She thrust out a white hand with rings on every finger, and I shook it briefly without identifying myself. I wasn't sure if the floral perfume was coming from her or from all the flowers or from both.

"Where are your people from, Mr. . . . ?"

Oy vey! I wasn't going to get off so easily or anonymously. My people? From all over half the map, but she meant the locale of my ancestral plantation.

"Adam Hult, from Brooklyn. Now I'm across the river in Manhattan."

She glowed at me. "A genuine Yankee! Praise *God* that He has healed all those hard old feelings. For we war not against flesh and blood, as the Bible says. Now tell me, Mr. Hult—no, you don't have to tell me, I can sense that something in your spirit has drawn you to this conference. Something in your spirit draws you to the holy Shroud, isn't that so?"

"I have an interest in it."

"Oh yes, and it has an interest in *you*, Mr. Hult—Adam, if I may. *He* has an interest in you."

The subject cried out for a quick change. "Your banner here says the pope stole it. What's that about?"

"You see, Adam? If there wasn't a *deep interest* going on here, you wouldn't even ask. Why, of course he stole it; we know all about that. Not the present pope, naturally, though I wouldn't put it past him, but the one back in the sixteenth century, at the time of the Great Reformation, you know? That was a great rising up of the Spirit, and the prince of this world took counsel with himself how he might overturn the table set up against him. 'Thou preparest a table before me in the presence of mine enemies,' as David testified. The devil took many measures, as we know, burning many innocent martyrs at the stake, but we believe his most dastardly stroke of all was to seize the Holy Shroud from its guardians and turn it into a superstitious relic, just one more way to raise money."

Whew! I had to ask, "Who did he steal it from?"

A slight frown dimmed her smile. "People are skeptical, we know that, when the subject of the angelic host comes up. But the Bible is not ashamed to speak of angels. God shall give His angels charge over thee, to keep thee in all thy ways. His angels excel in strength and do His commandments, hearkening unto the voice of His word. By entertaining strangers, some have entertained angels unawares. The Bible is full of angels."

"But the Shroud?"

"Well, we *have* the Shroud," she said triumphantly. "I mean, *we* don't have it, exactly, but we know it exists to this day. It has been preserved, even in *their* hands. And who preserved and guarded it through all the years of darkness? Who else but God's holy angels?"

"But then, how did the pope steal it from them?"

Her lips pursed in disapproval. "There isn't much they wouldn't stoop to, them with all their red robes and hats and crowns. They found a way. We know they took it at the time of the Great Reformation because there are paintings showing them standing on balconies and displaying it. They make their money from it, but at least they haven't destroyed it."

"No, they haven't destroyed it."

▮ ▮ ▮ ▮ ▮ ▮

After detaching myself from Mrs. Henrietta Harvey, I thought about getting some more good Belgian beer to fortify myself against whatever might come next, but decided that a sixteen-ounce latte was the smarter choice.

One thing was for sure: the exhibits here covered a remarkable range of topics and angles, everything from green vitriol and angels to the history of the ancient city-state of Edessa and high-definition digital photography. I was still in the process of absorbing it all when the hour hand rolled around to three, the time for the session on how the image might have gotten onto the linen. This was in one of the hotel meeting rooms on the floor above the exhibition hall, so I climbed the stairs and found the room. What I found was that they had changed to a larger room to accommodate all the people who were interested, like me. The new room seated around a hundred, but by the time I got there the seats had already filled up, so I joined the standees around the edges.

The session was entitled "A Scientific View of the Image on the Cloth." The lecturer was a German woman originally from Frankfurt, Dr. Erika Steiner. She was one of the world's leading biochemists and currently a professor at MIT—credentials so solid they could break your teeth. She was small; she wore glasses and had her black hair pulled back in a twist. She didn't begin her talk with a smile or a joke but went straight into her analysis of the problem, speaking English as Germans sometimes do, more precisely and musically than the British (forget the Americans). With the Shroud, as with most other things, she said, there are many possibilities, but only a few of these are probable. It is possible that it dates from the first century and is the actual burial shroud of Jesus or of another crucified man. It is also possible that it dates from a later period, and if that is the case, the later period is almost certainly the thirteenth or fourteenth century, as indicated by the 1988 radiocarbon test. And in that case, the image on the Shroud was caused not by any natural process—or supernatural event—but by some means of human artifice.

Dr. Steiner began, in her logical way, with the first possibility, that the Shroud dates from the first century. If the image were caused by a supernatural event such as a resurrection, natural science would soon hit a wall in trying to explain it. However, she said, the predominant, even the overwhelming experience of modern science is that events of this kind are so extremely rare and, in principle, so extremely doubtful, that their probability approaches zero.

As for the hypothesis that the cloth dates from the first century and the image was caused by natural means, there are only a few remotely plausible possibilities. Assuming that it was an actual burial shroud, one idea is that the urea in the man's sweat fermented into carbon dioxide and ammonia, and the ammonia diffused into the cloth as a vapor. A similar idea is that the image was caused where the linen came into direct contact with the body and was stained by some combination of perspiration, body oils, or burial anointing substances like aloes, myrrh, or olive oil. The main problem with such theories, Dr. Steiner said, is that they are inconsistent with the extreme superficiality of the image and cannot explain the three-dimensional information encoded in the image. Those matters, she promised, would be examined more closely toward the end of her presentation.

She then turned to the possibility that the Shroud originated more than a millennium later and was the work of human craft, presumably with fraudulent intent. Here again, she said, the difficulty was squaring the hypothetical method with the evidence provided by scientific examinations of the object. She briefly addressed and dismissed, as I already had, theories about some prodigy of medieval photography. As for painting, there was no evidence of any kind of pigment having been used. She then spent fifteen or twenty minutes discussing in some detail several variations of the powder-rubbing method advocated by Bob Mubala.

For most of this time, she had been moving around the front of the room, augmenting her words with her expressive hands. Now she came back to the lectern and leaned into it. As a teacher myself, I knew the body language: here comes the main point.

"All of these, as I have said, are possibilities. Some are more probable than others. On strictly scientific grounds, though for different reasons in each case, both the possibility of a supernatural miracle and that of medieval photography must be regarded as highly improbable. From the results of the carbon 14 testing, even though legitimate questions have been raised about how those tests were carried out, it is most likely that this piece of linen—fine linen, one must add—dates from approximately the thirteenth or fourteenth century. It is, therefore, almost certainly a wholly human artifact: both the cloth and the image on it were produced by humans.

"Having said this, however, we must immediately add that, as far as I am aware, all attempts thus far to explain or demonstrate how the image came to be on the cloth are severely deficient. Two characteristics of the image in particular remain unexplained. First, the image exists only on the outermost surface of the cloth. This fact was discovered and confirmed during the 1977 examination by the STURP scientists. To picture this correctly, imagine each strand in the herringbone weave to be the size of your forearm. In that case, the scorch-like coloring that constitutes the image would affect *only* the hairs on the top of your forearm. Those hairs correspond, in reality, to the microscopic fibrils on the surface of each strand. None of the image-forming methods so far suggested satisfies this condition. What perhaps comes closest to satisfying it is the idea of some form of radiation."

She paused, consulting her notes for only the second or third time during the lecture. "Now, the only radiation-producing technology known during the European middle ages, even in Germany"—this, her only laugh line, worked for her—"would have been some metallic object, possibly a sculpture, heated red-hot and brought in close proximity to the cloth. Unfortunately, though, in that case the scorching from radiant heat would have penetrated much deeper than the image on the Shroud. And so, on this count, from a scientific point of view, we remain baffled.

"The second unexplained characteristic of the image is perhaps even more baffling. Modern digital image-analyzing technology has revealed, quite conclusively, that the Shroud image encodes digital information for a three-dimensional representation of its subject. In short, it is a hologram. Even today we would not be able to encode such information on the surface fibrils of a sheet of linen. I would very much like to tell you how someone did it seven hundred years ago, but I cannot. If any of you can, there is a Nobel committee in Stockholm that is waiting to hear from you."

That concluded her formal presentation, and she spent the next half hour fielding questions. Most of these concerned points of fact, but some questioners were critical of her jaundiced view of all current proposals for how it might have been done. They obviously weren't going to agree on this, and I decided it was a good time to make my exit. It was almost dinnertime and I was hungry, so I headed downstairs for one of the hotel restaurants. I was paying no attention to the people or objects around me, being absorbed in processing Dr. Steiner's talk. Mainly I was gnawing on the apparent contradiction between her contention that the Shroud image must be a human artifact and her assessment that there was no conceivable way it could have been produced.

The problem was, I pretty much agreed with her.

. . . . . .

"Dr. Hult! Dr. Hult!"

I was in the hotel's main lobby when a woman's voice calling my name jerked me out of my mental spaceship. I turned to see an eye-catching young blonde in a bright-yellow suit with a cordless mike in her hand. Off to her side was a well-built black guy in scruffy jeans with one of those TV-grade videocameras on his shoulder, pointed at me.

"Dr. Hult," the blonde said to her mike, looking at me, "may I ask you a question?"

Just one question? I don't think I've mentioned that there was a full complement of media types at this conference, including several television crews like this one. They came from all over, but this honey's speech was standard American.

In a quarter of a second I mentally reviewed the situation. Some people, especially those with something to hide, such as embezzlers or philanderers, naturally wish to avoid media inquiries. Others, whose livelihood depends on exposure, such as politicians and other entertainers, need the camera time and need to answer the questions, however insincerely. Most of the camera-needers, of course, also have things to hide. Such as me. I had my personal no-go zones, but I was on an assignment where success was measured in media exposure. Doris Ballaster didn't want proof of the Shroud's phoniness just for herself. She didn't need it. She wanted the world to know.

The quarter-second hitch was enough for the intrepid reporter to feel the tug on her line. "Dr. Hult, I'm Mandy Blake with CBS News. Can you tell me, sir, what particular interest brings you to this Shroud of Turin Conference?"

"Well, Mandy, it's certainly an interesting thing—the Shroud, that is."

"Yes, but what is *your* interest in it, sir?"

A recollection flashed through my mind of Henrietta Harvey's quirky remark that the interest went both ways, but I didn't go there.

"Like many of the people here," I said, "I'd like to find out more about it, what it really is."

"Yes, but you know, Dr. Hult," she said with a smile that could enliven the entire male half of the population, "*you* aren't like many of the people here. You're a famous scholar and author, famous especially for debunking various popular but erroneous theories. Are you out to slay another dragon?"

"That's a colorful way to put it, Mandy, but misleading. The Shroud isn't a dragon, and I'm not into slaying."

"Tell that to the folks who think the universe began a few thousand years ago. But seriously, Dr. Hult, can you tell our viewers what your take is on the Shroud of Turin?"

"It's an amazing artifact, truly amazing. It's an incredibly difficult thing for anyone to pin down or explain."

"All right, but do you think it's a fraud, a hoax?"

I remembered that Doris Ballaster would probably be seeing this interview, or replays of it, rather soon.

"That's certainly the odds-on presumption. Proving it would be quite a challenge, though."

"Do you think you're up to the challenge?"

Ah, the price of being a public figure and also a paid flunky.

"Well, I'm here, aren't I?" I said without, I think, blushing.

CHAPTER 12

Mandy kept trying to push it a bit further, but when she found I would only repeat myself, she gave up and left me free to seek out a restaurant. I had noticed one that morning called Chez Cuisine and found it again easily enough. They would have a table for me in about ten minutes, and while I was waiting, a man came up to me and said, "Professor Hult?"

He was nearly a foot taller than me but almost skeletally thin with long, very blond hair draped across one eye.

"That's me."

"Pete vander Hoot."

He held out a hand, and I shook it. His name might actually be Piet van der Huit or something like that, but he didn't spell it for me.

"I overheard your interview with the television girl," he went on, "and when I realized who you are, I knew I had to intrude myself upon you. It is all right?"

His English was heavily accented, probably Dutch, judging by his name.

"Yes, it's all right," I said.

He nodded vigorously. "It is because I have read all your books—I think all—and I believe you are on the right track. There is maybe farther to go on the track, but it is the right one."

"Well ... thank you."

"If you are not meeting anyone here for dinner, may I join you?"

Why not? "Sure, if you like."

"That is excellent. We know already that we share an interest in the Shroud. Perhaps other things as well, yes?"

"Could be, I guess. What's your interest in it?"

"That is a good question."

He took out a pack of cigarettes then evidently noticed the restaurant's No Smoking symbol and put it back in his pocket, looking miffed. Smoking restrictions were less ubiquitous in Europe than in America.

"That is a good question," he repeated, "even for myself. What is my interest? I am a filmmaker, an independent filmmaker, based in Amsterdam, but I have made films all over the world—Kenya, Portugal, and other places. These films are in Dutch and German, however, so there is not so much chance you have seen them."

"Probably not," I agreed.

"To me," he went on, "the locale of the film is as important as the story or the characters. As place and as symbol, the locale is the main character. It is the center of the story. Do you not think so?"

"I suppose so. It would be hard to make a Vegas film in Poughkeepsie."

He stared at me for a second, trying to locate Poughkeepsie, and then said, "Yes, that is the idea, but more than that. It is a matter of the *Wesen*, the essence of the place."

"Like, for instance, the *Wesen* of Turin?"

He pursed his lips and shook his head, causing the drape of hair to sway.

"No, that is not the thing, I think—not so much the thing about the Shroud."

At this point, the host signaled that my table, now our table, was ready. He led us to a far end of the restaurant and seated us with our menus. The decor was much the same as high-toned restaurants everywhere—low lights, creamy tablecloths, sparkling crystal, and generic paintings and other art objects on the walls.

Feeling unadventurous, when our waiter came I ordered a slab of prime rib and a moderately priced (by Chez Cuisine's standards) bottle of Chateau Something. Pete ordered in French, so I didn't know what he was getting until the waiter eventually brought a dish that looked like pieces of liver in a yellow-green sauce over parsnips and watercress. I didn't ask.

Our conversation was odd. He did most of the talking, but we both seemed to be talking past the other, with little connection. I told him where I was from and what, in a general way, I was doing here. He recounted some of his filmmaking adventures, but even though he spoke English well enough, it was largely Dutch to me. I really wasn't giving him my full attention. This tête-à-tête hadn't been my idea, after all.

"But the Shroud, now," he said at one point, getting back to what we had in common, "you are a skeptic, of course."

That made me a little defensive. "Why 'of course'?"

"Well, your reputation, your books—on Shakespeare, on the new earth ..."

"In the Shakespeare book, I was skeptical of the skeptics."

He slapped the tablecloth with his palm. "But that is the point! You are the arch-skeptic! I think you see these things much the same way I do. You cannot believe what these people tell you. Take nothing at face value."

I thought that over before answering. "There's a problem with being skeptical of everything. If you 'see through' everything, there's nothing left to see. You come up empty."

"So what do you propose? Surely not something simplistic like 'seeing is believing'?"

"No, it's not simple. It's rarely simple. In one sense, the Shroud is 'simply' an old piece of cloth with some faint markings on it. But no one is satisfied with that because it explains nothing. We all—most of us anyway—want an explanation we can believe. If we could discover such an explanation, then seeing and believing might converge."

Pete mopped up the remaining gravy on his plate with his dinner roll, like a country farmer. "Have you seen it? The Shroud?"

"Yes, a couple of weeks ago."

He whistled. "You have connections. Not with the Vatican?"

"No." I didn't elaborate.

He drank some more wine. He had ordered a bottle of Australian pinot noir, which turned out to be very good—we had each tried the other's wine; he tried more of mine.

"I have studied many of the photos, many," he said. "I study them with a professional eye. They have much to tell that is not so obvious. I have also examined these would-be debunkers who try to tell us how some charlatan put the image onto the cloth. They are all full of *wurst*. Look at what they have done side by side with the original. It is a joke."

This was uncomfortably close to my own assessment. But it left an obvious question: "So what do you think the Shroud actually is?"

He looked around, as if checking for eavesdroppers, and then made very direct eye contact and said, "Most people cannot receive the truth about that, but I will take a chance with you, Professor Hult. I will tell you. As you must have noticed already, I am not a religious person. I do not believe in miracles, angels, or saints. No heaven or hell—this world is enough of both. And yet, here we have this remarkable thing, this strange and inexplicable object. Now, even though I am not a religious person, let me ask you: Do you think we are alone in the universe?"

Now here was a new slant. "I don't know. There has been no 'contact' thus far, of course. The problem isn't whether other intelligent species exist somewhere out there; the problem is the unimaginable distances that separate us. If they are as near to us, in cosmic terms, as a hundred light-years, that means even basic conversation would take a century each way. Not very practical."

"That is true, but it assumes their technology is no more advanced than our own. A weak assumption." He glanced around again. "A wrong assumption."

I was beginning to hear the theme music of *Star Trek*. I figured he wouldn't need any more prompting, and I was right.

"You are correct," he said, "that the other galaxies are too far off for contact. Within our own galaxy, though, the difficulties have been overcome, just as we will overcome them within another century or two. They *have* made contact. The Shroud is one of several messages they have left with us."

I thought it best to tread softly. "But then, why would they leave a 'message' in such a way as to encourage the growth of a huge, systematic world religion like Christianity?"

"Don't you see? Don't you see? They work *through* our own myths to reveal themselves. As we evolve to the point where we are able to demythologize our religions, we eventually find the kernel of *their* revelation of themselves to us."

"Which is ... a strange, inexplicable image of a crucified man?"

"No! No!" He almost pounded on the table, and I motioned to him to quiet down. He continued in a loud whisper, "That, the crucified man, that is the myth! The reality, the revelation, is that there is a technology—here, in the Shroud, we have hard evidence of a technology—that is as far beyond our own as ours is beyond the stone age. *That* is the message of the Shroud."

The waiter approached and asked if we wanted dessert. We both opted for just some coffee.

"You don't believe this," Pete said as he stirred cream and sugar into his coffee.

I just raised my eyebrows.

"Then, what do you believe? How do you explain it?"

"I don't know," I answered honestly, "yet. But I intend to find out."

CHAPTER 13

I flew back to New York the following afternoon. During the morning I had poked around the various exhibits some more, without learning much that was helpful. Except possibly one thing: I picked up several references to an artist in Boston who apparently was scathingly scornful of just about any and every fellow artist who tried reproducing the Shroud image by any and every method. This was one Dougal MacInnes, and none of the references to him was friendly. He was eccentric, cantankerous, talentless, and cracked. He had boycotted the Antwerp conference.

He stirred my interest.

But first I had to finish up my academic responsibilities—reading and grading term papers and final exams, filing grade reports, attending an Academic Planning Committee meeting, and so forth. All that took the better part of three days, with more coffee than food and not much sleep.

I did, however, steal an hour from this scholarly grind to present an in-person progress report to Doris Ballaster. I owed her such an accounting, no doubt, but the immediate stimulus was a brief, militaristic voicemail from Tom Freebinder telling me when and where. Nine o'clock that evening at her apartment (suite, manor, chateau). No question on either side that I would be there.

What should I tell her? I recalled Lara's view of this venture, that I was going into it expecting to leap tall buildings at a single bound, go where no man had gone before, solve the riddle that baffled all previous attempts to explain it. By and large, she had me pegged about right. The mental self-confidence scale barely reached as high as me. And Doris, at our first meeting, had certainly seemed to agree; if anyone could fulfill her wishes and expose the Shroud, it would be me.

But now ... the truth was, I was surprised at just how hard the task was turning out to be. So far, Bob Mubala was typical of the artistic forgery theorists I had come across: not very persuasive. Erika Steiner's extremely competent statement of the problem loomed in my mind. But Doris, I was sure, wanted to hear less about looming problems and more about promising solutions.

Gopal, her handsome Indian valet, opened the door to me with the same impeccable smoothness as before. This time he led me past the sumptuous living room into a smaller but equally elegant room where Doris awaited me in her wheelchair. Tonight she was wearing a gorgeous oriental outfit in patterns of gold highlighted with blue and buttoned up to her neck, probably worth half my annual salary. With great relief, I saw no sign of our mutual friend Tom. Maybe lurking behind the arras?

"Good evening, Adam," Doris said in her cultivated way. "Have a seat, please. May I offer you an especially fine manzanilla pasada, or would you again prefer coffee?"

"I'll try the sherry, thank you," I replied, primarily in order to show I knew what manzanilla pasada was—not just any sherry but a rare and fine one. Doris nodded to Gopal, who melted from the room.

"Now, Adam, let me again express my satisfaction at your willingness to work with us and my confidence in your ability. Tell me, what did you learn at the Antwerp conference?"

As much as I had already thought about what to tell her, I still wasn't sure what to say. My willingness to work with her was almost entirely financial, but as motives go, of course, few are any stronger. I temporized: "I learned quite a bit about the difficulties we face."

"I know the difficulties," she said impatiently. "Have you made any progress?"

I sighed inwardly. "All indications are, as expected, that the Shroud image was produced in the fourteenth century. If so, though, it was done by an amazingly original artist. As you pointed out at our first meeting, the attempts of current-day artists to reproduce it are less than convincing. As far as I've found so far, at any rate."

Gopal returned with our sherry, in crystal goblets—antique, I imagine—on a silver tray. I took a sip and found it, naturally, delicious.

"I see," Doris said. "I assume the chief thing that insight proves is the mediocrity of those current-day artists. Would you agree?"

"I suppose so. I mean, I agree that's the most logical inference. Pretty much the only logical inference."

"So you have defined a course to pursue."

I paused, framing a response. "Yes, but discovering that these guys aren't worthy to clean the old master's brush, or even proving it, only tells us about them. It wouldn't explain how the old guy did it."

She nodded gravely. "You will have to find an artist who is just as good as the old master. Find him or even, perhaps, invent him."

That took me aback. "Invent? As in, make him up the way Dickens made up Uriah Heep? Spin a hoax in order to debunk a hoax?"

A steely look had settled upon the prim old lady. "Success, Adam, success is what counts in the end. You are in a courtroom, the courtroom of public opinion. World opinion. You are the prosecuting attorney. Your job is not to determine whether the culprit actually committed the crime. We *know* that this fraud has been perpetrated upon the world. Your job is to convince the jury about the fraud. That's how you win your case. That is the only way you win your case. *Your* case, Adam. Am I making myself clear enough?"

Yes, ma'am, I get the drift.

▪ ▪ ▪ ▪ ▪ ▪

Finally the weekend came. May was half over; the school year was completely over. The weatherman promised two days of warm sunshine before the next rainstorm came to town, so on Saturday I snapped up an invitation to join Ari, Benny, Shelley, and Ari's daughter, Lucy, for a day at the beach. Romp in the surf, soak in the sun, and leave all your troubles in the old kit bag. It was Hannah and Chuck's anniversary, and he was taking her to a Broadway matinee and then out to dinner at Abboccato.

We went to Jones Beach out on Long Island. The drive in Ari's Toyota Highlander took a little over an hour, with the girls jamming pop songs most of the way. I recognized almost none of the songs, being old. We got there around eleven in the morning and unpacked our stuff—blankets, towels, picnic hamper, sunscreen, and Frisbee. A breeze was blowing but the sun was warming things up, and a good number of people were already on the beach and in the surf. We staked out our spot about a dozen yards from the wet sand, and the girls kicked off their flip-flops and scampered down to the water. Lucy, a nine-year-old with curly dark-brown hair, imitated her teenage cousin in everything down to the last prance, whoop, and shriek. Shelley didn't have the cast on her wrist anymore, and you'd never know she'd broken it. At thirteen, she switched moment by moment from hoyden to beauty queen.

Ari did some acrobatic stretching—he was fanatical about that stuff—then plodded down to join the girls. Benny and I eyed each other with, I think, mutual understanding, and sank down onto the blanket. I slathered on some sunscreen and offered it to him, but he declined. Skin cancer?—it wouldn't dare. Chalk it up to hubris or just old habit.

After a while, he said, "They are beautiful." He was watching his granddaughters.

"No other word for it."

"No. Does it make you the least bit envious?"

"About having children? I don't know ... maybe just a twinge. It wouldn't work so well for me, though. Who would stay married to me?"

Immediately I regretted saying that. Ari's wife, Joyce, had divorced him two years ago. The death of their young son Amos through leukemia had left her severely depressed, though how much that had to do with the divorce, I wasn't sure. That was one part of Ari's life that he shared with me only in an edited way.

"Not going to happen with you and Lara, I suppose," Benny said.

"No, I don't think so. Just as well."

Down in the water, Ari and the girls were jumping about in the small breakers and splashing one another. We watched them for a while.

"What do you think, Benny," I asked him presently, "about the chances for some sort of peace over there? How much longer can Israel avoid a full-blown war?"

After a minute, he said, "Israel has been at war for the better part of a century. The question is, how long can we avoid losing?"

"As bad as that ... "

"It's the same as with America, but much more local and therefore more intense. The same, I mean, in that having bigger and better guns doesn't guarantee victory any longer. Warfare has evolved beyond that."

"Not armaments any more as much as demographics?"

"Yes, that. And a certain tipping point that occurred when the suicide bomber mutated from the rare and solitary fanatic into the pious and patriotic hero. If the time comes when a thousand heroes are willing to infiltrate and explode themselves, Israel will become indefensible."

"And there's no way to stop that happening?"

"No way Israel can stop it. Hinder it, but not stop it. It depends on the Arabs, what they want to do with their children. Who are also beautiful."

Ari ran up and grabbed the Frisbee, and the three of them started flinging it among themselves.

"You made the newspaper again," Benny said.

"Not the obituaries, I hope."

"Your deal with that wealthy woman."

"Ah, geez, again. Tabloid?"

"The *Daily News*."

I exhaled a heavy and heartfelt sigh. "I know how that business slipped through the cracks. It started with that two-minute interview by Mandy Blake on CBS. I didn't mention any wealthy woman in that, of course. But then an ambitious local stringer decided to do some investigative journalism by pitching a question to one of my known associates, the socialite ad exec Lara Martinez. It isn't Lara's fault, though. I didn't swear her to secrecy. My bad."

He mulled that over and then said, "Your bad, huh? You mean blabbing to Lara or contracting with Mrs. Ballaster?"

Oops. It sounded like his view of it was going to be just as jaundiced as Ari's.

"Maybe both?" I said.

"Yeah. I won't say you've sold yourself out, Adam, but do you think you're going to be able to keep your end of the deal?"

"Like, prove the Shroud is a fake?"

"Like that."

"I don't know, Benny. I don't know. If I can't do it, they all say, nobody can. We'll see, won't we?"

I got up and went scrunching through the sand to join the Frisbee tossing. As if four was a crowd, though, Shelley and Lucy pretty soon decided to build a castle in the damp sand. Ari warned them that the tide was coming in and they had about an hour before their construction would be flooded out. They both stared at him quizzically. When you're young, an hour is a long time.

Ari shrugged, and we turned and started walking along the beach, where the successive waves just washed over our feet. We had both been so busy with one thing and another that we hadn't really talked in a couple of weeks. We had some catching up to do.

I began with, "Benny seems rather moody today."

He just glanced at me with a look that might have meant something.

I tried again with, "And as for you, any memorable musical gigs lately? Or have you hacked into Warren Buffett's investment strategy for the upcoming year?"

He smiled and shook his head. "Haven't succeeded with Warren yet. Last weekend I played a couple of nights with Sleek Ermine at Artemis. That was time well spent."

Sleek Ermine was a jazz group he had played with before, and Artemis was a new and popular Harlem nightclub. As far as I knew, this was his first time playing there.

"Moving up in the world," I said. "And speaking of time well spent, how did that stint with the Russian honcho go?" That bodyguarding gig he had told me about.

"Bah!" he grunted, kicking a small piece of driftwood as if it had offended him. "Not good. I thought he was a businessman, right?"

"A *Russian* businessman."

"Granted. I was giving him the benefit of the doubt. Should have done my homework better."

"What happened?"

"He'd set up a meeting with another 'Russian businessman' on the third floor of this roach hotel in the Bronx. Just he and I and one of his goons. By this point, I already don't like it. The whole setup stinks. My guy, first name Lev, knocks on the door, and I'm figuring what to do if we're looking down gun barrels. The dude we're supposed to meet is called Grigory. One of his goons—he had two with him, so we were balanced—opens up and lets us in. No gun barrels, guns all holstered. Some low-voiced, guttural Russian conversation between Lev and Grigory, too rapid and slangy for me to understand much of it, and then Lev's flunky pulls a nine millimeter Smith & Wesson and waves it at them. Lev pulls on them too, just to make sure. Lev tells me to frisk them and take their weapons. If I balk at that point, I'm in the privy with the other schmucks, so I do it—guns and a couple of knives. Lev has me empty the guns. He puts the bullets in his pocket, and we drop their weapons in the toilet tank. By now Lev has started to think about trusting me, and I snatch his gun and whack his comrade on the temple with it."

"Cementing a nice cross-cultural friendship."

"Like concrete. Lev's boy is down for the count, but Lev, now looking my own Walther PPQ in the eyeball, is breathing sulfur, first in Russian and then, when he remembers, in good creative English. The other three are looking at me like, 'Whose side are you on?'"

A pair of seagulls wheeled and dove in front of us, shouting *eek! eek!*, either courting or arguing.

"So then, whose side were you on?"

"The side with live ammo. I put the sleeper's gun in my belt and got out some plastic cuffs"—Ari always goes prepared—"and told Lev to cuff the four others. He refused unpleasantly, and I shot him in the big toe, and he went down. Then I told Grigory to do the cuffing. I guess he understood English, because he did it, and then I cuffed him. I told Lev I would never work for him again and reminded all of them that the weapons were in the toilet and the bullets in Lev's pocket. Then I left. I don't know how they sorted it out."

"You suppose Lev will be sending some of his chums after you?"

"If he still has a pulse. But he knows me by another name, no address. Whatever is, is. I try to learn from my oversights. Maybe Lev can learn from his too."

CHAPTER 14

We spent the whole day there at Jones Beach, ate our picnic lunch, goofed around, talked about things, and basked on the blankets. It was a great day. The only downer came in the evening when we were driving home and I turned my cell phone back on and listened to the voicemail from Tom Freebinder. It was about the stories in the tabloids mentioning Doris Ballaster's good name alongside my tawdry name, linked by a suspicious financial deal to throw mud at a famous religious icon venerated by millions of sincere believers. Tom was not amused. He threatened a lawsuit, serious physical pain, and worst of all, no more funding. My impression, though, with fingers crossed, was that these were only threats. Until I heard anything more definite, I figured Doris, however affronted she might be, was still in the game.

The following afternoon, Sunday, I got together with Lara at a Starbucks down in Lower Manhattan. It was her invitation, and I wasn't sure what to expect. Well, I hoped for the best and expected the worst. I arrived a little ahead of time and got myself a coffee and two of those crunchy, glazed old-fashioned doughnuts. Lara showed up a few minutes later, got her drink, and joined me at the tiny two-person table. She was in her normal power-suited, business-gal mode, but I thought that, if anything, she looked almost mournful.

"Hey, Adam," she said. Then, "Don't you ever change suits?"

"All the time. Every few days. Now and again. Good to see you too, babe."

"Yeah. You mad at me?"

"What about?"

"You know, those stories. Celebrity pundit's girlfriend spills secrets. I didn't mean anything by it, Adam. It never occurred to me it could be a story with legs."

"No problem, honey," I said with doughnut crumbs escaping from my lips. "Those rags make it sound lurid and sleazy; that's their business model. It's an ordinary, legitimate arrangement, nothing clandestine about it."

"You sure? It still sounds to me like they've got more cards in their deck than they're showing you."

"Doesn't everyone? That's the game of life. Basically this thing is just one more tangle I'm working to unsnarl."

"What, the Shroud thing or the mob-connected heiress thing?"

"Mob connected! Don't let the tabloids play with your mind."

"They didn't say that, as far as I read. It's just my idea. The whole business makes me wonder."

"Me too. There's always a bottom to these things, though, and I'll get to it eventually."

"Yeah, well … "

She gazed around the coffee shop. I could see the gears shifting, the subject changing. I was so right.

"You know, Adam," she said more quietly, "we've been a thing for a long time now, you and me. There's been a lot of stuff between us—I mean, pretty good stuff. Wouldn't you say?"

There's no really safe response to something like that. "Sure," I said, "a lot of good stuff. But?"

"I don't know … But what. Things change, you know, things happen. Sometimes it's things you don't plan. Things just come up."

"Whoa, Lara," I said, wiping my mouth with a napkin. "It's not like you to beat around the bush. Out with it, girl."

"Well, you know—I'm not the only woman in your life, am I?"

I almost laughed she was being so skittish about this, but fortunately I didn't.

"In that sense of 'woman,' yeah, you're pretty much it right now. But we're not exactly married. Does that help?"

"I guess. You see, there's another guy in the picture. Well, even guys. Is that going to be okay?"

I looked at her a bit and then reached across and took her hand.

"Yes, Lara, it's okay. We're free adults. Are you still open for a date now and then?"

She squeezed my hand but said, "Not for a while, Adam. Maybe sometime. But I love you for being such a good guy."

Occasionally, if you're lucky, you can come down with only a small bump.

' ' ' ' ' '

That evening a little after eleven, while I was at home listening to Errol Garner and rereading an old P.D. James mystery, I got a phone call from "the other woman," or another one at least.

"Adam, you beast, why are you dumping on me?"

"Good evening, Dina. I've been longing to hear your voice. I was just thinking—"

"Can it, sweetness. I've heard it from badder hunks than you. You know what I'm talking about. You'll suck up to any reporter with two boobs, but you won't give the time of day to the only editor who ever made you rich and famous. Any argument with that so far?"

"Look, that statuesque reporter just asked me what I was doing at that conference. We didn't sign a book deal."

"A book! Adam, you juicy peach, you brought it up without being prompted. How far along is it? You can't just be rehashing the same old stuff about that Shroud, you know. You've gotta dig new dope, stuff nobody's even thought about before. You know the drill, muscle boy. You've been in the zone. What've you got for your hottest banker?"

"Dina, there isn't anything yet, not even a title page. You're way ahead of the curve."

"The curve! Yeah, get fresh with me, whatever you want, lover, but as soon as you've got it, I've got it. You get it, my man?"

"As soon as I've got it—"

But she was gone.

▮ ▮ ▮ ▮ ▮ ▮

It was necessary, obviously, to throw cold water on Dina's ardor, but in fact I hadn't come away from Antwerp entirely empty-handed. Just almost. There was still that cranky Boston artist I've already mentioned, Dougal MacInnes. From Googling, I found that he didn't have a personal webpage, but there were several references to him and I was able to track down a phone number. On Monday morning I phoned him; no answer, no messaging. But I also found the address of his studio in the South Boston section of the city. I would just have to drop in on him unannounced—assuming I found anybody home.

Cutting things a bit close, I made it aboard the eleven-thirty-five shuttle from Newark to Logan International. I downed a fast-food burrito in the airport, and then one of those immigrant taxi drivers whisked me through the Ted Williams Tunnel to the Southie address.

After I paid the guy and he was gone, I noticed that maybe I should have had him wait. Parts of South Boston have been gentrified after long deterioration, but not this part. I was standing in front of a large nineteenth-century brick pile. The bricks were more black than red and tattooed with gang graffiti. Most of the windows were boarded up or just gone. The cabbie had dropped me at the main entrance, basically a large dark cave leading to tall double doors, one of which was missing. There was a row of mailboxes, and in the dim light I discerned that most of the residents were businesses, or had been. Some of the name slots were vacant, some had been crossed out, and the others were real old. Lo and behold, however, there at 4C was Aberdeen Studio, D. MacInnes prop.

The fourth was the top floor. There was an elevator shaft but no elevator. Just as well, as I would never have chanced it. The stairway smelled of old, foul things, and there were a lot of stairs because each story was around fifteen feet tall. With a huff and a puff I made it to the top, where the wide hallway was littered with trash, junk, dust, cockroaches, and probably rats. Stepping carefully, I came to 4C. Sure enough, the clouded glass window in the door—still intact—was etched with the same information as on his mailbox. Tacked to the wall around the door were faded notices for art exhibits in various places, none dating from the twenty-first century. Over the door was a tattered banner in red, white, and blue that declared: *"The Few. The Proud. The Billionaires."*

Anybody who wouldn't be intrigued by now would be predominantly dead. I rapped on the glass and then, on second thought, rapped again harder. I waited, but there was no response. I could hear no sounds from inside. I rapped again. Finally I tried the door, and it opened right up. Leaning in, I yelled, "Hello there! Dougal MacInnes? Anybody home?"

And then I heard a shuffling and more shuffling, and it came closer, and at length a grizzled old man came around a corner.

"Whaddya want?" he yelled back. "Go away!"

"Mr. MacInnes?" I wasn't yelling, just speaking up. "Did you hear me knocking?"

"I heard you. Don't want none. Go away. What is it?"

I stepped inside and shut the door.

"Dougal MacInnes!" I exclaimed like a besotted groupie. "It's been such a long time. Since the showing at that Back Bay gallery? What's it been, five, ten years? So amazing, I've never forgotten it. And now, here you are—the artist himself, in the flesh, still creating. I can't believe it!"

He came closer and eyed me with justified suspicion. On further inspection, he didn't actually look so old, maybe around sixty, but badly maintained. His gray hair was shaggy, his beard wispy, his breath fetid, and his eyes rheumy. But no glasses, though that didn't mean he could still see. He was wearing a voluminous, filthy smock.

"Okay, okay," he grunted, "don't push it. Whatcha got? Whatcha want? Don't mind me asking, but who the hell are you?"

"Adam Hult. You may not remember me, but I've always loved your creations. Do you actually create them here? I never imagined!"

I had no idea if this drivel would work; it was just what happened to come out.

He was scowling at me. "You never imagined, and you drug yourself all the way up here just to find out? That your story?"

"That's about it," I blurted, "and here I am!"

He eyed me some more then turned and shuffled off again. But I thought I heard him mutter, "What the hell… "

I followed him. As soon as we turned the corner, everything changed. We were in a large, high-ceilinged room with one wall—the south wall—all windows. This had either been designed as an artist's studio in the first place or remodeled as one. The window wall illuminated the whole room, and the other walls were covered with tapestries—at least what I, the art ignoramus, thought of as tapestries. They were works of art for sure, woven or embroidered in riots of color—purple, magenta, forest green, egg-yolk yellow, fiery red-orange—every sort of color arranged in curious patterns, some of them vividly pictorial and others more like dream pictures. The room itself was mostly taken up with large work tables on which were thirty or forty bolts of fabric and numerous pots, canisters, and a variety of implements whose purpose I couldn't guess. There were also a few pizza boxes with some unappetizing slices of old pizza. But one thing was no longer in doubt: Dougal MacInnes was a genuine artist.

Gazing around, I blurted again, this time sincerely, "Amazing!"

He turned back to me and twiddled his right hand. "It's all in the wrist, kid."

"Yes, but . . . do you ever exhibit these in galleries?" I didn't want to betray my total ignorance, but curiosity got the better of me.

He scowled so fiercely I was sure the game was up, but he just growled, "Samantha takes care of all that."

I would have loved to explore who Samantha might be, but I needed to bring things around to my real purpose. And that could be tricky.

I tried, "It looks like you could do almost anything in fabrics. Have you ever done, you know, imitations or reproductions of ancient fabrics—like, the colors and patterns and images?"

"What? Get real, kid. What else do you see? You got eyes?"

"I don't know . . . I mean, I didn't realize—"

"Hey, you been ogling my stuff so long, ain't that what you said, and you still don't know pesisir batik from oyster stew? Huh?"

"Pesisir?"

"Ancient fabrics, dint you say? Don't you know nothing? What else would pesisir be but this ancient technique? Okay, my stuff is my own variations on that stuff, but that—hey, whatted you say your name was?"

"Adam," I voiced meekly.

"So, Adam, maybe you could stop yankin' me around here and just come out with it. You don't know art from fart. Whatcha want with me? Or just get lost."

I sucked it up. "The Shroud of Turin. Have you ever tried reproducing that?"

He gaped at me and then started wheezing in what was probably laughter. When he caught his breath again, he said, "*That* merry-go-round. You're one of *them*. Go away. Beat it!"

Having come so far, having climbed all those stinking stairs, I wasn't about to cave in that easily.

"You haven't tried it because you couldn't do it. You're the best, and you couldn't do it. Dougal MacInnes couldn't figure out the Shroud."

He spat a loogie onto the floor. "Screw that. They waste their time, and you're wasting my time. Scram already."

"They waste their time? Who's 'they'? The artists who try to reproduce it? The ones with some gumption?"

"Gumption? What a crock! Gumption? Schappers has gumption? Portilla? Yunesky? Mubala? Sempel? Take a hike, Adam or whatever you are."

"I've seen some of their work, and it's pretty impressive—could almost be the real thing, the Shroud itself."

He spat again but got only a spray. "Phah! Who are you to say? Couldn't tell Picasso from Pogo. They're all a joke and you with 'em. Reproduce the image on that Shroud? Not a chance. Only one with half a chance would be Mersenne, and even he hasn't figured out how."

"Claude Mersenne?"

"Who the hell is that? *Michel* Mersenne. Now get out or I'll paint you green."

"Have you heard from Michel lately?"

He went and grabbed a canister. I didn't wait around to see if it was green.

CHAPTER 15

It was a slender thread, but it was the only one I had. An hour's toil on the Internet sufficed to distinguish my Michel Mersenne from twenty-six others. Two of them were artists of one sort or another, but only mine came up on searches including the Shroud. Mine—well, the one I was interested in—was in his mid-forties, residing in Lyon in southeastern France. MacInnes said he hadn't "figured out how," but I suspected that Dougal's information might not be fully up to date. Unlike MacInnes, Mersenne had a website for his art gallery—not a working studio, apparently, but a retail outlet. The website was in French, of course, but my collegiate French was up to the task. I considered phoning for an appointment but decided against it. Wasn't I doing just fine with cold drop-ins?

Free now of just about every other earthly responsibility, I booked a flight for Lyon, via Paris, and a hotel. This time I avoided the red eye, taking off from JFK just after 7:00 a.m. and arriving in Lyon, after losing all those hours in the time zones plus the layover in Paris, before ten that evening. With iron self-will, I avoided the airline booze and blitzed through a newly published history of the Tang dynasty in China.

After a restful night's sleep in a comfortable but not plush hotel and a leisurely breakfast in their cafe, I found a taxi and set out after my quarry. Mersenne's gallery was in the eastern section of the city known as La Part-Dieu. Both the sector and the gallery were many cuts above the shambles in South Boston. His establishment was called Callot et Mersenne; it occupied a prime location on a prosperous urban thoroughfare. A large and no doubt well-alarmed plate-glass window displayed smaller paintings and pieces of lovely glassware, as well as affording a dim view of greater treasures within. This was the sort of place where Doris Ballaster would browse and buy.

My goal, however, was information. I went in the door, triggering a crystalline-sounding chime, and a delectable young Frenchwoman (can you improve on that?) came forward to greet me—in French, naturally. I've mentioned my collegiate French, which at this point was passing its limit.

"*Pardonnez-moi*," I said, "but do you perhaps speak English?"

"But of course," she replied with a perfectly charming accent and a smile that warmed my heart and all its tributaries. "How may I assist you, sir?"

Instinctively I gave a slight and what I thought a Gallic bow. "I am Adam Hult, *madamoiselle*, a professor at Columbia University in New York City. I am here in quest of some information that I believe M. Michel Mersenne might be able to provide. If he is available, and if it would not be too great an imposition, might I be permitted a brief interview with him?"

Puttin' on the moves—the old guy hadn't lost it yet.

She—but what a fool not to ask her name!—smiled again and nodded. "That is possible, I am sure, but for that M. Mersenne is not here at this moment. But if you could return at, let me say, three in the afternoon, I am sure he will be here. I believe so, yes."

"Ah, that would be perfect. Thank you ever so much, Madamoiselle . . . ?"

"Camille. I am Camille Brabant."

"Thank you so much, Camille." I very nearly asked her out to lunch, but then I'm not, after all, French, so I settled for, "I hope to see *you* as well as M. Mersenne later in the day."

"Who can say?" she replied, downright flirtatiously, and turned on her heel. The retreating view was every bit as good.

Three o'clock was three and a half hours away. To kill the time, I strolled the streets, taking in the sights—trees in blossom, more French women. At a sidewalk café, I had a tasty French version of fish and chips with a bottle of Amstel 1870. After that, I found a pleasant city park where I sat on a bench beside a pond and watched the fish and ducks, both begging for a handout I didn't have. I also kept an eye on the French women, who weren't interested in handouts. The day was heating up, so I took off my jacket and loosened my tie.

I returned to Callot et Mersenne a few minutes after three and was greeted by a woman who wasn't Camille but might have been her overprotective mother, severe and unsmiling. She was punctiliously polite, however, and she spoke English. Yes, M. Mersenne was in; she would inquire about my request.

A few minutes later, a well-rounded, deeply tanned man with black hair slicked straight back came out and shook my hand and invited me into his office. He was wearing black designer jeans and a sky-blue silk shirt with the top two buttons open. He seemed to have one of those perpetual smiles that just make you wonder. His welcome to me appeared genuine enough, though; the trouble was that his English, while better than my French, was basic and so accented it sounded exactly like French. When he explained his method of Shroud-imitation, for instance, it came out like "Zees clote he ees poot ovair ze bouday…" Instead of an agonizing transcript, therefore, I will paraphrase our dialogue.

The good news, you will note, was that MacInnes's information was indeed out of date; Mersenne had completed his attack on the problem. He had no qualms about telling me how he did it—I gathered he relished any potential publicity—and, like Bob Mubala, he had photos as documentary evidence.

Rather than a sculpture or bas-relief, Mersenne worked with a live model who had long hair, mustache, and beard and hopefully was pretty well paid. A linen sheet was laid over the model and then rubbed with an acidic sepia pigment. The cloth thus stained was then artificially aged by slow heating in an oven, after which it was washed several times. In this way the pigment was removed, but an image remained, which, Mersenne assured me, was virtually indistinguishable from that on the Shroud. He showed me several photos that, admittedly, were more impressive than Bob's.

I had some questions for him, though. Having studied the matter for three months, I had a clearer grasp of the essential issues.

The first question was the same one I posed to Bob: Why did the original forger make a photonegative image? How could he have known what such a thing was? Mersenne's answer was that that wasn't his problem. His job was just to reproduce, nothing more.

The second question was one that Erika Steiner had mentioned, the matter of 3D digital information encoded in the image. This issue was made memorably vivid in a two-hour documentary on the History Channel in 2010. Mersenne said yes, he had seen that documentary, but again it wasn't his problem. "Not my problem" was sounding like his mantra.

The third question concerned the bloodstains on the Shroud. How had he reproduced those? The same way as the rest of the image but using a dark-red pigment. But was he aware that scientific analysis had established that the Shroud bloodstains were actual human blood? At this point, he seemed less comfortable with "not my problem." He said it would be neither practical nor tasteful for him to use actual blood.

There was little more that he could tell me or, by this time, wanted to tell me. Both of us, I think, were dissatisfied with the turn things were taking. He shook my hand again, smiling earnestly, clapped me on the back, and ushered me out.

▪ ▪ ▪ ▪ ▪ ▪

Lying in my hotel bed that night, waiting to fall asleep, I had much the same feeling of turning a corner as I had after Doris offered me the apple and I took a bite. A hairpin turn in the journey of life. This time, though, there was no temptress, no apple. I had, in fact, reached this turning point on my own steam. "Two roads diverged in a yellow wood," Frost's poem begins. Go one way, and I would keep on pursuing Doris's agenda, even inventing a solution if it came to that. Now it looked as if it might indeed come to that. One trouble with this road was that I really had no idea how I could invent a solution, spin a kind of anti-hoax, even if I wanted to. Could I be better at it than Michel Mersenne? Not likely.

If I turned and took the other road, however, the rich widow and her menacing enforcer would be seriously displeased. My ongoing investigation would no longer be funded. My sinking financial boat would no longer be bailed out. Old Tom would show the sharks where there was blood in the water. Could I handle that?

I forgot about going to sleep and switched on the bedside lamp. This hotel room wasn't a familiar place, and it took me a moment to orient myself. Then I got up and opened my suitcase and brought out the rolled-up poster, the black-and-white photo of the man in the Shroud. As I had done before, I unrolled it on the bed.

It was still the same: the crucified man.

Was this a hoax? I thought of Sareen and her obvious confidence that there was no hoax. What had she said? "I love the man in the Shroud." If I took this other road, would I be trying to prove that that misty image actually was the face of Jesus?

No, not quite that. This road would be different. I wouldn't be trying to prove something any longer. I would just be trying to find out the truth. There is a big difference.

No longer an academic whore. Whatever the consequences.

Could I handle that?

The truth was, I didn't know whether I would be able to handle it. Stormy seas, sinking boat. One frantic guy against the big, dark waves.

Oddly enough, this way felt better. I wasn't anywhere safe, but the voyage just might start being fun again.

I rolled the poster up again and put it away, got back in bed and switched off the lamp. The next thing I knew, it was morning.

MIDDLEGAME:
COMPLICATIONS

CHAPTER 16

It was morning, and I was in Lyon, France. I felt refreshed, energized. But also like I was on a tightrope halfway across Niagara Falls, with my tightroping skills. On the other hand, there might be a brighter-side way of seeing this mess. Maybe, if I just kept looking.

I showered and shaved and got dressed in fresh clothes. Before anything else, I needed to contact Doris and explain what was going on. As I reviewed what I had been thinking last night, it occurred to me that my change of course needn't be as drastic as it had seemed. At least I should be able to pitch it to her as a minor and reasonable course correction. Regardless of what she said or seemed to be saying at our last meeting, she could hardly be opposed to discovering the truth. Could she?

I opened my MacBook Air laptop and went to e-mail. The indispensable Gopal, of course, monitored the old bat's incoming e-mails as well as her phone calls, so she should get mine without delay. There were several new messages, mostly the usual nuisances. But one was from a certain S. Khouri with a subject line "wish to meet." I opened it and read:

> Hello, Adam.
>
> I am sorry. I believe I acted foolishly in Turin. Not so much because of what I said to you about the subject of our common interest but the manner in which I behaved. I am

> not actually as unstable as you may now think. Something has come up, however, which is why I am contacting you again. Is it possible that you are still in Europe? I know that you attended the conference in Antwerp last week.
>
> RSVP. Sareen.

It's a good thing I was seated in a sturdy chair when I read this. I had come to think I would probably never hear from her again, and now ... what? Something had come up?

I forced myself to slow down and think clearly, or try to. There was no doubt at all that I would reply. Even if replying were unwise—and I couldn't see why it should be—I would reply anyway. But I would keep it simple and direct:

> Hi, Sareen.
>
> It was good to hear from you. No, I don't think you are foolish. Yes, I'm still in Europe, or rather I'm back here after a short detour home. Specifically, I'm in Lyon. Whatever it is that has come up, I'm sure we don't want to discuss it in the cloud. I would be glad to meet; where and when?
>
> Best regards, Adam.

For some reason, that unexpected exchange left me a bit rattled. Sareen. Sareen Khouri. I decided to go eat some breakfast before tackling my missive to Doris.

The hotel restaurant served an excellent *soufflé au fromage* with croissants and good strong coffee. Feeling fully fortified, I went into their lounge and opened my laptop again and typed out the following message to Doris:

> Dear Mrs. Ballaster:
>
> Since our last meeting I have made progress, though it is turning out rather double-edged. I have met with two art-

> ists with expertise and experience in the matter of reproducing the Shroud image. Their efforts are impressive, up to a point, but still come short in significant ways of answering the critical question of how the medieval forger achieved all his effects. Certain of these effects are challenging in the extreme. For this reason, I am modifying my approach in the direction of trying to get to the bottom of these effects and their source, which may be quite different than we have supposed. I will continue with progress reports as appropriate.
>
> Intrepidly, Adam.

I took my time composing this message, trying for the right balance between honesty and flimflam. While I was in the midst of it, the program alerted me that I had a reply from Sareen. Already! I put the Doris composition on hold and read:

> Thank you, Adam.
>
> Would you be able to meet with me in Rome at the Caffe' Nostro on Via Teodoro Pateras at eight this evening? If you are not familiar with Rome, this is in the Trastavere district, south of the Vatican. Reply only if not possible.
>
> Sareen.

Well, no reply would be necessary; I would get there one way or another. On the Internet, I found a flight leaving here at one thirty and arriving in Rome before three thirty. Thanks to Doris's fifty thousand dollar retainer, I'd been able to pay down a couple of credit cards, so my credit was good for the ticket. Supposedly she would still be reimbursing these expenses, but the way things were going, I couldn't be so sure of that anymore.

Back in my room, I packed up my stuff—only a few clean changes of clothing left. Since there were still a couple of hours before I needed to be at the airport, I got out that book I mentioned before on the history of the Catholic Church in the late medieval period. Sitting by the window, with the sunshine on my back, I reread the section dealing with the early fourteenth century, particularly the part about the coup in which King Philip the Fair destroyed the Knights Templar.

The Templar knights were a religious as much as a military order, with direct allegiance to the pope. Philip's ostensible pretext for attacking them was suspicion of religious heresy, but the real reason probably had more to do with fear of their growing financial and political power. I was wondering again about the possible connection between them and the Shroud, the connection that Agnella Lozio had indicated, Geoffroi de Charny I and Geoffroi Zero. If I kept pursing this thread, of course, I would be moving farther away from Doris's agenda. Sooner or later, in that case, the chips would be falling.

Most likely sooner, as I found when I checked my e-mail again. Like Sareen, Doris was quick to respond, but rather less amiably:

> I am disturbed by the tone of your report, Adam. I should not need to remind you again that your brief is clear and specific and that one of the chief considerations is your own well-being, financial and otherwise. "Get to the bottom" of the matter by all means, but if you are wise, you will see to it that those means are such as conclude to our mutual satisfaction.

Not much greeting and no good-bye. At least I knew where she stood. I wasn't so sure where I stood—which, of course, was what vexed her.

The flight from Lyon to Rome was uneventful apart from turbulence over the Alps. From Fiumicino Airport, on the outskirts of the city, I took a cab to the Crowne Plaza St. Peter's Hotel, near the Vatican, where I had booked a room. It was within walking distance of the Caffe' Nostro, Sareen's chosen rendezvous. I was a few hours ahead of time, so, after consigning my used clothing to the hotel laundry, I set out on a tourist's tour of this ancient, picturesque corner of Rome, beginning with the Villa Doria Pamphili. This seventeenth-century villa—what most of us would call a mansion or palace—along with its extensive gardens, stretched between my hotel and the Trastavere district. I wandered through the beautifully landscaped gardens and then around the narrow, twisting streets of the old city, stopping off at a tiny trattoria to enjoy a crusty calzone with a bottle of spicy dark-red Negroamaro.

It was still twilight when I arrived at Caffe' Nostro. It occupied a ground-floor slot in a handsome pale stone building at least three or four centuries old. The cafe itself had been renovated relatively recently—perhaps not long after Mussolini and the Germans made their exit. Lamplight shed a glow over the sidewalk tables, but Sareen wasn't among the patrons there. I went inside and found her at a corner booth in the back, wearing a simple white blouse with a black pearl necklace—worth a bundle if genuine, but probably imitation. She held out her hand and greeted me with that uncertain smile that already seemed familiar.

"Hello, Adam. Thank you so much for agreeing to come."

"Wouldn't miss it for anything," I replied sincerely, squeezing her hand and slipping into the booth across from her. A waitress came and took our orders, cappuccino for her and coffee and a pastry for me.

"You look... happy," she said.

Happy to see you. But I replied, "I'm all right. How are you?"

"I am well. First, please, let me explain about that day in Turin. I did not encounter you there by accident. I had already read your book on Shakespeare's plays, which I much enjoyed. And then, I have a friend, Signora Fieri, who assists the Monsignor at the Turin cathedral. From her, I knew you were on the list of those to view the Shroud that day."

Aha! The frowning lady with the clipboard.

"Also," she continued, "after I knew you would be there, I read your other books as well. You see, this is how it is. I knew you were a famous author, also a scholar, who had made a name for himself by exposing false ideas, ideas that are popular but nevertheless wrong. And now you were one of those viewing the Shroud. This is a rare privilege, permitted only to a few people with unusual reasons or connections."

"And you thought ..."

"Let me explain. Signora Fieri and I both belong to an association dedicated to advancing a true understanding of the meaning of the Shroud. We had, I believe, some reason to suspect that you intended to join those who seek to prove that the Shroud is a fake. Unlike most of them, however, you came with powerful credentials. And, in short, that is why I followed you that day and ... said what I said."

The waitress served our orders, and then I replied, "I see. But I still don't see enough. I suppose you remember how you warned me about some sort of trouble the Shroud makes for people who, well, I don't know—who poke into it?"

"Yes, Adam, I realize how confusing that must have been. I'm sorry. The difficulty is that I still don't fully understand it myself. It's just that some things, holy things, are more dangerous than people think. Oh, I don't mean simple-minded curses or hexes or punitive lightning bolts. There are deeper dangers than that."

I smiled. "Deeper than a lightning bolt? Sorry. I don't mean to trivialize your concern. But if you don't understand it, can I be expected to?"

"No ..." She looked melancholy.

"And then, in your e-mail this morning, you said that something has come up, something that brings us both here. Well, here we are."

She sipped her cappuccino, taking a moment to glance around the cafe.

"Yes, and thank you again for coming. Perhaps I have overreacted, but I assume you're aware of the stories they've been writing about you and gushing over on morning talk shows. The queen bee and her stinger, as one of them put it."

"Really? I missed that one, but yes, I know the gossip."

"Is it true? This woman has ... bought you?"

I sighed. This was the hard part. "Not quite as baldly as that. It isn't bribery. I guess now it's my turn to explain. It's true she offered me a big payoff if I could prove to most people's satisfaction that the Shroud is a forgery. There's no law against that, maybe not even a moral law. And if I can't prove it, well, the rich lady is disappointed and I go back to my day job. Does that qualify as an emergency?"

This version, of course, was no nearer to full disclosure than what I told Ari. "Men are deceivers ever," as Shakespeare almost said.

"I don't know," she answered, "but it's little comfort. Your e-mail said you were in Lyon. Were you there to consult with Michel Mersenne?"

"You amaze me, Holmes!"

She shook her head but smiled in spite of herself. "So you were. Did he supply you with good ammunition? Unless it's a conspiratorial secret ... "

"Would you believe I have no secrets from you? No, I suppose not, but I'll come clean here. Really, Sareen, I think I have good news for you. The fact is, none of these guys even comes close to showing how that image on the Shroud came to be there. If anything, they demonstrate that it couldn't have been done that way. Certainly not by some rogue in the fourteenth century."

She looked at me intently for nearly a minute and then broke into the first unqualified smile I'd seen. Worth waiting for. "Truly?" she said. "You are concluding, then, it must be genuine?"

"Not so fast. I haven't concluded anything yet. There's a long way left to go. Frankly, at this point, I have no idea what to make of it."

She brushed that aside. "Oh, but you will. I am most confident you will. Do not forget, I have read your books. You are a tenacious investigator."

I scowled and growled, "Bulldog Drummond."

"Bulldog—yes, I think so. Have you thought about what your next step will be?"

"Sure I've thought about it. There's really only one line of inquiry left. If the Shroud isn't a fourteenth-century forgery, where was it before that? The one tangible suggestion I've come across is a connection with the Templar Knights."

"Yes, I am familiar with that idea."

"Why am I not surprised? What do you know that I don't know?"

"Perhaps not so much. But I know of someone who might. In the same group to which Signora Fieri and I belong, there is also another woman, an accomplished scholar who is employed here at the Vatican. Her particular specialization is exactly the connection you just mentioned, or at least it includes that connection. If you wish, I could probably arrange an appointment with her."

"Could you now? That might—*might*—be just the thing. At any rate, I can't be sneezing at the only lead I've got left. Sign me up, please."

"Sneezing? How oddly you speak. But I will see what I can do. Her name is Beatrice Dichter. Doctor, just like you."

"I'll look forward to it."

She contemplated me for a while again. "Adam, I must tell you, I am so glad that you are now moving in this direction."

"But keep in mind, moving doesn't mean reaching any preset destination."

She reached across the table and tapped my hand. "I will keep it in mind. I am still glad."

"By the way, how did you get my e-mail address?"

She squinted at me comically. "We too have our resources."

CHAPTER 17

Sareen promised to call me the next day, hopefully with news of an appointment with Dr. Dichter. I took a cab back to my hotel; one long walk per day is about my limit. Feeling keyed up and at loose ends and not at all sleepy, I took another shower. At hotels, I figure, you're paying for all that hot water. Then, wrapped in a bathrobe, I stretched out on the bed with a slim volume of those magically strange but strangely logical stories by Jorge Luis Borges, in English translation.

I was into the second story when my cell phone rang. Sareen already? The caller ID said "unknown." I took the call. A hoarse voice, almost certainly male, said, "This thing you're doing with the Turin Shroud, back off. Drop it or we'll drop you. We don't make empty threats. Wise up, smart boy." It clicked off.

When faced with sudden threats, the body automatically goes into the fight-or-flight response. Heart rate and breathing accelerate. Digestion stops. Muscles tense. Eyes focus into tunnel vision. I understood all this and knew what to do: breathe slowly and deeply, try to relax your muscles, stretching them slowly and easily. These things work to slow and calm your thinking process, forestalling panic. After a minute or two of this, I went to the bathroom and soaked a hand towel in cold water and then wrung it out and massaged my face and scalp.

It was working; I was relaxing.

I replayed the message in my mind. The voice, rough and male, probably hoarsened for disguise. Accent? Maybe British, but very likely put on for effect or for more disguise. As to who, the answer would probably come from figuring out why. What would be the motive?

What I was doing was called analysis, and I was good at it. Why would someone or some group want to stop me from investigating the Shroud? The plausible reasons were two, and they were, quite interestingly, opposite.

One reason would be to prevent me from discovering and publishing evidence confirming that the Shroud is a fake, a forgery. That, after all, as Doris tirelessly reminded me, was my mission.

The alternative reason would be if he or they had somehow been informed of my growing doubts that such a forgery was even possible. In that case, the motive would be to prevent me from looking into evidence that the Shroud might be authentic.

In either case, their reason for alarm was, as Doris had pointed out, that I'm a celebrated author with intellectual clout. The warning was by no means pointless.

Being chronically systematic, I considered the first motive first. Who was passionately against Shroud debunkers? Well, people like the pope and a few million other Roman Catholics. All sorts of religious fundamentalists (Henrietta Harvey's husband?). Sareen and her "association." Due to the nuisance of media coverage, any of these could know what I'd been up to. Sareen had just received an inkling that my mind might be changing, but that was still only an inkling.

Alternatively, who besides Sareen could know about that change? As far as I could tell, only Doris. And, inevitably, Tom. But would they use such a roundabout and melodramatic way to call me off? If Doris ever decided I was no longer her lap dog, she would just pull the money plug and alert the IRS vampires. She might even hold a press conference debunking *me* as a religious kook.

Bottom line (an awful cliché that I avoid like the plague), the odds seemed to favor the first motive. Beyond that, though, I didn't really have a clue. What I did have was a clear choice: play it safe and be warned off, or be a man, a scholar, an explorer, an Indiana Jones, and defy them.

I'm proud to report that I was, and remain, a man.

After all this, it took me some while to calm down enough to finally fall asleep, which happened somewhere in the wee hours. I didn't sleep well, naturally, and rolled out of bed sometime after nine in the morning, feeling physically exhausted but mentally jazzed to get on with it. I probably didn't need another shower but took one anyway, washing all those troubles out of my curly fringe of hair. Getting dressed, I realized I didn't have Sareen's phone number—didn't even know if she had a cell or what. But I could at least e-mail her.

I breakfasted on waffles and bacon in a restaurant adjacent to the hotel that catered to foreign tourists. While lingering over my coffee, I couldn't wait any longer, so I got out my laptop and e-mailed Sareen, "What's up?"

I had just finished paying the waitress when my cell phone sang its tune. The little window said "S. Khouri."

"Sareen?"

"Good morning, Adam. I received your e-mail."

"Great. How did you get my cell number?"

"Same answer as before. Listen, Adam, I have good news. Beatrice Dichter is willing to talk with you. She respects you as a scholar. She would even make time for you this afternoon. Is that all right?"

"Wow, you work fast."

"We, these people I mention to you, we keep in touch. So at four this afternoon?"

"Perfect. Where?"

"She works in the Vatican Library. Do you know where that is?"

"I can find it."

"I am sure you can. The doorman will be notified of your appointment and will show you the way."

"Thanks, Sareen. Thanks a lot—I'm looking forward to picking her brain."

"Picking?"

"Right. Sareen, look, can I see you again?"

"After you speak with Dr. Dichter?"

"Whenever. Where do you live?"

"Oh my. I live ... wherever I am. But yes, Adam, I will be in touch with you."

She clicked off. I saved her number to my cell's directory.

. . . . . .

The Vatican Library is huge, beautiful, and very old. The security man at the entrance signed me in and handed me off to a young woman in a blue uniform with a heraldic-looking insignia, who guided or guarded me up a curving staircase and down a couple of lofty halls to Dr. Dichter's office. The door was open; I thanked my chaperone and went in.

A middle-aged woman with salt-and-pepper hair pulled back untidily in clasps was working on a laptop computer at a large desk cluttered with books and papers, surrounded on every side by cases and shelves full of books and journals. She rose to greet me, introducing herself as Beatrice Dichter and inviting me to sit in an ornately carved, straight-backed chair beside her desk. Her blue eyes shone out through small rectangular glasses.

"I must say, Dr. Hult," she began, "when Signorina Khouri spoke of your wish to talk with me, I did not know what to think. There has been some gossip, you know, about your current enterprise. And your reputation precedes you."

Her English was excellent, but this didn't sound like a compliment. Even though Sareen said she respected me as a scholar, my reputation as an academic maverick probably didn't rate high with her. I stiffened my back and said, "However that may be, I really do want to find out the truth, whatever it might turn out to be."

She studied me with an appraising gaze. I had the impression of controlled intellectual vehemence, like a well-regulated volcano. I worked on not wilting.

"Very well," she finally said. "So then, your interest in the Shroud of Turin has led you to wonder about a possible link between it and the Templar order. This is correct?"

"Yes, it is. The gossip you mention is true up to a point. Until recently, I had been trying to confirm that the Shroud was created by some highly ingenious medieval craftsman. I've been discovering, though, that that explanation can't account for certain key characteristics."

"I see. Well, I would certainly agree with that. Such theories reflect judgments made in advance of the evidence. Now, I presume that what leads you to the Templars is the Charny connection, yes?"

"Exactly. Last month I had a conversation with Professor Lozio in Milan, and she steered me in that direction."

Her demeanor seemed to relax somewhat.

"So, so, I comprehend. She and I have a professional friendship. As for the connection between the Shroud and the Templars, I believe it is supported by two independent historical facts. First, of course, is the coincidence of names—one of the last Templar officials and the first historically authenticated owner of the Shroud, both Geoffroi de Charny, one or two generations apart. The second is a distinct array of reports and rumors from Templar sources, all concerning their secret veneration of a mysterious object usually referred to as a 'head.'"

"Secretive—that was the Templar Knights."

"Secretive and powerful. They were formed during the twelfth century in support of the Crusades. They built great fortresses across the eastern Mediterranean and ran fleets of supply ships.

In helping to finance the crusaders, they invented many of the techniques of modern banking."

"About this mysterious 'head'..."

"Yes. You know, of course, that the visage of Jesus that has become universally familiar since about the sixth century is, in all essentials, the image on the Shroud."

"The hair and beard, the calm demeanor. I saw an exhibit on that at the conference in Antwerp."

"I helped to assemble that exhibit. So that universally accepted likeness of Jesus is one more independent fact. All of this evidence, you see, is circumstantial. That is, all the evidence linking the Shroud as we have it—and have had it since the fourteenth century—the evidence linking that with the Knights Templar and, prior to that, with the Byzantine Empire, all the way back to Jerusalem in the first century, all this evidence is circumstantial, indirect. It is, nevertheless, quite strong. You might say there are a number of smoking guns."

I leaned forward, resting my chin on my fist. "Smoking guns, like that 'head' the Templars worshiped?"

"'Worshiped' is probably too strong. They were Christians, ignorant and superstitious in many ways no doubt, but not idolaters. They feared and venerated this object, according to their own testimonies that have been preserved."

"Okay, but do we have any hard evidence as to just what the object was?"

"We do, though you must judge for yourself how hard you think it is. One piece of evidence is a face painted on an old ceiling in a village in Somerset, England. The Templars had one of their regional headquarters there. The face on the ceiling is uncannily similar to that on the Shroud, and it is surrounded by stars. The most likely hypothesis, I believe, is that the painted face was the central focus of either an initiation ceremony or a nighttime vigil, during which a Templar knight would gaze up at the face, illuminated by candles or torches, to purify his soul in advance of trial or combat. It was a version of the beatific vision so essential to medieval Catholic mysticism."

I thought that over and then said, "The face may be similar, and the Templar knights may have venerated or even worshiped it, but that still leaves the connection to the Shroud itself pretty indirect."

She smiled almost wolfishly and leaned forward herself. "Yes, but none of these evidences exists by itself. They link together, build upon one another. Consider this one. One of the Templars, after his arrest by King Philip's forces and while under interrogation by them, described in some detail a secret ceremony involving an object that can hardly be anything other than the Shroud."

"Interrogation—probably meaning torture?"

"Perhaps, of one degree or another, depending on his willingness to cooperate. As you know, people vary greatly in this regard."

"Yes, but confessions elicited by torture can't be taken at face value."

"That is true. On the other hand, why would he invent such a story as this? Almost, how could he? Listen, and decide for yourself.

"This knight, François Gouttard, told of his initiation at a secret Templar hideaway somewhere in Provence. At the climax of a long and harrowing ceremony, he was blindfolded and led a long distance, changing direction many times through rough terrain, so that he was thoroughly disoriented. When they removed the blindfold, he was in a cavernous chamber lit only by two rows of candles on either side of a long linen cloth. On this cloth, he said, there was imprinted the figure of a crucified man. He was ordered to kiss the feet of that figure three times. He did so, he said, though he was utterly terrified. One may wonder which terrified him most, what would happen to him if he didn't kiss it or what would happen if he did."

"I can imagine; better him than me. But now, this Shroud-like length of cloth, mightn't it have been only a copy?"

She shrugged. "It might. But a copy of what? You see, again, we *have* the Shroud. Even if they were making copies of it long before the fourteenth century—and there are many such images—the genuine article is what they copied. It was copied so much because it was so highly venerated.

"Let me mention one such copy in particular, a drawing in what is known as the Hungarian Pray Manuscript, now kept in the national library in Budapest. The manuscript dates to 1192, more than a century before the Shroud image was allegedly forged. The drawing depicts Christ being laid out for burial. His form and figure are identical to the pose on the Shroud, even down to the hands crossed at the wrists. The fabric itself, in the drawing, is shown with the same herringbone weave as in the linen sheet in Turin. The same four burned holes are shown, in the same pattern as on the Shroud—not the burns from the 1532 fire but holes presumably burned at some point by a red-hot poker, for reasons unknown. A drawing made no later than 1192, Dr. Hult. To pass this off as mere coincidence defies credibility."

"Right. So this brings us to the question, if the Templars had the Shroud, when and how did they get it?"

"That is, of course, an important question, also a difficult one. As to the specifics, we can only make educated guesses. The general answer, however, we can be quite sure of. It was taken as part of the Crusaders' loot when they besieged and sacked Constantinople in 1204."

"Ah yes, the infamous Fourth Crusade."

"Indeed. As I am sure you know, that whole affair was even more misbegotten and tragic than most of the Crusades. Picture to yourself poorly organized armies streaming eastward from Europe on the relentless mission to reconquer the Holy Land. On the way, they come to Christian—though Greek Orthodox—Constantinople. They involve themselves in Byzantine politics, helping one would-be emperor depose a rival, for which they presume he will be grateful enough to subsidize their hugely over-budget expedition. He instead looks on them as dangerous and unwelcome barbarians. And they look on Constantinople as something they thought existed only in fairy tales, a city of wealth and splendor and sophistication beyond their imagining. There is, we may say, no meeting of minds. The outcome, if not entirely predictable, is scarcely surprising."

"So the Frankish barbarians sack, burn, and loot. How do we know the Shroud was there to be looted?"

She sat back in her chair and tapped a pen on the desktop, a triumphant gleam in her eyes. "This, I believe, is one of the most fascinating connections in the entire historical record. You are, of course, familiar with the Mandylion, also known as the Image of Edessa?"

"The most highly revered relic and icon in Byzantine history? I haven't studied it especially, but I certainly know of it."

"A piece of cloth imprinted, mysteriously, with the face of the Savior. At that time, at the opening of the thirteenth century, it was kept in the Church of St. Mary of Blachernae in Constantinople. Now, as to the identification of the Mandylion with the Shroud of Turin, there are many substantial clues, but the best of these comes in a book written by one of the crusading soldiers, Robert de Clari, after he was lucky enough to make it back home. He told of the wonders he had seen in Constantinople. Just a moment, if you please."

She went over to one of the bookcases and, after a brief search, took out a leather-bound volume. She paged through it until she found what she was looking for.

"Listen to this. Robert de Clari reports that in August of 1203, just a few months before hostilities broke out, he visited a church. Now I shall translate as best I can into English. The church, he says, 'was called My Lady St. Mary of Blachernae, where there was the burial shroud in which Our Lord had been wrapped, which every Friday stood upright, so that one could see the figure of Our Lord on it.' And then he added, 'No one, either

Greek or French, ever knew what became of this shroud when the city was taken.'"

She put the book back and came and sat at her desk again. "I would make three points about Robert's testimony, Dr. Hult. First, it is virtually certain that the object he described was Byzantium's treasured Mandylion. There could hardly be two such things in the same place at the same time. Second, he says that on Fridays the image 'stood upright.' This may mean simply that it was held upright for viewing. Alternatively, it may indicate that in its role as the Mandylion, it was normally folded in fourths so that only the head was seen, but on Fridays the full frontal figure was displayed for veneration. The Mandylion, as you probably know, when copied by various artists, was always a facial image only."

"Interesting. And the third point?"

"That concerns his statement that no one knew what became of this revered and treasured object. That is consistent with its having been taken into custody, one way or another, by the Knights Templar. They would have secreted it away, and very probably they did. It is also consistent with the fact that, following the disastrous sack of Constantinople in 1204, the Mandylion disappears from view in Byzantine history.

"Circumstantial evidence, Dr. Hult, can be very compelling. I remind you again, we *have* the Shroud. The one we have is not a copy, and it has a history. It has, if I may put it so, a story to tell."

CHAPTER 18

It was late afternoon and uncomfortably hot in Vatican City when I emerged from my colloquy with Beatrice Dichter. I stripped off my suit jacket and sat on a bench in the gardens surrounding the library. I got out my cell phone and called Sareen, but it went to voicemail. I asked her to call me back. Then I opened my laptop—I had figured I would want it today—and sent an e-mail to Doris. No matter how things shook out, it was time to come clean. I told her that, on balance, the evidence I had seen so far suggested that the Shroud was considerably older than the fourteenth century, and I wasn't willing to publish anything to the contrary. As far as I was concerned, I said, the deal we had arranged just wasn't going to work. I didn't add that she was free, therefore, to screw me financially. She would figure that out on her own.

I was at loose ends again and somewhat annoyed that I couldn't get through to Sareen. I considered e-mailing her but decided not to push it. I got up and wandered around St. Peter's Square, admiring the famous basilica. The whole massive structure was designed to overwhelm the small individual viewer with its magnitude, grandeur, and architectural beauty, as well as the immense wealth required for raising it. I was duly overwhelmed, but as many before me must have been, I was struck by the incongruity between this pinnacle of Renaissance pomp and the homespun, inglorious character of its namesake—a commercial fisherman named Simon, a peasant really, notable mainly for putting his foot in his mouth and denying any acquaintance with Jesus when the chips were down.

How things change.

As for Jesus himself, what would he have thought of this grandiose temple dedicated to his impulsive disciple? I wondered what Sareen would make of it; maybe I could ask her sometime.

Moving back in the direction of my hotel, I came across a likely looking restaurant, nothing fancy but probably good. So it turned out to be. I had the house lasagna, which was considerably better than American-chain-Italian lasagna. After that, sipping my straight espresso, I tried calling Sareen again.

Voicemail again. Bummer.

Along with the lasagna, I'd been chewing over all the stuff Dr. Dichter had served up. I agreed with her that the evidence, as she presented it, was impressive. I wondered whether the rest of the evidence, as she alluded to it, would turn out to be impressive as well. Evidence, as she said, builds itself cumulatively. I opened my laptop and made notes covering the essentials.

Where to next? She had suggested someone to follow up with on the saga of the Mandylion/Image of Edessa, an Australian specialist in Byzantine history named Rod Eglantine. He was, she thought, currently working in Istanbul. I had actually met him once at some academic forum or other several years ago. So, try to get in touch with him and maybe hop the Mediterranean over to Istanbul?

The old song ran through my mind: "Is-tan-bul was Con-stan-tinople, now it's Is-tan-bul, not Con-stan-tinople any-more." In between, it was the capital of the Byzantine Empire, or Byzantium. Now the problem was to get the tune out of my mind.

By that time, my last, mostly sleepless night was catching up with me, and I trudged back to the hotel. Better luck this time?

Yes, as it turned out. I took a cool shower and read a cou-ple more Borges short stories. No more menacing phone calls. I tried Sareen once more and then gave up and punched the pillow before ten o'clock.

Good things come to those who sleep. It was around seven, and I was just thinking about waking up when my cell phone jingled on the bedside table. My eyes were too bleary to read the caller ID, so I just said, "Hello?"

"Good morning, Adam. Is this too early?"

Sareen! "Never too early. I'm always an early riser."

I heard her chuckle; my voice sounded like an alligator. "That is to your credit, then. So tell me, early riser, have you breakfasted yet?"

"No, not quite yet."

"I see. You spoke with Beatrice Dichter yesterday?"

"Yes, I did. And thank you for the recommendation. She gave me plenty to think about."

"That is good. I was sure she would. Would you wish to join me for breakfast and tell me about it?"

Would I? "Your place or mine?"

"I can recommend a restaurant. Gino's. It's within walking distance of your hotel, and they serve breakfast earlier than most in Rome. Shall we say nine o'clock?"

I said nine o'clock, and she gave me directions. An hour later, showered and shaved and looking almost like Ben Affleck, I took myself out onto the streets of the Eternal City. It was Saturday morning, and things were pretty quiet—a few cars and bicyclists, an old lady sweeping the sidewalk, a few shopkeepers starting to set up. I came to a wide stairway, part of Sareen's directions, and started down when a voice behind me, right in my ear, said, "Last warning, smart boy!" and something like a fist thumped me between the shoulder blades, and I went tumbling down.

Part of the self-defense training I've done for years with Ari includes learning how to fall, and though I'm not as diligent as he is, I have picked up a few things. So I curled up like an armadillo and went with the fall, letting myself tumble to the base of the stairway, which, fortunately, was only six or seven steps farther down.

On the other hand, a fall is a fall, and stone steps are hard. By the time I stopped rolling, the world was spinning around me and I hurt all over. I sat up and put a hand to my face, and it came away bloody. A few people—I'm not sure who or how many—had gathered around me and were jabbering in Italian. I waved them off and tried to assure them that I was okay, okay, *bene*, *bene*. One of them gave me a large handkerchief, and I pressed it to my scalp, where the bleeding seemed to be. Then I got out my cell phone and speed-dialed Sareen (she had made the list). She answered and I told her I had taken a fall and needed help. I told her where I was. She told me to watch for a young man on a motor scooter with a red bandana around his neck. "You can trust him," she said.

I didn't feel like trusting anybody, but I was in no position to be choosy. I sat up against a wall and waited. Some people still stood around watching; I smiled and nodded. The bleeding seemed to be in check, and I mumbled thanks to whoever had given me the handkerchief. A few minutes later, I heard the popping whine of a motor scooter, and it bumped up the curb and wheeled right over to me. A young guy, sure enough, hardly more than a teenager, with sunglasses and a red bandana. He looked at me doubtfully and said, "You can arise? You can ride?"

"I can arise and ride," I said. I forced myself up and managed to swing my leg over the seat behind him, and we were off, bumping down the curb, which hurt, and away through the sparse morning traffic. I held on to him tightly; otherwise I would have taken another fall. Humpty Dumpty sat on a wall; Humpty Dumpty had a great fall . . .

After what seemed a long time but probably wasn't, we turned up a short driveway and through an open gate in a wall, into a courtyard with a fountain in the middle, which was just dribbling some water. Not a fountain, only a dribbler ....

Then some people were helping me off the scooter and into an apartment. One of the people was Sareen. They were steering me toward a bed, but there was also a large wingback chair in the room. I struggled toward it, grunting, "The chair." The bed would be too soft for a tough guy.

They removed my jacket and tie and eased me down into the chair. Sareen unbuttoned my shirt and stripped it off.

"It's not so bad, is it?" I said.

"Bad enough," Sareen said. "Besides the gash on your head, there are bruises and scrapes on your right arm and side here. How does that knee feel?"

The right leg of my slacks was torn at the knee. "It hurts," I said, "but it still seems to work."

"So perhaps you are very lucky and nothing is broken. What happened? How did you fall?"

I was finally tired of evasion. "I was pushed down the stairs."

"Pushed?"

"Yeah. It was a warning. Second warning, actually."

She bandaged the cut on my scalp and pressed a towel wrapped around ice cubes against it. It felt good.

"That should probably have some stitches," she said. "But for now, how do you feel? I mean, I know you feel terrible, but can you tell me what's going on?"

"Okay, it was after we had coffee, when was that, a couple days ago? After that, that night, I got this phone call. A man's voice warning me to stop looking into the Shroud, or else."

"Or else what?"

"He didn't specify. It was a short conversation. I never got in my licks."

"And what happened just now?"

"Just as I was starting down those stairs to the Via della Paglia, some guy came up behind me and said, 'Last warning, smart boy!' and gave me a hard shove."

"You didn't see him?"

"No, but I won't forget him. I'm just wondering who the hell these guys are anyway. Who cares that much about what I'm doing?"

She knelt down with a hand on my forearm. "I've said this to you before, Adam. The Shroud itself doesn't make trouble, but it attracts it. Power attracts trouble. There are, believe me, people who will do almost anything."

"To protect the Shroud?"

"Yes. Or to destroy it, one way or another."

I'd been thinking of it as an intellectual enigma, but she made it sound like warfare.

I looked around. I was in a small, plainly furnished bedroom in what appeared to be an old apartment. I asked, "Where are we?"

"Don't worry. This is a safe place."

"A safe house, like the CIA or FBI?"

She laughed. "Not as organized or official as that, but you will be safe here as long as you need for healing."

"Not long," I grunted. "Look, Sareen, I need to call a friend of mine in New York. Is my cell phone still in my pocket over there?"

She rummaged and got it out then handed it to me and went out of the room, and I dialed Ari.

"Adam, old sport. Top of the night to you."

"Sorry about that." I just realized it would be about 3:00 a.m. in New York. "Something's come up that's your sort of thing, and I don't want you missing out."

"Jolly good. You have my full attention."

I told him about it in the fullest detail I could manage. He wanted the exact words of the phone message; I had no difficulty there.

"So," he said, "this person who pushed you downstairs, you didn't see him or hear him coming up behind you?"

"Didn't I say so?"

"Just verifying, Adam. Plainly, though, you've been seriously nonchalant in your environmental awareness. If I have to bring

Benny in on this, he'll be disappointed. From this point on—right now, this minute—I trust you'll wake up and remember the disciplines. Okay, no more scolding. On a first assessment, it's apparent that these people don't want to have to kill you, because then I'd be talking to a dead phone. Killing is extreme and full of blowback on the perps. On the other hand, they obviously mean business and have some search and surveillance skills. With you stomping around over there like the Jolly Green Giant, of course, it hasn't been too much of a challenge so far."

"All right, all right."

"Next, just exactly who are they? Don't we have to presume they're members of some cult that doesn't appreciate you throwing doubt on the Holy Shroud?"

"So it would seem, though there's one other possibility, the other side of the coin. The thing is, all the research I've done thus far leads me to conclude that the Shroud is probably a lot older than the fourteenth century. Not a medieval counterfeit. Something else."

Ari whistled through the ether. "Don't tell me, Adam ... "

"No. I just don't know, okay? The other thing is, the only person I've told about this provisional change of plans is Doris Ballaster. She doesn't have to send hit men, she just has to burn my last dollar. Her doing it this way doesn't make sense. It doesn't feel like her style."

"I wouldn't count too much on style, but I agree that option seems less probable. Half the world now knows the great debunker has turned his gaze on the Shroud. There are fervent true believers of every stripe. This Joan of Arc of yours, for instance, she's bound to be connected to some of them. Have you considered whether she might be playing a double game?"

"Sareen? Dude, if you knew her other than by hearsay—"

"Do you know her?"

This wasn't getting us anywhere. "Not Sareen, okay? Some bunch of crazies maybe, but not her. Look, we're groping in the dark here. What we need is what you're best at. Haul yourself out of dreamland and dig into it, sift the cloud. Track down every den of saints or psychos that might have motive, means, and opportunity here."

"Your hound is on the scent. What about you? I recommend the first plane out of Rome, heading anywhere as long as you wind up back here where we can keep an eye on you."

"Waving a white flag, with my tail between my legs? Ari, now you're disappointing me. Oh, I'll keep to the disciplines, but I'm on the scent too."

"It's your funeral, though that would be my choice too. Where to next?"

"Better not say over an unsecured line. Unscramble this: I'll be singing to lords and ladies of what is past, or passing, or to come."

And I clicked off.

CHAPTER 19

One main hazard for people like me is we get too infatuated with our own cleverness. My closing clue to Ari, for example, was some phrases at the end of Yeats's poem "Sailing to Byzantium":

> ... to sing
>
> To lords and ladies of Byzantium
>
> Of what is past, or passing, or to come.

This tidbit was harmless enough by itself; the trouble is that clever people tend to become overconfident.

Assuming I could connect with Rod Eglantine, I would be sailing, or more likely flying, to old Byzantium, but first I needed at least a day or so to stop hurting. After I had finished with Ari, Sareen came back and asked me what I wanted to do. Was I still hungry? Did I need anything from my hotel room?

Hungry? I consulted my body and found it wanted rest more than food. As for my stuff, yeah, a change of clothes and my other suit. Plus, above all, my laptop. She said to give her the key card and she would take care of it.

Trust her? In for a penny, in for a pound. I gave her the key card and collapsed back in the chair. I wanted to stay awake, stay alert, but my body didn't.

I woke up groggily with no idea what time it might be. On the opposite wall I noticed a couple of religious paintings, a madonna and one of Jesus with the crown of thorns, looking, as the old painters always conceived him, agonized and calm at the same time. Not, it occurred to me, unlike the face on the Shroud.

I had a headache. But there, on a chest at the foot of the bed, was my suitcase. Evidently I had been zonked out for more than a few minutes. Looking around I saw an open closet with my one wearable suit hanging in it—not my only other suit, just the only other one I brought on this voyage around the world. And there, on an old round table, was my laptop. I was all moved in.

I struggled up from the chair and put on a clean shirt and my intact suit pants. There was a knock on the bedroom door, which had been closed, and I said to come in. It was Sareen, looking calm as usual but solicitous.

"Are you feeling somewhat better?" she asked.

"I'm back on my feet anyhow. Have you got any aspirin?"

"Of course. We aren't as primitive as you Americans like to think."

She turned to get some, but I said, "You say 'we,' but you aren't Italian."

She turned back, thoughtful. "No, I'm not. I suppose I meant 'we non-Yanks.'"

"Where are you from?" I hoped she wouldn't mind my probing.

She was slow to answer, though. Finally she said, "From Lebanon, originally. Perhaps I will tell you about it sometime. But now, come to the kitchen and I'll get you that aspirin."

The kitchen was evidently the most lived-in room in the apartment. It was fairly large with a big old gas range. Pots and pans and other implements hung on the walls, and a table with six round-back wooden chairs occupied the center. The kid who had rescued me on his motor scooter sat there contemplating a cup of coffee.

I said, "Hey there, my chauffeur. I probably never even thanked you."

"This is Marco," Sareen said. "He'll like practicing his English on you."

"Hey, dude," Marco said.

She gave me the aspirin, and I swallowed four with some water. She asked if I was hungry yet. It was just after noon, and food finally sounded good. She gave me a cup of coffee and set about frying up some onions and potatoes and lamb chops. Marco's mother, she explained, was at work at a clothing shop and would be back in the evening. She didn't say anything about a father.

Meanwhile, I brought out my laptop and did an Internet search on Rod Eglantine. Sure enough, he was currently at Istanbul University in the history department. An odd place for an Aussie, maybe, but home ground for someone studying the Byzantine Empire. I found a phone number for him and dialed it, and a definitely Aussie voice said to leave a message, which I did.

The fried lunch, along with some sliced tomatoes, left me feeling half-human again. I asked Marco to help me with my Italian, and we had a fine time doing rough-and-ready simultaneous translation. At one point, as casually as I could, I asked Sareen about her connection with this household. She replied only that they were old and faithful friends, and I didn't press it. Was this the headquarters of a zany, stop-at-nothing cult? It didn't seem likely.

After lunch, I thanked them for their exceptional hospitality but insisted on calling a cab to take my stuff and me back to the hotel. Sareen thought that would expose me dangerously and needlessly, but I said, in my reasonable way, that the bad guys would wait to see my next move before making their next move. Anyway, I hated the feeling of skulking, and I looked forward to practicing environmental awareness. I asked her if Gino's served dinner as well as breakfast. Of course, she said, and she agreed to meet me there at seven.

The move back to St. Peter's Hotel went uneventfully. In a nice soft chair in my room, I read a while and then phoned Ari to check on his progress. It was progressing, he said, but I wouldn't believe how many kooky crews there were out there. I assured him of my patience and went back to my reading.

A while later I got the call back from Rod Eglantine. He was definitely interested in my quest and would be glad to help however he could. Not being sure, I asked him what it would take for me to get a visa for Turkey, and he said I could get one overnight if I was willing to shell out a hundred and fifty dollars. I told him I'd give him a buzz as soon as I got that taken care of. And then, online, I made the arrangements for arriving in Istanbul just before noon the next day. Ain't the Internet amazing? And people under twenty take it for granted.

The bump on my scalp was throbbing, so I took some more aspirin. Get some stitches? Warrior that I was, I laughed at the thought. What would really make me feel better was some smooth single-malt Scotch. I still had a couple of hours before my hot date, so I took a gentle, warm shower, wincing all over, and then shaved and dressed and headed down to the hotel bar.

Not many things are as uniform the world over as bars, except in Afghanistan and Saudi Arabia and a few other places. This one could have been in Brooklyn, complete with the day-old-bearded Italian bartender. I've said before that I don't frequent bars much, and that's true, but there are times. I ordered a double Laphroaig and took it over to an unoccupied booth. Some kind of Italian pop music overlaid most other sounds. The whiskey was remarkably soothing and delicious. I thought about the series of strange permutations my life had taken since last February. Just three months. It seemed like three years. I wondered how Lara was holding up without me. More like, who was holding up Lara.

The Laphroaig was suddenly down to the last drop, so I got another double, resolving to nurse this one slowly. My head was feeling better. Everything else was too. I still didn't have kind thoughts toward the thug that pushed me down the stairs, but most everybody else was getting the benefit of the doubt. Good old Dougal MacInnes, crazy old coot. Then there was that young thing who came on to me at Mersenne's gallery—what was her name? Carmen? Definitely worth a return visit to Lyon. And Pete—was it Pete? Talk about crazy. Why so much craziness around these days? Too much streaming misinformation on TV and Twitter; makes everybody gullible.

My glass was empty again already, even though I'd only been sipping. What time was it? Wouldn't do to be late for a date with pristine Sareen. There, it was six forty. What time was that date? Seven, yes, seven. I got up and walked steadily over to the barman and paid him and asked him to call a cab for me. He nodded and speed-dialed on his cell phone—must call cabs a lot.

During the short cab ride, I wished I'd thought to bring some breath mints. I didn't want to make a bad impression, absolutely. I admonished myself to stand tall, walk straight, think clearly, and enunciate each word.

Gino's was a large place, an acre of restaurant. There was a hostess who took names and assigned tables. I asked her if she understood English.

"Yes, signor."

I asked her if a small but attractive Lebanese woman was waiting for me. No, she didn't think so. I told her I would take a table for two, secluded if possible, and wait for the small Lebanese lady. She nodded gravely and led me to just such a table next to a leafy potted tree. Would I like a drink while I waited? No—check that, how about a chilled bottle of Ferrari Spumante?

"Certainly, signor." She left two menus.

A haughty, saturnine sommelier promptly delivered the cold sparkly with two glasses and filled mine. I ought to wait for my date before trine the wine, but that arrogant steward hadn't offered me a trial sip like he was supposed to. I tried it. It was good—ginger ale for grownups. Cold and thirst quenching. Almost served the purpose of breath mints. I refilled my glass. We could always order a second bottle.

And there she was, walking across the room toward me with the grace of a ballerina. Could she be a ballerina? Just in time, I remembered to rise to greet her.

"*Buona sera*, Adam," she said. "I'm sorry to be late."

"You're not late! I'm early." I seated her and poured her wine.

"I see you found Gino's all right."

"Well, the cabbie found it. Anyway, as my pal Prince William would say, you look smashing."

She was wearing a black cocktail dress with silver hoop earrings and heels. What had become of demure?

"Thank you. You appear to be feeling better."

"Far better."

The waiter interrupted this sweet talk with a demand for our orders. I was about to wave him off when Sareen said I had to try their saltimbocca, so we ordered this for two.

"Have you discovered anything about who is attacking you?" she asked when we were alone again.

"Ari's on it—my friend in New York. If anybody can ferret it out, he can."

I stumbled over these syllables but, thank goodness, she didn't appear to notice. She asked about my conversation with Beatrice Dichter—which is what I had been going to tell her about over breakfast. I related this in as much detail as I could remember. It was frustrating how hard remembering was. Good thing I'd made some notes.

Then she asked about what I would do next, suggesting it might be prudent to lie low, at least for some time.

"Prudent, maybe," I said, "but not for me." I told her about Rod Eglantine and Istanbul.

The waiter brought our entrees. The saltimbocca looked as delicious as it smelled. I ordered another bottle of the luscious Spumante. Sareen doubted that was wise so shortly after I had suffered a probable concussion. I said I was fine and we needed something to wash down our meal.

What I really wanted to do was find out more about her. So when we were eating and I figured the time was right, I said, "Leman ... Lebas ... Lebanese, you said. Where you're from, I mean. That right?"

She looked at me a moment and then nodded.

"But you've been lots of places," I pressed on. "I can tell ... I can tell quite a bit about you, you know ... speak English like a Swiss finishing school ... been all the way around the block, haven't you?"

She finished a bite then looked at me again before saying, "I have lived my life. As we all do."

"We all do, sure enough ... sure enough ... and now this thing you've got with the Shroud, this ... this thing ... this fling ... I don't know, like ... like it was lowered from the sky by angels, and lightning flashes from it ... you know? I mean, it's intriguing ... intriguing ... sure, but angels? What's with that?"

"Adam, that's enough. It's time to get you back to your hotel for some more rest."

"Rest? The rest of my life ... hard to think of that without you ... so ... so essotic. Thass it, not essactly beautiful, but ... essotic. Wanna come back with me?"

I threw this pass making my best puppy eyes at her. Her eyes flashed back at me. Laughing? Angry? Hard to tell.

Suddenly she snatched up both wine glasses and the half-empty bottle of bubbly and took them over to the bar. Very nice walk. Not an angel. Ballerina. Belly dancer. Seven veils ...

She came back but didn't sit down. She said, "They are bringing you a carafe of strong coffee. Drink all of it and then use the restroom and take a cab back to the hotel. I hope you feel better in the morning, Adam. But"—she sort of smiled—"you won't."

CHAPTER 20

How do I despise thee? Let me count the ways.

Such was my self-talk the following morning, in grim survival mode. Had I ever felt worse? What about the time, at age twelve, when I broke my ankle running through a junkyard, fleeing from bullies. They laughed at my agony and kicked me for good measure.

But this was worse—total pain, physical, mental, and emotional. A hangover, naturally, which aspirin could hardly dent. Remorse and utter humiliation. A dim recollection of trying to pay the waiter only to find that Sareen had paid already. Could I despise myself more than she must despise me? Pathetic. The only silver lining was that I didn't puke on her. That was in the gutter beside the taxi. Some silver lining.

There was no way I was going to be world traveling today, so I called the airline and rescheduled for tomorrow. That was going to cost me an extra ninety bucks. I didn't ask why; I deserved it.

I spent the miserable day in the hotel room, mostly in bed. If my life had been turning corners lately, this corner was heading down. Chutes and ladders: down the chute.

Self-recrimination and self-pity are a toxic mixture; if they really could kill you, I would be dead. But, rather to my regret, I made it through the day. Suicide, I might mention, has never tempted me. Death by shame, okay, but not by bleeding or poison. It's just how I'm made, I guess. Who knows?

In the evening, I ordered club soda, coffee and a roll from room service. I read some more history of the medieval Catholic Church. Profound thought, mystical raptures, and continuous conspiracy, treachery, torture, and murder. Our thriller novels are only a pale reflection.

The next morning, Monday, I felt better, physically at least. "A sadder and a wiser man/He rose the morrow morn," the Ancient Mariner said. Sadder for sure, for me; only time would tell about wiser. I was too ashamed to call Sareen, but I touched base with Ari. He counseled more patience. New candidate maniacs kept cropping up, and some of these outfits were good at hiding their tracks. One better than them was on their case, however.

The flight from Rome to Istanbul aboard Swiss Airlines went without hitch, cruising most of the way high above an ocean of white cotton candy. Turning a new leaf, I drank only coffee. Following Ari's admonition, I also turned my mind to continually observing the environment. Who fits, who doesn't. Who shows up more than once, perhaps in different gear. This was Ari's specialty, but he had worked with me on it, partly just to hone his own skills. I was rusty at it, but like riding a bicycle, you never really lose it. If any assassins were nearby, though, I didn't see them.

We touched down at Atatürk Airport, just north of the Sea of Marmara, at twelve forty in the afternoon. After clearing customs, changing a hundred dollars into Turkish lira, and lunching at an airport restaurant on *su böregi*, a savory pastry made with phyllo dough, cheese, and parsley, I took a taxi over to the Grand Washington Hotel near Istanbul University. I chose the hotel because the name made it sound American-friendly, and it turned out to be friendly enough, though the name may have had little to do with it.

Once settled in my room, I gave Rod Eglantine a call, and he picked up. At the moment, he said, he was just chewing the fat with a few others in a faculty lounge. I asked him when would be a good time for a get-together, and he suggested four thirty at a coffee shop next to Beyazit Square, adjacent to the university. We settled on that, and he warned me to expect Turkish coffee.

"When in Rome ...," I said.

Still feeling the effects of my recent misadventures, I took a short nap and then at four set off on foot. The coffee shop was within a few blocks of the hotel, but I took a roundabout route, not so much for sightseeing as for counter-surveillance. Fortunately—or not, depending—I saw nothing but the sights. An onshore breeze was freshening the air and keeping the temperature moderate.

Eglantine had told me I could recognize him by his short curly hair and a white rose in his lapel. As for myself, I said, look for crossed band-aids on my half-shiny pate.

The coffee shop was busy with old men, young women—mostly in headscarves—and everything in between, but I saw Eglantine about the same time that he recognized me. He was guarding a small, square black metal table with a mesh top. We shook hands, and when a harried young waiter came over, he ordered for us in Turkish.

"So you speak the local lingo," I said.

"Not very well, they tell me. Rotten Aussie accent and bad grammar, but it's a have to if you're going to work here. For me, here is where the action is."

"The glory that was Byzantium."

"Too right. The Turks don't think it's so bonzer, though, because Byzantium was Greek. About as popular as the Greek end of Cyprus."

He had a merry round face, button nose, and sparkling black eyes. About half Aborigine, I estimated. "So do you run into political roadblocks?" I asked.

"No, not really. More like bureaucratic stalling and runarounds, and you can find that anywhere. Anyway, to business. You're digging into the Mandylion, you said? The Image of Edessa?"

Before I could answer, the waiter brought our order on a tray, two small cups and what I took to be a pewter pot. Eglantine poured for us. "Coffee," he said, "thick, strong and sweet. Either you get used to it or you don't." He grinned and rubbed his nose.

I sipped mine. I'd had Middle-Eastern coffee before. It's all right for a visit but not for every day. "Right, then," I said. "Actually, for the last few months I've been researching the Shroud of Turin. One strand in the investigation leads to the Mandylion, or the Image of Edessa. Is either term preferable, by the way?"

"Not really. The term 'Mandylion' refers mainly to its stay in Constantinople, from 944 up to 1204, when the city was overrun by western crusaders. Up till 944, probably going all the way back to the first century AD, it resided in the city of Edessa in what's now southeastern Turkey, around six hundred miles from here. Hence the term 'Image of Edessa.' 'Mandylion' is shorter—should we just call it that?"

" Call it that. A few days ago I talked with Beatrice Dichter at the Vatican Library, and she thinks there's reasonable evidence that the Shroud and the Mandylion might be the same piece of fabric. What's your take on that?"

He stared at me with a kind of mischievous smile and then said, "You know, don't you, we've met before. Briefly, six or seven years ago, in London I think it was. You recall that?"

"I do. I doubted you would, though."

"Oh get serious, mate. The famous Adam Hult, educator to the masses? Not quite so famous back then, but… Don't think I hold it against you, though. The masses need educatin'. Right, then, enough of this yabber. Do I think the Shroud and the Mandylion might be one and the same? I don't know. They might. It's a fair go. Quite the historical curiosity, in't it?"

"The Mandylion itself, then, how well established historically is it?"

"Oh, toss that. How well established is Julius Caesar? Same difference." He rubbed his nose again. Maybe it tickled when he got excited.

"Okay, but in the copies of it made by various artists, it's always just a head shot. Similar to the Shroud, yes, but, so to speak, where's the rest of it?"

He poured more of the coffee for both of us and then answered, "Now that is a fair question. The theory, of course, for those who reckon they're the same thing, is that the Byzantines normally kept it folded four times so that only the head showed. Keep in mind that they were, on the whole, extremely devout, what we would probably call superstitious. They weren't historically minded. They didn't think of the Mandylion as a historical relic, the burial shroud of Jesus, so much as a miraculously bestowed image, a direct revelation of the Lord. The face was what spoke to them—the face of God.

"Now, three specifics about how their chroniclers repeatedly referred to it. First, they used a term that, in all extant Greek literature, occurs *only* in reference to the Mandylion. This term translates literally as 'four-doubled,' or folded four times. As evidence goes, that's the true blue. Second, another term they used about it, a single word meaning 'not made by hands.' The image, they thought, couldn't have been made by any human artist. That squares with their belief about its miraculous origin, of course, but it also makes you think of the Turin Shroud and how all these blokes trying to reduplicate it are just so many no-hopers." He rubbed his nose and winked at me.

"And the third thing?" I prompted.

"Yeh, the third thing. It's another way they consistently described it. The image, they said, was visible but blurred, watery, indistinct. Again, that fits with their idea of a sort of divine shining-through. And it also describes the Shroud image to a tee."

"So it does." I sat back in my chair and took another sip of the bittersweet brew. At a table right next to us, four young blokes—

guys, that is, probably students—were arguing with great animation about something. I almost asked Rod if he could pick up on what it was about, but I didn't want to get him off point.

"What about the characteristics of the facial image itself," I asked, "the specifics of hair and beard and so on, and how that connects with the whole history of Jesus portrayal?"

Even seated, he gave a little jump. "That's one of the chief reasons I'm here in Turkey, on the ground where all this happened. In one way, it's an exercise in frustration, since so many artifacts from the Byzantine period have been lost or destroyed, often on purpose. But still a lot has been preserved, one way and another, and new finds are unearthed pritnear every month. A splendid one came to light recently, a fragment of a mosaic from the city of Urfa over in eastern Turkey. That's the same city that, in the ancient world, was called Edessa. The fragment, dating from the sixth century, contains a whole face, and it's undoubtedly the face of Jesus as it was known from the Mandylion. That is, it's the face that became the standard representation of him in Christian iconography—a rather long, oval face, shown frontally, with long hair parted in the middle, large dark eyes, a prominent nose, and a mustache and beard, the beard often being forked."

"Interesting," I said. "Dr. Dichter spoke about that 'standard representation' business too."

"Did she, now? The really interesting part is that, prior to the rediscovery of the Image of Edessa in the sixth century, that standard representation is never seen. Images of Jesus before that show him in different ways, typically young, round faced, and beardless."

"Okay, you said 'rediscovered'?"

"Therein lies a whole nother tale." Nose rub. "According to Eusebius, the fourth-century church historian, the cloth on which the Image is imprinted was brought from Jerusalem by the apostle Thaddeus to King Abgar of Edessa. This Thaddeus, Eusebius says, wasn't the one listed among the original twelve disciples but was one of the seventy-two recruited and sent out by Jesus some time later. Abgar is historically genuine, no problem there. By a vision he saw on the cloth, so the story goes, he was miraculously cured of a disease. As a result, he and his city-state converted to Christianity and the cloth became a holy treasure, the Image of Edessa."

I'd read about this in several sources, but I wanted to get it from the horse's mouth, as it were. "And this miracle cloth was none other than Jesus's burial shroud, I take it," I said.

"Well, the sources don't say so directly—believe what you will. But as to its rediscovery, that presupposes it was lost. And so it was, in a way. Under a subsequent king, Edessa reverted to paganism. In order to protect the Image, the local bishop had it sealed in a container and hidden over one of the city gates. Long story short, when the city returned to the Christian fold some time later, the Image was not forgotten, but its whereabouts were unknown. And then, dramatically, when the city was under siege by the Persian King Khosrau in the sixth century, the Image was rediscovered, and, as they believed, its power turned back the siege."

"And it became not only the Image of Edessa but the image of what, to the Christian world, Jesus looked like."

"Too right. And, of course, what he looks like on that strip of linen in Turin."

I poured the last of the coffee for both of us, remarking, "Stuff like this is why we're historians. So tell me now, how did the Image of Edessa become the Mandylion? How did the Byzantine Empire come to possess it?"

"Yet another good story, this one well documented historically. By the tenth century, Edessa was under the political control of the Muslim Caliphate of Baghdad. The caliph, though, one al-Muttaqi, was relatively tolerant of other religions in his outlying provinces, so the Edessan Christians were able to practice their religion and, in particular, to venerate their image. By that time, the fame of the Image had permeated to Byzantium and successive emperors had coveted it, but they had lacked the military power to enforce their wishes.

"By the year 943, however, that had changed, and the Emperor Romanos sent his great general John Curcuas at the head of eighty thousand soldiers to the gates of Edessa. The local emir, the caliph's surrogate, was duly alarmed, but he must have been amazed with relief when he heard Curcuas's terms. The Byzantine general offered to spare the city and turn over two hundred high-ranking Muslim prisoners in return for just one thing: the Image of Edessa. This news was relayed to the caliph in Baghdad, and his decision can surprise no one—the Edessan Christians would just have to make a sacrifice.

"And that, in one nutshell, is how the Image became the Mandylion."

CHAPTER 21

At the end of our conversation I thanked Rod profusely and insisted on paying for the coffee—small enough remuneration.

One doesn't get to Istanbul very often—first time for me—so I took a stroll around Beyazit Square, taking in the sights. There was an imposing mosque and a three-hundred-foot-tall super-phallic tower. Istan-bull. I was also engaging in Ari's environmental awareness program when my cell phone rang, and it was the man himself.

"You're over there singing to the lords and ladies, I presume," he said.

"Too cute by half—don't rub it in. What's up? Got something for me?"

"Maybe. But first, how's the body healing?"

"It's coming. I'm the walking wounded, but I'm walking."

"And watching?"

"As we speak. I just finished a quite illuminating hour with ... let's say, an Australian with an eye on the past."

"An eye on the present is more urgent at the moment—and that's me, baby. I've narrowed the search down to four or five most likelies, of which I'll just mention what seem, maybe, the top two. Ready for the good news?"

"If you think it's worth sharing with the National Security Agency snoops."

"Hi, fellas. I'll chance it; you need the info. Here they are—take your pick. In the Vatican bureaucracy, no less, there is one Cardinal Vitelli, a holdover from the Borgias. He's well connected among the rich and powerful all over Europe. He sees the Shroud as a potential monetary bonanza for the church and doesn't want it debunked. He takes no prisoners, and you can be sure he's no fan of yours.

"The other possibility is about as different as could be. Out in the far reaches of Wyoming, there is this nice rural church called the Church of the Right God. Sounds sort of spiritual, but they're skinheads with a perfect vacuum inside, led by a chief shepherd by the name of Dennis Quilt. Whatever religion he's got, Dennis got it after three stretches in prison. Rape and armed robbery, among other qualifications. I wouldn't walk in and question his conversion, though, without a loaded Uzi. Needless to say, these characters major in extreme views, and they believe in acting on them. Jews and non-whites are anti-American and therefore in the crosshairs. They lump all their enemies together in the general category of atheists. They see themselves as the only serious defenders of the one true religion—theirs—and for some reason I haven't fathomed yet, people who question the authenticity of the Turin Shroud are high on this list."

"But they're just a little country church?" I got in edgewise.

"More like the sharp edge of a movement. They've got plenty of followers and wannabes hither and yon, mostly under rocks. But also, surprisingly enough, they've got considerable expertise in com tech, like they've cornered all the bigoted hackers. These folks are trouble, my friend."

"Hey, ignorance was bliss. So what do we do about this?"

"As I said before, get you on the first jet plane to old New York. Tomorrow morning at the latest. Meanwhile, keep your guard up."

"Now that I have some incentive ..."

"One other thing. Have you seen any tabloids lately?"

"Just lately, everything I've seen has been in Italian or Turkish—oops, I let it slip."

"Never mind that. It seems that some eager-beaver reporter found out about your two-step with the lady Vatican scholar and held a mike up to her. Well, she spilled it—why not? So now the supermarket rags and tabloid TV shows have jumped on it: 'Celeb Debunker Adam Now Touting Miracle Shroud!' Pure grist to their mill, and you've made it onto their first-name-only list. All the more reason for you to hop on that jet home, bro."

"I'll take it under advisement. And then, after thoughtful consideration, I'll catch that plane."

"That's my boy. See you then. Keep safe."

I dropped the cell phone back in my pocket and kept walking. Glancing right and left, up and down. I saw lots of Turks. Most of them looked suspicious. If the cardinal's button men or Dennis Quilt's meatheads had my number, would they look like Turks? I wished I'd paid much more attention when Ari and I were working on this security stuff.

In any case, I was getting hungry again, and there was no reason not to eat. I didn't read Turkish, of course, but I could recognize a restaurant when I saw one. I headed back in the direction of the Grand Washington Hotel, and a block short of it I found what I hoped I was looking for. A restaurant, anyway, for sure.

I went on in. It was a small place with only about ten tables. They weren't all taken, though, and a waiter seated me and handed me a menu. In Turkish, naturally. I looked up at him, and he smiled and shrugged. I pointed at the menu, then at him, and then at myself.

"You pick," I said, "for me."

"Ah, nooey tooey rooey," he said, pointing at a menu item and nodding briskly.

"Thank you," I said, handing the menu back.

One benefit of traveling the world is getting to sample all varieties of national cuisine. I feel sorry for those people who go to Marrakesh or Jakarta and hunt for a McDonald's. Like being color blind in a rain forest.

When he served my dish, the waiter mimed drinking and said words recognizable as "*wine*? *beer*?" I waved that off, and he mimed, "I've got just the thing!" and brought me a tall, creamy-looking drink he called "ayran—ayran." Ayran turned out to be a tangy, slightly salty yogurt concoction—delectable. The meal itself consisted mainly of chunks of lamb in a puree of, I think, eggplant and a sharp cheese. Eat your heart out, Big Mac.

I took my time enjoying this while also mulling over what my next move should be. Ari was right, of course. If I had anything more to discover in this Shroud research, I could do it just as well from the relative security of my home base, at least for the time being. There wasn't much sense in insisting on playing the hero, shooting for that posthumous medal of honor.

I wasn't sure what to make of this tabloid celebrity business. I was used to being a popular, well-known author, but this would be popularity on another level, probably a less savory one. Celebrity means you're not just popular, you're a target. A target for bored and envious curiosity, for neurotic fantasy, and for fanatical devotion or fanatical animosity. Yes, indeed, Ari was right.

But. But my investigation into the origins of the Shroud was leading in another direction. Toward the center of events, toward the deep past. Toward, perhaps, the truth.

What would Indy do?

I paid the cashier, handing her half of my Turkish bills and trusting her not to short-change me. Then, on the alert again, I went to the front window and scanned the street. It was congested with cars and trucks in both directions, horns honking like agitated geese. Parked right in front of the restaurant was a European-looking sedan with tinted windows. Night was more than half-fallen outside, and I couldn't tell if anyone was in the car, but it raised my hackles. I looked around to check if there was a back way out, but then I recalled one of Benny's maxims:

prefer the danger you can see to the ones you can't. So I went on out the front door.

The car, I now heard, had its engine running. If I went to my left, opposite to the car's direction, I'd be going away from the hotel. Not the best. So I walked firmly to the right, coming immediately to a narrow alley beside the restaurant. Dark alleys are the prototype of hazard. I peered into the shadows but saw only shadows.

Then the car's engine roared, and its tires screeched, and it was lunging into the alley, right at me. I leaped back, and someone who must have followed me out of the restaurant grabbed me from behind around the chest. With my fingers I gouged at a nerve in his wrist, but the car had jerked to a stop and two men in dark pullovers or sweatshirts jumped out and came at me, piling into me and propelling me down the alley. I broke free of the first guy, but another one jolted me with a fist to my cheekbone. At that point the instinct gained from years of training finally caught up with me. I whirled on a low axis and kicked a heel into the side of one guy's knee, which buckled with an audible snap. Ten years ago I would have ended that move on all fours, but now I fell to the pavement on my side. The first guy kicked me in the back of the neck, and another aimed a kick at my groin, but I deflected it with a forearm. That threw him off balance and he flailed down on top of me, and we grappled for a moment like cage fighters until the first guy landed a hard kick to my kidney, sending a paralyzing jolt of pain to my brain's command center and from there to every extremity.

After that, they tenderized me like a tough steak until I heard a woman screaming like a terrified cat—the sound of hell's gates swinging open?—and then the three goons bolted to their car, or two of them bolted, dragging the third, and the doors slammed, and then I didn't hear much of anything until I felt a hand on my shoulder and a high-pitched, urgent woman's voice saying things I couldn't understand. But she was trying to help me to my feet, and I saw she was the same old woman I had seen working in the back of the restaurant, wearing a shapeless purple dress and a black headscarf. She was small and scrawny and must have been seventy at least, but she was surprisingly strong. Half-supporting me, she maneuvered me through a narrow door into a pantry off the restaurant kitchen and from there into a tiny restroom with a single toilet and washbasin.

She sat me down on the toilet and removed my suit jacket—one more good suit bites the dust. Turning the hot tap on full blast, she soaked a towel and wrung it out and ministered to my latest wounds, as many as she could find. The Turkish Good Samaritan. She touched the bandage on my scalp with a finger, clucking and shaking her head and saying, probably, "Are you making a habit of this?"

With as supreme an effort as I could muster, I caught my breath and, taking her by the wrists, thanked her effusively and assured her I would be fine. She knew better, but she let me stand up and peer at myself in the small, cloudy mirror over the washbasin. I saw a Halloween mask of Rocky Balboa after fifteen rounds. The woman's ministrations had helped, but there was only so much she could do.

I checked all my pockets. Sure enough, they had taken all my stuff—passport, cell phone, and wallet, which, along with everything else, had my hotel key card.

An undocumented, suspiciously banged-up alien in Turkey. This could spell trouble. In my shirt pocket, though, there was a scrunched-up piece of paper, cheap notepaper. I took it out and unfolded it and read, in penciled block letters: "Next time they wont find your body, smart boy."

A wave of panic washed over me just like that first phone warning had triggered. This time I had every reason to panic.

No cell phone—out of contact.

No ID—can't verify who I am.

No room key—out on the street.

No passport—can't travel.

No money—can't pay or buy or bribe.

What to do?

One of the cooks had come over and was chattering with the old woman. It looked like he was scolding her. I straightened my tie—amazingly, it was still knotted—and dusted off my scuffed-up clothing. Not quite good enough for a job interview, but it would have to do. The old woman was still going at it with the cook, so I sidled past them and let myself back out the door, the woman calling something after me that I wished I could decipher.

I found I could walk, slowly and painfully. If I could come up with a plan, now was the time. Taking deep breaths to suppress the panic, and thinking as hard and clearly as I could, I traversed the long block to the hotel without even getting mugged again.

Entering the main lobby, I stepped over to an unoccupied alcove. Wincing with the pain of movement, I slipped off my right shoe and, from under the insole, drew out a plastic card and put it in my shirt pocket. Then I limped over to the check-in counter. One of the advantages of the Grand Washington was that they spoke passable English. Behind the counter was a middle-aged man in a fez, perhaps for the benefit of tourists like me. Unlike me, most of them didn't have to rely on an ace in the hole, in this case an extra credit card, part of Ari's plan for Adam's survival.

I slid the card across the counter and said in a businesslike way, "I'm Adam Hult in room 314, and I'm afraid I lost my room key."

The man looked at me without flinching and then at the credit card. "Do you have any other identification, sir?" he asked.

"No, I don't. Look, I was foolish and went someplace I shouldn't. I got mugged—you know, roughed up and robbed. That card's the only thing they missed. But I don't want to make any trouble for anyone, no publicity. If you'll scan the card, you'll see I'm legitimate."

He stared at me impassively for what seemed five minutes and then finally turned to his computer and brought up my account. He gave a little grunt and ran the card through his scanner. It was a platinum card, good as gold. Looking back up at me with solemn eyes, he said, "I apologize for the bad elements in our country. There is bad in every country."

He handed the card back then turned around and opened a large case and plucked out a key card for room 314. Passing it over to me, he said, "Good luck."

That would be a novel experience, but nice.

I took the elevator to the third floor and hobbled down the carpeted hallway to my room. The key worked. I half expected to find the room ransacked—the thugs had my key, after all—but it looked just the same as I'd left it. Even so, I wasn't staying here a minute longer than I could help.

First things first. I sat on the bed and took the room phone and dialed Ari's number, willing him through gritted teeth to *pick up*. After a succession of buzzes and clicks, he said, "Ari's place."

"Ari, it's me. And it's trouble. They got to me again. Three of them jumped me in an alley and taught me a lesson and stripped my assets—passport and wallet and cell phone."

"But you're walking and talking. That's good. An alley, Adam?"

"I can explain that, but not well enough. What I need is Aladdin's Lamp."

"So you do. Consider it done. To what address?"

"It'll have to be this hotel, but I don't want to hang out here any longer than I have to."

"Understood, bro. It's two o'clock here now. The lamp will arrive in the morning, your time."

I gave him the address and hung up. I lay back on the bed, exhausted. So far so good, emergency-plan-wise, but there was no more to the plan. Now all I could do was wait.

Aladdin's Lamp? When us boys devise our schemes, we use names out of Tom Sawyer. This one was our masterpiece, the best we could contrive. Perfectly illegal too, for added spice. For each of us, we had produced counterfeit passports, driver's licenses, and credit cards. How? Mainly with Benny's reluctant help, pulled out of him like his own fingernails. Basically, I think, we managed to convince him that, given today's world and Ari's enterprises, we were marginally safer with them than without them. Ari would send mine by overnight FedEx to my hotel room. He would also cancel my stolen credit cards.

Not only was I beat up and exhausted, I was massively lonely. I couldn't help thinking of Sareen. Not quite beautiful but exotic Sareen. If I could remember her cell phone number, I could call her. Not that I would; she would just hang up on me.

It would be awfully good to hear her voice, though. If she would say anything at all. If I could bear her contempt.

Which would be worse, hearing her contempt or not hearing it?

Could I remember her number? I thought maybe I could—it was lodged somewhere in my memory as well as my cell phone's.

Oh, what the hell. I punched in the numbers that came to mind.

"Yes, hello?"

"Hello, Sareen. It's me, Adam Hult."

"Adam, I am so sorry about the other evening."

"*You're* sorry! My God, Sareen, I'm the sorry one. Can you forgive me?"

"Of course. But where are you now? Are you all right?"

Sixth sense? "I'm in Istanbul, the Grand Washington Hotel. And no, I'm really not all right. They got to me again, whoever they are. Three leg-breakers beat me up and stole my passport and everything else. No broken bones, though; that's just an expression."

She was silent, taking this in. Then she said, reminding me of my fourth-grade schoolteacher, "Listen to me, Adam, and do what I say. I am in Istanbul also—"

"In Istanbul!"

"Yes. Just listen, please. There is a safe house here also—as in Rome, more or less. Now, you must leave that hotel tonight. Let me think. All right, here is what we will do. At midnight, you must leave your room and leave the hotel. But tell me, Adam, are you able to walk?"

"Not very fast."

"Walk slowly, then, out the front entrance. Do not bring your suitcase—"

"I have to bring my laptop."

"Bring that, then. At exactly midnight. Walk west until a car stops for you. It will be a late model Volkswagen Passat, a white one. The window will be down, and you will see me. We will pick you up, and then Bashir will see to it that we are not followed."

"Bashir?"

"He is one of us. You must trust me, Adam."

Decision time. Easy decision. "Midnight. White Passat. Anything else?"

"That is enough. I will see you then, Adam."

"See you, Sareen."

I hung up, more than half stunned. Sareen in Istanbul? Following me again? What else could it be? And now more than ever, I was banking that she was on my side.

Suddenly my fuddled brain realized that our plans were crossing wires. Impatiently I punched in Sareen's number again.

"Adam?"

"Yes. There's one more thing, Sareen. Ari, the guy I phoned when we were at that other safe house, he's sending me a care package, overnight delivery. But it's coming to this hotel room. Can you give me another address he can send it to?"

"Adam, that's not… that's not… Very well, trust must run both ways. But you must not ever, *ever* reveal this address, except for this purpose. Do you understand?"

"I think, late in the day, I'm coming to understand perfectly. You have my word."

She gave me the address, and I phoned Ari back and relayed it to him with a brief explanation. Even at a distance, I saw his black eyebrows shoot up. He took it at face value, though. He said I got to him just in time, before the package shipped.

Trust.

CHAPTER 22

Midnight came around slowly. I hurt all over, definitely worse than after falling down the stairs. I thought there was little chance I would fall asleep, but I resisted the urge to lie down. I sat in an uncomfortable chair and watched the door. The door was sturdy and, of course, locked. If I were really Indiana Jones, I'd have a comforting .44 by my side. Maybe next time.

At five to midnight, I dragged my groaning corpse along with my laptop over to the door and scoped out the hallway. Silent and deserted, as it should be. I took the elevator down to the lobby and went, as inconspicuously as possible, out the door, turning left and heading west along the sidewalk. There was still some traffic and a few pedestrians, but things seemed quiet. I worked on environmental awareness, but it was hard with a stiff neck.

A moment later the white Passat pulled smoothly to the curb just ahead of me. The back door swung open, and Sareen got out. I shuffled over and hugged her with my free hand, the one without the laptop. She hugged me back, making me grunt with pain—no complaint, though—then she sort of helped and sort of shoved me into the car, sliding in behind me, and we accelerated away into the night.

Besides the two of us, there was just the driver, a tall guy with shoulder-length glistening black hair.

"This is Bashir," Sareen said loudly over the car noise. "He is a friend."

"Hey, Bashir," I said, "thanks for the rescue."

He answered something I didn't catch. He was driving fast, and I wondered if they had traffic cops over here. I figured he should know. We turned one corner and then another through the city; I was thrown against Sareen and then she against me, which was okay. After a while, we got onto some kind of expressway, and Bashir went even faster, passing one car after another. I knew what he was doing, watching for any sign of a tail. Just what Ari would do.

Sareen said something to me, but I didn't understand it very well. I was feeling a bit dizzy—not carsick, I thought (I really didn't want to puke on her), but shivery, hot and cold all at once. Tired, weak. A little dreamy.

I have no idea how long or how far we drove, but eventually we slowed and came to a stop. If I'd been asleep, I woke up enough to see, out the window, a stuccoed wall and behind it a house, its scalloped roofing tiles bathed dimly in moonlight.

"Adam, we're here," Sareen said. "We have to get out now."

I didn't want to move at all. Between them, she and Bashir lugged me out of the car and through a gate, up to the house. All around us I saw what looked like row upon row of grape vines, unless that was part of the dream.

Inside, someone switched on a lamp, and the light dazzled me. They laid me down on a bed with a hard mattress. I tried to tell Sareen I was all right, she'd gone to enough trouble on my behalf already, but she didn't understand. She, or the two of them, were undressing me, but I was beyond caring. A cool damp towel with Sareen behind it was bathing my face and chest and arms and legs, and it felt infinitely good except that pain was everywhere inside me now, and I couldn't seem to get warm no matter how hard I shivered. I tried to tell her I wasn't feeling so well but I was grateful beyond words and I wished things were different and I hoped she wouldn't go away, but I wasn't sure if she could hear me.

▪ ▪ ▪ ▪ ▪ ▪

When I woke up, there was some light—maybe it was the light that woke me—coming from behind a curtained window to my left. I turned my head on the pillow to look around and found that my head had become much heavier than it was yesterday. I couldn't lift it more than an inch, but I managed to turn it the other way. Sareen was there, asleep in a low cushioned chair. My slight movement must have awakened her, because her eyes came open and she sat forward, looking at me. Then she got up and knelt by the bed, putting her palm on my forehead.

"Your fever is down, thank God," she murmured. "We seem to be stuck in a repeating loop, so I'll ask you again, how are you feeling now?"

"Feeling?" I croaked. I cleared my throat feebly and said, "Better than last night, I guess, but weak as a slug."

"It's a wonder you're as strong as that. You're not much more than a bundle of bruises and scrapes and welts. It's amazing that no bones seem to be broken."

"It would take more than those three punks to break me," I blustered.

She pinched my earlobe. "Don't speak nonsense, Adam. They could have broken you if they wanted to. They could have killed you. The next time, they say they will. I read the note in your pocket."

"Oh, that." I had mixed thoughts about how much she was finding out about me and my follies. Part of me wished she saw only a stalwart, unfaltering front view, but the other part wanted her to know me more like I really was. If even I knew what I really was. Endlessly curious, I would say. Intellectual. Headstrong. Rash, sometimes. Cynical, certainly. Largely clueless, as I've said before, about women but needing what they have to offer. Maybe even what they offer beyond (but not excluding) sex.

Needing. Needy. I wouldn't have thought so before ...

"I don't know," Sareen was saying quietly, "who is being harder on you, Adam, these fanatics who threaten you or you yourself by your own choices."

Ouch. Like making drunken passes on first dates? I wouldn't bring it up, though, if she didn't. I said, "You mean like not taking the first threats seriously enough?"

She sighed. "I think so, yes. These are not nice, civilized people. They value human life only as far as they can reach."

"That's pretty much Ari's assessment too. That's one reason why he's sending a care package, besides the fact that the bad guys stripped me clean."

She stood up and then sat on the bed by my feet. "This package, what will it contain?"

"Beef jerky and a few quarts of whiskey. Sorry, it's that lame joke reflex. It'll contain replacement ID, money, cell phone—the basic necessities." I held off from mentioning that the ID would be a new me.

"I see. All right. Probably you should rest some more. But first, you must be thirsty. Some water or tea?"

"Tea sounds good, but boil the water." I didn't want to add Montezuma's Revenge to my trials.

When she brought it, she helped me sit up a bit, propped by pillows. The tea scalded my tongue at first but tasted good.

"Thanks," I said. "Thank you, of course, for everything. And by the way, where exactly are we?"

She giggled, the first time I'd ever heard her do it. "That is what you kept saying last night, over and over again. That and a few other things. Fever talk, we call it."

"In that case, you can't trust anything I said. So anyway, are we still in Istanbul?"

"The outskirts of the city; it doesn't matter exactly where. A safe place, as I told you. We weren't followed here. Bashir was certain of that."

"Okay." I thought about how to phrase the next question. "Look, Sareen, it can't be just coincidence, you showing up in Istanbul like this. Why were you following me?"

She gave me a wide-eyed, innocent look. "You needed me. Isn't it obvious?"

"Not obvious at all. How could you know I would need you? I mean, need this overly dramatic sort of rescuing?"

Her face clouded. "I have said it to you before, but I think you don't listen. You are stirring up scorpions you are unaware of."

"But you are aware? Aware of what?"

"I don't know exactly. But I am not naive. And you mustn't pretend to be more naive than you are."

That stung. "Okay, no more pretending. What do you know about these mysterious Shroud terrorists that I don't know?"

She put a hand on the covers over my ankle. "Please, Adam, be calm. Don't waste your energy. As to specifics, I know no more than you do. But I know the Shroud stirs strong passions—not the Shroud in itself, but he who is in the image. The crucified man. Of all those people who know about Jesus, few are indifferent to him."

I grunted, petulant and unconvinced.

"You know about the fire in 1997, don't you," she continued, "when the Shroud was nearly destroyed—that was certainly arson, and it nearly achieved its purpose. It was the same with the fire back in 1532. The conflict is perennial, and it is about more than an old length of cloth."

The tea had cooled enough that I could take full swallows, and I finished the cup. I wasn't sure how to respond to her religious intensity—not just what to say but what to think. She relieved me of this difficulty by taking the cup from me and saying, "You should rest again. See if you can sleep some more, but rest at least."

I don't always follow doctor's orders, but this time my body said yes. I laid aside the covers except for the sheet, since the day was warming, and settled back.

. . . . . .

I slept till around noon. When I woke up, I didn't see or hear any sign of Sareen or anyone else. Earlier in the morning, I hadn't paid much attention to my surroundings, so now I looked around. I was in a good-sized bedroom with white plaster walls, two of which had windows, now open to let any breeze in. There was a large chest of drawers and a mirrored dressing table, another small table with a vase of flowers, and that low chair in which Sareen had apparently spent the night. The only wall hanging was a small, plain wooden cross.

Gingerly, I experimented with rolling out of bed. It was a noble idea, but it didn't work out well. Everything hurt all over again, muscles and joints and toenails. Just sitting erect made me wobbly.

"Adam! Do you think—"

It was Sareen coming through the doorway.

"It's time to rise and shine? I just wish," I said, easing myself back down. She helped me adjust the pillow.

"You mustn't rush things," she said. "The body heals on its own schedule."

"So it just informed me. I'm thirsty again, though, even a little hungry."

"That is a good sign. I'll bring you some water. Then, perhaps, some rice and vegetables?"

"That'll do. Bottled water?"

"Yes, in ten-liter jugs."

A while later she brought the meal on a tray. I was able to sit up enough to balance the tray on my lap. I took small bites and ate them slowly.

"Let's see," I said. "You know what I do for a living. What's your gig, other than midnight special ops?"

She smiled. "Those I only do for desperate professors. Normally I work with an international non-profit group seeking to promote democracy and religious freedom, especially in places where they are absent or under threat."

"Ah … well, that sounds commendable. And ambitious."

"I suppose so … but much less colorful than all these things you write such memorable books about. How did you happen to go from academics to these diverse bestsellers?"

Was she deflecting my inquiry into her own life? Oh well, don't push it.

"Sort of a freak thing," I said. "I was always something of a freak."

"Freak? No, Adam, you mustn't think that."

"But it's true. I can't help it. You know the thing about being in the top percentile, the top one percent? I just happened to be in the top millionth. I was reading and combining fractions when I was three, without even trying, just for fun. When most kids were struggling with long division and *James and the Giant Peach*, I was reading Wittgenstein and playing around with integral calculus. Other than that, I was fairly normal—at least I sure wanted to be."

"It must have been difficult, wishing to be normal when, in some essential ways, you weren't."

"I guess so. Well, yeah, I know so. To start with, I was the freak in my own family. My parents were … no disrespect, you know, and it was no fault of theirs, but they, I'll just say, they started life in the basement and barely made it to ground level, for all their effort."

"Are they … gone then?"

"No, but worn out ahead of time. My pop is dying of emphysema. Just always been working and smoking himself to death. His father was a coal miner in eastern Pennsylvania, one of those people who barely survived the Depression. He died before I was born. So my pop grew up rough. No education to speak of; had to be a tough scrapper to make it out of his teens. But he toughed it out and wound up making a decent living driving trucks. A bare-knuckle brawler, but a good guy in his way. Really proud of being a family man."

"And your mother?"

"Oh, my mother. Another hard story. Her mom was one of the original hippies, back before there were hippies. I think she, my grandmother, was abandoned somehow by her parents—I never learned any details about that. She was floating around with some homegrown gypsies, mostly older than her, and she got herself pregnant for the first time, with my mom, when she was about fourteen. That was in the early fifties. Then when my mom was just a kid, they started forming these rural communes, shabby and primitive. They grew pot, smoked it, and sold it. Dealt some other drugs too. It wasn't the good life, anything but. By the time my grandmother burned herself out and died, they were in some commune in upstate New York—hell of a place to live rough in the winter. My mom was around fourteen herself then and damned lucky not to be pregnant herself. The commune died a natural death about the same time, and she wound up down in the big city, living, I think, in some flophouse with other street kids. Again, I'm hazy on the details here. She's never been very forthcoming about it, understandably. It's amazing she survived as well as she did. It's amazing that I'm even here.

"She and my pop met when she was sixteen and he was eighteen. There may have been romance in it, I don't know, but they've stuck together ever since. They got married after a couple of years, and I came along a few years later, the freak, and my brother, Sam, three years after that."

"So you have a brother. Any other—"

"No, just Sam." And in another tone of voice, I added, "Sam."

"Why do you say that? What about him?" She had picked up on that tone of voice.

CHAPTER 23

"Sam, my kid brother, was normal like most of the other kids. And we started out with the usual brotherly relationship, shoving and challenging and fighting and clowning around. At first, as the younger, he looked up to me as the alpha male in our pack of two. But then—maybe when he was four or five—he began to realize I was different. Partly, I'm sure, he picked it up from how the other kids treated me and talked about me. 'Wizard' and 'brainiac' were two of the nicer things they called me.

"That put Sam on the horns of a dilemma, a clash of loyalties. Who would come first, older brother Adam the wiz or the other kids in the hood? It wasn't easy for him, and in fact I don't think he ever really decided. I think it tore him up inside, along with some other things that tore at him. In just about every way, he was my opposite. He wasn't brainy, but he was strong and athletic and he resembled a young Brad Pitt. It's not surprising, I guess, that he went after those things, his strengths—sports, street fighting, hot girls. He was the kind of cocky, rule-smashing kid that school administrators hate, except that he was their top athlete. In the same year, his sophomore year, he broke the conference record as a running back in football and nearly got kicked out of school for knocking up the vice-principal's daughter—and she was a senior.

"He gave our parents a lot of early gray hairs. Our mom tried to hold herself up as an example of wasted youth, a disaster to avoid at any cost, but he didn't see any parallel at all. Well, kids almost never do. Our pop was proud as a rooster about Sam's athletic feats but beat him black and blue because of all his rebellious ways up until Sam was too strong and fast to take it anymore. After that, Pop just cussed him like the truck driver he was."

"What about your relationship with him?" Sareen put in.

"That's hard to define. Being so different, we could never be very close. But we were brothers, and that meant something to both of us. He thought of me as half idiot savant, half space alien. He was bewildered by me and kept his distance, but I suspect he also admired me, sort of in the same way primitive tribesmen admire airplanes. I'm sorry. I shouldn't put it that way..."

"It's all right. I understand. What has become of him?"

"He took off after his junior year with, get this, two of the choicest local young hotties. The idea was they were going to surf and party all summer on all the Florida beaches. I don't know about the girls, but for Sam it became a way of life—surfer, beach bum, skin chaser, boozer and junkie. You blow through your prime in a hurry that way. By the time that Sam discovered he wasn't the golden boy any longer, the truth was he hadn't been for several years. He woke up one morning, I would guess, surprised that people wouldn't give him handouts anymore and didn't want him at their parties. The last time I talked with him, he said he had a job as a bail bondsman. But that was a couple of years ago, and he might have been blowing smoke."

"It makes you sad, doesn't it?" she said.

"Yeah, sure, of course."

We were long since done with our small lunch. Sareen cleared the stuff away and then came back and told me I should rest some more. Even if I couldn't sleep, just rest, the fastest way to heal. In fact, all that talking had depleted my tank, and I didn't argue.

▪ ▪ ▪ ▪ ▪ ▪

I may have slept some, but mostly I just lay there with my eyes closed and let random thoughts bump around like pinballs. My poor unenviable family. Me, the freak. Me, the world beater. Me, the academic whore. Me, breaking Doris's chains and coming out ... where? On the lam, pounded into hamburger, hiding out in some sort of safe house somewhere in old Byzantium. Safe house? Have to ask more about that. Have to ask more about a lot. Not fair, me doing all the talking. All the others talked to me—Bob, Henrietta, Pete, crazy old Dougal, Beatrice, even slick Mersenne—why not Sareen, our lady of secrets. Altogether too many secrets in this affair.

Secrets. Secret adversary. Why threaten me and assault me from the dark? Come out into the open and we'll settle things, mano a mano.

Old Byzantium. Old Edessa. Camel caravans, dusty roads, tinkling bells.

At the center of things, one looming cryptic secret: the man in the Shroud. The crucified man.

Why is that image a photonegative? Why?

How?

When?

Who, what, when, where, how, why—all the reporter's questions were in play here.

I must have fallen asleep because I woke up and noticed the light had changed, the sunlight coming at a different angle through the window. I checked my watch: four twenty. Hoping for better things this time, I eased my legs off the bed and sat up. Better: the world stayed upright around me. There, laid across the chair that Sareen had slept in, was a well-worn but apparently clean gray sweat suit. Not mine but evidently for me. Good thing, with only my undies between me and nudity. Leaning forward, I was able to reach it and, slowly and with care, I put it on.

Just in time too. Sareen leaned around the doorway. "Adam? Oh, this is good, you're up. Is it all right this time?"

"Good as new. Decathlon ready."

"Not quite. But look, your care package has arrived." She brought in a FedEx box big enough for six doughnuts. She had already torn off the address label and either burned or swallowed it. Excessive caution, maybe, but who was I to talk?

"I'll let you open it in private," she said.

"No, please stay. I'd rather you stay. If I can't trust you, I'm a dry melon."

I opened it. On top, under the bubble wrap, was a handwritten note.

> Yo Ken, note the two cell phones. The black one is encrypted, use it only for dialogue with me. The other is an ordinary Droid; use it as sparingly as possible. Sealed orders: head for home.

"Yo Ken" wasn't weird Asian code; it was me. Kenneth Clark. Our first thought had been Clark Kent, but that, or even Kent Clark, seemed over the top. But Kenneth Clark, now; could an alias be more innocuous? Besides the two cell phones, the package contained a passport and a new wallet with several credit cards, an international driver's license, and about a thousand dollars in cash.

Deciding to come clean all at once, I handed her the passport. She opened it and saw the name.

"Kenneth Clark?" she queried.

"My latest incarnation. 'Ken' to friends like you."

She paged through it and saw the various national stamps, including the most recent one courtesy of Turkey.

"Adam, this is... this is flagrantly illegal. What are you thinking?"

"To be precise, changing identities. The villains are dialed in on Adam Hult and waiting for him to re-emerge. But Ken Clark, who's he?"

"I won't call you by that name. If the Turkish authorities see through this, even the American Embassy may not be able to rescue you this time. Five years in a Turkish prison? Adam, you are insane."

I took a deep breath and let it out slowly. "Okay, Sareen, now here's something *you* can't reveal. Absolutely. Are you ready for this?"

She looked slightly offended. "I will reveal nothing."

"I believe you. All this"—I gestured to the care package—"is Israeli product. The best there is. It will pass muster."

"Israeli!" She was dumbfounded.

"Yes. Ari's father has been an agent with the Mossad most of his life, and Ari has, to a degree, apprenticed to him. They have deep connections and resources. But, again, keep it under your hat."

She shook her head, muttering, "Men are idiots. You play children's games with live grenades."

"It's the only way, Sareen. These characters we're up against, they're too good at intelligence to play it any other way. But look now, I've shown you all my cards, laid myself pretty bare for you, figuratively and literally. I think you owe me some explanations too. For starters, whose house is this we're in? Whoever they are, where are they? Where's Bashir?"

She sat down beside me on the bed. Today she was wearing royal blue slacks and an intricately patterned, collared shirt in shades of orange. Good to look at.

"You are right," she said. "We've already established that trust must go both ways. Very well. This house is actually owned by the organization I work with. As I told you before, we work to promote democracy and religious freedom. It is called the Global Organization for Democratic Faith. Its origins and focus are in

Lebanon, but, especially over the last decade, it has grown well beyond that. There is an older couple, Mansoor and Iris Sahadi, who normally live in the house and take care of it. Just now, because of you, they are in a small apartment behind the house. Don't let that concern you, though. You are important to them, and their first prayer is for your full recovery."

"Important to them?" I wondered.

"Oh yes. Part of our mission is providing succor to victims of religious persecution."

Religious persecution? Well, maybe. I said, "That's generous of them, but I don't plan to displace them much longer. And Bashir?"

"Oh, Bashir. He is one of us, as I told you. He works as an airplane mechanic here in Istanbul. He is married; they have a baby girl."

"Okay, but when you say 'one of us' and when you talk in terms of safe houses, your organization sounds more secret than open. Which is it?"

"It is both. The open and the secret organizations overlap somewhat—myself, for instance. As for the secrecy, we need it because of the world and the times we live in. Various factions, Islamist ones especially, do not value democracy or religious freedom and will go to extreme lengths to combat them. In your own way, you also are discovering this, though I doubt your adversary is Islamist."

"No, beliefs about the Shroud would be low on their priority list. As to who it really is, I've had to change my thinking. This latest attack came well after the news was splashed all around that I've started delving beyond the theory of artistic fakery. What I'm doing now, talking with people like Beatrice Dichter and Rod Eglantine, is more likely to comfort the true believers and alarm people like Doris Ballaster. Why she would resort to highly organized thuggery, though, eludes me. Perhaps she could, through Tom Freebinder's connections, but it doesn't quite compute. Something more is in the game."

"As to that, time will tell—or else it won't. Aside from that, would you like to try walking a little? If you can, it will be good for you."

With her taking my arm, I stood up and took a few steps. A little creaky, but I was walking again. By tomorrow I'd be training for the marathon.

We went from the bedroom down a short hallway to the main room. It was spacious and airy with a high, slightly arched ceiling. Beautiful carpets, Persian or Armenian or even Turkish, were arranged around the floor. The furniture looked solid and un-American, which was fine with me.

"How about the bathroom?" I said. "It seems my body really is working again."

After my potty break and a face wash, easy on the scrapes and swellings, she showed me the kitchen, also airy and roomy and evidently well provisioned. I sat at the table, and she put water on to boil for some more tea.

Over tea, we talked about where I might be at in my Shroud research. Sareen was glad, of course, that I was edging beyond the fraud hypotheses. All the information I had gathered from Drs. Dichter and Eglantine had persuaded me that somewhere, starting perhaps right here in Istanbul—Byzantium, Constantinople—there probably existed "the rest of the story." The hints and clues were too many and too substantial to be nothing but coincidence. I was eager to dig more deeply into this fascinating, enigmatic Image of Edessa and its possible link with first-century Jerusalem.

She asked me if I was ready for some dinner, and I said, "By all means." While I slept the morning away, she had done some shopping and brought back a plucked chicken, some fragrant fresh pita bread, and ingredients for a Lebanese salad. While she worked on this, I gazed out the window, taking my bearings. As

I had vaguely noticed last night, there were indeed rows of grape vines all around; the house seemed to be set in the midst of them. On my asking, Sareen explained that the vineyard was owned by a winery conglomerate but managed by Mansoor and Iris and worked by locals.

Beyond the vineyard in one direction, there were low hills sprinkled with farms, while in another direction the city skyline could be seen. It all looked peaceful and unthreatening. If only life were that simple.

Darkness had fallen by the time we sat down to our meal. It was worth waiting for, the chicken deliciously roasted, the pita soft and chewy, and the salad, for a food lover like me, to die for. Keeping me firmly on the wagon, though, she served only apple juice. It wasn't Chateau Latour, but it tasted good.

As we were finishing, I asked her about her own family background.

And she told me.

CHAPTER 24

"My family is very old," she began. "Well, all families are, in one sense, but ours is traced in family records. We are Maronite Christians, a tradition founded by the Syriac monk Maron early in the fifth century. I was born in Beirut in 1980, in the middle of the civil war. Relations between the various ethnic and religious groups in Lebanon have always been tense, but in 1975, things fell apart. It was terrible, especially in Beirut, and it went on year after year. Historians write about phases in the struggle, but for ordinary people, most people that is, it was one long nightmare of gunfire crackling in the streets, rockets whistling in and exploding, screams and more explosions outside your window in the night. There were times of relative calm, but you never knew when all hell would break out again. It could be any moment, anywhere. Out in the streets and markets, you could never feel safe. You never were safe.

"We lived in a middle-class, predominantly Christian neighborhood in East Beirut. Our family was my father, Rafiq, my mother, Jamila, and my older sister, Mariam. Family was all-important to us—the four of us, together with an innumerable network of grandparents, uncles and aunts and cousins, then cousins of cousins. It seemed as if everyone we knew back then was related somehow.

"I am sure that in times of warfare, if families are not torn apart, they draw even closer. I have said my father's name was Rafiq, but to me he was always Baba. He was not a large man, but he stood ramrod straight, and to me, from when I was a toddler, he was like Hercules. He had dark eyes and a carefully trimmed brown mustache. He was, in my recollection, an intense, solemn man, driven by conscience and purpose."

"You keep speaking of your family in the past tense," I observed.

"Yes, past tense," she said, solemn like her father. "I will come to that shortly. But first I want to tell you the good memories. My mother—Mama—was slender as a young tree. She was Egyptian on her mother's side and had that sun-polished coloring. She did wonderful needlework, which she sometimes sold on consignment in the markets. She also played the piano and sang like an angel. She laughed often and made me laugh. I adored her, wanted to be exactly like her.

"My sister, Mariam, took more after Baba, I think—earnest and conscientious. She was two years older, so sometimes she bossed me around, but otherwise we were almost like twins; our lives were completely intertwined. Like Mama, she had a beautiful voice, and they would sing these duets together, either planned or just spontaneous.

"On holidays, and especially on Easter, we had these huge, boisterous family gatherings, usually at the home of my Jiddo Youssef up in the hills—'Jiddo' is grandfather; Youssef was Baba's father. Mariam and I ran wild with a dozen or more cousins, Mariam trying to organize everything. The grownups ate and drank for hours and then sang and danced. I was too excited to eat much of anything.

"Although I didn't start noticing it until I was five or six, however, the civil war was constantly menacing all this and eating away at it. The war was crazy, chaotic, with eight or ten factions fighting each other or fighting among themselves—Palestinians, the PLO, Sunnis and Shi'as, Christians, Syrians, Israelis, Hezbollah, you name it. Many parts of Beirut were blown to rubble, and after that they kept shooting at the rubble.

"I didn't know about it until afterward, but Baba worked behind the scenes on behalf of the Maronite militia. He was an investment banker with Credit Lyonnais in Beirut, so he was well placed to arrange loans and fund transfers and such things. Was it legal? Under such conditions, legality becomes blurred and confused, wrangled over like everything else. But it was certainly dangerous.

"And then one day, the fourth of October, 1987, Baba didn't come home in the evening. We waited. Mama placed telephone calls. They said he had left the bank around the usual time, six o'clock. He commuted to work in his Peugeot, and both he and it were missing. We grew more desperate, more frantic, but to no avail. Weeks passed with no word, nothing. He apparently had been, as they say, 'disappeared.'

"Mama was devastated, though she tried to hide it from Mariam and me. Our life went on, hollowed out but resolute. For our sake, Mama sometimes still forced herself to play the piano and sing with us, but it was never the same as before."

She stopped, gazing into dark memory.

After a while, intuiting what would come next, I whispered, "You don't have to tell me any more."

She sat up straight and said with controlled ferocity, "But I will. I want to tell you. I think I need to tell someone, someone who ... but no, I just want to tell it to you. I'm sorry, there is no explaining this. Please, just keep listening. I can get through this. I will get through this.

"So, Baba was gone. We clung to hope, or at least we professed hope, but he was gone. The war went on. Life went on—but not for much longer. One day, another one day—I have since learned that it was June 22, 1989—Mama and Mariam and I were crossing a city street to where our car was parked. I ran around to get in on the far side when the world erupted and I was thrown onto the sidewalk. Our car was thrown too; it landed just short of me. The noise was deafening, and all was smoke and dust and shock. I remained conscious, I think, and I must have been screaming for Mama and Mariam. People were shouting and running all about, but not Mama or Mariam, mostly men. Then I was up and running in sheer panic, crying for Mama. I don't know exactly how it happened, but as I ran, a man was holding me by the arm. I didn't want to go with him, but he was much stronger. There were other men running with us, down narrow, twisting streets and then through a gate into a courtyard and up a flight of steps and along a balcony and into a room, an apartment, apparently someone's living quarters.

"I was gasping for breath and screaming for Mama. There were some women in the apartment, of different ages, cloaked in black hijabs, though with their heads now uncovered. They tried to calm me down, but I was out of my mind. The men who had been running with me crowded into the apartment too, some of them carrying guns and brandishing them fiercely, as if they were going to shoot at all of us, but they didn't. Some of the men wore headscarves, others perhaps had lost theirs in the turmoil.

"I knew they were Arabs, of course, and though I didn't know which faction they might belong to, I was naturally terrified of them. The women kept stroking me and trying to pacify me. Their Arabic was, for me, strangely accented, but I understood them easily enough—'Peace, child. Quiet yourself now. It's all right now. They won't hurt you. Would you like some tea and cakes?'

"How long that went on I couldn't say, but eventually I must have fallen asleep or just passed out from exhaustion. When I woke up again, it was dark and I was momentarily disoriented until shattered fragments of memory chased in my mind and I cried out again. Immediately someone was cradling me to her breast in the dark, no doubt of it being a matronly breast, and cooing to me. I knew it wasn't Mama, and it felt almost disloyal to accept this comfort, but I desperately needed comforting. I relaxed into her warmth and presently fell back asleep.

"It was light again, daylight assisted by lamplight, when I woke up once more. The place was astir, people moving about and murmuring, coughing, grunting. I was on a cushioned couch, wrapped in a quilt. The night's sleep seemed to have relieved my panic, but certainly not my fear and distress. One of the older women, who must have been watching, came over and knelt beside me, saying, 'Poor child, poor poor child. It will be all right, little chick, but you must be brave, be a young lioness. The valiant ones have rescued you, but no one else could have survived. I must tell you this; we cannot pretend this world is even a finger of paradise.'

"I shook my head, still clogged with slumber. 'Mama? Mariam?' I mumbled.

"Tears welled from her old eyes and slid down her cheeks. 'If they were with you, they are now with Allah.'

"I shrieked in protest, but it was weaker than the day before. I knew she must be right. How could they have survived that horrendous explosion?

"Perhaps because of my outcry, a young Arab in military fatigues came and squatted next to the old woman. Seeing him, with his enigmatic dark eyes, brought it home to me. 'The bomb!' I shouted. 'The bomb that blew up—you set off the bomb that blew up, that blew them up! You killed Mama and Mariam!'

"'No, no!' the woman gasped, horrified.

"'She's right,' the man said to me, 'it wasn't us. If you've suffered loss, we're very sorry for you, but the bomb wasn't ours. The damned Israelis probably, or the Christians or the Syrians, but not us. They were trying to kill us.'

"'Christians?' I stammered. 'No, that can't be . . . '

"'Ah,' he said, 'that's how it is. I thought it must be so.' And to the old woman he said, 'Your kitten is a Christian. It's no fault of hers, it's just where Allah has assigned her.' He tousled my head and bounced to his feet and strode off.

"The woman leaned closer and said, 'Never mind him. They talk big, but if we didn't feed them, they would shrivel and die like a weed in August.'

"So they fed me and bathed me and found fresh clothes for me. There were, as it turned out, three other children there, but they were all younger than me, and we didn't interact much. Rubbing shoulders with all those people, I was still lost and alone, and in my agony, I began the drift into Samarkand."

"Samarkand?" I asked.

"My word for it. I had heard the name, and it sounded distant and magical. It became my refuge, my hiding place. But also my desert place.

"What was real? What was fantasy? I don't know; to me it was all one thing, where memories, current events, and dreams were equally real or unreal. When immediate life—the real world—became too painful or terrifying, it just blended into Samarkand. It was like drifting through wide, empty spaces where the light was filtered through pastel-hued mists. Sometimes I would eventually come to an oasis surrounded by palm trees and giant ferns. Camels would come to drink there, and other animals too—zebras and antelopes and giraffes. I would stand there and watch them for hours; it seemed so peaceful. But sometimes, not always, predators like enormous hyenas or tigers would come and attack the other animals and chase them off.

"Other times in Samarkand I would come to a city with fantastic architecture and tall, dreamy towers. People were milling in the streets, but they ignored me or didn't see me as I wandered among them. At least once, I remember, there was a beautiful Indian princess about my age dressed in a gorgeous sari. She was in this elaborate procession, and as they went by, she looked directly at me with a sober gaze, and I thought she understood."

She fell silent. Presently I asked, "What happened? How long did the Arab group keep you?"

"About a week, perhaps, I'm not sure. The same young soldier—his name was Muhammed—questioned me about my family. At first, I was afraid he might mean them harm, but then I realized he and his cohorts hadn't harmed me. Anyway, of course, I was frantic to get back to them, to whoever was still alive. So I told him as much as I knew about where Jiddo Youssef and Teta Bahar—that's Grandma Bahar, Mama's mother, a widow—about where they lived. I don't know how, but they located Teta's house. She lived in a village perched on the city's edge and slowly being absorbed into it.

"One day the black-clad women hugged me and wept over me, and Muhammed took me outside into the dusty courtyard. It was a hot, windy day. An ancient, decrepit-looking motorcycle was there with a sidecar attached to it, probably something abandoned by the French when they left in the nineteen forties. It took Muhammed some doing, but he got it to fire up, snapping and popping erratically. He sat me in the sidecar and off we went.

"I must say that, for all the distress I was in at the time, that ride was exhilarating and even fun. We careened through half the back streets of Beirut, or so it seemed; I assume he was avoiding the various enemy-controlled sectors. But finally we came to an area I began to recognize, and Muhammed pulled up in front of an open-air market stall displaying leatherwork and various fruits. He gave a shout and pointed and waved, and another hijab-cloaked woman came out. He talked rapidly to her, pointing some more, and then told me I must go with her. She would take me to Teta Bahar. He scowled at me, manfully refusing to show any sentiment, and entrusted me to the mercy of Allah, and then hopped back on the bike and sped off.

"The woman took me by the hand and led me down some alleys and across a few wide streets, and before I knew it, there was Teta Bahar's house! I cried out for joy, and the woman looked all around apprehensively and then gave me a wet kiss on the forehead and pushed me toward the house. I didn't look back to see if she was still there. I just ran through the gate and up the winding pathway to the kitchen door, the door we always used. I banged on the door and then opened it. It wasn't locked, which meant she must be home. I shouted "Teta! Teta!" and ran through the kitchen to the front room. Teta was struggling to rise from her chair with a look of alarm, and when she saw me, she screamed and fell back into the chair in a faint. I rushed to her and hugged her and smeared her face with my tears until she came around, and then she hugged me for a long time, murmuring, 'My angel, my angel' about a hundred times."

CHAPTER 25

"Teta was torn between wanting to find out what had happened to me and not wanting me to be upset by telling her. I wound up giving her an abbreviated version—but truly, that was about all I knew. Having believed me dead, she was now aghast and rejoicing at the same time. She was a dignified and cultured lady but not physically very robust. Her face was like an overripe fruit, sweet and full of wrinkles.

"She of course told the other members of our family of my survival and miraculous return, and they came to visit and cosset me and marvel over me, but I stayed with Teta Bahar for the next nine years. With her, really, I grew up.

"Even though occasional horrors like our bombing still occurred, at that time the civil war was finally winding down into an uneasy peace, and Teta felt comfortable taking me on short walks in the direction of the countryside. She let me help in the kitchen, chopping vegetables and making hummus. She had a good idea of how much I was suffering from my loss, if not exactly what I was suffering. I was, I think, recovering from the first stunned shock but struggling as the reality of what had happened forced itself on my mind. Having found Samarkand in those first days with the Arab fighters, I now was trying more deliberately to keep finding my escape there. In a way I found it—I knew how to get there—but it was gradually changing, against my desires, from an enchanting and magical place to a place of desolation and lostness, with endless barren hills and gullies. I kept trying to find the right pathway, but boulders would block the way or the path would just disappear.

"So Teta was trying to draw me out of this dreamland that was turning nightmarish. What helped most in the long run were the stories she told. Teta always had stories to illustrate anything and everything. To a degree, I suppose, her stories were like my Samarkand, a way of coping—except that she was in control of her stories. They were safe for her because they were rooted in the one who is security itself. She needed that security—well, in the end, we all do—but she knew she needed it because she had had a difficult life. Her husband, my Jiddo Hakim, died of a heart attack when I was only two, so I don't remember him. I have learned, though, that he was a jovial but erratic man who jumped from one career to another. He was what today we would call bipolar, swinging from energetic activity to depression and bitter anger. I am sure he beat Teta Bahar. And I believe it was her faith in Christ that saved her, mentally as well as spiritually."

Again she paused. After a while, I prompted, "What kind of stories?"

"What kind? Oh, every kind, though they were always about Jesus. They are now my stories. I know them all by heart. Would you like to hear one, just to get an idea of them?"

Did I want to hear a story about Jesus? I very much wanted Sareen to keep talking, so I said, "Please."

"Very well. Let me see. This will be the story of Jesus and the Lost Children.

"Jesus lived with his mother, Mariam, in a humble two-room house. Although the house was humble, it was built of indestructible Lebanese cedar. It kept itself miraculously clean, and it always smelled fresh and spicy.

"His mother, Mariam, was slender and dusky and perfectly beautiful. God's own brightness shone around her; flowers, when she walked by, bloomed and released their fragrance. She sang like the angel of the waterfall."

Here Sareen interrupted her story to tell me she now understood that these details were meant to remind her of Mama and Mariam, indirectly but comfortingly. The story went on:

"One day Jesus found a baby sparrow fallen from its nest. He took it in his palm and brought it home to Mama Mariam and asked her what he could do for it. 'Sing to it,' she told him. So Jesus sang to it until the baby sparrow could answer him with singing, and soon enough it gained enough strength to fly away on its own. Ever after that, he could hear it singing to him.

"On another day, Jesus found a baby rabbit lost from its burrow. He brought it home to Mama Mariam and asked her what he could do for it. 'Run with it,' she told him. So Jesus and the little rabbit ran and ran together until, one day, the rabbit found its burrow. It was home.

"Then one day Jesus found a boy about his own age who had been orphaned from his parents. His name was Izhar, and they talked for a while until Izhar became comfortable with Jesus, and then Jesus brought him home to Mama Mariam and asked her what they could do for him. 'My son,' she told him, 'it is time for you to decide.' And Jesus said immediately, 'He is my brother.' And just like that, Izhar had found his new home.

"So that's the story of Jesus and the Lost Children. What do you think?"

"It's ... touching. I can see how it might have helped you when you were, what, nine years old?"

"Yes, the stories certainly helped. Perhaps I could tell you just one more, if you have the patience for it."

"For you, I am all patience," I said honestly.

"Good. Well then, this will be the story of Jesus and the Poor Farmer.

"Once, when Jesus was ministering up in Galilee, he went off from his disciples for a time and journeyed by himself across the world to the kingdom of Persia. On the way, he walked across the three great rivers—the Tigris, the Euphrates, and the Nile. At that time, Persia was a kingdom of great wealth and splendor. The king's palace was all of gold and crystal encrusted with pearls, emeralds, and rubies. Court officials and prosperous merchants lived in houses made of marble and ivory. They ate four meals a day, their tables groaning with roasts and melons and grapes and pastries, and each meal lasted three hours.

"Yet, as everywhere, there were poor peasant farmers in Persia too, and one day Jesus met one of these.

"'I am poor,' the farmer said. 'I have no seeds to plant.'

"'Ask God,' Jesus told him.

"So the farmer prayed, but when his prayer seemed to go unanswered, he begged some seeds from a neighbor and planted them. That season, however, there was a great drought, a famine of rain, so the farmer went to Jesus and said, 'There is a famine of rain, and my seeds will not grow. What can I do?'

"'Ask God,' Jesus told him.

"The farmer prayed for rain, but none came right away, so he dug the hard earth for four days until he found water for his seeds. His plants grew, and he reaped a harvest, but even with a full belly, he soon died and went to heaven.

"In heaven, he saw Jesus and said to him, 'You told me to ask God for seeds, but none came, and I had to beg for them. Then you told me to ask God for water, but it didn't rain, and I had to dig a well. Then my plants grew, and I reaped a harvest, but I died anyway. Please tell me now: am I treated so poorly because I was only a poor farmer to begin with?'

"Jesus asked him, 'Who moved your neighbor's heart to share his seeds with you?'

"The farmer was mute, and Jesus answered, 'I did. Who gave you the strength to dig the well? I did. And now that you have died and come here to heaven, tell me, who has brought you here?'

"And that," Sareen concluded, "is the story of Jesus and the Poor Farmer."

"You're a good storyteller," I said.

"Only because of Teta Bahar. But thank you for listening. Would you like some coffee?"

"Coffee would be just right. Not the Turkish kind, though."

"We have some French roast here. There is a good deal of France still in Lebanon, and we tend to carry it with us." She got up and set about preparing it.

"Let me guess—you speak French along with English and Arabic?"

"Oh yes. Also some Italian now. As a child, I absorbed some French and English along with Arabic, which was my first language. And then in school we learned basic French and English grammar and vocabulary.

"Perhaps I should finish telling you about my stay with Teta Bahar. As I said, I lived with her until I was eighteen. The war destroyed my childhood, but she took the remains and restored them. She became both grandmother and mother to me, and though she was elderly and increasingly frail, she remained my rock of refuge. It took around a year, but with her help, I gradually left Samarkand behind and learned to cope with life as it really is. I returned to school and became, as far as possible, a normal child."

"Somewhat better than normal," I opined.

"No, I think not, only somewhat different. We are all unique."

I had been relishing the aroma of brewing coffee, and now she served it in good sturdy mugs. She took cream, but I had mine black.

"So your Teta Bahar survived till you were eighteen?" I said.

"One year beyond that, after I had enrolled at the American University of Beirut. She always told me the Lord would spare her until I was able to leave the nest, and she was right."

"I see. Well, the American University—a good place to land. Did you have a scholarship?"

"No, but there is family money that I inherited from my parents. My father may have been a daring partisan, but he was a shrewd and careful banker. Anyhow, yes, the American University was a good place for me. I majored in International Relations. I developed a number of good friendships, but the one with the deepest influence was probably Sherrill Lansdowne, my French literature professor."

"Aha."

She smiled; she had the best of all possible smiles. "No, not like that. Sherrill was in his mid-seventies and the courtliest of men, with silver-white hair always perfectly groomed. He was originally from Tennessee, and when *he* turned eighteen, it was just in time to join the army and take part in the invasion of Normandy."

"Which he survived."

"Which he survived, but no one survives war unscathed. The high point of his war experience, however, was the liberation of Paris. After the war, he returned to Paris to study and stay for some years. He married a Frenchwoman, but she died shortly before I met him. He referred to himself as an 'intellectual Baptist,' and he introduced me to what I suppose you could call intellectual Christianity, along with the glories of French literature. There was Molière and Montaigne and especially, for me, the *Pensées* of Pascal. I pored over his insights into human life and death and all the depths and nuances of their meaning until they became a part of me."

"A great philosopher," I put in rather lamely.

"And much more. So anyway, Sherrill—Professor Lansdowne—he, more than anyone else, introduced me to the life of the mind. And beyond that, he spent time with me and seemed to value my company. In his office, he served me iced tea made with mint and honey, along with small French cookies and pastries. He made me feel both thoroughly feminine and intellectually capable."

We sipped our coffee for a minute, occasionally looking at each other.

"Sherrill was a discerning man," I said.

"I hope so."

I stood up from the table and went around it and took her by the hand and said, crazily, "I hear music. Shall we dance?"

She came up to me—gracefully, the way she did everything—and then she was in my arms, and we were moving in a slow dance and she asked, "What are they playing?"

I heard it then, a quiet jazz combo playing a slow-tempo "Sophisticated Lady" with Ben Webster on sax. Stretching out the craziness, I murmured this information to the top of her head. I wondered if she could hear the music too, or if it was only in my mind. She moved with me as if she could hear it. All my aches and pains were far in the background.

As if reading my mind, she whispered, "You seem to be feeling better."

"Better than you know." And I kissed her. We kissed.

Heaven.

We danced. "I don't deserve this," I muttered.

"No, we don't deserve it. We give and receive it."

We danced.

"I've never really done well relating with women," I said, "never quite got it right. I understand most other things, but not your fearsome and wonderful gender. It's always been trial and error, trial and error … "

We danced.

"I can't answer all your questions, Adam, but there are a few basic things about us. We desire to be desired, and also we love to be loved. From that first day, back in Turin, I saw your desire for me, and it felt good, though it also—what is the word?—*flustered* me."

"That first day? It was that obvious?"

She kissed me. We kissed. And danced.

"Oh indeed, that obvious. But I also began to sense, even then, a possibility of love."

"There's a difference . . . "

"Yes. Desire is for *what* the other person is. It's full of hormones, blood rushing around, breathlessness, all aiming for ecstasy. Each in our own way, we all experience it—the desire, at least, if not the ecstasy. But love is for *who* you are, the inner person, who you *really* are. And love gives all, even dies, for the other."

We danced more slowly.

I said, "Of course you're right about the desire. If it wasn't love at first sight, it was certainly desire at first sight, there at that park, you over by the rose bushes. I still don't understand much about love, but I may have started loving you that day too. It's all so hard to fathom . . . "

"Don't *fathom*, Adam, not now. 'Adam,' you know, means 'man.'"

"Madam, I'm Adam ...."

She chuckled. "You remember that."

"And much more. But you said, 'Not Eve.'"

She took my face in her hands, leaning up to kiss me again, whispering, "Eve."

CHAPTER 26

When the morning sunlight woke me, my arm was curled around her and I had a new situation in my life. Not a problem, necessarily, but certainly a situation. I was launched on a new and fundamental learning curve. Up till then I had thought of "making love" as just a physical activity, something like gulping down an instant energy drink and then running a mile. But now my previous experience was being subsumed in this new, wholly other thing.

What thing? What is this thing called love? Part of it was opening yourself up on the inside, the region I suppose they mean when they talk about the soul. Opening up your soul for the other person to probe, search, explore, critique, appreciate, and try to understand.

Giving and receiving, but above all giving your soul. If such a thing exists. I was starting to wonder if it might.

If there was a problem here, however, it would be better not to dodge it. Over morning coffee at the kitchen table I brought it up.

"I'm wondering, Sareen ... please level with me about this. Did I take advantage of you last night—you and the whole situation?"

She contemplated the question for a minute then replied, "No, Adam, not at all. I chose it as much as you did. But I did not choose it easily or without some anxiety. It has been a long time since I last decided to trust a man in the way I have decided to trust you."

I didn't know how to respond to that, but it didn't matter, as she continued, "When I was telling you about my background yesterday, I didn't get beyond my college days. Now I must mention some of the rest. When I was twenty-five, seven years ago, I married a man, a fellow Lebanese, a Maronite like me. He was a medical student with a passion to discover a cure for AIDS. He was passionate in every way—for certain political causes, and for me. A year into the marriage, I found out he also had a passion for one or two nurses. We fought—there is no need to say more—and there was a divorce.

"Ever since that experience, I have been wary of romantic relationships. There was one man, but I broke it off before ... before I let it go as far as last night. So you see, that is why last night was, and is, important to me. I had doubted whether I could ever trust a man again."

Again it was hard to find words. She was trusting me, but was I truly trustworthy? Not a question to answer lightly. I said, "I'm honored, Sareen, and very glad. It's important to me too. So, now ..."

"We will live one day at a time. As Jesus said, each day has trouble enough of its own."

"I think I love you," I said.

She smiled. "We will work on that one day at a time too."

She rustled up an American breakfast for us, or maybe mostly for me—bacon and eggs with hash browns and cantaloupe. Watching her at the stove, the awful thought occurred to me, *What if she is as useless at cooking as I am?* Bahar's God, I mused, enabled her to live until Sareen was grown up; maybe he enabled Sareen to cook.

Morning-after philosophy.

Over a third cup of coffee, I called Ari on the encrypted super-cell. Just a whisker too late, I realized it was the wrong time again over there.

"You dork," he began, "this better be another bleeding emergency."

"I'm afraid things are looking up."

"From six feet under?"

"Nope. Just finished a terrific breakfast prepared by a brilliant but alluring female." I winked at Sareen. She just smiled that wonderful little smile.

"If she loves you, your count is up to one. All right, I'm awake. Fill me in."

"The short version is, Sareen and a buddy of hers rescued me from that hotel and drove me to what she calls a safe house. She and her buddy and their safe house are on the side of the angels. I'm convinced of that, and if I'm wrong, I was toast yesterday. Okay, that's that. The reason I'm disturbing your beauty rest, apart from forgetting the time, is that while I appreciate all your efforts in tracking down my nemesis, I'm pretty sure we've been barking up the wrong tree."

"Already deduced that, bro."

"It's not the praise-the-Shroud crowd, it's the hose-the-Shroud crowd."

"To a ninety-four percent probability. I have two or three possible hits on that side of the ledger, but I do need an hour or so of slumber every twenty-four to keep the edges sharp. I'll get back to you as soon as the data firms up a bit more."

"And I'm everlastingly grateful. Good old Tom Freebinder wouldn't head that list, would he?"

"We don't give out that information until we have higher resolution. Can you stand the company of your *femme fatale* for another ten or fifteen hours?"

"Hours? Try years."

He rasped, "You got it bad, and that ain't good."

And we left it there.

"How much of that did you follow?" I asked Sareen.

"Some of it, I think. I am brilliant and alluring. The rest is unimportant."

"The rest of it was about how we can save my personal endangered species."

"I have done my part, I believe. I did notice, however, that you now realize your adversary is not interested in defending the Shroud's reputation."

"Too true. The attacks have escalated since I began moving in that direction."

I finished my coffee and declined her offer of a refill.

I asked, "Would you be willing to tell me more about this Shroud-defending association you belong to?"

"Oh, it's not as formal or formidable as you make it sound. We are really no more than a group of friends who have discovered a common interest in the Shroud of Turin. For most of us, as for me, the enthrallment is with the man in the image."

"As you've said before. Okay, good. But as for you, how did you come to have this enthrallment with it—or him?"

"One thing at a time. Him, Jesus, I came to know and trust through my family's faith and most of all through my Teta Bahar, as I have told you. With regard to the Shroud itself, I learned about it from another teacher at the University, a young woman who taught your subject, history. She is Pamela Lapham, from England, and she has become one of my closest friends. From her, I learned the kind of things you are now discovering, the significance of the Shroud for the Christian faith as well as the controversy surrounding it.

"How can I express it? As nothing else does, the Shroud speaks to me of the crucified man and the meaning of his sacrifice for me, for all of us. Jesus didn't lose his life, he gave it up willingly so that by trusting in him we can share in his new life. I don't know how to say it any better than that."

"You say it well, and believe me, I respect your faith. You must understand, though, that for me, this whole possibility that the Shroud might be the real thing and the image on it the result of a supernatural miracle, a resurrection—that whole speculation still strikes me as outlandish and extremely improbable on several grounds."

"Several grounds," she said, nodding. "Such as?"

"Just consider the implications, the consequences. If that were true, at a single blow it would lend credence to all the superstitious humbug and all the ruthless power plays by the whole religious hierarchy, all the hollow bishops and predatory priests and hooded Jesuits over thousands of years. Back in Rome last week, I was looking at St. Peter's Basilica and wondering how Jesus, the peasant rabbi, would fit in there.

"And then, it isn't only the Catholic and Orthodox juggernauts in the picture here, but all the wild-eyed, fire-breathing preachers and all the culture-destroying missionaries and every lunatic leader of a hundred screwy sects. It's Pandora's box, Sareen."

I paused to catch my breath. As noted before, I'm good at overwhelming and alienating people with rational arguments. Would our nascent relationship survive this one?

Sareen was shaking her head. "I think you are mistaken, Adam. You are identifying two different things. To believe in Jesus—his person, his incarnation and miracles and resurrection—to believe in him and love him, that is one thing. But in no way does it require accepting or condoning all the things that self-proclaimed Christians have done over the centuries—all the absurdities and follies and atrocities. In the Maronite Christian community in which I grew up, many of the leaders were hard, corrupt, violent men, a form of mafiosi. To them, the term 'Christian' designates a political sect, and salvation is a fairy tale suitable for women and children. Or to mention one other example, your American Ku Klux Klansmen. When not wearing their bed sheets, they gloried in being outspoken Christians. They may even have actually thought of themselves as Christians. But were they followers of Jesus? He, of course, will make that judgment finally, but he leaves me free to make my own provisional judgment. He has even given us grounds on which to form that judgment: 'By their fruits you will know them.' On that basis, no, I do not accept so-called 'Christian' gangsters or Klansmen, or many others of that sort, as genuine followers of Jesus. Did he not warn us about wolves in sheep's clothing? And I commend to your attention, Adam, the parable of the wheat and the weeds.

"As for St. Peter's Basilica, it is pompous and pretentious, yes, but think of how human it is. There are surely better ways for us to memorialize what Jesus did, but when you consider *what* he did, monuments like the Gothic cathedrals become understandable. Jesus overcame death itself, and he did it for us. All of the other things we humans dread—pain, sickness, hunger, violence, rejection, aging—all of these are portents of the primal fear, death, the final extinction of this life as we know it. Jesus rose from the dead so that, trusting in him, we can rise and live forever with him. No wonder people sometimes get carried away. St. Peter's is a mixture of the worldly and the spiritual, just as we ourselves are."

By this time, I had caught my breath and, indeed, was taking a succession of defensive deep breaths. Either out of fear of losing an argument or fear of jeopardizing this amazingly good but vulnerable thing we were just starting, I decided this was a good moment to change the subject.

"Good point," I said, granting a small concession. "And then there's this democracy organization you're part of, Global Something, that does spy work and keeps safe houses. Tell me more about that and how you got involved with it."

She began clearing away the breakfast dishes but demonstrated female multi-tasking by also answering.

"It is the Global Organization for Democratic Faith, or GODF for short. Its origins were in the Lebanese civil war, even before I was born. Its central tenets, I would say, are that political democracy has been, historically, an outgrowth of religious faith, and that freedom and faith nurture each other. Take away one and you will undermine the other. When I say religious faith, however, I do not mean religious institutions that have evolved into political institutions. This is basically the distinction I just made with regard to Christianity and its history. The same distinction applies even more obviously to Islam. Since the inception of that faith, the faith itself has been corrupted and oppressed by political despotism and violence. Yet within the Islamic world, the only thing that has any chance of truly changing that political culture is the power of the faith itself. If in fact, that is, the faith itself actually possesses that power. It may, it may not. I do not know."

"But Christianity does?"

"Oh yes. More precisely, Jesus does, absolutely."

"Right. So then, how did you hook up with this organization?"

"That was also while I was at the university. The civil war was over as regards wholesale fighting and bloodshed, but it kept on simmering just beneath the surface. All those factions I mentioned before, they still distrust and even hate one another. Yes, even the Christians, and not only the gangsters in their midst. Christians are human too, with all the same fears and failings. Jesus calls us upward to a new and better life, but we are still waist-deep in the mire of this world, and some of us deeper than that. Human life is complicated, as you must know."

"I'm working on it. So you were at the university . . . "

"Yes. And, of course, my life to that point had sensitized me both politically and religiously. I kept abreast of what was going on in my country and in other countries in the Middle East and around the world. I imagine that all times in human history have been times of ferment—you would know better than I—but this was certainly one of them. Political oppression and religious persecution were terrible in so many places, mostly places not visited by the evening news. Anyway, I had many friends, some of whom were politically active. In particular, two of them belonged to the Global Organization for Democratic Faith. I attended some of their meetings, and it seemed a good fit."

"I guess it might be. And you went through their initiation?"

She laughed. "With blindfolds and ordeals? No, nothing like that. A pledge of commitment and confidentiality, yes. If you didn't know it a month ago, you surely know now that some secrets need to be kept secret. As I told you before, our organization operates both openly and secretly. Neither democracy nor religious freedom is universally popular—any more than, as you are finding out, investigating the true origin of the Shroud."

"Are you suggesting I should investigate it secretly?"

"I may suggest it, but I haven't started it. There is this stealthy alter ego called Kenneth Clark."

Bingo. "Yeah, right, there is that. How quickly we forget. So anyhow, your outfit started out in Lebanon but now operates all over the map. Is Lebanon still your home base?"

"Yes, but we have developed ties with compatible groups and funding sources, and while we have no direct connection with the Catholic Church, we are increasingly using a department in the Vatican as a confluence of pipelines. It's complicated and steadily evolving. In fact, I must return to Rome tomorrow on just such business."

I sighed. "Tomorrow?"

"Tomorrow. And you will be returning to New York?"

"I'm not sure. I'm thinking more about Jerusalem."

That stopped her, and she sat back down. "Jerusalem."

"Openly or secretly, I'm going to track this thing down. According to this theory that Rod Eglantine inclines toward, the place of origin may well be Jerusalem. The source. Ground zero. Supernatural miracle or something else—whatever it is, I've come this far and I've got to figure out the rest. It's who I am."

"Yes, I believe it is. Well, your forged papers are Israeli product, you said. Is their handiwork good enough to fool even them?"

"I'm leaning toward finding out."

"The Israelis won't laugh at the joke if they find you out."

"No, they wouldn't. Would I be right in guessing you're one of those who prays?"

"Definitely. And you have already made the list. But first, whichever way you jump, we must take you shopping for some new clothes. You can't go world traveling in Mansoor Sahadi's old sweat suit."

She was so right; I was still in those gray baggies, and both the good suits I'd brought from New York a week ago were in sad shape. I should try to stop falling down stairs and scrapping in alleys.

"Okay. Have you got an idea about where to shop?"

"The woman is always one step ahead. There is a large Carrefour a few miles from here."

Carrefour is the French version of Walmart, or just a bit more upscale, but gray sweats wouldn't be too outré there. We washed up the dishes together—a new height or depth of domesticity for me—then went out and got in the same white Passat that Bashir had driven us in two nights ago.

Two nights? My sense of time had been thrown completely out of whack, but that's what it was.

The day was warm but cloudy with some misty rain. On the way, Sareen, ever concerned for my safety, brought up the possibility of a disguise. My assailants had seen me, and anyway pictures of me were easy to come by. We discussed it and I decided that without a head rug, I was basically undisguisable, and no way was I shopping for a head rug. She went along with this, but we agreed we should change my wardrobe from the academic suit to nondescript casual. We settled on several pairs of bland khakis, several bland shirts and pullovers, a generic windbreaker jacket, and, in lieu of a toupee, a few varied hats—a cloth bucket hat, a straw Panama, and a Red Sox baseball cap that I'll never wear in New York. We also outfitted me with a new set of toiletries and stuff like that. If I were a woman I would go into detail, but I'm not. I'll just mention the new suitcase to put all this stuff into.

As we were driving back, Sareen said, "I know we just bought you a new shaver, but why not let your beard grow out? You've already got a couple of days' head start."

I said, "A beard? I've never worn a beard; that's probably why it didn't occur to me. The most basic appearance changer. But would you find a beard . . . you know, attractive?"

"I don't know. Life is full of chances. Are you willing to chance it?"

"No, I'll break in the new shaver as soon as we get back."

"Adam!" If she weren't driving, she would have stamped her foot. "I will not find you attractive if you shave any time soon."

Living with women, you see, is a matter of continual adaptation.

We got back to the Sahadi's safe house without further incident. We got me an e-ticket for Ben Gurion International aboard El Al, departing just before ten in the morning. Being one or more steps ahead, Sareen had already planned our meals and shopped for them while I was sleeping it off yesterday morning. We had a leisurely lunch and spent the remainder of this fortuitous furlough building our newly deepened relationship.

CHAPTER 27

Ari's revenge came just before dawn. Fortunately I'd put the black cell phone on the beside table, but its ring was like those grade-school fire alarms. I groped for it and fumbled around trying to switch it on. His voice came as a slight improvement to the alarm.

"You want the good news or the bad news first?"

"Huh?"

"I guess you need the good news. One of your suspects has floated to the top of the scum pool."

"Hey, Ari. If that's the good—"

"Correct. It came up from the deep scum. Like most of these fraternities, it has a harmless-sounding name, Free Action for Clear Thinking. The name was probably devised from the acronym, FACT. Give you a clue?"

"No, just get on with it."

"As you wish. FACT is a voluntary association of the type of folks that during the Enlightenment were called freethinkers. Having spent over two centuries freethinking their way through just about everything that can be thought, they now believe in absolutely nothing but their own free thought. Oh, did I say a voluntary association? You might join them voluntarily, but you don't leave them that way."

"Okay… but what's the problem with free thought?" That came close to describing how I regarded myself.

"How did I know you would ask that? The problem is that if you're a FACToid, your thinking is free, and so is everyone else's to the degree that they agree with you."

"Intolerant."

"That would be a reasonable euphemism for it. For public consumption, they promote secularism, atheism, science, and progress. In their heart, though, these fellows are pure nihilists. The intellectuals among them quote Nietzsche—"

"The demented prophet," I interjected.

"—who provided the Nazis whatever intellectual foundations they had."

"Rotten, noxious foundations."

"Cemented with the idea that the strong not only do in fact dominate the weak, and not only ought to dominate the weak, but they should be laughing in triumph while they trample on the weak."

"Charming. But what brought these winners to the top of your list? What's the connection with the Shroud?"

"Simple and straightforward. Religion tops their extensive hate list. That includes any and all religion, but what naturally provokes them most is successful and persuasive religion. Being as there is a great deal of that all over the world, FACT is constantly and fiercely provoked. And when Adam Hult, the world's foremost debunker, tackles the Shroud of Turin but then appears to have turned traitor and begun actually investigating its bona fides, that betrayal triggers all the alarms at FACT headquarters."

"Which is where?"

"London, but with branches all over Europe and coastal America and with outposts far beyond."

"Yeah, okay, now that I'm awake, I recall I've heard the name but never paid much attention to it. But look, have you got any evidence that these bozos send out trained hit men?"

"Still working on that, but the preliminary answer is probably yes. Hence this thoughtful wake-up call. So, when do I pick you up at the airport?"

"Sorry, change of plans. Ken Clark is off for Jerusalem later this morning."

Ari's reaction, predictably, echoed Sareen's: "Jerusalem! Adam, that's nuts. You may as well arm the grenade and stuff it in your mouth."

"You don't trust the goods you sent?"

"Not the point, dude. Ah, bananas, you're serious, aren't you? Just remember to pack a body bag for when they gather up your pieces."

On that promising note our chat concluded. By then Sareen was fully awake beside me, and I filled her in on the other half of the conversation. She, of course, was in full agreement with Ari, but my motivational thought remained: *What would Indy do?*

▪ ▪ ▪ ▪ ▪ ▪

It was noon on Thursday, May 30, when I deplaned at Ben Gurion International Airport, located between Tel Aviv and Jerusalem. Sareen was off to Rome and yours truly to Israel. Half an hour later there was a bounce in my step: two high hurdles had been surmounted, the security checks leaving Turkey and entering Israel. Security doesn't come any tighter than that. Thus far at least, Aladdin's Lamp was producing genies, and Ken Clark might be real after all. Sareen and Ari were excessive worrywarts.

Inside the airport it was pleasantly cool, but as I discovered soon enough, outside it was scorching hot. Owing to foresight I was wearing my coolest drab shirt, accessoried with my Panama hat and three-day-old stubble. At Carrefour I had also picked up wraparound sunglasses which, apart from concealment, were a practical item under the glaring Jerusalem sun.

High on my agenda at this point was keeping a low profile. Pursuant to that, I had booked into a good but reasonably low-profile hotel, the Eldan. To make the winding, climbing fifteen-mile (as the crow flies) commute, I chose a "monit sherut," or share taxi. The deal is you have to wait until the taxi fills up before it leaves, but then it drops you off at your own destination. I had to wait a sweltering twenty minutes, but I made no complaints to the driver, a woman who probably spent her off days as a prison guard.

The Eldan is on King David Street, close by the Old City. I checked in and took the elevator up to my room on the fifth floor. From its window, I could see out over part of the Old City, along with a crowded, probably Palestinian neighborhood.

I stood there for a long time, absorbing the view and pondering its endless significance. An array of sun-bleached buildings, a jumble of ancient and modern architecture and everything in between. A jumble of civilizations and religions. Not a melting pot but more like a high-energy particle collider.

What I could see was only the tip of the iceberg. The remains of most of the city's five thousand years of human habitation were another jumble, ten or twenty feet beneath the current pavement. Bronze age villagers, Canaanites, Jebusites, the Davidic kingdom, Assyrians, Babylonians, Hasmoneans, Romans, Byzantines, Abbasids, Fatamids, Seljuk Turks, Crusaders, Mamluks, Ottomans, European colonialists—it made the history of New York seem a matter of months.

The Promised Land. The Holy Land. The bloody holy land. Holy to the three great monotheistic religions. If their God was a jealous God, they were certainly made in his image. Blood and thunder and smoke. Smoke by day and fire by night.

The navel of the world, that was what medieval Europeans called Jerusalem. And how right they were. In terms of abstract geography the earth has no navel, but human history isn't abstract. By common consensus and common sense, we see the world divided into north and south, east and west. "East is East and West is West," Kipling wrote, and only mindless modern political correctness would fault his analysis. The Chinese sure wouldn't.

The navel of the world, where all four directions on the human compass intersect. Converge. Interact. Explode.

The navel of the world. Not just the focus, but the origin, the birth, the nativity. Biologically we may have come of age in Africa, but spiritually the source is Jerusalem. Michener picked the right title for his great novel on the city—*The Source.*

Spiritually. The word poses that eternal question: Is humanity's whole tumultuous spiritual quest merely a psychological and anthropological phenomenon, or is there more to it? If there is more, the more will be immeasurable, unfathomable, uncontainable. That's what Sareen had been trying to tell me. I wondered if, even during the next few weeks, I might discover whether or not she was right.

Down in the streets, people and cars and motorbikes moved and jostled much like in any other city, but this wasn't any other city. *Jerusalem.* Scholars debated the distant origins of the name—perhaps something like "place of the presence of God and peace."

Peace? No. During its long history, according to historical statisticians, Jerusalem has been destroyed twice, besieged twenty-three times, attacked fifty-two times, and captured and recaptured forty-four times. The Prince of Peace came to Jerusalem and was executed for blasphemy. What an interesting world.

So anyway, what was I really doing here? What could I do that I couldn't do at least as well in a New York library and on the Internet? There was no scholar or other human resource here that I wanted to talk with. Is there any investigative value in just "being there"? Thinking so seemed naive and even superstitious, but I had a feeling about this place, a hunch. Normally I resist hunches on principle; why not now? Because of Sareen's influence? No, if she could have kept me away from here, she would have. Because the Shroud was getting to me and softening up my brain?

Yes, that was the real question, and with all the grit I could muster, I steeled myself to answer it. Truth and reality without prejudice—that had always been my lodestar. Follow the evidence wherever it leads, using the mind God or nature gave me, using it as conscientiously as I could. Was I doing that in this instance?

I thought so. I had examined a great deal of evidence over the last few months, and this was where it led. Some quite solid evidence too, like Dr. Toomey's presentation, back in Antwerp, on pollen samples taken from the Shroud. That exhibit on the conclusions of several forensic pathologists. Dr. Dichter's evidence linking the Shroud with the Templars. Dr. Eglantine's evidence providing the links between Constantinople, Edessa and Jerusalem. Closely considered, a hunch like this could be the mind's subconscious evaluation of that evidence.

It could also, of course, be the influence of that crucified man in the Shroud. That would be Sareen's conclusion. Who knows?

I seemed to be asking that a lot lately.

I had picked up a tourist's map of historic destinations in and around the Old City. The ones I was interested in were all within about a mile of the hotel, easy walking distance for a strapping young stud like me. With vague notions of confusing surveillance, I changed my shirt and switched to the Red Sox cap. No one who knew me would expect that. From behind my sunglasses I could inspect everyone and everything. Out on the street I came to a vendor peddling falafel and veggies in pita pockets, reminding me that I was famished. I bought two of them and a bottle of Pepsi, and then found a vacant end of a bench to park on while I ate.

My first destination, arrived at through the narrow, twisting, noisy streets of the Old City, was the Western Wall, the holiest site—or the holiest remaining site—in Judaism. Sixty feet high, it's actually a section of retaining wall for Herod's Temple, which was still under construction when Jesus drove the moneymen out of it. The Romans under Titus Flavius Vespasian razed it to the ground at the conclusion of the Jewish War in AD 70.

The large plaza in front of the Wall was, as usual, teeming with people. The bearded, coat-and-hatted Hasidim, either impervious to the heat or raving masochists, were the most conspicuous, but they were only a few among the assorted hundreds.

The Wall was an obvious choice for the average tourist, but what about me? As I've said, I was following a hunch more than a plan. What was I looking for? Vibes?

That's about it. I meandered, I viewed, I meditated. Or I tried meditating, but it didn't seem to be working. Meditation, of course, isn't designed for quick results. I would have to be patient.

I exercised patience for thirty or forty minutes and then gave up and headed back to the hotel. An itch was starting, an itch to get on the Internet and see if I could find anything more about the connection Rod Eglantine had suggested between Jerusalem and Edessa, with an apostle named Thaddeus just remotely possibly bringing the Shroud fro and to.

Meditation, hunches, itches. What would the faculty members of the Columbia University History Department say?

But itches must be scratched, so once back in the relative coolness of my room, I booted up my laptop and went to work. The search turned out to be difficult on account of both the scarcity of genuine source materials and the abundance of oddball stuff. Anyone who Googled "apostle" or "Thaddeus" would see what I mean.

Eventually, though, the wheat started separating out from the chaff. The real Edessa, when you stripped away all the clutter, was a small city-state lodged uneasily between the powerful Roman and Parthian empires. It was four hundred miles north of Jerusalem, and it prospered by being a nexus of trade routes from the south, east, and west. Two of its notable kings were named Abgar. Abgar V reigned from AD 13-50, which includes Jesus's ministry years and the early period of apostolic journeying, most famously by Paul but involving others as well. Then there was an Abgar VIII, who reigned from 179-212. The stories or accounts connecting Thaddeus with Abgar don't specify which one it was. That was one puzzle I could try to solve.

A similar puzzle, more easily solved, was that the apostle's name was recorded in two different forms. In the earliest surviving history of Christianity, written by Eusebius of Caesaria early in the fourth century, he's called Thaddeus, the Greek form of his name. But in the nineteenth century some early documents in ancient Syriac were discovered which included an account of the same event, and there the apostle is called Addai. We have the same thing today, when John or Giovanni or Ivan are forms of the same name. This Thaddeus/Addai has been revered by the Assyrian church as its founder from the earliest times, perhaps as early as the first century.

The story essentially is this: Abgar was suffering from a disease beyond the skill of his physicians, and he heard of the healing miracles Jesus was performing down south in Israel. That part is plausible, considering the trade-route grapevine and the sensational character of the alleged healings. Abgar then sent a courier to Jesus with an appeal for him to come to Edessa and heal the king. Jesus declined, explaining—as the canonical Gospels record—that his calling was limited to Israel. But he commended Abgar's faith and promised that after being "taken up," he would send one of his apostles, anointed with the same healing power.

Addai—using the Syriac form—duly arrived in Edessa in the same year that Jesus was crucified and resurrected, a date given by both Eusebius and the Syriac version as AD 30. Modern scholars concur in that dating of the crucifixion, with AD 33 as a possible alternative. According to the New Testament book of the Acts of the Apostles, written as a companion volume to the Gospel of Luke, persecution from the Jewish authorities in Jerusalem caused regional scatterings of the first Christians (before they were even called that) during those seminal years. So it seemed reasonable to me that Addai could have pursued his mission to Edessa as early, or very nearly as early, as the sources claimed.

At that point, the story gets to its most intriguing and challenging part. In Eusebius's version, King Abgar saw a wondrous vision in the face of Addai and was instantly cured of his disease. The other version, the Syriac one, identifies this vision with the face on the Image of Edessa—the face of the crucified man imprinted on the cloth, which, as Eglantine told me, in its status as the Edessa Image, was undoubtedly historical. This second version says that Addai "placed the Image on his own forehead and went in thus to Abgar. The king… seemed to see a light shining out of his face, too bright to look at, sent forth by the Image that was covering him." Abgar was healed, and he and his court, and consequently most of the kingdom, converted from their paganism to faith in Jesus.

Now my meditations had plenty of fodder to chew on. First I went back to the question of which King Abgar was the actual one the story was about. Was it the one contemporary with Jesus or the one who reigned nearly two centuries later? Many scholars preferred the latter on the grounds that there is no solid evidence that Christianity came to that region prior to the late second century. On those same grounds, however, there is no evidence that it didn't. By the middle of the first century, Paul and his companions had taken the gospel farther afield than that. All things considered, the balance of probability favored the earlier Abgar.

I was jerked out of this erudite cogitation by the black cell phone ringing.

CHAPTER 28

"Double oh seven here."

"And I am Dr. No. Silly games can get you dead, Adam. Wise up. You always were too juvenile for the real world."

"Who dreamed up Aladdin's Lamp?"

"We did, me as the adult for serious purposes and you as Peter Pan. Now, are you braced for some more grim realism about your antagonist?"

"I'm sitting down anyway."

"Good. I should have said 'most likely antagonist.' There are others on the short list, but these chaps are the ones I think we need to concentrate on. I recall to your attention FACT, cute acronym for Free Action for Clear Thinking. Pseudo-intellectual nihilists presenting themselves as the only truly consistent rationalists. Still with me so far?"

"Jerusalem station tracking."

"Aagh ... So, you'll be surprised to learn that FACT is structured as a pyramid, like the Vatican but smaller and even more squirrelly. At the tip-top is one Morris Griffin, an interesting character. Briefly—I'll supply more details once you get your miserable body *home*—our friend Morrie is a millionaire shipping magnate, now in his sixties. He heads a mega thing called the Griffin Group. He started out as a deckhand in Bristol and worked his way up the ladder, using hard fists and a hard head. Rags to riches, with the losers strewn in his wake. Along the way, he developed his personal philosophy of life and, along with a few others, got FACT started during the 1980s."

"That philosophy of life—different from Gandhi's?"

"You could say so. He claims his great hero is Darwin, but he's less interested in biology than in social Darwinism—natural selection and the survival of the fittest as applied to human relations. Dog eat dog in order to become bigger and stronger dog."

"Well, that's how lots of folks get by. At least he philosophizes about it."

"Yeah, give him credit. As I mentioned in our previous parley, FACT devotes its strongest vitriol to dissolving the chains of religion. Griffin published a book just last year on that topic, ghostwritten but representing his ideas. A catchy title too: *Bury the Zombie God.* Here's just one quote so you can get the flavor, from the Preface: "Belief in any kind of god or any kind of miracle is, by definition, insanity."

"Aha, Sherlock, a clue! Morris Griffin is no fan of the Turin Shroud."

"Sure, but none of this so far is why you should be sitting down. Griffin and his chums don't just have a philosophy, they act on it. That word *action* isn't in their name just to be pretty. Which brings me down to the true grit. FACT is their public face, but there's another one on the back of their head, and it ain't smiling. They keep that one so well concealed that it took me, even me, several hours in deep cyberspace to uncover it. They've got an even cuter name for it, just among themselves—F/ACTION."

He spelled that out for me with the front-slash.

"Okay," I said, "what's F/ACTION's game?"

"As far as I can tell at this point, things like vandalizing or burning or blowing up various mosques, synagogues, churches, and Salvation Army posts. These fellas are ecumenical bigots. I'm still running down that sweet stuff, but I figured I'd better alert you before you slip on their poop."

"Well, as ever, Ari, I appreciate your concern, but how could they possibly twig Kenneth Clark?"

"*As ever*, bonzo, you have this aggravating habit of underestimating the foe. You're the amateur here; Griffin's boys are working on turning pro. They've already demonstrated their dislike of you in ways even you can grasp. They've *seen* you, dude. When's the next flight from Ben Gurion to JFK?"

"I'll check it out, but there are still one or two things I want to do here. I'm getting closer to figuring out this whole Shroud business. I'm not there yet—I may never even get there—but I'm too close to call it off."

"Do it from here. Finish it from here."

"Tomorrow, probably. Maybe before noon."

"Stone head. Brain-dead. Can you keep just one thought in mind?"

"Environmental awareness?"

He terminated the transmission.

I was hungry again, and no wonder, it was already seven thirty. Donning the Red Sox cap again, I went down to the hotel's main restaurant to get some dinner. The menu was in English as well as Hebrew, and I ordered some chicken meatballs, called *albondigas*, from the Sephardic branch of Jewish cuisine, in tomato sauce over couscous. With that, I had a single glass of Israeli Gewürztraminer, a nice spicy white wine. Notice I wasn't on the wagon any longer. While I had no intention of repeating my former overindulgent follies, a glass of wine isn't a bender. Unless it's the start of one, as I conscientiously reminded myself. For dessert, I had a slice of Linzer torte with coffee.

I didn't linger over the Linzer, though; the itch to get back to Edessa was too demanding. And an hour later, hovering over my laptop once again, I unearthed another chunk of historical evidence for the apostle Addai and his early connection with Edessa. As early as AD 190, Clement of Alexandria, in his book outlining the spread of the church during the second century, listed the known burial places of Jesus's disciples. Among these he included the tomb of Addai in Edessa. This wasn't proof that the King Abgar in question was the one contemporary with Christ, but it fit with that inference and gave it weight.

Moreover, to Clement's mind, and probably also in the mind of the historian Eusebius, Addai wasn't only connected with Edessa and with bringing a distinctly Shroud-like cloth there, but he was also flesh and blood enough, non-legendary enough, for his burial site to be remembered and recorded.

I got up and walked around the room, sifting, contemplating. Maybe it was the contemplating that brought Sareen to mind. I hadn't talked with her for the better part of a whole day. I got out the Droid that Ari had sent and punched in her number.

"Hello, Adam."

"Hi there. So you recognize my Droid all right."

"And your foolish alias."

"Foolish maybe, but will you remember it always?"

"Just as I already remember your birthday. When is your birthday?"

"The sixth of November. When's yours?"

"We women keep age-related things to ourselves."

"Hey, you already told me you were born in 1980. What about the date?"

"I think I will make you guess."

"What, 365 guesses? Come on. I told you mine."

"It's in the spring."

"Early or late?"

"Early if you are in Helsinki. Later, maybe, in Athens."

"I give up. Are you still in Rome? Can you tell me that?"

"It's in April."

I groaned dramatically. "One, two, three, four ... "

"Stop at twenty-three."

"April twenty-third?"

"What a good guesser you are!"

"That's Shakespeare's birthday."

"Then you will buy me two presents?"

"More than that, sweetheart."

She laughed—I loved making her laugh—and said, "No-o-o ... "

"That was Bogey."

"I know. Bogey to you too. Yes, I'm in Rome. And you, I imagine, are still in Jerusalem."

"How wise you are. Now that we've got the preliminaries out of the way—"

"We can speak of more important things. Let me guess this time. I guess that you have spoken with your friend Ari again during the day."

"Amazing. He called a couple of hours ago."

"I thought he might. And he still wants you to go back to New York."

"On the first plane out."

"He's right. Ari is a good friend, Adam. You are taking this matter too lightly."

"Ah, Sareen, our first disagreement, and it persists. I'm not taking it lightly, really. But like I told Ari, I'm making genuine progress in the Shroud research. Being here is helping. I'm not sure exactly why, but it's helping."

"How much longer?"

"You and him both. I told him tomorrow, maybe even by noon."

"I don't believe by noon."

"By sundown then? When Shabbat begins on Friday. Speaking of you and Rome and your business there, whatever it is, how's it going?"

I heard her heave a sigh, and there was a silence, and when she spoke again her tone had altered. "My business here has run into difficulties—even, perhaps, difficulties as serious as you are in. Please don't ask me for the details. But I have good friends also, and I pay attention to their advice."

"Ahh," I sighed back, "message received." I almost added, "Take care of yourself," but being a blackened pot myself, I settled for, "There's never a moment when you're out of my thoughts, Sareen. When will I see you again?"

"In your dreams perhaps? Are you one who dreams?"

"Sure, but that ain't the same thing, and you know it."

"No, it isn't. But for the present, it may have to suffice."

"I could come back to Rome when I'm done here."

"No. Truly, Adam, that is not a good idea. Go home. The world is small; time is long."

"She's not only brilliant and alluring, she's a philosopher. But that's a hard philosophy, Sareen. I don't know if I can—"

"I love you, Adam."

"You do?"

But she was gone.

But it was all right. Everything was all right. Just right. I called room service and ordered some coffee. Until it came, I stared out the window at all the moving and twinkling lights of the city, seeing stars.

What a romantic rascal.

That mood lasted until I recalled what she had just told me, that she was in a predicament of some sort, even a serious one. She was reluctant to share the details, but maybe I should have pressed her anyway. As it was, I felt not only clueless but helpless, useless. I wished, fleetingly, that I believed in prayer the way she did.

After the coffee came, I went back to my laptop and diddled around some more, but rather aimlessly. I didn't need more information so much as to digest all the information I had. The sooner I pushed this task to its conclusion, the sooner I could…

But she said not to come and join her in Rome. Why?

I wasn't seeing stars any longer. With a headshake and in a sober frame of mind, I forced myself back to work.

I thought about Jerusalem and its burden of history. Blood, sweat, toil, and tears. The whole Middle East, the cradle of civilization.

Cradle. School. Marketplace. Forge. Battleground.

Graveyard?

And Edessa, a small but essential part of the intricate tapestry. Like Jerusalem, a crossroads. Year after year, century after century. How many caravans? How many bearded men? How many swordsmen on horseback? How many brown-skinned boys driving goats down the road? How many women, either in the vibrant colors of the East or in the black veils of Islam, each one with her hopes and frustrations and secrets?

I felt a frustration of my own, something that had occurred to me before but that I had never felt as poignantly as now. It was about the modernist vanity, the modernist historical prejudice. In their own time and place, people have probably always entertained it, especially superficial intellectuals. It's the silly prejudice that leads us to imagine that people who lived and events that occurred a few thousand years before us were hardly more real than the land of Oz.

For such people, including myself at times, the long ago appears to be a tissue of mists, myths, legends, tall tales, and superstitions. All those people, if they lived at all, were benighted, ignorant, and credulous. Maybe they never did live at all. The past never really happened.

Except, of course, it did happen. They did live, love, procreate usually, and die. They were as real and particular as me and Ari and Sareen. As Mom and Pop and Sam. And they weren't stupid—they invented civilization.

Edessa. King Abgar, diseased and in pain. Jesus, drawing crowds on the hills of Galilee. Addai, sent on a healing mission. Mary Magdalene and those other women at the tomb owned by Joseph of Arimathea. Peter and John running and finding the abandoned grave clothes.

Were Peter and John real? Even as real as I am?

But those are just stories, inventions.

At this point, my historical training came into play—or maybe just common sense, coming to the rescue of my historical training.

They are stories, yes. Inventions, only possibly.

All our written history boils down to stories. My family history, or Sareen's. Iceland's history. Magellan's voyage around the globe. The past can only be remembered and related as a vast compilation of stories. Our stories are the heritage of our human heart and soul. Absent human stories, the remnants studied by archeologists are mute, while in company with our stories they serve a valuable function, confirming or correcting.

Remnants ... like the Shroud of Turin. With a story to tell. Or a witness to the story.

These days, though, our trendiest sages are those postmodern super-skeptics who claim that all our stories are sheer invention. But are we really that impoverished, cut off, derelict?

Obviously not. Those people lived. Through accounts, recitals, diaries, letters, chronicles, journals, and narratives, we can be as in touch with them as I am with, say, Queen Elizabeth II of England.

In all this musing, I kept cycling back to Beatrice Dichter's point that we *have* the Shroud of Turin—an irreducible, durable, undeniable historical *object*. All my research thus far tended to the conclusion that it was probably not a medieval forgery; it probably had a longer history. As she said, it has a story to tell.

And as for the serious complication of that radiocarbon dating? Erika Steiner, no intellectual lightweight, accepted it. I would have to tackle it.

But not now. It was midnight. I made my ablutions and went to bed.

CHAPTER 29

I went to bed at midnight but not quite to sleep. My healing body was worn out again, but my brain was on overload. I told it to shut off, but it wouldn't obey; way too much was happening in my life. I tried all the tricks: thinking peaceful thoughts, imagining the sound of gentle waves lapping up on the shore. *Susurration* is the word for that sound, one of those perfect words.

I rolled over, trying to get more comfortable. I thought more good thoughts, peaceful thoughts, peaceful sounds.

I rolled over again, and some more, and somewhere in the dark hours I must have fallen asleep in spite of myself, because it was full daylight when I woke up again, slowly and groggily. After rubbing my eyes and fumbling for my glasses beside the bed, I checked my watch and saw it said a quarter to ten. Unless the watch had gone haywire, I was getting a late start on a big day. But at least, apparently, I had got some sleep after all.

I was recently discovering that the old morning prep goes faster when you don't shave. Twenty minutes later I was down in the hotel's coffee shop, wearing a different new drab outfit, with the bucket hat and a wino's beard. They served me anyway, good strong coffee and a couple of *burekas*, pastries made of a flaky dough and stuffed with cheese, spinach, and mushrooms. I left crumbs all over the table, but I was fully awake and good to go.

I had two possible hunch-inspired destinations: the Church of the Holy Sepulchre and the Garden Tomb. The first, in the

Old City, is the traditional site of Jesus's crucifixion, burial, and resurrection. It was so identified as early as the fourth century, when the Emperor Constantine ordered the construction of a magnificent basilica to enshrine it. The monument has been damaged, destroyed, and rebuilt several times over the intervening centuries—this is Jerusalem, after all—but the current church occupies the same site.

The Garden Tomb, half a mile north of the Holy Sepulchre and outside the Old City walls, is the alternative site for those momentous events. It was found and identified in the nineteenth century by some Protestant scholars who doubted the traditional siting on several grounds. These include the Gospels' testimony that Jesus was crucified and buried outside the city walls, and the fact that the traditional site had been dominated for centuries by the Roman Catholic and Greek Orthodox churches and still was. Politics gets in everywhere.

In any case, my option was to visit both sites or just one or the other. For no particular reason, certainly not religious partisanship, maybe just on account of my late start, I decided to simplify things and just walk over to the Garden Tomb.

As I walked through the streets and among the people, under the searching sun, I questioned once more—as Ari emphatically would have—my motives for doing this at all. The hunch explanation was inadequate and maybe even evasive. The truth, which I was dubious about swallowing , was that this was exactly where my whole Shroud exploration seemed inexorably to be leading.

If the Turin Shroud was the cloth that the Knights Templar hid and venerated, and if before they looted it from Constantinople it was the Mandylion, and if before the Byzantines ransomed it from Edessa it was the Image of Edessa, and if it was brought to Edessa by the apostle Addai in the first century, then the Old City of Jerusalem was where I should end up. I had no solid proof of any of those transactions, but I did have a preponderance of evidence and reasoning. The Shroud came from somewhere.

But if it came from here, the implications could shatter whole worldviews. Sareen was at peace with those implications, but I wasn't yet. I was high up in the air, without a wing and a prayer. It was, just about literally, dizzying.

Along with the other tourists, I paid my fee at the gate and went over to inspect the Garden Tomb, not without goose bumps. The tomb is a cave carved into an ancient rock wall, undoubtedly intended as a burial site. The evidence from the Gospels indicates that Jesus was buried in a tomb like this, if not precisely this one, and there is no evidence to the contrary.

And then the Shroud—or maybe, at that point, just the shroud. The Gospels say that Peter and John found it lying there, left behind, abandoned. The body, the man, the Master was gone, one way or another, but the grave clothes were left. What would the disciples have done with the shroud? They had far bigger matters on their mind at the moment, but would they have ignored it? Tossed it out? Forgotten about it?

Another question: Was the image we see on the Shroud today, which evidently has been seen for the better part of two thousand years, already visible to those bewildered fishermen? It seemed there was no way to know.

And then, whatever they may have seen in it and whatever they thought about it, if the disciples took custody of the shroud, why don't the Gospels say so?

On the other hand, the Gospels are mum about a great many other things as well, things that stir our curiosity to the boil. What became of Mary's husband, Joseph? What took place during those two silent decades between Jesus's boyhood and his ministry? And perhaps above all for my purpose, what did Jesus look like? Did he look more or less like the man in the Shroud? The Gospels don't say. So their reticence about what the disciples did with the Shroud is consistent, if frustrating.

And then, after the crucifixion, what happened to that frightened, grief-stricken, demoralized group of men and women to transform them into a jubilant band that fanned out spreading the good news, risking everything and fearing nothing? Whatever it was, it must have been something extraordinary. They said they had seen Jesus alive again, fully and bodily alive, such that death could never touch him again.

If that happened, it was beyond extraordinary.

If it happened. If it wasn't some sort of mass hallucination.

Hallucinations, though, don't leave images.

None of this amounted to an epiphany, but it was more grist for my mental mill. By then it was past one o'clock and the heat was becoming oppressive. Somewhat at loose ends, I was muddling over what to do next when the Droid rang. It was Sareen.

"Sareen?"

"Yes, Adam. Where are you now?"

"Still in Jerusalem. At the Garden Tomb."

"Very well, I am familiar with the place. Wait for me outside the gate."

"Wait for you! You're here, in Jerusalem?"

"Yes. I'll be in a taxi, in perhaps fifteen minutes."

I went out to the gate. I would need at least fifteen minutes to figure out how I felt about this latest twist. Or this latest rescue effort, if that was what it was. It was like being caught up in "The Perils of Pauline" in reverse.

The taxi came, she paid the driver, and he drove off. I must admit she looked awfully good in a blue-trimmed white sundress and a white hat with a curving brim. Some sixth sense told me to enjoy it while it lasted. She just stood there, glaring.

I opted for the attack: "It's great to see you, Sareen, but why do you keep following me around?"

She gave a little jerk of the head. "Come. We will walk back to your hotel."

"Why not keep the taxi and have him take us?"

"That would be a good idea, Adam, but I was too preoccupied to think of it."

I caught up with her and fell in with her rapid pace. I didn't have to ask her how she knew which hotel, since I was with her when I booked it. But I still wanted some answers.

"Why, Sareen?"

"You know why. Don't pretend otherwise."

"I know how you see it, and how Ari sees it, but you have to understand how I see it. It's a lame cliché, but there's light at the end of the tunnel. I don't understand it all yet—far from it—but the Shroud is starting to make sense."

"Fine, excellent." She was scanning the way ahead; maybe I should too. Environmental awareness.

"Listen, Sareen, do you know anything at all about the Image of Edessa? Do you know where Edessa was, what it was? Have you heard about the apostle Thaddeus, aka Addai?"

"I'm glad you're making progress, Adam. I truly am. But this is not the way to do it, not under these circumstances. This is not a time for action-film heroics or male stubbornness. I'm sorry if my coming offends you, but—"

"I'm not offended. I'm glad to see you. Look, it's lunchtime. Have you eaten?"

"I haven't thought about it."

"On the way over here, I passed a promising-looking cafe, not too far ahead up here. What do you say?"

"Whatever you like, as long as we're not out in the open."

We came to the cafe and went in. It was crowded and noisy, but we got a table that two older Jewish men were just leaving. A busboy came and removed their stuff and wiped the tabletop with a damp cloth.

By this time Sareen was in a state I'd never seen before, angrily swiping the tears from her eyes. Belatedly, it occurred to me that there might be something going on here besides me.

"What is it, Sareen? This isn't just about my stubbornness, is it. It's also whatever's been going on in Rome. Can you tell me?"

She sat down, almost flopped down, on the wooden chair and looked daggers at me. Evidently just holding herself together, she said, "I should tell you, shouldn't I."

"That's up to you. But I hope you'll tell me. I want there to be ... less and less between us."

She kept glaring and fighting back tears. A waitress came over to take our order, and Sareen shook her head. I ordered some bottled water and pita bread and hummus and olives for both of us; if she didn't want to eat anything, fine.

"All right," she said, "I will tell you. But just listen, please? Don't ask questions."

I leaned forward to hear her over the surrounding noise.

"We, our organization, we have a team over in eastern Ethiopia. Three people, three friends of mine. They have been working on a dispute between two tribes over water rights, in a region experiencing its fourth year of drought. The dispute is complicated by the fact that one tribe is Muslim and the other Christian, so there is little trust between them.

"Over the last several weeks it seemed like our team was close to brokering a deal between them. One of the reasons I needed to return to Rome was that I am part of the oversight group. The team itself has authority to make decisions on the ground, but we try to back them up with information and advice.

"Shortly after I arrived in Rome, however, we learned that the situation had taken a turn for the worse. A young man of the Muslim tribe was stabbed to death, and they are blaming it on the Christians—who, of course, deny it absolutely. Our team was caught in the middle, trying to forestall an all-out battle while catching blame from both sides. Being outsiders, we are never deeply trusted ourselves. Things were deteriorating so rapidly and unpredictably that we—the oversight group—decided the best thing was to temporarily evacuate the team. We have a small plane and a pilot over in Addis Ababa that can be used for that purpose. But all three team members have agreed to stick it out for the time being. So all that we, the others, can do for now is watch, and pray."

The waitress had brought our food, but neither of us was eating.

"So anyway, even with all that," I said, as quietly as I could and still be heard, "you came here, to Jerusalem."

Her tears erupted and she pulled some tissues from her handbag. "They are in danger," she said shakily, "you are in danger. At the moment I could do nothing more for them. Perhaps it was stupid and impulsive, but ... "

I took her hand, the one not daubing at tears. "We should all be so stupid and impulsive."

She shook her head, her lips pressed together, then burst out, "They were so close! So close to reaching a settlement—so close to finding a way to share their water. And now this. But this is so often the way it goes."

I squeezed her hand, not finding anything to say. Probably best.

"Well," she said, noticing the food on the table, "you should eat something. You must be hungry."

I was hungry. I ate an olive and scooped up some hummus in the pita. While chewing I said, "Hungry or not, you should eat something too. At least drink some water."

She forced a smile. "Yes, I suppose so. You won't want a fainting lady on your hands." She drank, then started nibbling on an olive, pensively watching me stuffing my tummy.

"So what next?" I asked after a while.

She tucked the tissues back into her handbag. "We have to get you out of here. If you are ready, that is."

"Ready and willing. I just have to get my gear from the Eldan, and we can check on the flights."

She paid our bill and we went back out into the hot brightness. Slipping my sunglasses back on, I scanned one way down the sidewalk. A lot of pedestrians were coming and going, but I noticed a man leaning against a signpost reading a newspaper. Looking the other way, I saw another man about thirty yards up the street, peering in a shop window. He glanced toward me momentarily from under a billed cap. He was dressed much like I was, nondescript, but he knew he'd been made the same instant I recognized him from our recent rumba in an alley in Istanbul. I grabbed Sareen's hand and pulled her back into the restaurant, but not before seeing both men lunging into action. We dodged through the customers and banged through the double swinging doors to the kitchen, where a couple of cooks gaped with faces like big question marks. I grabbed a large dishtowel off a hook and thrust it to Sareen, saying, "Toss the hat and put this over your head and start chopping something."

"But … no—"

"Do it!"

I had noticed a narrow hallway leading to a rear exit. Ducking back out of the kitchen, I made for that exit just as the two men barged in the front door. It was like being in Sareen's action film, but this wasn't make-believe. I flung the door open, shouting "Move it!" to no one in front of me. Then I was in another alley. It's one of those facts we may register but never notice, that every row of shops in every city in the world has a dark, stinking alley behind it, along with the rear end of another row of shops. I flipped a mental coin and headed to my left. I heard the two guys come thrashing out behind me four or five seconds later.

Where they would try to run me to ground would be a place with no spectators. So far, this looked like their lucky day. I stumbled around some garbage cans and was just picking up speed again when one of them caught me by the arm and spun me around. I managed to scoot a few more yards into an open area behind one of the smaller shops, but the back of it was boarded up.

Box canyon. I turned to face them. One of them, the one I didn't recognize, had pulled a knife with a clean-looking six-inch blade.

Long enough.

Why not a gun? Probably because if they catch you with a concealed knife in Israel, you're in trouble. If they catch you with an unregistered gun, you're al-Qaeda.

The other guy, my thuggy buddy, shuffled around behind me, but he didn't try to tackle me or anything. Maybe they were in the mood for a little cat and mouse. I took off my sunglasses and tossed them aside. I breathed deeply in an effort to settle my nerves.

The one in front of me, with the knife, was taller than the other. He had close-cropped blond hair and old acne. Catching his breath, he said, "Where's the girl? Ah! In the restaurant."

"Not anymore."

"Doesn't matter. You're the one that made the appointment. Mister Smart Boy himself."

"Could be I have room for getting smarter."

"Sorry, out of room, out of time," blondy said, twitching the knife blade. Behind me, buddy snickered.

"Something I've done offends you?" I said reasonably. "Maybe we could work out our differences."

He shook his head slowly, like he'd seen in a hundred TV dramas.

"Some of us learn," he said, "some of us just don't. You think you're so bloody clever, *Doctor* Adam Hult, but we're not impressed. The miracle sheet isn't coming to save you. You seem to be the praying kind—now would be the time." A working-class British accent, maybe Norfolk.

Cat and mouse. I think he enjoyed this. He moved closer, two feet away, the blade pointed toward my belly button. I could smell buddy's garlic breath behind me.

"Manchester United? Arsenal?" I asked.

"What?"

"Just wondering which football club you yobbos fancy. Two or three more sentences and I'll nail it down."

"Bloody stupid Yank, it's you that's being nailed down and stuffed in a bloody dustbin, where nobody—"

As he spoke I wasn't studying accents but filling my lungs with air, and now I yelled suddenly, as loud as I could. His reaction was very slight but involuntary while I made a move similar to the one in Istanbul, falling and spinning all at once but in the other direction. My right foot caught his ankles and swept his feet aside, and this time, as he hit the ground with a thump, I landed correctly on all fours, facing buddy, who was snarling and launching himself at me, but I was lower than he expected, and as he sailed over, I scored with a short hard uppercut to his nuts. His whole body jerked, and he flopped onto the pavement in a fetal clench.

Blondy scrambled back onto his feet, waving the knife, and I faced him in what I think of as the Ari crouch. I feinted to the left and kicked to the right, past the blade, driving my heel into his kneecap. As the knee buckled, he screeched and collapsed to his left, supporting himself with the hand clutching the knife. I stomped on that hand and the knife skittered away. Buddy's free hand, the one not clutching his groin, clawed at my back pocket. I spun and kicked him in the side of the head, and he fell over, no longer enjoying this.

Fair fights are for amateurs. I kicked blondy in one ear and then grabbed the other ear and banged his head onto the pavement, interrupting his thinking process. Buddy was trying to scuttle away, but I kicked him in the kidney as a remembrance from our last encounter and then banged his head down as well.

I emptied their pockets. They both carried passports, probably as phony as mine. Blondy had a curious signet ring on his right ring finger; I took the ring and pocketed it with the passports. A quick search of the area turned up a coil of old rusty wire. Retrieving the knife, I used it to cut off pieces of the wire, probably dulling the blade, but I didn't care. I bound their wrists behind them and then bound them together by the necks, loose enough not to strangle them if they behaved themselves. So far, at least, they were behaving.

I wiped any prints off the knife, tucked it under blondy's belt, then headed for the Eldan Hotel.

Mighty Mouse!

ENDGAME: COMPOSITION

CHAPTER 30

We were well out over the Atlantic aboard a Boeing jumbo jet before Sareen gave any signs of cooling down. Hell hath no fury, for sure, even if the woman in this case hadn't been scorned. I had long since given up trying to explain myself to her, or for that matter to myself. Was I just by nature a heedless, manic risk-taker? I never would have thought so. I hoped I had gotten it out of my system.

Sareen, no doubt, hoped so too, but with no optimism. She had barely spoken to me for the last eighteen hours.

As soon as the three of us—me and the two goons—had gone out the back door of that restaurant, she had gone to the alley and looked around, but she decided that if she followed us she would only increase my problems. I told her that was absolutely right, but she wasn't mollified in the least. Her least-bad option, she decided, was to call the police and then to go to the Eldan Hotel and wait in the lobby and, I expect, pray, though she didn't admit to that. When I showed up there fifteen minutes later and a little scuffed up, she went into a sort of controlled meltdown. I took her up to my room and got a towel from the bathroom for her to cry into.

The details of that night are unromantic and hardly bear recounting. My best estimate was that she would never believe I could behave sanely until I demonstrated the ability for some unspecified period of time—reckoned in days, I hoped, but I feared it might be years. By playing the crazy hero, had I scuttled our whole relationship? Under those circumstances, though, what else was I supposed to have done?

Rational arguments like that weren't cutting it here.

On the other hand, here she was beside me, en route to New York. That must count for something. We had changed planes in Rome, but not before taking a brief detour to her apartment, where she repacked her suitcase and packed a second one. Why? Because she insisted on accompanying me the whole way. Possibly she didn't trust me on my own. Whatever, I wasn't contesting the case.

As I said, she started thawing (or cooling) somewhere over the Azores. She asked me about Ari, in that female way that prefers personal information to factual. I gave her some facts and tried to sweeten them with some flattering comments about his good nature, sense of humor, and so on. Ari's sense of humor is about as merry as the Terminator.

But the palaver seemed to be working. She nodded and hummed and kept asking questions. Meanwhile, to stay alive, we ate some contemporary airline food—we were flying business class—and drank bottled water.

It was five o'clock on Saturday afternoon in New York by the time Sareen Khouri and Ken Clark had passed through customs at JFK. And there was Ari Halevi waiting to greet us; I had of course given him encrypted information about our travel plans along with a summary of recent developments. He looked Sareen over with, I think, due appreciation and shook her hand. He didn't shake my hand but said, "Mr. Clark ends here. You carry the bags."

What price heroism? Thinking it best not to whine, I went along with their punitive games. Ari drove us in his Highlander along the Southern Parkway into Brooklyn. It was nearly as hot in the city as in Jerusalem and more humid, but the SUV's AC kept us comfortable. We stopped off at one of our favorite joints,

Hank's Diner, for some real food with local microbrews. While we were there, Sareen phoned one of her GODF contacts for an update on the situation in Ethiopia. When the call was done, she gave Ari a quick briefing, with the news that there had been no significant changes and the situation was still tense. She wasn't happy, but she wasn't crying either. When we finished eating, Ari took us over to his place to unwind.

The first thing I needed to do while Sareen and Ari got acquainted was to call my mom. Ari had given me the news, bad or good, it's hard to tell, that my pop had died several days ago while I was incommunicado. The funeral had been yesterday, about the time I was… but it wasn't worth trying to figure it out with all the time zone changes.

So I called her, and she was home.

"Hi, Mom. It's Adam."

"Oh, Adam! I tried to call you, but you never answered."

"I'm sorry. I lost that cell phone. It's probably in a landfill somewhere by now." I wasn't sure about that, but I was glad the thugs hadn't answered.

"Have you heard… about your pop?"

"Yeah, Ari told me. I just got back from a long business thing in Europe."

"It's a shame you couldn't be back yesterday when we had the service."

"Yeah. I'm sorry. I just didn't know."

"I understand, Adam. The people from Hillside Baptist, they took care of everything."

Hillside Baptist was a neighborhood church that Mom occasionally attended, without Pop, for unexplained reasons of her own. I was glad they seemed to have taken her under their wing.

Now, though, she was going to be more my responsibility. Not my strong suit, but I thought I was willing to try.

Ari was giving me a high sign. "Just a moment, Mom," I said.

"Tomorrow, Sunday," Ari said, "we're having a family pow-wow here, with dinner thrown in, say around four o'clock. See if your mom can make it."

I asked her, and she could; I think she sounded relieved. The two houses were within walking distance, but I told her Ari would pick her up.

With that taken care of, I joined them for coffee around the kitchen table.

"Why is it," Ari asked, "that some men's taste in women excels some women's taste in men?"

"Beware of jealousy, the green-eyed monster," I said.

"But I like his green eyes," Sareen said—to me.

I shrugged. "He's cute enough, for a leprechaun."

"A Jewish leprechaun?" Ari said.

"Beyond all the nonsense," I said, "we are going to have to figure out what to do about this hornet's nest I seem to have stepped on. Just a minute."

I went over and opened my suitcase and rummaged around until I found those two passports and the funny ring, wrapped up in a dirty T-shirt. I tossed them on the table. Ari looked them over briefly.

"From your late assailants," he said.

"Hey, I didn't—"

"Correction, latest assailants. Frederick Baines and Anthony Young. Phony baloney. The ring is interesting, though. What do you make of it?"

"Signet ring," I said. "Which would fit with an outfit like FACT, especially their clandestine nasty branch. I've never seen quite this symbolic design before, though."

It really was a curious design. The symbols worked into it seemed to include an eyeball (but not the eye), a hammer (but no sickle), and a ruler, with some other stuff I couldn't make out.

"It's new to me too," Ari said. "Well, I'll pass these goodies on to Benny, and if I hit him in the right mood, he'll pass them on to some people who are *really* good at finding things out."

"So you think this FACT bunch is our boy scout troop?" I asked.

"Definitely the most promising candidate. This stuff is a good haul, could pin it down for sure. But look, as far as tomorrow goes, let's just do the family thing. Your research into this Shroud business, no problem with that, but we'll keep the rest of this to ourselves for now."

"Just so we deal with it," I said. "I'm tired of being their target."

"Then steel yourself to mind your own business for just a few days, and lock your doors, vary your routes and times, and for God's sake recall what you've learned about passive self-defense. Like, you know, see trouble coming and step around it?"

"I have been trying," I sulked.

Ari looked at Sareen, and they both broke up laughing.

"And—and," I said, trying to get us back on track, "we can quietly and discreetly keep digging into FACT and all its dirty secrets."

"Yeah," Ari gasped, "yeah, sure, bro, you betcha, right on, we're gonna be doing that ... " And the heartless duo lost it again.

At the front of my mind, understandably I think, was the as yet undiscussed question of where Sareen would be staying. Our sleeping arrangements. Ever since yesterday's blowup, our relationship seemed to be finding its way tentatively, one step at a time.

I was a bit surprised, then, when Ari upended his coffee cup and announced, "Enough already. I'll take the two of you over to Adam's quarters before I begin wasting another night solving Adam's problems."

The real surprise was that Sareen made no fuss at all over this but just cleared away our coffee stuff to the counter.

I waited until we were actually up in my comfy-like-an-old-shoe apartment, with the door locked securely behind us, before I said, "I'll say it one last time, Sareen. I still have this huge blind spot when it comes to reading you—you as a female in particular."

She turned to me with her characteristic Mona Lisa expression. "I know, Adam, I know. Please just be patient with me, and trust me."

"I do trust you. I love you."

"I know that too." Her face broke into sudden amusement. "Put this towel over your head! Chop something! Do it!"

"It seemed like the best idea at the time."

"It was, perhaps, the least bad option—in any event it seems so now after some time for reflection. Along with everything else, I still can hardly believe that you managed to take down those two hit men. Really—how did you do it?"

"Hit men? Tough talk, lady."

She grinned. "Tough lady."

"No argument from me. But I'd rather not replay that scene; just let it fade with the credits. How do you like my humble abode?"

She looked around. "I like it very well. Becoming more familiar with it will give me much more insight into you. My advantage over you in that regard will only increase."

A large wave of relaxation came over me, body and soul. She wanted to become familiar with me, my apartment, and my life. But the relaxation reminded me how exhausted I was, and she must be too.

"It's still rather early," I said, "but you must be tired. After you look the place over, time for bed?"

"I think so, yes. Tonight, Adam, just hold me. I want to be held close and sleep a long time."

Which we did. Sometime late in the morning we woke up, and making love again was like a reunion.

After a leisurely shower, I shaved my cheeks and neck, grooming the dark-brown mini-beard. Sareen, meanwhile, went and inspected my kitchen. Since I don't cook much more than microwave popcorn, she was disappointed and told me we would have to do some major shopping before breakfast. I said I couldn't wait that long, and we compromised on breakfasting at one of my old familiar haunts in the hood, Peg's Place, and then on to Citarella, an elite supermarket for do-it-yourself gourmets. We—make that she—loaded two large shopping carts brimful with foodstuffs, largely unfamiliar to me, plus numerous culinary specialty gadgets. If at some point Sareen chose not to hang around any longer, it would all go to waste.

We paid the extra fee to have all our booty delivered to the apartment an hour later. And I was determined to waste none of it.

While we were walking back, Sareen phoned for another update on the situation in Ethiopia, but there was still no change. They would call her as soon as there was news.

CHAPTER 31

The family bash at Ari's place drew quite a crowd. Along with Ari and Sareen and me, there was Benny, my mom, Hannah, and her husband, Chuck—a big, overweight, outgoing guy—and superteen Shelley. Ari's nine-year-old Lucy was there too, shadowing Shelley. My mom had fixed herself up for the occasion and looked many times better than the last time I saw her. Though Pop's death was a profound grief for her, not having to live any longer with his decline from robust vigor into medicated, tubed-up frailty had to also bring some measure of relief. One of the peculiar trade-offs of human life.

Hannah was doing the cooking, assisted ably by Shelley, who in turn had Lucy as her apprentice sous chef. Chicken was frying, corn meal muffins were baking, potato salad was being made, and an elaborate veggie tray was under assembly. Though it goes without saying, I will just mention that people like me who don't cook owe a lot to those who do. In restaurants, we pay cash. Here? Well, I helped set up the tables and chairs. The dining room table was supplemented by a fold-up table at one end, jutting into the living room, all covered with unseasonal red-and-green tablecloths.

We sat or stood around in all three rooms, with groupings and conversations shifting and mingling. Some were drinking wine; Chuck and Benny had bottles of beer, and there was also iced tea and lemonade. I was sticking with the lemonade.

One of the first conversational stops I made was with Mom and Benny. By then, Mom had caught wind of my affair with the Shroud and was full of curiosity.

"I've never heard of this," she was saying. "Oh, I may have heard of it, but I took no notice of it. And you're going to prove it's a fake, or is it the other way around?"

"Neither, really. Or else one or the other. I mean, I just want to find out what it really is. If I can, that is. A lot of people have been trying, one way and the other, but it's a tough nut. Genuinely mysterious."

"I suppose so. The *Today Show* said that some rich heiress is paying you to prove it isn't the real thing."

That cat was long since out of the bag, and there was no avoiding it.

"Yes, she did pay me to get started, but then, a week or two ago, I sort of veered off the reservation, so I expect that funding source has dried up. It's all been happening so fast that it's hard to keep up with the changes."

"Not to mention all the languages," Benny put in. "From what I've overheard, you've been hopping between Belgium, France, Italy, Turkey, and Israel on this quest. Have I missed any stops?"

"Italy two or three times, I think. I may be going over the top on this, but it just seemed best to go to those places where the Shroud may have been, century upon century. Along the way, I've been able to confer with some people who know more than I do about it and the detailed history surrounding it."

"Including your lovely young friend over there?" Mom inquired with a smile, not a frown.

"Including her, the souvenir beyond price. You'll love her, Mom."

"If you do, I will."

As simple and final as "whither thou goest." Everything in life should be as simple as that. Everything in life, of course, isn't mother and son.

A while later, Hannah shooed and clucked and herded us all to the table, now loaded with savory luxuries starting with two heaping platters of crispy, golden-brown, finger-lickin' chicken. The Colonel is good, but homemade is better.

I wound up sitting between Lucy and Hannah, with Chuck and Ari across from me. We were a small enough group that, for the most part, we all got in on the same table talk, though sub-conversations sprang up now and then. We talked about the heat wave currently setting records across the Midwest, and from there the conversation veered to climate change and from there, somehow, to dinosaurs, broken state budgets, and stage magicians.

Eventually no one was helping themselves to seconds or thirds any longer, and Hannah announced, "Well now, it looks like we're about ready for some dessert here, unless you'd like to wait till later. I've made some strawberry shortcake, and, of course, there's coffee or tea."

We looked around at one another until Shelley piped up, "Now?"

Chuck held out his hands like Marilyn Monroe was walking toward him. "Strawberry shortcake? Bring it on!"

Several of us joined in clearing the table—or I should say them, as I got involved in discussing with Lucy the possible overlap between dinosaurs and magic.

Strawberry shortcake is hard to do badly—though I speak only from the consumer's point of view—and Hannah does it very well indeed, topped with real, not ersatz, whipped cream. The conversation was trending off into the potential perils of cyber warfare when Ari's cell phone rang, and he stood up and turned away and answered it. Then he handed it over to me, saying, "For you."

For me? I took it into the kitchen.

"Adam Hult here."

"You bad *bad* boy, do you have any *idea* of the trouble I've gone to trying to run you to ground?"

Dina Pallas, my carnivorous book editor.

"Dina, I'm sorry—"

"Sorry buys you squat, Prince Charming. If I hadn't remembered about your exciting friend Ari, I might never have heard from you again. You ditched your cell just to avoid me?"

"I lost it. I mean it got stolen—"

"The dog ate it. Relax, peach fuzz, all is forgiven now, as long as you never do this to me again. You're still my valentine. And just to prove my love—I trust you're familiar with that expression—I'm going to assume you're not holding out on me."

"The thought would never occur to me—"

"Because, look, sugar, I'm in the business, kapeesh? The gutter press, late night, social media, none of it gets by me, you think?"

"I never doubted—"

"Ding! *'Celeb Debunker Adam Now Touting Miracle Shroud!'* Ding!"

"I realize you must have heard—"

"You realize corn chips, Superman. Haven't I always been square with you? Now you've got thirty seconds or less to square it with me."

"Whoa there, Dina. I might be on to something with this, yeah, but I'm not there yet. Getting close maybe, but—"

"But no cigar. I love you, but I hate cigars. So you think it's the goods?"

"Maybe, Dina, maybe. You want more than maybe, don't you?"

"Maybe I want to squeeze your cheeks and kiss your juicy lips. How much longer the tease, Adam?"

"When I know, you know, Dina. Soon, I hope. Now—"

"Not so fast. The number."

"Number?"

"You think I wouldn't figure you for a new cell, lover?"

I gave her the new number and escaped. The ransom might have been far higher.

. . . . . .

The next morning, decadently late, Sareen bustled around in my newly stocked kitchen and then brought breakfast in bed for both of us—French toast, probably with some Lebanese influence, and sliced mangoes with yogurt. And coffee. I didn't have the kind of bed tray with little legs like you see in those old Tracy and Hepburn movies, but she found a couple of large serving platters and we balanced them on our thighs. She was, naturally, better at that than I was, but through extreme care, I managed not to dump her creation on the sheets. I hope she appreciated my effort, or rather I'm sure she did, since she doesn't miss much.

That afternoon I took her ice-skating. It was either that or hanging around my apartment, and I figured the fun would be worth any marginal increase in risk. We were, it seemed, in an odd interlude, a sort of limbo, between all that had happened since we first met and whatever might come next—particularly what our friends at F/ACTION might be cooking up.

An odd interlude, maybe, but mostly a pleasant one, dimmed only by the uncertainty over her team in Ethiopia. The dreamlike eye of the hurricane. We took a taxi to the Sky Rink at Chelsea Piers down in Lower Manhattan, one of the few year-round ice-skating venues in the area, the others being pools and ponds that freeze in the winter. I'd been ice-skating since boyhood and was fairly accomplished, but this was Sareen's first time. She roller skated, though, and I assured her that the ice version is nearly the same thing, only better.

We strapped on our rented skates and ventured out onto the ice. There were other skaters whizzing or wobbling by, but it wasn't crowded. I took her hand, and we gave it a try. She wobbled a bit at first—similar action as in roller-skating but different footing—but by the time we'd circled the rink once, she was into it. By our third or fourth circuit, I turned and skated backward, holding both her hands. Her brown cheeks had a reddish glow, and her eyes sparkled up at me, and I thought, *Let's do this forever.*

Life is about compromises, though, and we skated for an hour before moving on to the next thing, which was another get-together with Ari, just the three of us this time. He was going to make his special tacos for us, and we were going to talk some strategy. It would also give the two of them a chance to get to know each other better.

Another taxi took us across the Brooklyn Bridge, an old friend to me but new and fascinating for Sareen. She said it looked stately and almost Roman. She would be about as good a judge of that as anyone.

Ari's row house, when we got there, was already aromatic with the chili con carne he had prepared with stewed and shredded beef, jalapeños, garlic, cumin, and other goodies he might not disclose. He gave us our choice of chilled regional microbrews to start off with. Sareen and I sat at the kitchen table while Ari did his chef act at the counter. Sareen asked if she could help, but he said he had everything under control. Being Ari, he would say that under any circumstances and almost always be right. My continuing hope was that the "almost" wouldn't catch up with him one of these days.

"Yes, I can see," Sareen said. "I like your kitchen. A Goldilocks kitchen, not too small, not too large."

"Yeah, it works for me. A man of simple tastes."

"Except, perhaps, in the matter of tacos," she said.

"And enchiladas," I added, "and lasagna and gefilte fish and pierogi and blintzes. Don't let that simple-tastes front fool you. Ari likes to master things, and since he has to eat food, he attacks it and tries to master it."

"You make me sound like Genghis Khan in the kitchen."

"Your analogy, but I'll accept it."

Sareen laughed, and I noticed him glance at her with a small appreciative smile. Then she said to him, "I understand that you and Adam have been friends since childhood. He has told me something of his, what shall I say, rather unusual childhood. What was it like for you, knowing him then?"

"Him? You mean the freak?"

"That is the term he also used, but I don't like it."

"Okay, then, the geek, the prodigy. I'll say this: he was a pretty ordinary kid except for the brainy part. He went along with our games, our pranks and fights, our sports."

"Ah, sports," she said. "So, Adam, you did other sports along with ice skating?"

"Well, skating as in ice hockey. I was never a figure skater, never wanted to be. Come to that, I wasn't any great shakes at hockey either."

"He played baseball with us too," Ari said. "Any boy who wanted to be in the pecking order at all had to play baseball."

"I have seen it once or twice on television, but that's all," she said.

"Hey, that reminds me," he said, turning toward us while his razor-sharp knife was bouncing up and down mercilessly on an onion, and I figured his finger would get diced with it, but apparently it didn't since he went on, "there was this one time when Adam's special talents on the baseball team really shone out."

"No, don't . . ." I said in vain.

"It wasn't actually out on the diamond; it was in a team meeting, a training session. We were in middle school then, seventh grade I think, eleven or twelve years old. I say 'we' were in middle school, meaning the rest of us. Adam by that time was about a senior in high school and way beyond that in math and stuff like that, but they kept him back in extracurricular activities so he could lead some semblance of a normal kid life. So, for instance, he was on the ball team with the middle school kids. Well, the high school boys would have used him as the third base bag.

"So anyway, we're in this team meeting, and the coach, a pot-bellied guy who couldn't touch his knees, is explaining the mechanics of batting a ball. 'Keep your eye on the ball, and swing like this,' he says. But Adam raises his hand, and the coach says, 'What is it, Hult? You got a better idea?'

"Adam gets up and goes to the white board and draws a cylinder to represent the bat and a sphere for the ball. Then he goes into all these numbers and Greek squiggles, explaining the differential equations that govern the physico-geometric interaction between cylinder and sphere. 'Just simple Newtonian mechanics,' he tells us, 'nothing more than that,' and he concludes that the level swing is fourteen percent more effective than the uppercut.

"By that time, I think, the poor coach didn't know whether to strangle him or hire him."

During this embarrassing narrative, Sareen was looking at me with undisguised merriment and no hint of pity or compassion.

"Wonderful!" she praised him. "You tell it so well that I can see it happening."

"Oh, it happened," he said.

"How are those tacos coming?" I said.

"He's perfectly normal when it comes to eating, you see," he told Sareen.

"Yes, I have discovered that."

"Tacos?" I reiterated.

"Yes, sir, and would you like those with or without the sour cream?"

"Either way, just as long as it's before tomorrow."

He had been heating or cooking (see, I don't know the difference) the corn tortillas in a device like a waffle iron without the waffling. Now he was sliding the tortillas onto plates and spooning on some of the hot chili mixture.

"The rest you can add on for yourselves at your own discretion," he told us. Spread out on the counter were bowls of shredded extra-sharp cheddar, chopped onions and black olives and lettuce and tomatoes, sliced avocados, cilantro, salsa, sour cream, and extra jalapeños if we wanted even more heat.

All kidding aside, Ari's tacos were the very best. And at their best, when you pile on all the extras, tacos are deliciously messy, with aromatic goo dripping every which way.

Except if you are Sareen. Her delicate fingers managed to hold the thing in such a way that nothing escaped or even oozed. She took delicate bites, and nothing ran down her chin. The feat astonished me, but I had no inclination to emulate it. My chin and hands dripped freely. So did Ari's. There is probably some explanation; or maybe not. Wiping his face and hands with paper towels and passing out a second round of beers, Ari said to Sareen, "Adam tells me you work with some kind of international relief organization."

"Yes," she said. "Well, partly what you could call relief. Also political education and advocacy for religious tolerance and freedom."

"I see. What parts of the world are you active in?"

"Various places, and more all the time. Our organization started out in the Middle East and then got involved in North Africa. That was years before all the uprisings and turmoil broke out there. I won't say we triggered anything, but then I also won't say we didn't." She smiled. "Ambiguity is often necessary in our work."

"I'll bet," said Ari. "And now other regions as well?"

"Yes, we have branches, either established or being planted, in Central Asia and Sub-Saharan Africa. Even, believe it or not, in Europe."

"Oh, I believe it. The Nazis' efforts notwithstanding, Europe has never been ethnically 'pure,' but over the last few decades, they've become thoroughly multicultural."

"And troubled by the changes," she added.

Swallowing a bite but not bothering to wipe my face, I said, "Like some other, maybe less commendable organizations I could mention, Sareen's group operates both openly and covertly. Understandably, of course, as the dangers are obvious."

"Ah, so you're beginning to notice," Ari said—a gratuitous dig.

To Sareen, I said, "You mentioned to me before that you've been involved in the covert side of things too. So I'm wondering, am I the only one here who's been risking his neck? Check that, I know Ari has; that's his territory. But what about you? Unless ..."

She was chewing a bite and shaking her head till she finished it.

"It's true," she said, "the work certainly has had its hazardous moments. Perhaps Ari and I have been a little unfair to you, Adam. It's just that we—he and I—even though we have just recently met, we have both been much concerned about what appeared to be unnecessary risks you were taking. I still think you stuck your head out too far, even though the cause is admirable. I think you understand this."

Ari glanced at me, and I glanced back at him.

He said, "Sareen, you're under no pressure or obligation to respond here, but I think both Adam and I would really be interested in any particulars you might feel comfortable in relating."

She sighed. "If the two of you were women, you would be interested in other kinds of secrets. As it is, however ... very well, being as it is you two and what you mean to me, I believe I should tell you something. Something true, of course, though I won't use any names.

"For many years now, we have been active in various parts of Iraq. The place where I was involved is in the far western part, near the border with Syria—in both countries, actually. The border there is porous, especially if you have good documents and cash for bribes."

"Forged documents," Ari said.

"Naturally. So my role was to be a liaison between some Christian leaders in the area and some of the Muslim mullahs and tribal leaders. The church there is very ancient, going back to the first centuries after Christ. Owing mainly to political conditions in both countries, especially the wars and sectarian violence in Iraq, relations between the Christians and Muslims have deteriorated recently. There has been much tension and mistrust; some of the Christians have been beaten and even killed, and churches vandalized.

"Many of the leaders on both sides of this divide, however, wanted to resolve the problem as far as possible and avoid further violence. The main obstacle was communication, or the lack of it. That was where I came in, an Arabic speaker and a woman. And though I am a Christian, I was not affiliated in any way with those churches."

"Being a woman was an advantage?" I asked.

"On balance, I think so, yes. Wearing a head covering and long dress, a woman there is relatively anonymous and much less likely to be perceived as a threat. I was able to pass among them, even across the border at times, bearing messages they could not deliver directly."

"You survived, I see," said Ari, "for which Adam is even more thankful than I am. Any real trouble?"

"A few close calls, when they questioned my papers or threatened to arrest me because the bribe was too small. On one mission I was threatened with rape—though it's hard to tell for sure sometimes with Arab men—but nothing came of it."

"Thank God," I muttered with other than religious feelings.

"And do you think," Ari asked, "that your courier service made any difference?"

"That is hard to tell also—hard to tell how things might have been otherwise. I hope so, but such matters are extremely tangled and difficult there, as in so many other places. These fears and suspicions and hatreds go back fifty generations and more."

"Being a Jew, I can't argue with that," he said. "Well, thank you for indulging our curiosity, Sareen. And being a Jew, I know there's no point in advising you to quit the struggle. Just keep safe. But now I think it's time to clear the table, literally and figuratively, and get around to our current problem."

If Ari had a club, Sareen had joined it.

CHAPTER 32

"War council in session," Ari said. He had opened his laptop on the kitchen table.

"You've passed those hard-won assets on to Benny?" I asked.

"An hour after you passed them to me. And for some odd reason, he thinks your case is priority one. He has handed them over to his 'friends,' rest assured. We'll just have to await their assessment."

"Worth waiting for if it confirms F/ACTION as the opposition. If it disconfirms it, though, we're back to square one."

"No," he said, "I think Benny's boys will ID one group or another. And I'd bet my toaster on Morris Griffin and company."

"He sounds like an unpleasant man," Sareen said. I had summarized for her what Ari had told me so far.

"Unpleasant like a tarantula. Here, I snagged a copy of his book. His picture's on the dust jacket, inside back cover."

The book was *Bury the Zombie God.* On the front cover, the title was in large, runny blood-red letters on a granite gravestone. We turned to his photo on the back. He glared back at us through eyes like black holes over a bulbous nose, a wide, flat mouth and a receding chin. Sareen crossed herself. I hoped it might work.

"I've pulled together some more career details," Ari said. "Shipping tycoon, as you know. Parents were conventional, buttoned-down middle-class folks in Bristol. Morris seems to have been a rebel from the womb. In and out of juvenile court. Ran away after secondary school and signed on as a deckhand on a ship hauling things like lumber and machine parts. He was no slouch, though, more like a force of nature. By age thirty, he skippered his own ship. By forty, through as yet unknown means, he acquired the funds to become a partner in a shipping firm operating in the North and Baltic Seas."

"Why do I think I wouldn't want to have been his partner?" I noted.

"I doubt the word is in his dictionary. From that point, he diversified into things like shipbuilding, mining, and armaments. A major player in the booming trade in illegal weaponry, though nothing's been pinned on him yet."

"But why does he write books like this?" Sareen asked. "What does he care about God?"

"Well, he traces his thinking to Darwin, but it's really a dumbed-down version of Nietzsche. God is dead, religion is for weaklings, the world belongs to the strong—basically the skinhead and swastika beat. There is some logical confusion, of course, if our greatest social scourge comes from weaklings."

I was peeking at his computer screen. "Are those some more quotes you've copied out there?"

"Just a sampling. If it whets your appetite, you're free to read the whole book. The first one's the one I gave you over the phone."

He turned the laptop so we could both read:

> Belief in any kind of god or any kind of miracle is, by definition, insanity. *Homo sapiens* is the cleverest animal, but we're all animals and when we die, we're just dead.
>
> Their god is the zombie god: it's been dead for centuries, and they keep trying to pump life back into it.
>
> This whole god thing is nothing but a big con—the biggest and worst confidence racket in history. They dangle the promise of life beyond the grave, eternal bliss, in front of the stupid, gullible crowd—just bow down to us and

> sign over your bank account. It's long past time to stamp out these racketeers once and for all.
>
> There are two main categories of irrational people. First there are the sub-rational, all the morons, mongoloids, cretins, and retards. Their intelligence quotient is just too low for rationality. The second category is the anti-rational people, those that refuse to accept that the advance of science has proved that there is no God, never was any God, and never will be any God. These people are the dangerous ones because their irrationality is deliberate and purpose-driven. All of these pea-brains get in the way of scientific progress and the advancement of the race into a rational future free of ignorance and superstition.
>
> Of all the irrationals, the Jesus freaks are the worst scourge. They hype their god-man to the ignorant masses the same way McDonald's hypes hamburgers. The only answer is to wipe the slate clean, wipe the miracle man out of human memory. We need to raise a generation that never saw that hollow-eyed, bearded face.
>
> The only foolproof way to eradicate superstition is to enact selective breeding and birth control and education on a thoroughly rational and scientific basis.

"Note the 'hollow-eyed bearded face,'" I said. "No wonder the Shroud gets under his skin."

"It's strange," Sareen commented, "he claims to be an atheist, but his bitterness and ferocity against believers is exactly the same as the bitterness and ferocity of the most hardcore fundamentalists in the Middle East or Northern Ireland. It's like a disease that affects a certain fringe of people no matter what their religious views."

"Uh-huh. But the particular rabid dog we're concerned with is trying to bite Adam," said Ari.

"There's a strain of eugenics in the mix here too," I said.

"Eugenics?" Sareen asked. "I have heard the word, but what exactly does it refer to?"

"It's a social movement that gained quite a bit of traction in Europe and America during the first half of the twentieth century," I said. "Its main idea was to achieve racial health and vigor by identifying the genetically inferior strains and sterilizing them so they couldn't reproduce themselves. And when they do manage to reproduce, snuff out their babies."

"Like Griffin's morons, mongoloids, cretins, and retards," Ari said.

"All mercifully disposed of. For Griffin, though, the first cattle cars in the train are reserved for religious believers."

"Cleanse the world and make it fit for the Hitler Youth to grow up in," he added grimly.

"I see," Sareen said. "I have come across other ideas just as obnoxious and poisonous in our world today. But if we have some concept now of what we are up against, what can we do?"

"To do or not to do, that is the question," I quipped.

"That's about it," Ari said. "The first choice, I think, is between passive and active strategies."

"What would a passive strategy look like?" I wondered.

"Well, the fully passive thing would be to stop antagonizing them—stop pursuing this Shroud business."

"Knuckle under, you mean."

"Semantics. It could be a way of prolonging your life."

"Yeah, but is that what you would do?"

He grinned. "No. But it's not me they're after."

"After what happened over there in Jerusalem," Sareen said, "might they not be licking their wounds?"

"Sure," Ari said, "but they're not going to back off from this any more than Adam is. They understand kill or be killed; they don't understand being intimidated."

"So you don't think I'm going to back off and knuckle under."

"Of course not. I only brought up the passive strategy to be sure we cover all the options. But there are active options as well."

"Like what?" I said. "Form ourselves into a three-man—sorry, three-person commando unit? Hunt down the F/ACTION goons in the dark streets of a dozen cities?"

"No, that one doesn't play into our strength," he agreed.

"So we need to identify our strength, or strengths," I said.

"But let's do it over coffee," Sareen suggested.

Ari hopped up. "I'll take care of it. One of my strengths."

I looked at Sareen. "So, ma'am, you and me—any strengths we can identify?"

She smiled. "Yes, but it might embarrass you."

"I mean," I snorted, "any strengths that might help me wriggle out of the jaws of the great white shark."

She thought a minute.

"Well, I've been told you were a child prodigy. What about sheer intelligence?"

"I'm trying … I'm trying … "

There was a lull in which, I suppose, we were all trying. The coffee had been smelling good, and now Ari poured it for us.

"For any active strategy," he said, "whatever weapons we might have and use, what we first have to identify are their weaknesses, their vulnerable points."

"If any," I said.

"Oh, every person, every group, every faction has its weaknesses. These clowns certainly do. Think about it."

"They're ideologues, fanatics," I suggested.

"Which implies a narrowing of mental vision," he said. "There will be ways to exploit that. We simply need to find the ways."

"Simply," I muttered.

"Dark streets," Sareen said.

"Yes?" said Ari.

"One of you mentioned the dark streets of a dozen cities. These people need the darkness—literally, but even more to the point, figuratively."

Ari put down his coffee cup and poked me in the chest. "Keep this lady around, particularly when you're in need of intelligence. Now, bright lady, would you mind expanding on that thought?"

"It just occurs to me that people like this, especially people like Morris Griffin, prefer concealment for their activities and even need it. They can't bear too much exposure. This thought is expressed in the Gospel of John, the third chapter."

"Ahh," Ari breathed, "yes, Sareen, that could very well be it. The Gospel of John? Well, whatever, it may have a bearing on our favorite sinners. Not only with regard to the crude, violent stuff, vandalizing churches and synagogues and mugging college professors, but Griffin's business and financial deals too. Exposure could be a problem for him."

"It could," I agreed, "but we'd have to do it carefully and the right way. He's sure to have a pack of top-dollar lawyers whose main brief is fending off exposure."

"First we will have to find out much more about him—his businesses, his finances, his possible criminal activities, and his exact connection with FACT and F/ACTION," Sareen said.

"Yeah. I've got quite a lot in here," Ari said, patting his laptop, "but we'll need more. It'll give us something to do while we wait on Benny's results."

We sipped our coffee and pondered all this.

"Those lawyers," Sareen said, "there are some forms of exposure that they would be very good at neutralizing, but others that they might not be."

"The ones they're good at ..." Ari prompted.

"Would be the ones they're used to. Lawsuits. Civil suits. Cases where they can bring countercharges of libel. There may even have been criminal charges brought against him that they've defended successfully; we'll have to see."

"And the ones they wouldn't be so good at?"

"Those might be some of the newer forms of exposure. WikiLeaks, things like that."

"Social media," Ari said, "blogs, maybe Twitter."

"But can we do it," I wondered, "and would it work?"

"It could work," he said. "Cyberspace is a whole new world, and one of its favorite things is plain old gossip on a scale never before imagined. Innuendo, slander, scandal, where it's all but impossible to sift the truth from the lies."

"Partly because there's so much of it flying around so fast," I said.

"And the people who attract the most attention in the scandal-sphere," he added, "are those who are already celebrities or bigwigs."

"Senators and governors and French politicians who get paparazzi'd with their pants too far down," I said.

"But is Griffin a big enough wig?" Sareen asked with a wink at me.

"Well," Ari considered, "he's big enough as a business magnate and one of the leaders of FACT. He's a well-known international figure. He's just managed to keep a relatively low profile thus far."

"I do believe we might rectify that," I said.

"I do believe so too," he agreed.

"How excellent!" Sareen laughed, clapping her hands. "We are all believers together."

"Whoa, don't jump to a conclusion too far," Ari said. "And anyway, kids, homework first, then play."

"And keep in mind," I said, "these aren't children's games. If we shine some floodlights on Griffin in his lair, that'll be the same as smoking them out."

"Of course it will," he said. "We will have to be prepared for that."

Sareen's cell phone rang and she looked at it and said, "GODF." She talked in a low voice and mostly listened for the next ten or fifteen minutes, moving randomly around the room while Ari and I waited and wondered.

When the call was done, she looked at us, heaved a huge sigh, and said, "It's over, it's done. They've settled it."

"How? What happened?" we both asked.

"Well, first, our team managed to persuade the elders of both tribes to meet together before things fell apart completely over that young man who was stabbed to death. And then by the time of that meeting, the Muslim tribe had figured out among themselves what really happened. It turned out to be the old matter of honor. The young man in question had seduced a girl, or she seduced him, whichever, and her older brother found out about it and avenged the family honor. The familiar old story."

"What happened to the girl?" Ari asked.

"She ran off into the bush. They will find her fairly soon, dead or alive."

I asked, "What happens to her if she hasn't killed herself?"

"That will be decided by the tribal elders according to their customary law."

"And her brother?"

"The same. I don't know about their customs."

"It's a hard world," Ari observed.

"Yes. But now they appear to be ready to resolve their dispute over water rights, both sides do—more ready than before this happened."

"It's a hard world, but we make our way through it," he said.

She sat down and propped her chin on her laced fingers so that her head bobbed a little when she said, "Yes."

CHAPTER 33

We agreed that I should lie low, as far as possible, until we got the goods on Morris Griffin and F/ACTION, presuming we got enough goods to do any good. Sareen, bless her heart, was willing to lie low with me, but as we had determined yesterday at Ari's place, it wasn't going to be all fun and games. So after we rolled out of bed shortly before nine and got ourselves washed and dressed, and she made crepes with peaches and yogurt for our breakfast, we got to work. She worked on my home computer and I on my laptop. Relying heavily on my mathematical brilliance, we divided the job into thirds. Ari, as the only serious hacker among us, was tasked with trying to hack into F/ACTION's e-mails and any other stuff they might have left lurking on the web. Sareen was looking into the religious and ideological side of things, statements that Griffin or FACT had made in the public record. And I was going after his business and financial dealings, with a particular interest in the shady or downright illegal.

In the more obscure sectors of multinational business, I discovered, he was a player with a reputation for buying distressed companies, selling off all their assets, and spitting out the husks, like investors and employees. He did this in small enough bites, though, that it didn't attract as much attention as, say, Enron.

I was well into this edifying exercise when Ari called.

"What's up, dude?" I said.

"Have you given any thought to the university's Media Relations Office?"

"Not yet, but since you—"

"Why not?"

"Well, I'm deep into MG's nefarious wheeling and dealing."

"Okay, but think about it now. Any chance that he and his cronies might have infringed on your precious academic freedom?"

"Now that is a thought. I could make a case, I guess, if we had any proof that anything happened and they were the perps."

"Ah, my son, proof is only the very final stage in this sort of stratagem. It may never even come to that. To begin with, we have your outraged testimony along with a few fading but still visible scabs and bruises. And then we have a virtual eyewitness with the most impeccable credentials."

"I'm not bringing her into this, not publicly. Too dangerous."

"Very gallant of you, I'm sure, but doesn't she have the right to decide that for herself? Hasn't she earned it in the heat of battle?"

"Oh man, go ahead, stick me in an impossible position. But we still don't have any real evidence, let alone proof, that it was them that did it."

"That may be arriving shortly, particularly in the form of that signet ring. But as I just suggested, it doesn't necessarily need to come to that. Rumors will be swirling on Twitter, on Facebook, in the tabloids, and on talk radio. Then the renowned Professor Hult, joined on the podium by the exquisitely admirable Ms. Khouri, expresses his passionately righteous indignation at these shocking assaults upon academic free inquiry. The heat will be on; who needs proof? What is 'proof' anyway?"

"I get the point. But the university won't like it, mainly on account of me running amok and messing with something as politically incorrect as the Shroud of Turin. They'll prefer to cover the whole thing up."

"Sure, they might prefer, but we won't let 'em. Anyhow, what's it to you if they've got their family jewels in the vise?"

"Cripes, Ari, you're a menace to society. But I still don't like involving Sareen that openly."

"Her decision, bro. Ask her."

"If you insist. How's the search progressing?"

"How high is your security clearance?"

"Go swim in the cesspool."

I switched him off. I was working at the breakfast nook, and Sareen had been on the computer in my study, but now she was in the doorway.

"I heard most of that," she said, "and his side of it isn't difficult to infer. Thank you for your gallantry, but Ari is right. The truth is, most women have never really wanted to be protected in the harem."

I looked at her and then smiled at her. "God help Morris Griffin."

"God will, if he asks." She took that kind of thing seriously.

We worked for another hour or so, then she fixed lunch, and after that we went back to the grind. I found that Griffin had indeed been sued over various financial shenanigans and even indicted twice, but his lawyers had always come through for him. Also, through a series of fronting companies he hid behind, he was heavily involved in the international bazaar in military weapons. Much of that was probably more or less legal, but not all of it. It made me wonder about still being alive, though I recalled Ari's point about my public visibility being a problem for them if it came to murder.

Then I remembered they'd already tried once.

I was into this cheerful meditation when my phone rang again—the Droid, not the encrypted one. Everything brightened up when I found it was Tom Freebinder.

"How did you get this number?"

"Please, Dr. Hult, remember who I am and be serious."

"Whatever. How may I be of service?"

"Mrs. Ballaster thinks you owe her an accounting."

"Look, I told her, or as much as told her, that our deal just isn't going to work. I can't prove the Shroud is a medieval forgery. I think it most likely isn't. It's older, though I'm still not sure about the real provenance. I'm not going to *invent* a hoax for you people. I probably couldn't if I tried."

"There are, if you recall, certain consequences if you back out of the bargain."

"As the Duke of Wellington famously said, 'Publish and be damned!'"

"If that's your position, Dr. Hult. Damnation, I'm afraid, takes many forms. In any case, are you averse to explaining this to Mrs. Ballaster in person?"

"I suppose I could do that, sort of for old times' sake. When should I announce myself at the Paterno?"

"She suggested tomorrow afternoon at four."

"All right, I'll be there."

After he rang off, it occurred to me that, even though he might be capable of siccing the IRS hounds on me, he probably had nothing to do with F/ACTION. We take our comfort where we can.

Sareen took a break from the investigative drudgery to put together a turkey and oyster pie with dill sauce for our dinner. At this rate, I could get used to eating at home.

But how long would she stay? I was reluctant—make that too cowardly—to ask. Was she conventional enough to want me to make an honest woman of her? Or rather, if your thinking tended this way, should I make an honest man of myself? Anyhow, if not conventional, she was religious. And yet, here she was. In a childish way, I wished we could just freeze the status quo and not change anything.

Life, of course, doesn't work that way, and in my admittedly spotty experience, neither do women.

As for myself, the long exposure to my parents' marriage dimmed my view of the institution. It worked for them, I suppose, and they stayed together, but their stifling, monotonous, tortoiselike existence gave me the shudders.

On the other hand (I am big on other hands), they would probably have lived the same kind of life without a marriage certificate. Blaming the wedding cake for it was illogical.

A new thought washed over me like a cold shower: Maybe they stayed together all those years because of love. Mom and Pop—what a thought.

Would Sareen connect love with marriage? Would she stay in my life if I didn't marry her?

Was she having second thoughts about trusting me? Should she be?

Would she say yes if I popped the question?

These thoughts scared me as much as Morris Griffin did, maybe more. So, over dinner, I didn't bring it up. Instead, we compared research notes. I told her about Griffin's corporate skullduggery and gunrunning. For her part, she had read as much as she could stand of his zombie book and then done some study on the history of eugenics.

"It's so disturbing," she said. "It's the same as you told me, this whole plan or policy for forcibly sterilizing people they class as 'unfit.' What is almost worse than the policy itself is the attitude in which they promote it, this hearty confidence that they are being modern and scientific and progressive and liberating."

"Right—about as liberating as Auschwitz."

"Who are these all-wise ones," she went on, "who divide the rest of us into categories. And where does this categorizing end—who is fit to live and who isn't? Who stops it? Who controls it?"

"Whoever is making the decisions, I guess. In the world as we know it, that usually winds up being those with the greatest wealth and political power."

"Who might have no scruples about anything."

I reached across the table and gave her hands a squeeze. "But I still have scruples about you."

That brought a smile. "Yes, and I treasure every one of your scruples. But still, this whole business ... much of my work in GODF amounts to resistance against attitudes and policies like this."

"That's so, and I haven't forgotten. Anyway, I expect you noticed similar themes in Griffin's book."

She nodded. "The man is evil. Anything we might do to hinder him would benefit everyone else."

"Well, we probably can't persuade him to change course, but maybe we can shoot his tires out."

She squeezed my hand back and said, "We must shoot his tires out."

▮ ▮ ▮ ▮ ▮ ▮

The following morning, around an hour before noon, Ari showed up at my apartment with a predatory gleam in his eye. He flopped down on the couch and opened his laptop on the coffee table, and Sareen and I joined him.

"You wanted proof?" he began. "Now we've got proof squared. I'll start with the passports and signet ring. The passports are counterfeit, of course, but Benny's nameless ones traced them to a top-of-the-line London specialist. The ring is our clincher, though. Only initiates of F/ACTION who've 'made their bones' can wear it, and every initiate swears on his own blood never to reveal the source or meaning of the symbols. They take this seriously enough that no one has ever broken the code of silence."

"How did Benny's friends break into it, then?" I asked.

"Don't know for sure, but my bet would be that 'no one ever' has shifted to 'until now.'"

"And the ID is definite?"

"Benny says so."

"Good enough for me. So we're good to go?"

"Yeah, but I've got more. I got into their e-mails. They use a substitution code, but it's not all that sophisticated. In their messages over the last few weeks, they referred to 'the fake sheet,' 'the professor,' and a certain unspecified location in Istanbul. These roaches are our roaches."

"Okay then," I said. "And here's another thing. Earlier this morning, Sareen dug out some info on Griffin's relations with the Inland Revenue—the British IRS. He and his lawyers have been battling with them for years, giving up a little ground now and then, but still holding the fort. If somehow we could tip the balance there ..."

"Good, we'll work that into our campaign," he said. "*Campaign*, you know, is really the word for it, since our operation is going to have both military and political aspects."

"Military?" Sareen asked doubtfully.

"In the sense of strategy and tactics. Our bullets will be words, allegations, rumors, and the like, but the strategy and tactics will be essentially military. Confuse the enemy, shake him up, distract him, disinform him, overload him, and take him down."

All of this got my blood pumping, spiked with some adrenalin, but after having laid out Griffin's tax problems, my conscience couldn't take it any longer.

"Guys," I said, "before we go any further, I've got a confession to make."

They both looked at me with expressions that said, "What now?"

"It's about that deal I made several months ago with Doris Ballaster. About half of what I told you was the truth. She *hired* me—that's the word for it—to prove once and for all that the Shroud is a forgery; that's true. The money she offered, including the fifty grand she paid up front, that was the carrot. What I neglected to mention is the stick. She had—still has, for that matter—some leverage over me. Morris Griffin isn't the only one in a tangle with the feds over taxes. Me too." Here I winced, cringed, and maybe groaned. "So Doris, with her enforcer Tom, were holding that over me. If I succeeded in debunking the

Shroud, they would fix it for me with the IRS—pay them off or whatever. But if I failed or welshed on the deal, they would shove me into the feds' shooting gallery. Will shove me, now, I guess. So … there you are."

Ari's face was wreathed in this irrepressible impish grin.

"Dude," he said, "I'm shocked, *shocked*!"

"You mean … this isn't news to you?"

He shook his head in the manner of a high school vice principal. "Adam, my old friend, you have your secrets, and you can keep them from those academic types at the university, but not from Ari. And, may I suggest, don't expect to be keeping them from Sareen."

My turn to shake my head. I made faces and probably blushed. Wished a hole in the floor would swallow me and was glad it didn't.

"So now, to business," he said, going back to his laptop.

CHAPTER 34

"Like any well-conceived campaign, military or political," Ari said, "ours will develop in stages. Three stages, to be exact. I've taken the liberty of labeling them. First will come Insinuate, then Aggravate, and finally Infuriate."

"The last one being the point at which we'll have to cover our backs, or cover our heads," I observed.

"Definitely. We'll go into that when the time comes. It'll depend on what emerges in the meantime."

"What happens in this first stage, Insinuate?" Sareen asked.

"It's already happening. Rumors have broken out at numerous points in the Twittersphere and will soon metastasize. On Facebook and Google+ also. The points of origin in both these venues are well-connected and plausible ones."

"These points of origin," I said, "these are people, I presume. How are you getting them to cooperate?"

"I didn't. They aren't."

"So you hacked them?"

"Proprietary secret."

"But what happens when they notice it and start issuing heated denials?"

"Too late by then. The battle and the noise and the lights and cameras, all the mindless greedy excitement, will have moved on by then. No one will pay them any attention, at least not until our skirmish is settled, one way or another."

"But after that, will they be able to trace it back to you?"

"Another proprietary secret, but the answer is no."

I was glad he was on our side. At the same time, feeling a qualm, I said, "But now, are we deciding here that the end justifies the means?"

He sat back on the sofa. "You mean, involving civilians in our private war by hacking their accounts."

"Yeah, that. This ethical stuff sounds like your turf, Sareen. What do you think?"

She looked at Ari for a while, then at me. We both watched her thinking it through. Finally she said, "The basic question is whether the end, the goal we seek, is important enough to justify the means we think are required to achieve it. One of my heroes, Dietrich Bonhoeffer, decided he was justified in joining a plot to assassinate Hitler. Ours is a much smaller matter, but the issue is the same."

"Or in terms a simple guy like me can follow," Ari said, "is it better to cheat a little and have a shot at bringing down these rodents, or is it better to keep our hands clean and just wish them bad luck."

Now Sareen and I looked at each other. I'm not sure if she nodded first or I did. I said to Ari, "How about this: The cheating we've done so far is proportionate to the goal—Morris Griffin is a certified rodent—but we keep on with this means testing as things progress."

"Works for me. So next—immediately, that is," he went on, "you call the *Post* and tell them who you are and tell them you've got the scandal of the month. They'll send a reporter over before you've even hung up." The *Post* was one of the city's more sensationalist tabloids.

Sareen fixed us a simple lunch of ham and cheese sandwiches on Jewish rye—an alarming combination, but Ari is kosher only when he wants to be. And he was right about the *Post* reporter, who rang the doorbell before we had finished eating. I gave him a *Post*-appropriate version of the affair.

During the afternoon we monitored the progress of our campaign. The rumors were spreading around the social media, rumors about Griffin's alleged links to illegal arms shipments and to organized crime, and rumors about FACT having a terrorist wing that bombed and burned churches, synagogues and mosques. At first there was a lot of "Who's this Morris Griffin?" and "What's this F/ACTION?" By and by, however, people chattered as if they'd known Morris all along and F/ACTION was as familiar as the YMCA or al-Qaeda. A few widely read bloggers speculated on the links between FACT's agenda and its background in the horror show of eugenics. I didn't ask how Ari had arranged that.

I called the university's Media Relations Office and made an appointment for tomorrow morning at ten. I didn't tell them what it was about, just that it was important.

After a while, the various rumors started generating exaggerations, contradictions, and denials. All according to plan. The more discord and noise we could cause, the more attention it would draw, which before long could grow into pandemonium. At some point, all this had to cause trouble for Morris Griffin. Or so we figured.

A little after three thirty I sucked up my nerve and headed out into the big bad world for my showdown with Doris Ballaster and Tom Freebinder. I wasn't looking forward to this, but some things have to be done.

Gopal showed me in for the third time; we were getting to be old mates. Doris and Tom were both in the living room, as at our first meeting. Today the drapes were open and the picture window displayed its expensive view of Riverside Park.

Doris's costume was subdued this time, almost funereal, a gray blouse with a strand of pearls. The opening salvo in her message to me, no doubt.

“Sit down, Adam,” she said.

I sat. Evidently neither coffee nor cognac were going to be on offer.

“I am hoping you will be able to clear up my understanding of things,” she went on. “In particular, I hope you can help me decide whether to interpret your behavior as failure or as betrayal. Or as both.”

I took a deep breath and said, “I’ve spent the last three months investigating the Shroud to the best of my ability. My ability in things like this, if not second to none, isn’t far behind. I started out on the assumption, shared with you, that it must be a fake. The 1988 radiocarbon testing indicated an origin around the fourteenth century, but there are doubts about that test, which I need to look into further. The real problem, however, is the nature of the image itself, the image on the Shroud. Three problems, to be precise.

“First, the image is actually a photonegative, such that only when it is photographed and developed as a negative does a positive image emerge. How would a medieval artist have had any concept of a photographic negative, let alone understand how to depict one?

“Second, the image is extremely superficial, existing only on the outermost millimeters of the fabric. How such an image might have been created is still completely open to question—possibly some type of radiation, as yet undetermined—but it is essentially impossible to imagine how any fourteenth-century craftsman could have done it. The various modern-day craftsmen who have attempted to demonstrate how it was done have, in my opinion, only shown how it wasn’t done. Their efforts to solve the mystery only serve to deepen it.

“And third, the image has been shown to encode three-dimensional digital information. It is, in effect, a hologram. That *has* been demonstrated. No medieval artist could have produced that.

One theorist I talked with thinks it was done by space aliens, but I won't go into that."

"There is no need to be flippant," she said sourly.

"I don't feel flippant in the least. Because the day after I sent you an e-mail about my growing doubts, I got a phone threat, warning me to stop investigating the Shroud or face the consequences. I didn't imagine he meant a lawsuit.

"He didn't. I continued investigating, and two days later I was pushed down a flight of stairs in Rome. The man on the phone had called me 'smart boy,' and that's what the guy who pushed me said—'Last warning, smart boy.'

"I survived, obviously, but I was banged up. I'm a stubborn cuss, though, so I kept on with it. The historical traces led me to Istanbul, where I was jumped and beaten up by three goons. They left a note in my pocket; its wording has stuck in my memory: 'Next time they wont find your body, smart boy.' They left the apostrophe out of 'won't.'"

"I had nothing to do with any of that," she said. "It must have been one of these fanatical fundamentalist religious groups."

"I don't think so. I went on to Jerusalem, a possible place of origin for the Shroud, of course. There I was jumped again, in an alley, by two men, one with a knife. They called me by name and also by 'smart boy' and advised me to say any final prayers. I managed to take them down—stubborn survivor—and then I lifted a few souvenirs off of them. One was a signet ring from an organization calling itself Free Action for Clear Thinking, or FACT for short. Ring any bells?"

Her face fell momentarily, but she was nothing if not self-controlled.

"I am a member of FACT and proud to be one."

"FACT has a darker side to it," I continued, "a terrorist wing designated F/ACTION, which is overseen by a rich Brit named Morris Griffin. Any more bells ringing?"

"Terrorists? That is hysterical nonsense."

"The signet ring, Mrs. Ballaster, that's specific to F/ACTION. Now, tell me about Morris Griffin."

"This is absurd. I am ... acquainted with Mr. Griffin, but ..."

I took the ring out of my pocket and showed it to her then to Freebinder, who examined it carefully and then grunted.

"How well acquainted?" I asked.

She shook her head.

Rather to my surprise, Freebinder said to her, "You phoned him, Doris?"

She glared at him and snapped, "I may have done."

"After Dr. Hult's e-mail?" he asked.

"After, before, what's the difference? Morris has always championed our cause."

He handed the ring back to me, saying, "I'm sorry about this. Things obviously got out of control."

"Those chaps seemed under control to me. Controlled by your friend Griffin, to be specific."

"I doubt if you can prove that," he said.

"I'm not interested in proving it, as long as the three of us are aware of it. As long as Mrs. Ballaster's understanding of things has been cleared up."

▪ ▪ ▪ ▪ ▪ ▪

Ari and Sareen and I, now in full operational mode, stayed in my apartment for dinner. Sareen served up something she called *samkeh harra*, which was grilled blackfish marinated in a sauce with oranges, chiles, and cilantro. It was delicious—Ari said so.

While I was jollying it up with Doris and Tom, Ari had unearthed some more, potentially useful, intel on Morris Griffin. Our ultra-rationalist, it turned out, had his superstitions. I don't know exactly how Ari roots out things like that; he just does.

They were quirky superstitions. One of them had to do with numbers. Not with the usual suspects—three, six, seven, or thirteen, for instance—but with prime numbers larger than thirteen (these things can't be explained). The primes above thirteen start with seventeen, nineteen, twenty-three, twenty-nine, thirty-one, thirty-seven ... Morris didn't like these numbers, was afraid of them. To deal with this fear and try to allay it, he had memorized all the primes up to a thousand, and he avoided them as far as possible. Of course he couldn't avoid them altogether, but he wouldn't, for example, stay in a hotel room with a prime number or schedule important business on any such days of the month.

He was also afraid of blackbirds—and crows, ravens, and so on. He believed they were looking at him, watching him. We spent a lively hour plotting how we might pepper him with blackbirds and prime numbers.

As the evening matured, further results of our Internet campaign bubbled up to the surface. It was almost like watching election returns. People took sides, made up stories, warned about hoaxes, and expressed alarm, umbrage, and rancor. The bigger it got, the uglier and more chaotic it got.

It wouldn't do to stay up all night, though, as we had a big day coming tomorrow. Ari went home around eleven, and Sareen and I went to bed. None of us, safe to say, fell asleep right away.

▪ ▪ ▪ ▪ ▪ ▪

Ari came over again at eight in the morning for breakfast, with plenty of coffee. He announced that the second stage in our campaign, Aggravate, was commencing. One indication of this, apart from our own capers, was that the target had started reacting. FACT had issued an angry official statement, denying everything and threatening record-breaking slander and libel suits. There was a certain vagueness to the threat, however, belying their frustration over being ignorant of the source, the instigator, the villain, the quarry. For them, I imagine, it was like being in a wild west cavalry fort with arrows flying in from every direction.

Another sign that the murk was stirring was a copy of the *New York Post* that Ari had brought with him. The headline screamed: "Adam Charges Shroud Bash!"

I dressed in my academic regalia, or suit and tie at least, for my ten o'clock appointment at the Columbia University Office of Media Relations. Both Ari and Sareen insisted, as per Ari's scenario, that she should accompany me. And so she did, looking like a million dollars in a dark-blue power suit. Media Relations was over in the northwest corner of the campus, only a fifteen-minute walk from my apartment. Outside, it was one of those regrettably rare perfect summer days in Manhattan, sunny but not too hot. With Sareen walking beside me, I seemed to attract more than a few glances.

After a brief wait in the receptionist's area, we were shown into the supervisor's office. This person was a tall woman, well turned out, also in a power suit, naturally. Her auburn hair was so immaculately styled that it looked plastic. She introduced herself as Tracy Schippers and offered us coffee, which we declined.

Ms. Schippers probably knew of me already and certainly, since I made the appointment yesterday, had read my file. With a concerned expression, unfeigned I would guess, she asked me what this was about.

"Over the past several months," I began, "I have been researching a historical object of uncertain origins but of great scientific interest and with immense impact on the human imagination. I refer to the Shroud of Turin, reputed to be the burial garment of Jesus Christ but regarded by most experts as a medieval forgery. My goal, as a historian, has been to ascertain the truth about it, whatever that might be.

"In the course of this research, about a month ago, I received a phone call threatening me with violence unless I abandoned the project. I was alarmed, naturally, but I refused to be intimidated by crude fanatics. When I persisted, however, I was physically assaulted on three separate occasions. On the last of these, they expressed the intention of murdering me in order to put a stop to my research. I survived all these encounters, as you can see, but like Coriolanus, I could show you my scars."

I didn't think she would recognize the Shakespearean allusion, but I was trying to sound as academic as possible.

"That is certainly ... disturbing, Professor Hult," she said, "but do you have any knowledge of who these ruffians might be or their motive for attacking you?"

I figured that those ruffians had earned me a small degree of poetic license.

"They said they were sent by an organization called Free Action for Clear Thinking, or FACT, which, ironically, presents itself to the public as a champion of free inquiry and scientific progress. Moreover, I have physical evidence in my possession to corroborate that identification. Far from being a champion of free inquiry, I'm afraid, FACT turns out to be a violent enemy of academic freedom."

"I see," Ms. Schippers temporized. "This is indeed a most disturbing allegation, Professor Hult. In fact, you see, I am somewhat familiar with FACT, and I have never—"

"I was there!" Sareen broke in furiously. "I was there when Dr. Hult was assaulted by those cutthroats! He prevented them from killing me—or worse. They are ... unspeakable!"

This outburst perturbed the Media Relations supervisor.

"Well, Ms.... Khouri, is it? Are you an ... academic person also?"

"I am a senior official with the Global Organization for Democratic Faith, headquartered in Beirut and Rome and with offices and operations across Europe and the Middle East. My credentials are here for your inspection."

Her voice trembled with affronted indignation as she rummaged in her purse.

"That won't be necessary, Ms. Khouri, I'm sure. I can assure you that the university will wish to settle this matter as expeditiously as possible. Now, Professor Hult, can you tell me why you have come to this office? Why not to, say, the Office of Academic Affairs?"

"That will be my next stop. But I insist on publishing an official protest through Media Relations. This is a flagrant violation of academic freedom, and as such it is an attack on the university itself."

"I understand, Professor Hult, but—"

"I must insist, Ms. Schippers. If this sort of atrocity isn't publicly exposed and officially condemned, what next? Will we shut down the university when they threaten to bomb us?"

"Oh, I doubt it will come to that. Really, I'll need to consult with my superiors—"

"Otherwise I will go directly to the *Times*, the *Daily News*, and *USA Today*, not to mention *The Today Show* and *Letterman*, and tell this outrageous story in my own words, including the fact that Columbia University's Media Relations Office refused to go public with it."

"And I will call my editors in Rome, Paris, and London," snarled Sareen.

Ms. Schippers swallowed a parrot and turned to her keyboard. "If you could just give me the particulars ..."

CHAPTER 35

While Sareen and I were steamrolling Media Relations, Ari phoned a friend of his who was an investigative journalist in Tel Aviv and Jerusalem. He asked him to check with the Jerusalem Police and find out whether they had turned up any evidence to confirm my story of having thwarted a mugging there.

Next we focused on a sub-operation we called Bedevilment. Griffin's corporate headquarters were in London, and he lived in a suite occupying one of the upper floors of the Dorchester. Ari, with his uncanny powers in cyberspace, had penetrated all their computer networks. Using a sophisticated graphics program, he created hordes of blackbirds, ravens, and crows, each one with beady black eyes staring back at the viewer. Sareen suggested that the eyes should flicker with light at uneven intervals, and Ari made it happen. The birds would come and go on their computer screens, unpredictably and uncontrollably. After that, he hacked into their corporate communications, inserting prime numbers randomly and liberally—a prime contagion, he called it. He did the same things with Griffin's personal Internet connections.

After another working lunch in my apartment, I called Chou Li-Cheng's cell phone. Over the past several weeks, I had been considering and refining the follow-up questions I wanted to ask him about that radiocarbon dating of the Shroud. The call went to voicemail, and I asked him to get back to me at his convenience.

By two that afternoon, the BBC, CNN, and FoxNews had all picked up the story, treating it as a potentially explosive hybrid of serious allegations, wild insinuations, and celebrity zaniness. On CNN's Cafferty Report, Jack Cafferty asked his viewers which was the bigger story, Adam Hult becoming a believer in the Shroud of Turin, or Morris Griffin and FACT being accused of terrorism. As usual, the responses were mixed. One viewer speculated that when I visited the Vatican I must have been abducted and brainwashed. Another wondered if Griffin was a figment of my paranoid imagination. A third viewer was convinced that the whole affair had been concocted as the lead-in to a new reality show.

Although my Droid was a new number, that was little hindrance to the media, and the cell had been ringing steadily for the last hour or two. In order to keep control of events as far as possible, I screened out all except a few personal calls. Keep 'em guessing.

We were watching Bill O'Reilly fulminate a comparison of Morris Griffin with Saddam Hussein when Chou called back.

"Thanks for getting back to me, Li-Cheng. Are you free to talk?"

"Free as bird. Hey, you in the news, man, crazy stuff. Any of it true?"

"A kernel of truth covered by husks of wild speculation. In a fairly direct way, all that frenzy in the news is connected with what I want to ask you about. You remember when we talked a couple of months ago about carbon 14 testing?"

"Sure I remember. More than remember. Today not the first time you in the news. After we talk last time, I see them get all excited about famous guy Adam Hult investigating famous Shroud of Turin. So, not-so-famous physics guy Chou add it up in fraction of one second. You talk to me about dating some old cloth. This shroud, it some old cloth."

"I can't put anything over on you, can I?"

"Not much likely, man. So after that, I check out this shroud and the test they done on it back in 1988. Hey, great year, '88—you know what happen then?"

"Lots of things, I guess. What've you got in mind?"

"That the year Chou Li-Cheng first come to America, grad assistant in physics lab at UCLA. In LA, you know?"

"I know. Congratulations, Li-Cheng. You've come a long way."

"Too far maybe. But too late now for fortune-telling business. So anyway, I check out this shroud, like I say. I go over their testing procedure. But also, I check out previous history of this piece of cloth. Long history, known about back for more than six hundred years."

"Right. I'm glad you went to that trouble because that's just what I want to ask you about. The thing is, a number of questions have been raised about the exact section of the Shroud from which they took their samples, as well as the way in which the tests were carried out."

"I know, man, I know. I examine all those questions. Some of them really good questions, tough ones. But biggest question, I think, is one you say about corner of cloth they cut samples from. People, lot of people, been grabbing that corner to hold up cloth for showing. Look like Catholic bishops with those tall hats, you know? On the Internet I found old drawings and paintings of them doing that. Even bishops got sweaty hands. They do this maybe twenty, thirty times over few hundred years. You know what that do to cloth?"

"Carbon contamination?"

"Sure. Now, those scientists doing test, they might be able to clean that out—only might, only maybe, still big error factor—but they don't even take into account that corner of cloth been grabbed and squeezed. So now we got big problem, Adam. Error factor way too high, who knows how high. So sorry, too bad."

"No, Li-Cheng, maybe not too bad. If we're scientists, we want the truth, right?"

"You scientist too now, Adam?"

"In my own way. Thanks a bunch, Li-Cheng."

I rejoined Sareen and Ari in monitoring events. Griffin's lawyers had issued several statements categorically denying these vile and unfounded accusations. They especially denounced my charges of having been assaulted, or if I had been, it wasn't by anyone remotely associated with their client. They mentioned countercharges of libel and slander, but things were moving too fast and the facts were too high up in the air for them to take any specific action.

Meanwhile, the ferment continued on Twitter, Facebook, countless blogs, talk radio, and the TV news channels. It was mostly out of our hands now, but that was all right at this point. For dinner, we phone-ordered a couple of pizzas, washed down with more local microbrews. While we munched, I filled them in on what Chou had told me, adding that it lined up with my own conclusions.

"So, my mentalist friend," Ari said, "just how big a conclusion are we jumping to here?"

"Tentative, tentative, ever and always tentative," I qualified, "especially with an object as incendiary as the Shroud."

"Tentative conclusion then."

"At this point, the balance of probability indicates a history going as far back as the first century. But that, of course, is still considerably short of affirming a supernatural event."

"Considerably short? Doesn't sound that way to me. What are the other options? Jesus or some other guy got crucified and bled and sweated onto the sheet? I thought you said it couldn't have happened that way."

"That's right. That is, the image itself wasn't caused that way. If the Shroud covered Jesus or, as you say, some other poor dude, he would have bled and sweated all over it, right enough, but that would have soaked through the fabric. The bloodstains on the Shroud, by the way, do seem to have been made exactly that way. But the image of the man himself is extremely superficial. Determining what *did* cause it turns out to be one whopper of a challenge."

Sareen wiped her mouth and smiled at both of us. "The answer is so simple that it eludes our understanding," she said. She didn't say any more, and Ari changed the subject, warning us that the time had come for us to redouble our precautions. He judged that Griffin might be sending more of his torpedoes our way at any time. He asked us whether we minded if he bedded down on my couch. We said of course not, and he, ever prepared, went out to his Highlander and brought up a gym bag. There was probably a Glock tucked in with his underwear, but I didn't nose around.

We spent the rest of the evening watching events continue to unfold. At one point, Sareen brought up a concern about my mother.

"She's alone now, isn't she?" she said. "In that same house that you grew up in?"

"Yeah, she is."

"She probably gets lonely."

She didn't say any more about it, and neither did I. Since nothing new seemed to be breaking in our troublemaking campaign, we decided to make an early night of it and get an early start in the morning. We made sure the deadbolt was engaged, and I got out a blanket and pillow for Ari.

▮ ▮ ▮ ▮ ▮ ▮

He was up just after dawn, which comes early in June. I heard him stirring around and got up to join him. Sareen got up too and went to the kitchen to brew some coffee. We checked the Internet and the media and found that Griffin, feeling the pressure, had agreed to a live interview with a tame journalist who always treated him favorably. Whether or not his lawyers favored this move, we didn't know. The interview was scheduled to begin in half an hour at seven o'clock our time, which would be noon in London.

The interviewer was a veteran British reporter named Ian Chandler, and the venue was Griffin's luxurious London office. Before the show began, the camera panned around, lingering on the vanity wall featuring photos of Griffin on safari, Griffin deep-sea fishing, Griffin with the queen and with a couple of prime ministers and other luminaries. If clout counted for anything, Griffin had plenty of clout.

Then we came to the two principals, seated near each other in cushy leather chairs as if for a cozy chat. Chandler was slender and angular, birdlike, with bottle-brown hair, gold-rimmed glasses, and a pencil-line mustache. Griffin looked like a somewhat older and angrier version of his picture on the book jacket. If looks could kill, as they say, I would be a stain on the wall. I reminded myself that while I could see him, he couldn't see me.

I crossed my fingers.

Chandler began (plummy voice): "Good morning, everyone. I am Ian Chandler, here at the corporate headquarters of the Griffin Group. We're here to sound out the views of Morris Griffin himself concerning this sudden and extraordinary uproar that has seized public attention. Thank you for granting this interview, Mr. Griffin, under what we know are trying circumstances."

Griffin (grunt): "Welcome."

Chandler: "A remarkable flurry of the most absurd and outrageous charges involving you and your business affairs seems to have erupted almost overnight. Do you have any idea, sir, how this has come about?"

Griffin: "I know it's bloody nonsense."

Chandler: "Yes, sir, frightfully distressing. However nonsensical, though, it has exploded over the last twenty-four hours. There must be some explanation, wouldn't you think?"

Griffin: "Don't think, mate, I know. It's that weasel snoop Hult. Nothing else it could be."

Chandler: "Ah, yes. You refer, of course, to Adam Hult, the Columbia University historian who *allegedly* was assaulted by certain persons who *may* be connected with one of your organizations."

Griffin: "If he claims that, he's a damned liar."

Chandler: "Indeed, indeed. I am uncertain whether he himself has claimed the link directly, but others certainly have. There also appear to be some bizarre allegations of illegal arms sales to foreign nationals. Can you clear that up for us?"

Griffin: "More stupid lies. My solicitors will squeeze the last farthing out of every halfwit who tries it on."

Chandler: "Yes, sir, I have no doubt of that. So then, are you denying any involvement in weapons trafficking?"

Griffin: "Morris Griffin has nothing to deny."

Chandler: "Um, I see. Well, sir, perhaps we can move on to these *unsubstantiated* claims that you have violated certain Inland Revenue statutes. What is your response to that?"

Griffin: "Talk to all those accountants and lawyers on the payroll. Maybe we can find out if they're worth what I pay them." (Tooth-baring grin.)

Chandler: "I'm sure they are. Now, there is also a charge of another sort that seems to gain intensity by the hour. This hysterical slur concerns your recently published book, *Bury the Zombie God*. People are saying—or at any rate tweeting and blogging—that you advocate sterilizing those who may be 'unfit' to propagate themselves. It must be malicious slander, but they say you advocate what amounts to exterminating people of low intelligence or with physical or racial abnormalities. Can you refute these appalling and ridiculous smears for us, sir?"

Griffin (harsh laugh): "Anybody that whimpers about it can go to the head of the line."

Chandler (blanching): "I-I'm not sure I understand, sir. Could you explain that, please?"

Griffin: "Clive, my solicitor over there, the one waving his arms, he doesn't want me to explain it. Anyhow, I think my meaning is plain enough. I'm a plain man."

Chandler: "Yes, sir, no one will dispute that. Well, er, we, ah—well then, it looks like we'll have to wrap it up here. I'm Ian Chandler, and we've been hearing the views of Morris Griffin, board chairman and president of the Griffin Group. Thank you, Mr. Griffin, for being so candid with us."

Griffin: "Umph."

They went to an anchor's rehash and commentary. Ari leaped up with a fist pump, spilling his coffee cup and whooping, "Gotcha, Morrie!"

"Easy, boy," I cautioned, "we're not there yet."

"No, but Operation Aggravate is in full swing. Now that it's rolling along, we'll give it a few extra pushes."

So while Sareen fried some bacon and potatoes and scrambled some eggs, Ari monkeyed around in cyberspace, inciting mayhem—mainly, I assumed, with particular reference to Morris's unguarded remarks.

Shortly after nine o'clock, CNN flashed the "Breaking News" that Columbia's Media Relations Office had issued a formal statement protesting vicious assaults on a member of the university faculty, Dr. Adam Hult, while he was engaged in serious academic research. Pending further investigation, preliminary indications were that the assailants were connected with an extremist wing of a hitherto unimpeachable organization, Free Action for Clear Thinking, or FACT. This extremist wing was thought to operate under the name F/ACTION. The University demanded an inquiry into this deplorable violation of academic freedom.

And in a sidebar, CNN reported that the Jerusalem District Police had just announced the arrest of two men on suspicion of an armed attack against the very same Adam Hult. Acting on a tip from Israeli journalist Zeke Golman, detectives were looking into links with a group called FACT or possibly F/ACTION. As the suspects, who carried no identification, spoke British English and apparently nothing else, the Israelis were forwarding their fingerprints to New Scotland Yard.

"Now," the CNN anchor exulted, "we're getting somewhere!"

CHAPTER 36

With these developments, Ari informed us that Infuriate, the third and hopefully last stage in our campaign, was commencing. Meanwhile, we had decided I should take calls from both CNN and CBS's *60 Minutes*. These were, you might say, the lucky two piranhas that got tossed a goldfish. While they didn't overtly offer heaps of cash for an interview, they covertly offered heaps of cash for an interview. We stipulated that, for security reasons, the interviews had to take place at my apartment.

Anywhere, they both said, and the sooner the better. We scheduled CNN for noon and *60 Minutes* for two.

In the meantime, the three of us conferred over coffee in the kitchen about the status of this private war that we were turning into a public one.

"It's gotten bigger than I ever anticipated," I said, "and faster."

"The nature of the new beast," Ari said.

"Which beast do you mean?" Sareen asked.

"Information and communications technology. But remember, the tech explosion is a human artifact. We've made it, we control it—mostly control it, that is, for now—and so it's an expression of who we are. For better and worse."

"And it's still exploding," I said.

"Day by day. Its future course is unpredictable, but it's certain to become harder for any individual or group or government to keep it reined in. Like you said, Adam, too big and too fast. Nanotech, IT, neuroscience, pharma, cyber—all those and a dozen others are growing too fast to be predictable or, possibly, controllable. Add to that that they're getting smarter too. It's like what Satchel Paige said: 'Don't look back—something might be gaining on you.'"

"Sounds like the plot line of a hundred sci-fi novels," I said.

"But this, as some character usually observes in such novels, isn't a novel," Ari observed. He stood up and pulled his iPhone from a pocket.

"Consider this little toy," he said. "More computing power than the Apollo astronauts had. In a few seconds and with a little know-how, I can access more information than the CIA could back then. But five years from now? Ten years? Literally, no one knows where this is going. The experts' educated guesses are just guesses."

"Back to the present," Sareen said, "it appears that what we have set in motion is already beyond our control. What are the chances that it might turn and attack us?"

"Just so we're clear here," Ari said, " the 'it' we're talking about is the media firestorm. Griffin and his troops will be fighting back as best they can, and we'll have to deal with that the best we can. As for the media monster... well, yeah, we can't really control it. The challenge of the game is to steer it better than they can."

"The game?" Sareen queried doubtfully. "In the way that bull-fighting is a game?"

"Something like that. Yes, something very much like that."

▪ ▪ ▪ ▪ ▪ ▪

The CNN crew arrived at 11:30 and set up their equipment,. The interviewer was another of these young women who, if beautiful and articulate enough, gravitate to that profession. She started by tossing a couple of softballs to set me at ease and then cut to the chase.

"Now, Dr. Hult, you haven't just stirred up a storm here, you've made some pretty serious allegations. But do you have any proof or evidence that either FACT or F/ACTION is responsible for the attacks on you?"

"Yes, I do. After subduing the two men in Jerusalem, I took their passports and also a signet ring that one of them was wearing. Our experts have determined that the passports were counterfeit and made in London. The signet ring, which I have here, has an insignia bearing the secret symbols of F/ACTION."

"According to experts in your camp or in your pay?"

"Your own experts are welcome to have at it. That's what it is."

"We may do just that. Now, Dr. Hult, you must be aware that the rumors circulating—no, make that swarming—all over the web are implicating a British businessman by the name of Morris Griffin with this so-called F/ACTION group. Can you comment on that?"

"I can. Anyone who checks it out will find that Morris Griffin is one of the founders of FACT and has been their head of operations for over a decade. Dig a little deeper, and you'll find he's also the godfather of F/ACTION, their hit squad, responsible for the torching and vandalizing of numerous churches, synagogues, and mosques in the UK and across Europe."

"That's quite a serious charge, Dr. Hult. Can you substantiate it?"

"You're CNN—dig into it yourselves."

"That's happening even as we speak. Will you be pressing charges?"

"My attorney is considering all our options." Well, maybe he was.

Not long after they left, and while we were munching a quick lunch, the *60 Minutes* folks showed up and we went through much the same drill, though they probed a little deeper into my academic background, my deal with Doris Ballaster, and my investigation of the Shroud. I answered their questions honestly, though of course with some spin. Our bet was that all this exposure was our gain as much as MG's bane. The idea was to keep ramping up the pressure.

"Hey!" Ari yelled when *60 Minutes* was folding up their stuff. "Get this—Griffin's press secretary has just announced that he, the man himself, is going to give a wide-open press conference beginning at eight this evening, their time."

"That's, let's see, three o'clock here," I said. "Fifteen minutes! Check it out on CNN."

We did, and CNN was just interrupting their own commentary on my interview to flash this late-breaking development.

"His lawyers cannot have advised this," Sareen observed.

"Over their dead or choking bodies," Ari said.

"The man wouldn't have gotten to where he is without a mind of his own," I noted.

"A mind of his own," Sareen mused. "Perhaps we shall see."

We stayed with CNN, who of course were scuttling their regularly scheduled programming and scrambling to set up the feed from London. Their act was impressive; within two minutes, their chief London correspondent appeared live on camera, rather breathless but professionally put together. We saw the press corps busily taking their seats and checking their notes and smart phones. There were dozens of them, with more filling in around the edges. A battery of microphones bristled in front of a large podium with the Griffin Group logo on it. The logo was similar to the F/ACTION insignia but more abstract.

As the top of the hour approached, there was a bustle of technicians and flunkies around and behind the podium. Finally a pinch-faced man in a dark-blue suit came out from the anteroom, glancing behind him, and came to the podium and leaned into the mikes.

"Ladies and gentlemen of the press," he said, "thank you for coming on such short notice. This evening Mr. Griffin has graciously consented to entertain any questions you may have, but I believe he will open with a prepared statement.

"Mr. Griffin."

The introducer's body language was almost that of an eighteenth-century French courtier as he welcomed his boss to the podium. Griffin himself looked much the same as in the Ian Chandler interview that same morning, but more tired, exasperated, and wrathful. Moving stiffly and trembling all over, he slapped a sheet of paper down on the podium and cleared his throat harshly. Along with a whole lot of other people, we were on the edge of our seats.

Griffin: "Here I am, let's get on with it. I know I'm not talking just to these pencil-pushers but to all you people all over the planet who've been sucked in by the feeble-minded lies of a gaggle of pipsqueaks who think they can take me down. We'll see about that tonight. We'll see who's taking who down, and just how far down.

"Now, before you start with the questions, I've got this prepared statement I'm going to read. And just in case you're wondering, this wasn't written by any ninety-pound lawyer. This is me, Morris Griffin."

He read: "If you think I was born with a silver spoon in my mouth, you're dead wrong. It was the mean streets of Bristol for me. Nobody gave me anything. I had to fight for whatever I could get—fight to get it and fight to hang on to it. But I'm a good fighter, always have been, always will be. Not everybody can make it to the top, but I did. Nobody gave that to me either. I fought for it and won it fair and square.

"All along the way too, I explained to the people I was dealing with just who I am and what I stand for. I don't believe anybody gives you anything for free in this world, nor should they. I believe in Darwinian natural selection and the survival of the fittest. Who else but the fittest—the toughest and the best—ought to survive? What kind of a world would that be? A world of losers and whiners and beggars, the kind of human garbage the world has been drowning in all my life. The kind of human garbage that can't make it on their own, so they invent gods and heavens and guardian angels to call on so they can be protected and comforted and provided with all the things they're too lazy or weak or stupid to get for themselves. The worst trouble with the human garbage is they hump like rabbits and spread themselves like an epidemic, and their stupid gods and guardian angels spread with them, and they all get organized into these help-me, pity-me societies, these praise-God, glory-to-God plagues.

"So I, along with some like-minded people, took a stand against all that puke. I stood up for self-help, self-reliance, and self-domination. I stood up for reality, what you can see and touch and grab hold of. I stood up for reason and science and freethinking, over against all their damned spiritual mumbo-jumbo. I founded Free Action for Clear Thinking. That's FACT to you, ladies. Me and people like me, we think clearly and we act on what we think. You want me to apologize for that? Not on your life, sister.

"Now, any questions?"

Journalist in front row (outshouting many others): "Thank you for speaking so frankly, sir. What can you tell us about these rumors that have been surfacing about your troubles with the Inland Revenue?"

Griffin: "You shouldn't pay attention to rumors."

Same journalist: "But what are the *facts*, sir, the *reality?* Do you think they'll be taking you to court?"

Griffin: "They'd be fools to try. That's not to say they aren't fools."

Journalist in fourth row: "Yes, sir. What is your response to all these allegations that your organization, Free Action for Clear Thinking, or FACT for short, has been involved in numerous acts of arson and vandalism against various religious sites?"

Griffin: "More stupid nonsense. Just who are all these cryba-bies? I could give 'em a cold shoulder to cry on."

Same journalist: "Within the last few hours we've learned that two men have been arrested in Jerusalem under circumstances that seem to support the charge that they assaulted Adam Hult there. What's your comment on that?"

Griffin (glowering): "Don't know who they are, no connection to me, but it looks like they botched their job."

Journalist in third row: "On another subject, sir, questions have been raised about your involvement in the international arms trade, and specifically that some of that involvement may have been illegal. Can you comment on that?"

Griffin: "That's my own business. It's only candy-striped politicians and bureaucrats that dream up those laws anyway."

Same journalist: "One of our sources reports that you've done an arms deal with North Korea. Can you confirm or deny that?"

Griffin: "Is that a joke, son?"

Over the room's audio system came a loud, disembodied voice, a resonant baritone, pronouncing: *"The countdown is at seventy-one."*

Griffin (flinching back a step): "Jesus Christ! What the hell is that?"

Technician (from off-camera): "Don't know, sir. We're working on it."

Griffin (furiously): "Clear away all the damned blackbirds while you're at it!"

I looked a big question at Ari. He shrugged and said, "A cohort of mine in London. I put a flea in his ear on the off chance that something like this might develop. He's a wizard of a technician. The numbers, of course, will be primes."

Corporate aide (at Griffin's elbow): "It's only a glitch, sir. We're live on camera, remember."

Griffin: "Back off, junior. No one's ever beat me yet, and these fairies won't beat me now. Next question!"

Journalist near the rear: "Continuing with the subject of arms deals, is it true that during the recent bloody civil war in the Congo, you sold weapons to both sides?"

Griffin: "I'm a businessman, son. We sell products to people willing to pay for them. We don't examine their politics."

Same journalist: "Are you aware that such arms sales are contrary to international law?"

Griffin: "Same answer as before. If those international girl scouts can't enforce their rules, they should just shut the hell up."

Same journalist: "Those deals were for millions of pounds or euros or dollars, and that's an impoverished nation. Can you comment on the claim that the money was raised by extortion, child slavery, and sexual slavery?"

Griffin: "Not on my end of the deal. How the woolies handle their end of the deal is none of my concern."

Black female journalist in front row: "Woolies?"

Griffin (wide grin): "Can't use the N-word, can we?"

Disembodied voice: *"The countdown is at sixty-seven."*

Griffin: "What the hell, I told you weenies to fix that! Don't you get what they're doing? The numbers, the *numbers*!"

Loud sound of birds squawking.

Griffin: "The hell? *Stop it!*"

Journalist in second row: "Sir, if you don't mind, I have a question about your book, *Bury the Zombie God*. In it, you seem to be advocating what amounts to a sort of general euthanasia. And just now in your prepared statement, you were talking about eliminating what you referred to as human garbage. Are you saying that there is no special value to human life?"

Griffin: "No special value except what you can make of it by your own effort. And even that's only a temporary fix. In the end we're all garbage anyway."

Same journalist: "That sounds rather harsh. Do you mean it to sound that way?"

Griffin: "Sounds like what it is."

Black female journalist in front row: "But most of us are garbage already, right? Can you explain that or elaborate on it?"

Griffin: "Elaborate? Do I have to explain everything to you slow learners? Do I have to spell it all out for you? What is it you don't get about the difference between people like me who stand on their own feet and people like the bleeding hearts and cripples and religion freaks who crouch down on their knees and beg and pray for anything and everything? The difference seems plain enough to me."

Same journalist: "So are you saying, sir, that people in that second category should be eliminated?"

Griffin (harsh laugh): "I know, I know, trick question. Give the man enough rope and let him hang himself. But not Morris Griffin, sister. The answer is, just quit with the handouts to the garbage and it'll rot away all by itself."

Same journalist: "Rotting all around you, sir. Wouldn't that cause quite a stink?"

Griffin: "What we build bulldozers for."

Same journalist: "After the garbage has rotted, sir, or before, while it's still in the rotting process?"

Griffin: "Before, during, after—"

Disembodied voice: *"The countdown is at thirty-seven."*

Griffin (shouting): "You skipped some! You're trying to mess with my mind! Who do you think you are? Who the hell are you?"

Technician (off camera, frantically): "We're working on it, sir!"

Griffin: "They can't mess with my mind! Nobody messes with Morris Griffin's mind!"

Journalist in sixth row: "A minute ago you mentioned blackbirds. There are weird reports of blackbirds appearing on computer screens all over this building. Can you tell us just what's going on?"

Griffin (purple faced): "Nothing's going on, damn you! They want you to think it's these demons from hell, but science has proved there's no heaven or hell or freaking demons or twenty-four blackbirds, and those numbers you can't divide can't hurt you even if you can't divide them. They only want you to *think* they can hurt you, but the mind makes its own reality, and the mind of the strong man and the superior man makes its own strong and superior reality, and nothing can touch it or shake it or get to it, none of these damned blackbirds or grinning ghosts or staring numbers. They just want you to think there's a hell gaping at the end, but there's no such thing, and Adam bloody Hult, I know you're behind all this and you can just go to hell, or better yet I'll send you there myself on a one-way ticket—"

Disembodied voice: *"The countdown is at nineteen."*

Raucous bird squawks.

The reporters scrambled for their smart phones.

CHAPTER 37

"Holy Birkenstocks," I said. "We made all that happen?"

"He has done most of it to himself," said Sareen.

"No fist pump this time, I notice," I said.

Ari wasn't smiling. "Infuriate is working, obviously, but it isn't over with yet. Just now, and the next twenty-four hours maybe, will be our extreme hazard zone."

Sareen was pouring us all some more coffee. "You don't mind this, do you," she said to him. "In fact, I think you rather enjoy it."

He thought about that and then said, "I'll put it this way, Sareen. I didn't create or order up this world we live in. Like everyone else, I inherited it. I also inherited certain skills with which to deal with it. I've worked to develop those skills. And I'm lucky enough to have a few friends, like your friend Adam here, and now you too. If I can use my skills to help a friend out now and then, I feel good about that. Enjoy it? I guess maybe, in the way a high diver enjoys doing a twisting two-and-a-half somersault from ten meters."

"I can understand that," she said. "But I don't enjoy it. I want it to end, hope it will end. Twenty-four hours, you said?"

"My best estimate. For F/ACTION, it's coming down to now or never. There are no certainties, though. Like you, I'm hoping."

For dinner, we ordered out again, this time from a local deli that delivered roast beef sandwiches on sourdough. We had beer on hand but limited ourselves to one bottle each, and Sareen had orange juice.

While we were eating, Sareen said, "If they try to attack us here, how will they get to us? During the day, there is a doorman, and when he leaves, isn't the building alarmed?"

"All true," Ari said, "but for resourceful people, there are ways to get around those defenses."

"Like taking out poor old Thomaz?" I said.

"That would be a bad choice," he said. "Too apt to draw attention. They will want to be quiet about it until they can get close to us."

My Droid rang. The caller ID showed, of all people, Tom Freebinder.

"Adam Hult here."

"Good evening, Adam. Been an interesting day, hasn't it? Something like Hurricane Katrina for the media."

"May you live in interesting times," I quoted.

"More of a curse than a blessing, I think. And you have a certain talent for making them more interesting."

"Some talent. What's on your mind, Tom?"

"Just want to clear the air, I suppose. I trust you realize that we, Mrs. Ballaster and myself, had nothing directly to do with those attacks against you."

"The operative word being *directly.*"

"That's right. She talked to him, told him what you were doing, told him when you expressed doubts about the project and about the origins of that troublesome old piece of cloth. But that's all. The rest is down to him. Well, we all saw the Great Griffin Meltdown Show."

"Broke all their ratings records, I imagine."

"Probably. Okay, with that out of the way, I'll only bother you with one other thing. About those allegations of Griffin's tax evasion and fraud. The agency I used to work for has a lot of sources.

I suspect they could turn over that pile of dung and see what's crawling underneath it."

"Better sources than the Inland Revenue?"

"Let's say additional, complementary resources. Griffin has a lot of business interests over here."

"I see. And why would you want to turn that pile over?"

"Good question. Maybe, after all the fun we've had together, I owe you one."

"One."

"Just one."

"Even steven," I said and switched off.

Ari and Sareen looked the question at me, and I filled in the blanks.

"Even the devil himself has a soft spot, it looks like," Ari commented.

"No, he doesn't," Sareen reproved him. He raised his eyebrows but then nodded.

"Where were we?" I said. "Weren't we figuring out how our assassins are going to sneak up on us?"

"So we were," he said. "But we don't even know for certain that they will, let alone exactly how. The readiness is all, as someone put it."

"Hamlet," I noted pedantically.

"Hamlet, then. So we will make ourselves as ready as we can."

He went over to his gym bag and brought out not one but two dark-gray pistols.

"Twins," he said, "Heckler & Koch .38's. They'll do the job if we need them."

"I don't need them," Sareen said.

"No, I wasn't thinking of you. Do you mind if Adam and I both keep one handy tonight?"

She regarded him pensively. "I have been here before," she said. "Do what must be done. If I am the only one praying, God has a big ear."

So we laid our plan, such as it was, the best we could do. Sareen would sleep, or at least stay, in the bedroom. Ari and I would plant ourselves on large pillows in the two corners of the entryway adjacent to the front door. The lights would be out, and I would be next to the switch. In an attempt to make sure we weren't both asleep at the same time, we broke the night into two-hour shifts. I took ten to midnight, he took midnight to two, and so on.

Best-laid plans.

Just after ten we emptied our bladders of the coffee, trusting that the caffeine would stay with us, and took our stations.

Lights out. All quiet on the western front. I had the first watch, but I doubted that either of us would fall asleep. Caffeine mixed with adrenaline.

Time went by slowly on my wristwatch's luminous dial. Lots of time and nothing to do with it but think.

Being mine, my mind drifted first to mathematics. Arcane, endlessly complex, beautiful mathematics. Diophantine equations. Fourier analysis. Polytopic tessellations. Zeroes of the zeta function in the complex plane.

My thoughts turned to Galileo's remark that mathematics is the language of nature. The language of science, the study of the natural world—real science, not Griffin's perverse sham.

But why? Why is there this apparently total correspondence between the mathematical constructs developed in the human mind and the vast universe outside our mind? Everything from nuclear fission to fluid dynamics to planetary orbits is described and analyzed mathematically. Why? Mathematics is the distilled essence of human rationality, but why should the universe itself be so utterly and thoroughly rational? As Einstein put it, "The most incomprehensible thing about the universe is that it is comprehensible."

The ancient Greeks and Hebrews, as different as they were, agreed on this matter. The world is rational, and we (at best) are rational, because God is rational, they said. As the Hebrews put it, we have been made in his image.

They were right, I thought, to this extent at least: if God isn't the true explanation, we are left with one enormous, indigestible coincidence. The universe at large and we ourselves within it—mental prodigies all—are either an extreme, incalculably improbable coincidence or else a reflection, in some unfathomable way, of the mind of "God," or at any rate of how God works in the natural universe.

Evolution could explain it. But that was yes and no—explain it in one way but not in another. Explain the bare facts, sure. This led to that and to that and to that. But that reasoning never gets us any closer to the massive human question: Why? *Why* is the supremely human question because it goes to purpose. If there is no God, there is no answer to *why*, no purpose, no reason, just meaningless stuff.

No reason.

But there *is* reason. The universe and the human mind are suffused with rationality.

That phrase recurred to me: the image of God.

The Shroud. The image. My strange and unsought quest for it over the last few months.

Ari went "Tst" and tipped his watch face my way. Midnight. I could catnap with a clear conscience.

Fat chance.

Then there is that curious circumstance that scientists have labeled "the anthropic principle." The fine-tuning of the universe. If the natural universe weren't precisely the way it is, we couldn't exist, couldn't survive biologically. More than a score of physical parameters have to be exactly what they are, and not a million-millionth different, or we wouldn't be here. Another fantastic coincidence?

Ah, but suppose our universe is only one of an uncountable number of universes, and ours happens to be the solitary one in which we won the big lottery. We can't detect any of those other universes, but they must be there or we wouldn't be here. The big lottery must be out there, somewhere.

Because otherwise ... God. No third option has ever occurred to anyone, not yet at least.

A rational, self-disclosing Creator or an endless, mindless, invisible lottery. Which one strains your brain harder? Until very recently I would have said *Creator* reflexively. Why was I now in two minds about it? The Shroud business, obviously. And Sareen ... yes, even more, Sareen.

My thoughts turned back to my quest for the Shroud and its meaning. According to the Christians, that meaning has everything to do with God.

The God-man. The crucified man. The image of God.

Sareen thought of Jesus as the dividing line between despair and hope. Being alienated from God, she thought, and being sucked inexorably into the black hole of death, we are all wrapped—you might say enshrouded—in hopeless, existential despair. As the atheist philosopher Bertrand Russell put it, defiantly but bluntly, the thinking man can only base his life "on the firm foundation of unyielding despair."

According to Sareen, we usually mask this despair in denial, through pop psychology or drugs or sex or career or religion—even religion. Religion, she said, is our effort to reach beyond our world and placate or manage whatever powers may be there—an understandable effort, but as futile as it is burdensome. Jesus is God reaching in to rescue us from all that.

It struck me that if I had never embarked on this quest to decipher the Shroud, I would never have met Sareen. One more phenomenal coincidence? I shivered at the thought of all those zillions of world lines in which she and I never crossed paths, never coalesced.

Never were in love.

Love, that amazing, priceless action of the human soul.

The human soul. But if such love exists, such love as that between Sareen and me, the soul must exist. Physical chemistry, sure, but more than that. To deny that would be to deny my own most precious experience.

If we have souls, though—Sareen and I and Ari and all the others—if we *are* souls, then all bets are off. The crucified man could have done whatever he did in order to leave his image for eighty generations of people like me to see and wonder about.

Wonder about… What was it Erika Steiner said? Just about the only thing that could have caused that image is some form of radiation.

Radiant love. The resurrection, theologians say, verifies and clinches the love that motivated Jesus in his crucifixion. Death, that final thing, is no longer final—as Sareen had been trying to tell me.

Resurrection. I had always had it tucked safely in the psychology-of-religion category. As Sareen seemed to keep reminding me, though, life isn't all that safe. If the resurrection actually happened ....

The limits of reality. Who knows? But for me to try to set limits to reality would be artificial and ridiculously presumptuous. Might not reality contain more than I had encountered up till then? It might.

Somewhere before two o'clock, there was a deafening bang and the door flew open and two men entered in a crouch. As Ari's disciple I had my .38 ready, and I flicked on the lights and Ari said, "Drop the weapons, girls. This one is loaded."

They spun toward him, raising their guns, and he shot them both before I could react, and they lurched back and thudded on the floor. One of them got off a shot before he died, and I had a hole in the hardwood floor to prove it.

All that planning and waiting and thinking, and it was all over in five seconds.

CHAPTER 38

Sareen came out of the bedroom and saw the bodies and saw us. She looked at me, and her face crumpled. I went over to her and held her against my chest, feeling her convulsive sobs and the wet warmth of her tears.

How did I feel about it? Two dead men, recently alive. Actually, I felt okay. If I hadn't done what I could to protect my home and her—and us—I would have felt a lot worse.

"I'll call 911," Ari said. Half a dozen other tenants would have called already, but it had to be done.

The first police arrived a few minutes later, announcing themselves with a loud shout and coming through the doorway with their guns out but pointed down. We had left our pistols on the coffee table. Ari raised his palms. I was still holding Sareen, but she stopped crying as soon as the men in blue showed up. She sucked it up and faced them with a chin like Rocky Marciano, but prettier.

Before long, my apartment was crowded with detectives and scene-of-crime techs and a police physician and photographer. The media hounds were kept out in the hallway; score one for the cops. The detectives separated the three of us and questioned us for the next couple of hours. Since they weren't from Mars, they knew enough about the whole Adam Hult-Morris Griffin hullabaloo to know two things right away: this was one hell of a big case, and they had better not screw it up and make it bigger.

By morning, when I was completely exhausted and I'm sure Sareen was too, and even Ari was feeling it, the lead detective had put his head together with his bosses and the District Attorney and decided there weren't enough grounds for any charges against Ari or me. If it wasn't open-and-shut self-defense, it was close enough. More pertinently, the D.A. and the police brass were attuned to the politics of the case. Trying to make heroes out of F/ACTION assassins wouldn't play well.

Later on we found out, through the media, that the two creeps had gotten by Thomaz by posing as electricians, with the usual forged work order. Once inside, they hid out in a utility closet until the small hours. If they could have picked my lock quietly, they would have, but the deadbolt forced them to blast away. Presumably, they figured they would still catch us asleep and would be able to dispatch us before we could react. By that time, I imagine, they felt too committed, mission-wise and felony-wise, to back out. What their escape plan was is anybody's guess.

We were beat, as I said, and after the bodies and the authorities were gone, around 8:00 a.m., and after we shoved my recliner against the door to keep it shut—with a note tacked to the outside warning the paparazzi that we were armed and overwrought—we collapsed on our respective sleeping spots. I can't say that I exactly slept, but I drifted in a delirious semiconsciousness until early afternoon.

When I got up, punch-drunk and hung over, Sareen and Ari were already up. Ari was fixing something in the kitchen—start with the coffee, please—and Sareen was watching TV.

"Adam," she said. She held out her hand to me, and I lumbered over and took it, flopping down on the couch beside her.

"What's happening?" I asked.

"Morris Griffin has been arrested. The charges at this point are tax fraud and evasion, but the news people say more charges are sure to come, relating to his involvement with F/ACTION."

Ari brought us coffee and doughnuts. During the next week, we, along with half the other people on the planet, learned that F/ACTION, for all its nastiness, was really rather small potatoes, around fifty "made" members altogether, two of whom resided in an Israeli jail and two more in the morgue. The rest had either been rounded up or soon would be. Their professionalism didn't extend much beyond hooliganism.

But for now we just ate a lot of doughnuts and drank a lot of coffee. Good nutrition could come later.

Good old Ari had already called an outfit that did door repairs or replacement, and they were due to arrive any time. With that, he figured his duty was done, and he took his leave. Sareen hugged him and kissed him and cried on him. I didn't. I gave him the full male intimidation stare, and he winked at me.

' ' ' ' ' '

When the door fixers came, Sareen and I took the opportunity to get out of what had come to feel like a siege bunker. We walked across 116th Street to the university campus and strolled through its landscaped acres. I pointed out certain landmarks, and she pretended to be impressed.

After we had passed the end of our loop and were heading back, she said, "It appears to be all over with now, does it not—your private war with those demented people."

"I hope so. I think so too."

"Good. It may have been exciting for Ari and even for you, but I am only glad it is done with. Other than that, though, I have enjoyed my time here in your city. I like New York. It has many layers, and even, for so young a city, a sense of antiquity."

Something in her tone bothered me. I said, "I suppose so."

"I like your mother also, Adam."

"Yes ... I've been thinking about that—I mean her situation now with Pop gone and all. If I can somehow find the money, maybe I should get a better house to move her into."

She turned and regarded me with an expression of amusement or exasperation.

"Not that, Adam. Don't you understand? I talked with her during that family gathering at Ari's house. She loves her home. To her, that's what it is, her home. Her husband bought it for her when they were married. For better or worse, she raised her boys in that home. She doesn't want to be moved to some strange new place, Adam. What she does want, I am absolutely sure, is for you to visit her more often."

I took all that in. Being that she was her and I was me, there was around a 99 percent chance she was right.

"Okay," I said, "you're probably right."

"I am right. As I said, I like your mother. I would like to visit her whenever I come to New York."

"Whenever you … come to New York?"

"Yes." The word came out like a purr.

"Well …"

"Naturally I can only visit her when I come here."

I didn't respond to that. We were on a paved pathway between two rolling lawns. The pathway to hell, someone said, is paved with good intentions. What, if anything, paves the pathway to heaven?

Too tough for me. I was only on a path on the university campus near St. Paul's Chapel. Deal with it, buster.

"Look, if you want … we could get married?"

"Is that a question?"

"It's *the* question."

"Well, Adam, do you want to marry me?"

"I do! Absolutely. But you … do you … ?"

"For a certainty, I believe in marriage as much as I believe in love, but not for the purpose of pinning each other down like butterflies in a collection."

"Do you think that's how I mean it?"

"I think not, but … is that how you mean it?"

"No!"

"Good. I think we understand each other, then—so necessary for a good marriage."

If she thought I understood her, she was wildly wrong. To pin *it* down, not *her*, I said, "So you will marry me?"

"I will marry you."

Just like that. "I guess we can discuss the particulars ..."

"Yes, but not now."

"But not now. Look, Sareen, you were just talking about 'whenever you come to town.' But hey, this town is where I live and work. And you live and work pretty much all over the rest of the world. How's that going to ... work?"

She, strange creature that she was, seemed amused all over again, as amused as I was perplexed.

"*It* doesn't work, Adam. *We* work it out. You love me. I love you. We both have hearts and minds. We have options, possibilities, opportunities. We decide what is best for both of us—both of us together. Do you not think we can do so small a thing together?"

"What if we can't agree?"

She stopped and turned to me. "Do you trust me?"

"By now? Yes."

"And I trust you. If we have love and trust, then we *can* agree. Don't you see it?"

I tried strenuously to see it.

"I don't know. Does this have anything to do with faith?"

"It has everything in the creation to do with faith. Faith is trust. And love isn't a what; love is a who. Such fun—so much to discover. Come."

She took my hand, and we walked on, back to 116th Street and then up to my apartment, where the workmen were just finishing up. They had been able to repair the door but had to replace the hardware. I paid them, and they left. I wasn't sure whether, according to the rental agreement, the tenant or the management was supposed to foot the bill for damage of this sort. I would have to hash it out with the building manager and, probably, lose.

By then, it was evening. Both of us were tired, both of us were engaged to be married, and both of us, we discovered, were hungry. Sareen went to the kitchen and got out a package of frozen tamales, which she had purchased, I expect, for a time just like this. While they were steaming on the stove, we sat at the breakfast nook and held hands, either like teens on a first date or like oldie weds.

But in the back of my mind, those old money problems kept calling themselves to my attention, like a jackhammer.

"Since my deal with Doris Ballaster fell through," I said, "I'm back to square one on the financial side. The IRS and all that."

"But Doris and her friend Tom won't be feeding you to them any longer, isn't that right?"

"Yes, but the IRS is like radioactive waste; it doesn't go away."

"Listen to me, Adam," she said energetically, "your financial situation is perfectly manageable. You just haven't managed it well. That can change. I am quite a good money manager, I believe. And anyway, there is that money I inherited from my father, a good deal of money."

"That's your money."

"No. If we don't share our money, we won't share those things that are even more important. That is wisdom, Adam, believe me."

Wisdom! Always in short supply here. I'd found the right girl.

"So," she said a minute later, "is your Shroud research drawing to a conclusion?"

"I think so. I've done all the legwork and spadework, as we say. And last night, sitting there in the dark by the front door, I did a lot of thinking. And as unthinkably radical as the idea seems, the cumulative evidence points where you all along have thought it points. The R word. The image on that linen cloth is unquestionably an image of a crucified man. But no normal human body leaves behind such an image, one with such unique and extraordinary characteristics. I won't say there's no other possible explanation, but there is no better one. No other explanation can account for the facts as well as the fantastic one. Resurrection."

She said quietly, "I'm glad, Adam."

"This is going to be hard for me, though. This changes everything."

"Of course it does. When the sun comes up in the morning, doesn't that change everything? And now, what an adventure for you! You will find, when you join the cosmic dance—as, you may have noticed you are doing—the wonder of it is the music, because the musician is Jesus, the fountain of everlasting love, and when you hear his voice, his music, and come to him, your heart and mind become free to dance like you never thought of dancing before, in perfect rhythm and grace, for the sheer joy of it."

"Wow, that's ... poetic," I stammered.

"Yes, isn't it? But, of course, since we are human, there will be growing pains, downs along with the ups—poor choices, failures, heartbreaks, frustrations—but in the end, it will be good. Very, very good."

"You mean ... between you and me?"

"In all our relationships—between each of us and God, and, yes, between you and me. For all who put their hope in Jesus. The good news is truly good and should be treasured; Jesus actually does have our lives in his perfect control. That's why in marriage—the way marriage was meant to be—we aren't pinned down, but we dance to the music, like butterflies, because it's so much fun." She laughed and squeezed my hands. "You look like you think I'm out of my mind."

Well... But I answered honestly, "Maybe, but if so, I want to be out there with you."

"Don't look now, but you already are."

Then it struck me. My Shroud investigation all but complete ... the responsibilities of marriage ... money ...

Dina!

I whipped out my Droid and punched her in.

"Adam, you lovely brute! *You* calling *me*—I can't catch up with my heartbeat! Dish it out, handsome. Tell Mama whatcha got."

"Stop the presses, Dina darling. I'm ready to roll with this thing, and it's a can't-miss killer. Pop the champagne corks, baby!"

"The Shroud thing? The Shroud thing!"

"Got it in one, chickadee."

"Perfect, lover man, just the first paragraph's already radiating the media like a neutron bomb—funky terrorists and loony Morrie—perfect! Now, cookie, I need the full story, your story, the whole enchilada!"

"Only for you, Dina. So here it is. It all began one miserable day last February while I was sitting in my office at the university reviewing a rather tedious statistical economic history of the French Third Republic, and this big, heavy, horse-faced guy walks in and sits himself down and takes his time looking everything over, the books and the potted plants and all, and then finally he fixes me with these eyes like dull brass buttons, and I figure I'm in the river with concrete boots on, financially, because for the last dozen years I've been deducting my marginal ETPs through a series of collateralized nominal amortization derivatives integrated under a hyperbolic distribution curve but differentiated by a paralogical logarithmic algorithm—"

"Mute it!" she shouted. "Gimme a break, sugarplum. That pig won't squeal."

ACKNOWLEDGMENTS

This is a work of fiction, but the focus of the story, the Shroud of Turin, is an actual historical object. All the characters are invented, though some are based loosely on real people. Most of the organizations and events are fictional except for a few, such as the Shroud of Turin Research Project (STURP) and the 1988 radiocarbon testing of the Shroud. As to the historicity of any portion of the Shroud's saga prior to the fourteenth century, the reader, like Adam Hult, must judge for herself. Guys can judge too.

Apart from some minor fictional elaboration, all the pieces of evidence that Adam tracks down are genuine. Robert de Clari's memoir of the Fourth Crusade, for instance, and the quote from it in the novel, are historical artifacts.

My first notable introduction to the Shroud came in 2008 when I first read Mark Antonacci's *The Resurrection of the Shroud* (M. Evans and Company, 2000). Prior to that, like most people who have vaguely heard of the Turin Shroud, I assumed it must be some kind of medieval fake, part of the well-known cottage industry in ersatz relics, which Chaucer, for one, made sport of. Antonacci's book hit me as a tentative but fascinating revelation. I wanted to find out more.

My chief source on the subject has been Ian Wilson's comprehensive study *The Shroud: The 2000-Year-Old Mystery Solved* (Bantam, 2010). Anyone who has read that work as well as my novel will realize that I parcel out Wilson's insights piecemeal to Adam Hult over the course of his research. Why not just have him read the book? Because then the game would be over around the second inning.

To Donna Chumley and Rachael Sweeden and Ashley Luckett and all the other allies at Tate Publishing, one huge Thank You.

To everyone: the truth is better than we can imagine. Come and see.